A BULLET
FOR ME

Terry Atkinson

For my beloved sister, Pat Allen
(Mary Patricia Atkinson, 1950 – 2017)

Acknowledgements:

My wife, Elaine, for allowing me the time and space to follow an often selfish hobby.

My ex-colleagues and Bacchus/Lady Grey friends who are an inexhaustible source of inspiration and ideas.

My wife and my brother, David who, along with others, advise me on the content of my books.

A World of Payne trilogy:

Book 1: A Bullet For Me
Book 2: A Kill Too Far
Book 3: The List

ONE

The rifle sights were lined up perfectly. He had been there twice before to check whether his plan had legs. His shots at the test target, a dandelion head at the far edge of a neglected, patchy square of lawn, the largest of a cluster little more than ten feet from where the intended target's head would be, had sent up plumes of earth within two centimetres of one another. All that remained of the stricken flower was the shattered stem, oozing its white milk. Even allowing for unkind weather, his aim was going to be accurate enough to hit the target.

It was matter-less whether it was the right eye or the left, the mouth, the nose or the throat, for beyond that lay brain matter and the spinal cord. The result would be just the same. Utter devastation, the ending of a worthless life. Within minutes, the police would have an idea of where the shot had come from within an arc of a hundred feet, but it would more difficult to locate the exact spot, apart from disturbed ground or any forensic evidence carelessly left behind. There would be none, of course, he would see to that.

The only other physical clue, potentially, would be tyre patterns in the mud. But there was no mud. It had been dry for days and the prevailing north-easterly August breeze had removed all but the tiniest grains of soil and sand nestling in the crevices of the coarse blacktop. In any event, tyre patterns would rarely provide conclusive evidence without features known only to that tyre. A cut here, a nick there, picked up along the way.

A painstaking search of the scene, if carried out professionally, should eventually uncover the practice bullets. That could not be helped. Probably three to four inches deep and no more than a foot from the entry points, depending on how compacted the earth was but, without the weapon they were fired from or a link to a suspect, they would be of no help to the police. Their journey through the soil, maybe striking a few stones and pebbles, may or may not have distorted the unique barcode striations caused by the missiles' passage through the rifled barrel. Nor would there be any ejected cartridge cases. They would fall within the vehicle itself, then be gathered up to be disposed of many miles away.

The vehicle, a grey, drab to the point of being almost invisible, Ford Focus nearing the end of its life, had been bought for cash from an *ask no questions* car dealer from Hanley, near Stoke on Trent, and would be sold to an equally iffy scrap metal dealer in Darlington. It had been acquired for its anonymity with used, untraceable £20 notes and there would be no love lost when it parted company with its owner. Even if the police found a witness who could give them the make and registration number it would be like looking for a needle in a haystack.

In the likely event that police enquiries would extend to beyond the local force boundary, it would take them some time to find the vehicle. But this scrap merchant was chosen because of his tendency to grind out identifiable features, then crush it almost immediately once the recyclable parts had been removed. He allowed his crew no more than an hour to render it unrecognisable. It was how he stayed in business for so long. His family had been in the business for three generations, not one prison sentence between them. They knew a thing or two.

The target was Tony Molloy, a retired semi-professional super middle-weight boxer turned thug. His speciality was *taxing* other criminals who were not within the protection or

4

employ of Ray Morrison. Molloy's weapons of choice ranged from fists, feet, knees, head and sharp instruments. His favourite was a carpet knife for slashing faces or backs of hands and, if he wanted to be particularly vicious, he would use a machete. He would occasionally tape three or four craft knives side by side to create parallel wounds so that the medics could not find enough stable skin to stitch them together. They would have to use tape, with varying degrees of success. The wounds would take forever to close-up, often leaving deep, purple scars. This was Molloy's intended consequence. He wanted his victims to be reminded, every time they look in the mirror, that it pays not to cross him. He had no conscience. It had been bought from him.

Morrison, of course, was now a gentleman criminal with a number of legitimate businesses funded from the outset from ill-gotten gains. He had started by shoplifting and burgling commercial property as a schoolboy, eventually progressing to 'cash-in-transit' robberies. His hauls, rarely less than £20k and often nearer £60k, gave him the till to buy recreational drugs in bulk and set up his own empire. This upset a lot of people, but Morrison was unfazed. His enemies were out-muscled, outnumbered and out-gunned. For now, there was tolerance and mutual respect. There was enough spoil to go around and, as long as no one became too big for their boots, the co-existence was working fine.

Morrison, a six-footer weighing seventeen stones, much of it around his middle, had been fit in his earlier days. He needed to be to stay alive and remain in business. Morrison liked to put it about that he was personally responsible for two killings, but those close to him knew that Mr. Teflon would never get his hands dirty to that extent. Sure, they had despatched people on his behalf, but that is as far as Morrison's involvement went. He was ruthless enough to issue death warrants but never around when the executions took place.

The police were unconcerned when villains were on the receiving end. They would go through the motions but, in the scheme of things, it was one less for them to worry about. Actually, two less. The killer and the victim.

Finally, Morrison went into property ownership. Pubs, clubs, care homes and anything that would turn a quid, but his past would preclude him from managing any of them himself. No matter. He preferred to count the money and order the occasional slap if takings were lower than expected.

Not content with the lucrative and seemingly legitimate businesses, he still enjoyed the risk of overseeing the running of the drugs limb of the business. And, of course, the insurance business. Insurance against something indelicate happening to clients' businesses or loved ones. This was far more exciting for a man who liked to throw his weight around. It was personal because he knew who the victims were. But, as with everything else, he kept his distance. If the shit ever hit the fan, none of it would stick to him, but the stench was unmistakably there. He got even more kicks from knowing that the police were aware that he must be involved but could do nothing about it without some serious investment in time, money and resources, all of which were in short supply. Times were hard for the police and the days when they could sit on a target for weeks on end had long passed.

This killing was a message for Morrison. He had it coming for making matters personal. That was uncalled for and he would answer for it, but now wasn't the time. It was far too soon for his own day of reckoning. He had to know real fear first. As his henchmen fell one by one he would come to realise that, one day, it would be his turn.

The assassin knew that Molloy was being released from hospital that day, probably around four in the afternoon after the consultant surgeon had completed his rounds. In many cases the patient was more than ready to go home, physically and mentally, and the final check would be a formality. For Molloy, however, it was touch and go. The surgeon's nod was far from assured and Molloy would have to be convincing. And convincing he was, as much as it pained him to force a reassuring smile and give the thumbs up. With a final few words of warning to take his medication on time, get plenty of bed rest and do no more than make the odd mug of coffee, the surgeon allowed him to be discharged. But the surgery and intense aftercare were about to be wasted. It had all been in vain. There would be a tinge of sadness on their part, but not for long. Someone else would need patching up and Molloy would become a distant memory.

The journey home would be between twenty-five and forty minutes, depending on the volume of traffic. Rush hour, these days, started around 3pm, so delays were inevitable, although on any day and in the centre of town, the traffic was always heavy. The assassin would take no chances. He would observe the release from the hospital grounds then race ahead to the chosen spot, hoping that Molloy would indeed go straight home and not take a detour. He should be in position a good ten minutes before the ambulance would arrive and, as long as no one had parked in his spot, everything should be fine. There were no schools close-by so the school-run parents and grandparents would not be a problem.

There would be no blues and twos, Molloy was just a low-life giving up a hospital bed for a more deserving case. Besides, he was out of danger and on the mend.

He looked at his watch. He had made good time. Ample to set up. Molloy's jaw was healing nicely, although the metal plate and the five-inch opening along the jaw line where it was inserted were going to be permanent fixtures. His smile, if ever he could manage one, would be crooked and painful. It was of little consequence. It would not be for much longer. Today would be his last day on Earth.

The route had been studied meticulously during the seven days in the high dependency and intensive care units and now, five weeks after the failed attempt on the assassin's life and the beating Molloy took in return, he was due home to continue his convalescence. To the Health Service, he was just another patient who merited the same first-class care that every citizen was entitled to. Except that Molloy was no model citizen. He had not paid a penny in dues. His National Insurance stamp was paid by the government due to his inability to find work following a debilitating injury during his boxing days, and were none the wiser. His family, who had exploited loopholes since the introduction of the benefits system, had schooled him well.

The spot chosen was perfect, less than one hundred metres from the front door of Molloy's house, from an elevated position and across unobstructed landscape. Through telescopic sites that had been painstakingly set up days earlier, it would be an easy shot. Success was assured.

From another vantage point close by, the ambulance could be seen approaching, giving the assassin plenty of time to get into position. He would not bring the rifle to his shoulder until the last minute. There was little point in exposing himself at the ignition point longer than necessary. There would be no need for him to leave the driver's seat. He would just lower the front passenger electric window from the switch on the driver's side, then raise and aim the rifle, just as he had practised. The barrel would not extend beyond the car's outer shell. Molloy would be dead before he heard the crack, if there was a crack to be heard. The noise would be little more than the tap of the hammer on the cartridge rim. Had Molloy been looking directly at the muzzle of the rifle, he would have seen the flash about one quarter of a second before the small cone of lead penetrated his skull just above his right eye, and circulated several times inside his dome, making blackcurrant jam of everything in its way.

Another look at the watch, a final check that the sights had not been disturbed. Moments later, the ambulance came into view, albeit five minutes later than expected. The assassin took a deep breath and exhaled slowly, followed by another, then another. The ambulance crewmen, both wearing their dark green uniforms, left the cab and went around their respective sides to the rear door. The driver opened the door and lowered the mechanised lift with hand-held controls and climbed onto it. He then held the yellow button, raised the lift until it was level with the floor, then discarded the control box and disappeared inside. Two long minutes went by. More deep breaths. *Had Molloy relapsed? Was he even there? Had he been dropped off elsewhere?*

Another minute passed, after which the driver emerged and backed out onto the lift, towing the government-issue wheelchair with Molloy on board.

The assassin breathed a sigh of relief. He quickly glanced around for any unwanted intrusions then, coast clear, brought the sights to bear, just in time to see Molloy crack a painful smile. He winced and raised his left hand up to the jaw to gently cradle it. He was going to take a long time to mend, but he was still being paid so there was no need to rush back to the maiming business. He had not been home for weeks and longed to put up his feet and watch his fifty-inch flat screen with the latest surround sound, not crowded by confused old screamers in wheelchairs and dressing gowns, begging for a cigarette. No buzzers, no cries through the night, no stinking bed pans, no retching or vomiting, no restless, bored kids visiting under protest, being threatened by equally restless and bored adults.

His first priority would be a quick, longed-for girl on top romp. His tank was full, but he was not yet strong enough to take too much of an active part. His next priority would be a small bottle of lager in front of the television, watching the cage fighting programmes that his loving Carlie had recorded for him. He longed for a glass of cold Carlsberg Export, just like they'd drunk at the end of Ice Cold in Alex before they marched off the German spy who'd played a valiant part in saving them from the desert. It was one of the many movies he'd watched from his sick-bed. It had had a lasting effect on him, or at least his thirst. He was going to be disappointed on both counts.

The lift having come to a halt on the ground, the driver removed the safety chain and wheeled Molloy backwards up over the kerb, then span the wheelchair around and onto the short pavement leading to his front door. Before he reached it, a young woman appeared in the doorway. The lovely Carlie. She was heavily made up as if for a night on the Quayside, wearing a short white skirt that left little to the imagination. Her unidentifiable, much-expanded tattoos were just visible on her bare, puffy midriff and a white boob-tube, with some undecipherable, washed out logo highlighted in silver sequins completed her outfit. Her hair was dyed black and lifeless, having been subjected to years of self-applied products where no account was taken of what the labels warned against. Another smile, another wince.

This guy was easy to please, thought the assassin, but she was his choice. Someone's cherished daughter. She took over the wheelchair, thanked the crew, and spun it around to allow Molloy to wave them goodbye. Probably a little too quickly for Molloy's liking, as his head rocked and forced him to grab the right wheel to brace himself against whiplash. With his left hand already occupied, cradling the injured jaw, he released his grip on the wheel and raised his right arm in a friendly wave.

It was now time. The assassin expelled the air from his lungs to slow down the heartbeat and prevent any unwanted movement of the cross-hairs on the telescopic sights at the wrong moment. He gently squeezed the trigger, applying ever more pressure until, past the point of resistance, the released spring brought down the hammer.

The shot came only once the crew were inside their cabin and were pulling away. They did not hear it above the clatter of the increasing revolutions of the three-litre diesel engine. Neither did Carlie, whose first indication that something was wrong, was when Molloy's head jerked sharply backwards, followed by the sight of a scarlet trickle then a spurt of dark red blood from the neat round hole in his forehead. The spurt slowed to a steady flow, weakening by the second as the heart struggled to cope. And then it stopped altogether. Ideally, the victim would see exactly who had terminated him but it would not be wise to let that happen. If Carlie had seen the assassin, she would have to go the same way too. As a man with a conscience, the killer felt that she did not deserve that. It would be wrong. Murder in cold blood. On this occasion, distance was his friend. By the time Carlie realised what had happened, the Ford Focus was slowly disappearing from view.

Within thirty minutes, the Ruger .22 calibre rim fire rifle with its telescopic sights and silencer was back in its hiding place, all traces linking it to its handler removed with a clean rag.

Three down, but many more to come. The first had been unintended and the second, justifiable. This one had been pre-meditated and carefully planned. It would certainly not be the last. There was no remorse, no regret, no pangs of conscience. On the contrary, he was strangely satisfied with his day's work and he would keep going until the threat against him had diminished. Who would know how many more victims the same weapon had seen off in its lifetime? Its previous owner, after all, had been a professional hit man, from whom it had been taken by lethal force.

TWO

It was one of those April days when you feel you don't have a care in the world. Winter over for another year, temperatures in the mid-teens, clear blue skies and all the time in the world to do whatever you want to do. There had not been many days like that in Charlie Payne's life and he had no way of knowing, at that time, that it would be the very last. But, for now, the sun was shining and he was doing exactly what he wanted to do. He was taking a well-earned rest on a rustic wooden bench made with his own hands from driftwood he had rescued over the years from Northumberland beaches. It had been a virtual lifetime's collection, but the bench was only a year old. When they began to clean up the beaches to restore that coastline and its resorts to their former glory, the driftwood became less and less available, and he had to make do with what he had already collected. It was a sturdy bench, drilled and bolted, not nailed, and it would take all of his fourteen plus stones. And probably another two of similar weight.

He had been digging the hole where the garden pond would be, shaded by trees so that there would be a mixture of light, shade and almost perpetual darkness, to attract a range of creatures. It was a sizeable hole that had taken him many days to dig by hand. He could have rented a digger for half a day and achieved the same result, but the sense of achievement would be, somehow, lost. The rubber pool liner, unused, sixty square metres of it, was about eight years old and today was the day it was, at last, going to be put to use. Charlie was always well-intentioned, but work seemed to get in the way of his domestic life. Either that or it was just a convenient excuse. But, no longer. He had not long been retired from the police service. Only two months, in fact. A full thirty years he had served, most of it in one branch or another of the CID. He had not chosen an easy path. Remaining in uniform had its challenges but there was too much of it that did not provide the excitement he craved. Lost children and minor disputes or disturbances, and petty crime, as important as they were, were the staple diet and unless they involved murder, rape, kidnap and general mayhem, there wasn't enough to hold his interest.

His promotions came through taking scalps rather than keeping his head down and his nose clean. Had he kept his nose a bit cleaner he may have made another couple of ranks, but he was not one to play a political game, and preferred to call a spade a spade. Besides, he was happy. Results and reputation mattered to him more than the safety of a desk job, sometimes, no matter how those results came. But that was all past him now and he was enjoying having whole days to himself.

The one remaining barrier to total closure on his distinguished career, was the final trial. It had been a long, arduous investigation, with many highs and lows, but it had ended well, with five of the main players on remand and awaiting sentence after entering guilty pleas. They knew that they would spend many years behind bars, but not as many as the number one man, Freddie Simpson, who was fighting it all the way. He had not been long out after doing a ten-stretch for drug trafficking, and that would not go down well with the judge. A life sentence was the most likely outcome, even if he pleaded guilty, so Simpson had nothing to lose in fighting to the end. The evidence against them all was tight. Charlie had made sure of that and all bar one had thrown themselves on the mercy of the judge, expecting credit for not spending more of the public purse on a costly trial.

Freddie had a number of choices, the first being to accept his fate. That was unlikely, since his arrogance would not permit him to admit he had been done over. The other options were to discredit the investigation or the investigators, nobble or discredit the witnesses or nobble the jury. Murder would not be out of the question either. In fact, it could work to his advantage since he and his colleagues would all be banged up at the time of the execution. Proving that he was complicit in murder, while being entertained at Her Majesty's pleasure, would have been unquestionably difficult.

His barristers had pulled strokes to extend the trial deadline in the hope that something would turn up, and there were still some months to go. Anything could happen.

Witness and jury protection were down to others now. It was no longer his responsibility to ensure the integrity of the case, or that it went off without a hitch. Even if Simpson were to walk away a free man, it shouldn't matter to Charlie. He was untouchable and his bosses no longer held power over him. But it *would* matter. Of course, it would. He did not spend thirty years fighting for justice just to hang his boots up when they stop paying him.

There was plenty of time for Charlie to rehearse his part and to worry about how it would all pan out. There wasn't a great deal to his statement, which consisted mostly of how the interview went, and since it was all on tape, it was there for everyone to listen to. But, as Charlie knew only too well, any attack would be against the way the investigation was handled and not what was written in his statement.

It was difficult to second-guess how they would come at him. Simpson was bang-to-rights, so he knew they must have a trick or two up their sleeves. But there was no point in his worrying about that. Not yet, anyway.

In the meantime, Charlie's long-suffering wife, Julie, had agreed that they would spend three days a week together, apart from going on holiday, and during the other four they would do their own thing. Charlie's *thing* included tending to their large garden and messing about in his boat, a 10.5 metre Sole Bay Ketch, more than thirty years old, but still in beautiful condition. Stormy Monday was named after Charlie's favourite recording, an Eric Clapton number played while he was with John Mayall's Bluesbreakers, and she was moored at Amble Marina. Charlie had chosen this marina because of its vibrant sailing community. Its nickname, The Friendliest Port, was well earned. With around 250 berths for mixed use, and surrounded by idyllic scenery, there was no other like it.

Occasionally, Charlie would go out fishing with a few friends, mostly colleagues but occasionally not. He was a competent sailor and could sail her single-handed, but he preferred the company of friends. With old colleagues, they would always rake up the past, the good times and the bad, and they would agree that they could not possibly survive as coppers in this day and age. There were too many rules and regulations and they would have fallen foul sooner or later. No, they were around for the better times, they agreed, when they occasionally made up the law as they went along.

The conversation would invariably turn to who was no longer with them. It was an alarming fact that few of their colleagues got past the age of seventy and, in fact, the last six funerals were of men who were not yet eligible to draw their state pension. Theories abounded as to how that could be but, deep down, they all knew it was lifestyle related. Adrenalin and alcohol clearly do not mix, certainly not in the quantities that came their way. They had all slowed down, of course, but every few months, as they attended yet another funeral, they were reminded of their own mortality. The damage was already done and irreversible. If there was one consolation, it was that at least it gave old colleagues a chance to meet frequently and, callous and strange as it may seem, they kind of looked forward to the next, although none would openly admit that. In any event, Charlie was determined to enjoy himself and make the most of what time he had left.

He was no gardener, but he liked to potter. It gave him time for private thought and the occasional rose-tinted reminiscence. He remembered the good times more than he did the bad. Mostly.

Julie's *thing* included shopping and lunches with her two sisters, Sue and Jenny. Sue was good looking and petite, probably a size eight and thirty-four double D. She was a couple of years younger than Julie, but you would not know it to look at them. She was inclined to be bossy, a trait that caused Charlie to keep his distance and not to engage her in conversation for fear of being put in his place. She had once told him to shut up, half in jest, but Charlie decided then to limit his comments to greetings and pleasantries, and not to offer an opinion. Like Julie, who was slightly bigger boned and much more to his taste, she looked good in whatever she wore.

Julie kept her red hair quite long, just off the shoulder, and her make-up was subtle, just sufficient to highlight her best features, her cobalt-blue eyes. In fact, there was nothing to complain about, he loved her just as she was and would not change a thing.

Jenny, on the other hand, was an altogether different prospect. He would put her at a size sixteen, if not more, but her main attraction was her personality. She earned a first at Oxford in politics and could hold her own with anyone, on any topic, and was at the top of the list for any party invitations. Perhaps one of her more endearing features was that she had little interest in clothes other than they were a necessity in this climate. Nothing she wore appeared to match or to fit. She was unconcerned about what people thought. She was plain at best, certainly no oil painting, and she knew it. *Why try to polish a turd?* she would say, when her sisters berated her for not making an effort. But Charlie loved her company and felt at ease with her. In some ways, she was a better match for him than Julie. So, it was much to his shame and guilt that he would refer to her sisters as Beauty and the Beast, whenever they cropped up in conversation and, although he had the bottle for most things, he was not prepared to risk life and limb by revealing either of those opinions to Julie. Especially the opinion that Sue was really, rather tasty. That would open up an unnecessary line of never-ending unpleasantness, as Julie was not feeling particularly secure anyway, not after many years of living with a career detective, who only showed up at home when it was convenient.

She was aware that many of his colleagues had parted from their wives, mostly because of their own infidelity, but she had not ever been in danger of losing Charlie to another woman. She was not to know that, but it would not do to reassure her of that fact too often, or it could have the opposite effect. The truth was that Julie was as exciting now as she had been when Charlie first met her in Tiffany's dance hall years previously. They were both in their thirties when they met. She, shy and reserved, with little confidence, and he, the confident, ebullient and charming white knight on a steed. They were meant for one another.

For all she did not see a whole lot of Charlie over the years, at least she could not say he left her to bring the kids up on her own. Regrettably, they were not blessed in that department. There was no point in worrying about that now, the chance had passed them by. Adoption was talked about, but he doubted that he would ever have made the grade. Too unstable a lifestyle and probably too old. Besides, coppers' kids tend to be bullied or to dish it out themselves. Either way, they could have done with the hassle and it would probably have ended in tears for all concerned.

Now, two days after his 52nd birthday was one of those days, 19th April, he and Julie had agreed to do their own thing. It was around 11am on a Tuesday and she was about to meet Sue and Jenny in town. Tuesdays always meant a light lunch at Mark Toney's in Grainger Street followed by a little unnecessary shopping, then a snifter in The Old George, Newcastle's oldest pub. They liked the cocktail menu there, but Julie would only have the one as she almost always took her car. Charlie could never understand why she would not let him drop her off and get a taxi back. She probably just needed to have an excuse not to drink too much, as she still had the evening to get through and she preferred to keep her wits about her at all times.

Julie was always full of catch-up gossip when she returned home and Charlie would join her for a gin and tonic or a glass of Rioja, before they made a start on preparing dinner. Once in the house for the night, she was less fussy about what she would drink.

She would not let Charlie cook dinner himself. Charlie's culinary skills left a lot to be desired, so it was probably for the best that he left the cooking to Julie. But she would allow him to prepare the vegetables. This, he could do, as long as he did not try to cook them. His carrot julienne looked factory prepared, no more than five centimetres long and five millimetres square. All done with a clean-bladed Stanley knife and a steel rule, of course. But it would take forever.

On the conversational side, in years gone by, he was so wrapped up in his own world that he only pretended to be interested in what Julie had to say. These days, he genuinely listened to her and so much looked forward to her returning from her days out, to take centre stage. Charlie did not know whether she appreciated that, she didn't say, but her actions spoke louder than words and the more she appreciated his efforts, the more animated and affectionate she would become. Charlie's crust was breaking and he was beginning to mellow. She liked that.

Of the two of them, Julie had been the more successful, certainly financially, and had owned a string of upmarket trendy hairdressing salons in the north of England, as far away as Cheshire where many of her clients were WAG types with more money than sense. She revelled in the scandal, the fall-outs and the tales of woe.

Her mother, herself a hairdresser, had owned and grown the business and passed it on to her as a thirtieth birthday present. But Julie extended and transformed it into a trendy boutique chain while her parents concentrated on their property lettings portfolio, running at in excess of eight hundred properties, just before they died, some of them very upmarket indeed. And three retirement homes.

After years of interest from other hairdressing chains, Julie succumbed and sold the hairdressing business. She was now tiring of the travelling. Besides, she had a third share partnership in the multi-million -pound property empire to keep her busy.

Strangely, their good fortune changed neither of them. The house was already long paid for and her hairdressing windfall had been invested wisely. She would not need to touch that money. Ever. If she bit the dust before Charlie, he was well cared for, although with his own police inspector's pension and his own retirement lump sum also wisely invested, he was already quite comfortable in his own right.

In contrast to their wealth, they both had simple wants and needs. Expensive cruises and fine dining were of no use to them. Their one indulgence was Stormy Monday and a day's sailing or a long walk, mostly along the Northumberland coastline, would do them, as long as there was a sandwich and a glass of something at the end of it. Julie shared Charlie's lack of ambition for the high life. She had experienced it all. Balls for this charity, dinners for that charity, hobnobbing with local celebrity and, like Charlie, just wanted to put her feet up and enjoy what, to them, was an idyllic lifestyle. Their beneficiaries would have to be her three teenage nieces, daughters of Sue, and Charlie's younger brother, Steve. If he survived Charlie, that is.

Steve had been a Royal Marine turned mercenary, turned close protection security officer, turned hard-man. At some stage during his military career he joined a parachute regiment, but he was reluctant to talk about those days. He would hide behind The Official Secrets Act, which only led to more mystique and suspicion. Try as the family may to uncover his secrets, he would not budge.

In the Marines, he cut a dashing figure and his family were extremely proud, all attending his passing out parade and making a fuss. All, that is, except for his parents. Like Charlie, he did not really know who they were. He and Charlie were, effectively, brought up in a Barnardo's home before being fostered out and there was no contact with their biological parents. They had both died during early adulthood, or so they had been told, probably from over-indulgence in one substance or another. The subjects of lineage and ancestry were taboo, so were never discussed. His full dress-code photograph still took pride of place on Charlie's dining room wall.

Gradually, over the years, with one campaign after another, Steve changed. He had witnessed barbarities he could not have imagined possible. The capacity for man to inflict such suffering onto his fellow human beings had staggered him. He became withdrawn, silent for long periods, and developed a short fuse. When he blew, everyone would run for cover, then afterwards he would carry on as if nothing had happened. His wife, Wendy, understood him, but her patience had worn thin. It would take only one final straw.

On his discharge and lured by an ex-colleague with the promise of riches, he joined a small band of mercenaries bound for some God-forsaken part of Africa. It almost cost him his life and he still had fragments of shrapnel in his upper right thigh and backside. It was not something that could be treated back home, or the medical authorities would have been obliged to report their findings. Being paid to fight for one side or another in a civil war was frowned upon. He had to put up with the occasional pain and movement of sharp, if tiny, slivers of metal. One day, they would work themselves to the surface, he thought, so no real drama, unless they nicked something vital en-route. Charlie would gladly have given him the twenty grand Steve had made for his couple of months' work, just to stop him from going. But Charlie didn't know he had gone until he had gone. Even Wendy did not know until she found his letter leaning against the kettle, where he knew it would be found quickly, by which time he was already in the air and on his way to Paris to meet others for the first leg of their journey to Nairobi.

Back home, job done, Steve's contacts arranged for him to join a team of close protection security officers, for celebrities who wanted to draw attention to their importance by the size of their entourage. It was the easiest money he had ever made. All he had to do was wear black, look hard and muscle anyone out of the way who got too close. He was good at that. He had kept himself physically fit and, although he was well into his forties, his experience, courage and fondness of the pre-emptive strike compensated for his relative lack of speed or stamina. He could still leave Charlie standing, although Charlie could teach him a thing or two in other arts.

With recreational drugs so readily available in showbiz circles, Steve developed a liking for cocaine. Best of all, he didn't have to pay for it.

His clients took a liking to him until, one day, when he was having one of his mood swings and a little worse for drink, he gave one of them a dig. It was a left punch to the solar plexus that travelled no more than twelve inches, but it was followed by a right uppercut as the head came forward and down. The nose, already weakened by extensive rhinoplasty, stood no chance. Steve was so far gone that he claimed he could not even remember what started it.

'You jumped up little twat!' he'd said, finally losing his patience when the guy, yet again, snapped his fingers to demand attention. *'Don't you snap your fucking fingers at me!'* he'd said. At least that's what he was told he'd said, after the mist had lifted. With the celeb's nose out of shape, it put an end to his engagements for two months. After that, no one in show business would touch Steve. That was almost four years ago and he had not worked since. Well, not legitimately. He ran doors and a few errands for a different kind of people. Fortunately, the celeb was too embarrassed to make a fuss and legal proceedings would have made him a laughing stock.

In the meantime, while lost in his own little world and full of his own importance, later turning to self-pity, Steve lost sight of what was going on elsewhere in his life, the things that really mattered. His family. In particular, his son, Paul. Steve was never there when Paul needed him, and it came as a huge shock and wake-up call when Paul suddenly died of barbiturate poisoning. No one had seen it coming. Steve tried to persuade himself that it was unintentional, just an accidental overdose, but deep down he knew that no one washes down a cocktail of

60 Diazepam and Temazepam tablets with a bottle of whisky in a twenty-minute window just to get a night's sleep. The coroner eased the family's suffering by recording a verdict of misadventure, but they knew the dreadful truth.

Steve blamed himself. So did Wendy. She was utterly wretched. Despair didn't even begin to cover it and that was the final straw. With Paul, disappeared her hopes, her expectations, her only chance of future happiness. Steve had become a liability but she'd had high hopes for Paul, who had studied drama and, she had persuaded herself, was about to break through onto the big stage. She lost weight, weight she could ill-afford to lose, going from just over eight stones to just under seven. Although she and Steve remained married, they lived apart and neither had the will nor the strength to make things official. Steve had not seen her since she left. That was two years ago.

Charlie felt guilty about his brother's dire situation. It was not money that Steve needed, although it would help a little. He just needed a reason to live. He was determined, one day, to help Steve get his head together but, to his shame, he had nothing planned. He had no idea of where to start other than to keep offering Steve the chance to set up in a business of his choosing, something like taxis or limousines, nothing too taxing, until he regained his confidence. He lived in the fervent hope that, one day soon, Steve would accept his offer or that another solution would come to him. It would help if he were to meet someone else, perhaps someone with similar baggage, but Steve was not particularly bothered about female company. Or any company, for that matter.

Contrary to Charlie's perception, Steve was quite content these days. He made his army pension, as little as it was, and his benefit money, as little as that was, stretch until the next payment. His allotment, which he visited most days, provided him with not only an abundance of fresh produce, it occupied his time and allowed him to keep his sanity.

In contrast, Julie's success had bought Charlie and her a large house in Darras Hall, with an acre and a half of land, bordered by a variety of evergreen and deciduous trees and bushes. Rhododendrons lined the drive and the garden had been planted to ensure that there was colour all year 'round. Only God knew how much it was worth these days. It was something they had never really considered.

They had no intention of moving house, and since Julie would obviously outlive him, as women often do, especially when they are younger than their husbands and especially when their husbands have lived in the fast lane, it was hers to do with as she pleased. Steve would be well cared for, she would see to that without any persuasion from Charlie and whether Steve expected anything or not. She loved Steve as she would a little brother, and pitied him at the same time. Steve regarded her as a big sister and would regularly tease her, much to her delight. Charlie was aware of this warm relationship and it had crossed his mind that, should he go before her, there was the possibility, the hope even, their relationship would develop into something else entirely.

The front door to the house was hardly ever used. Only the postman and those who were not in the know used it. For all the back door led directly into the kitchen-come-family room, everyone else used that door. It was the most welcoming and homely of entrances, with an arbour and mature Wisteria framing it. The large front garden was screened from the main road and the driveway curved around to the front of the house, allowing enough parking for at least twenty cars and, if parked sympathetically, only the last two could be seen from the road.

Which was very quiet. The large wrought iron gates were rarely closed.

Mainly residents and their visitors used that road, and the occasional rubbernecker interested in how the other half lived. The back and side gardens were separated from the front by a six feet tall solid wooden shiplap fence with a wooden gate. The nearest house was just over sixty metres to the east, the next nearest in the other direction, nearly one hundred metres. They did not really know any of the neighbours in spite of having lived there for many years, and it was what you could call, without fear of contradiction, a secluded spot.

'Bye, then!' said Julie, after plonking a mug of coffee beside Charlie, causing it to slightly overspill. 'See you around six-ish.' She gave him a peck on the cheek, her hair tickling his slightly exposed neck and he responded, taking care not to soil her clothes with his muddy, rough hands. He resisted the temptation to squeeze what he occasionally referred to as her *fabulous arse*. She did not like that term, even when they were alone. She did not mind the occasional fondle or a quick grope but there was a time and place for everything and this was neither the time nor the place. She always dressed elegantly and would make a bin liner look sexy. She always looked a million dollars, certainly in public. Appearance meant everything to her, especially as she had been in the fashion business and still mixed with the *fashionista aficionados* from time to time.

And off she went, watched by a lustful Charlie, taking her lovely rear through the gate, her blue dress contrasting with the red Audi TT sports car.

He did not hear her start the motor, a combination of the distance between them, the sound insulation provided by the tall wooden fence and hedge. And the fact that his mind had already turned to how deep he should make the hole for his pond. The spring frosts had subsided and if he did not make a start now, it could be another year gone.

THREE

Charlie had no idea of how long Julie had been gone, five, ten or fifteen minutes, when the garden gate swung open behind him. He was not expecting anyone. His friend and ex-police colleague, Jed, normally called for him around Friday lunchtime for a coffee and a chat, but other than that, he did not normally get visitors through the day. He looked up. It did not take him long to register. He had changed little, but it was unmistakably Tommy Layton, a man whom Charlie had put in prison for fifteen years, about ten years earlier, for armed robbery. This bore the hallmarks of a very bad day, and he swallowed hard. Tommy must have walked along the edge of the lawn, otherwise Charlie would surely have heard his footsteps on the gravelled path. It was of little importance how he had managed to find where Charlie lived, that would wait for later. Tommy grinned from ear to ear, but it was far from friendly. The hatred in his eyes gave him away and Charlie, for once, was lost for words.

Tommy had prison pallor. He was almost white. His face clearly had not seen much sunlight for many years. He was not the sort of man to toe the line and Charlie imagined that he would spend a lot of his time in solitary confinement, exercising mainly in a high walled yard. Nor was he the sort to engage in sports, from Charlie's recollection of his lifestyle. He was more inclined to be a spectator. Which would partly explain his increased girth. That and the high carbohydrate nature of a prison diet. The legs were still skinny, though, he noticed. His denim jeans appeared to be empty and featureless as if they'd been hung out to dry in a heavy frost.

'What brings you here, Tommy?' he said at last, trying to conceal his alarm, and as if he did not already know. Charlie's grip tightened around the spade shaft. Not that he was thinking about using it on Tommy, it was a subconscious reaction brought on by the rush of adrenalin. Tommy had verbally threatened Charlie when he gave him the bad news on the charge sheet and again, with a menacing stare, when he was led off down the Crown Court stairs to wait for the prison bus to take him to *his Nanna's*. He hadn't done any jail time as an adult, up to that point, such was his ability to evade capture. He was one of the wiser villains, if such a creature existed but, with this length of prison sentence, he was entering uncharted waters. And to say that he was pissed off would be an understatement.

'Unfinished business,' came the curt reply, 'I promised you it wasn't over.'

'I take it you are on parole ... or did you escape?' Charlie asked. He knew it was a feeble remark, but it was all he could think of at the time.

Charlie's eyes were all over him, and behind him, looking for any kind of weapon. *And where is Danny Pritchard, his co-accused? Is he there? Is he waiting on the other side of the fence? Is he checking the place over?*

'Parole. A week ago, not like Pritch, poor bastard. Died of complications following a cocktail of stuff about a year ago. Didn't you know? Don't you read the papers?'

Charlie shook his head, 'Honestly, Tommy, I didn't hear about it. I'm retired now.' It was a lame excuse, but it was true.

'You ruined my life, you know that? And Pritch's. And Cleggie's!' Globules of saliva left his mouth in all directions as he vehemently spat out his words. Then, after a brief moment, he took out a dull, grey, sinister looking handgun, from inside his distressed, brown leather bomber jacket. The hammer snagged on the faux fleece lining before he impatiently tugged it free, fuelling his anger further. In different circumstances, Charlie might have sniggered at his ineptitude but, at that moment, amusement could not be further from his mind.

The colour drained from Charlie's face. This was a game changer and he began to tremble involuntary as the adrenalin told him to prepare for flight or fight. He had been in many fixes but nothing as bad as this. He could handle himself in a one to one but, on this occasion, he had nothing going for him, just his wit and his tongue, both of which could make matters worse if he misjudged the mood. The spade was no good for the ten-foot distance between them, and Tommy could have dropped him before he even had time to lift it. The gun was well-worn, probably a forces' piece from the Cold-War era. It had history.

'C'mon, Tommy, this is crazy, you've done your time! You don't want to go back inside!' said Charlie, unconvincingly. 'Life means life for a second serious offence. Tommy, you were guilty as sin and you bloody know it.'

There was not a flicker of emotion from Tommy, just a passive, emotionless, cold stare. His anger had subsided and he was now focused on the task ahead. Whether Charlie was guilty or not was irrelevant.

Charlie was not sure whether he was doing himself any favours, and decided on a change of tack. Maybe a massage of the ego would have the desired effect. It was worth a try at least, he thought.

'You were the all-time number one robber in the north of England, and you got away with dozens. You know that, but so did everyone else. Even the Crime Squad couldn't get near you, with all their resources. That's how good you were! They told me I was wasting my time and there was nobody more surprised than them at the result. I just got a breakthrough, that's all. You can't blame me for doing my job. Remember when your mate Forster was abducted and tortured? – It was me who locked up the team who did that! I do my job, that's all. I even work for the bad guys when they get some shit.' Charlie tried to bite his tongue. Running off at the mouth like that would let Tommy see his frailty. But it was true, Charlie had put away one of Tommy's old colleagues' enemies, and Forster and Charlie actually got on quite well after that. Forster would give him information and Charlie occasionally turned a blind eye to his activities, in return. He did not condone them, he just chose not to see them in the same light that a judge and jury may have done. He always led Charlie to bigger fish, which is why Charlie told himself it was okay.

'Who was the grass?' said Tommy, unmoved.

'There was no grass, Tommy, absolutely none, but the court rules prevented me from saying whether there was or wasn't. I'm telling you now, there *wasn't*, and that's the honest truth.'

It was the truth. Charlie had correctly guessed the identity of the gang, based on his study of the modus operandi of historic crimes, and what was known about Tommy and his team. After that, everything fell nicely into place. He just got lucky. He knew it, but Tommy would take some convincing.

'There was five of us on the video at that garage. Me, Pritch and Cleggie. You couldn't see who the others were, but us three were obvious, so how come Cleggie didn't get locked up?'

'We honestly didn't know who he was, Tommy. My team wasn't from your neck of the woods. I showed the video around but about a dozen different names were mentioned as possibles, hardly enough evidence to knock on anyone else's door. If cops couldn't make up their minds who it was, how could we expect a jury to?'

'You're lying!'

'No, I'm not, your barrister must have told you. At least he should have. He had every aspect of the investigation disclosed to him. They had copies of every document, video and everything. The prosecution knew the situation and they always talk to the defence. They're all mates, have dinner together, for Christ's sake, and do deals. I swear, the bloke who was paying rent for the garage saw your car in it and reported it to the local plod because it shouldn't have been there. They checked the car number and it was stolen. Plod watched it for a couple of weeks and put a video on it. They identified you, and because their gaffer knew I was interested in you, he passed the job over to me. There's no grass, it was just circumstance!' Again, Charlie felt that it sounded as if he was pleading for his life. He was doing just that, but he did not want to give Tommy the satisfaction of knowing that the once formidable Charlie Payne, wasn't the hard-nosed detective people thought he was.

'You also played us like fools, getting rookies to interview us then dropping shit like that onto us.'

Charlie's head dropped. It was true, Charlie had indulged in a little gamesmanship. Ten years earlier, the evidence was so good that he did not need confessions. For the interviews, he chose relatively inexperienced officers who would stick to the script and not get carried away with their own agenda. He gave them a game plan, the questions to ask, how to ask them and when to ask them. Both officers were instructed to appear nervous, out of their depth, and one of them, Joe Elliot, threw in a practised and perfected stammer for good measure. Layton and Pritchard were in for a treat. Charlie knew from experience that criminals tend to relax a little when they realise that they are in the hands of novices. Some deride their inexperienced interviewers and become cocky, while others tend to play along and humour them. One thing for certain, Charlie felt, when they are relaxed or think they have an advantage, they tend to talk.

Often rubbish, and mostly lies, but at least they talked. This would often open up new lines of enquiry or tempt them to tell silly, unnecessary lies, which would later enable him to hang them out to dry.

It worked for this pair. They hadn't known what to expect, but were so relieved to find their opponents appeared to be going through the motions, before their inevitable release. Jill Thomas made a big issue of losing a false finger nail and switching between curses and giggling while trying to remove the cellophane wrapper from the tape just before Layton's first interview, and Joe Elliot's stammer was worthy of an Oscar.

At the time of arrest and during the hours they waited in the cells for interview, Layton and Pritchard had worried about what evidence the police had. This was only natural because they weren't to know what evidence the police had against them. The microphone from the interview room to an adjacent office allowed Charlie to listen to the proceedings. Everything was going to plan. The questions were about where they were at the time of the robbery, no more. There was lots of laughter, and the more their confidence soared, the more they talked. That is, until the interviewer's last, scripted remark.

'That's all for now, but when we come back, we want to speak to you about that stolen car you had holed up in a Gateshead garage.'

Tommy said nothing, but looked at his solicitor, who remained expressionless. He was used to maintaining a stony face for effect but, up his sleeve, had several well-versed outbursts suited to the occasion. An inexperienced officer might be impressed, but not so Charlie. He'd heard it all before.

When it came to Pritchard's turn, the effect of the disclosure was watered down. He knew what was coming. His solicitor had warned him. Joe Mangan, a big shot with the criminal fraternity, occasionally a handler of stolen goods, although that was never tested, was acting for both suspects. He was allowed to do so because there was no conflict of interest, as neither was blaming the other. But Pritchard denied all knowledge of the stolen car just the same, in a way that prevented him from altering course later. They *did* have a stolen car hidden in a garage in Gateshead, they both knew that. It had been there for at least a month, but how did the *filth* know?

The second interview was pretty much as the first. Both denied any knowledge of the robbery or the stolen car tucked up in a garage in Gateshead, and because the interviewers were still playing the dim-wits, Layton and Pritchard repeatedly cemented their denials. The joviality, on the other hand, had disappeared. And then came the interviewers' parting remark:

'Well, we'll take another break, and when we come back, we want to talk to you about who was seen messing around at the car. You do realise that we have been videoing the comings and goings at this garage for weeks, don't you? You're on it, plain as day!'

This time, Layton's glance towards his solicitor was met with a startled look. Guilty or not, the solicitor had allowed them both to respond to questions that would help seal their fate, certainly as far as the stolen car was concerned. It was a foot in the door. The thin end of the wedge. And he'd fallen for it, just as they had.

During the interval, Mangan demanded full disclosure of all of the evidence.

'Detective Inspector Payne,' he started as soon as he saw Charlie in the custody suite, 'I must protest at the way these interviews are being conducted. It's unprofessional and does the police no credit, let alone you. I demand full disclosure of the evidence!'

Charlie looked him up and down. His face, with the complexion of a pepperoni pizza, was now purple. He wasn't used to being outsmarted. Compassion and diplomacy weren't in Charlie's vocabulary, certainly not for the likes of him.

'On the contrary, it does us a lot of credit,' fired back Charlie with a grin. 'You will get full disclosure in due course, Mr. Mangan. You and I both know that I can control the pace of disclosure, so don't try and bullshit me. Only a fuckwit would show his hand before the betting starts. I don't have to tell you more than the reason for arrest for openers and you know that. I have a copy of the solicitors' rule book if you want to refresh your memory?'

'In that case, I'm instructing my clients not to answer any more questions. If you have the evidence to charge, you must charge.'

'Actually, the law doesn't really say that either, does it?' said Charlie. 'Look at the wording! At this time, I don't know if there is the reasonable prospect of a conviction so I'm duty bound to continue.'

Mangan said nothing.

'There are still some questions I have to ask,' Charlie continued. 'It's up to them, whether they want to answer them. Frankly, I don't give a monkey's either way. You know the score. I'm surprised you even raised it. And, by the way, don't quote the law at me unless it's factual or I'll be making a complaint to The Law Society.' Charlie was having difficulty in hiding his delight.

There were now three possible scenarios. They would either tell the truth, tell more lies, or refuse to answer further questions. It was a win, win, win situation. The first was unlikely, Charlie knew that. The second was also improbable, once Mangan realised what was happening. He would have advised his clients to stop digging their graves. The final option would be to say nothing. If they chose that path the trial judge would be entitled to invite the jury to consider why a person would not wish to answer questions, especially when they had already been freely answering questions, but clammed up as soon as the questions got harder. The fact that they had also told provable lies about the car in the garage would not go down too well, either. The jury, even without knowing the pair's offending history, might begin to realise what kind of people they really are.

Both Layton and Pritchard knew that they were in for a charge of car theft, alternatively handling stolen goods, at the very least, nothing on the scale of things to follow, but that would hinge on whether the video recording at the garage was good enough for an identification. Charlie knew fine well that it was, but the defence would not find that out until later, by which time it was too late for them to come up with a plausible alternative explanation. Both were offered the chance to view the video recording during interview, but declined, as Charlie thought they might. In front of the television screen it would be difficult for them to deny what was painfully obvious. *If it looks like a duck, quacks like a duck and waddles like a duck, it is probably a duck.*

There was no mistaking the identifications of Layton and Pritchard. They would later regret not seeing the video because, had they watched it, they would have been able to identify the third man, Clegg, and wonder why he wasn't facing the same treatment. At that time, it could have made a difference to the outcome, but the chance had passed.

At the initial showing of the footage to the defence barristers who, as usual, left everything to the last minute, they agreed that it was, indeed, Tommy Layton and Danny Pritchard. They also knew that the third man was Clegg. Not only did the barristers know him themselves, Tommy and Danny confirmed his identity to them after the trial, while they were preparing for the appeal. Which failed. The appeal judge ruled that everything had been fair and above board, and that the trial judge's summing up had, if anything, been overly fair to the defendants. They had nowhere else to go with it.

The next interview was about the finer details of the crime. Joe Elliot and Jill Thomas were now giving more disclosure, as planned. Elliot's stammer had miraculously cured itself and Thomas's giggling had stopped. She was now a serious opponent and Layton and Pritchard knew they'd been conned. All they had been told on arrest was that it was for a £5 million attempted robbery at a security depot in Newcastle, and the time and date it happened. Now the detectives were able to tell them, as if they didn't already know, the intimate details of the crime. The vehicles that had been stolen and used, including a van capable of transporting about 3 cubic metres of banknotes. And probably seven people, in all, were involved. But how did the police know all this?

The enquiry team had found all of the vehicles, and pieced together the details of an elaborate, well planned crime. Well planned, except for two mistakes. The first was that the wagon stolen to ram the defences, was not big enough. It was only a five tonner, whereas at least a seven tonner was required to breach the security rated bollards. Even the larger vehicle would have to have been doing almost 50 mph at the point of impact to get through. Its speed at the point of impact was, in fact, no more than 25 mph, according to road traffic collision investigators and tachograph experts.

Secondly, although there were no forensics, they were too good for that, they were not good enough to detect the listening device Charlie had arranged to be placed in the stolen car while it was garaged in Gateshead, the car in which they had discussed the intimate details of their plan. They could not have spotted the device. Police technicians had broken into the garage without leaving a trace and worked on the car for several hours to bury it where even a mechanic would not find it without stripping the car down completely. It was probably still there, although by now the car would have been scrapped, crushed, melted down and re-incarnated as part of someone's washing machine. The only misfortune was that the connection between the attempted robbery and the stolen car was not made until after all the dialogue had been transcribed, weeks after the actual event. But what a connection.

From the recording at the garage housing the stolen car, three people could be identified, Tommy, Danny, and another of their gang, James Clegg, although Clegg's identification was far weaker and was unlikely to convince a jury. None of the investigation team knew Clegg. They had been recruited from different areas, not in Clegg's manor, but the defence team knew him well enough. The defence barristers were not convinced that there was insufficient evidence to arrest and charge the third man and, during the trial, both they and their juniors, four wigs in all, gave Charlie grief for three whole days, while being made to stand in the witness box. Protocol dictated that they were not permitted to ask Charlie directly whether there was an informant, but they tried every trick in the book to make him drop his guard and create an opening.

Charlie was better than that. He knew the score and withstood the interrogation. The remaining figures in the video were just shadows and could not be identified at all. In truth, Charlie was fairly certain that the third man was Clegg, but chose not to arrest him, for two reasons; firstly, his team was fairly small and already stretched. Headquarters were becoming impatient and the overtime had dried up so Charlie chose to stick with the ace and king rather than twist and risk drawing a joker; secondly, and he sometimes regretted this but it seemed like a good idea at the time, when Tommy and Danny were shown the videotape, which they were entitled to see, they would have instantly seen that the third man was James Clegg. Unlike the police on the investigation they knew him intimately, even though the identification wasn't as clear cut as their own. He would be labelled the snitch and, at the very least, it would cause a huge fall out in the team. Clegg may have even turned *Queens* in exchange for a shorter sentence and a new identity.

At the time, Clegg's wellbeing did not concern Charlie. He was a low-life that had ruined many peoples' lives, and any bad luck that came his way was well deserved. He was part of a team that had maimed, tortured and terrorized mostly innocent people. The families of victims and witnesses had been put through ordeals that often resulted in breakdowns, as they struggled to cope with their situation. Not a good idea to mention any of this to Tommy Layton just now but, with all of that in mind, it was clear that Tommy had good cause to ask questions. As of now, Charlie wished he could turn back the clock.

'Tommy, okay,' Charlie conceded, 'I accept that the interviews were not what you are used to, but methods change. We wanted you to deny something that we could prove, so we got you talking and denying so that you could hardly go back and change your mind. It's the way things are done. Let you talk yourself into a corner. You want to blame Mangan for that. And honestly, there was no snout, we just couldn't identify your buddy well enough to put him to a jury. He's a very lucky man'.

Tommy shook his head. The remark irritated him. 'Lucky? That's a fucking joke! When did you retire?'

'Two months ago. February.'

'It's 10 years since the case, did his name ever crop up again?'

Charlie thought for a moment. 'No, I don't believe it did. I wouldn't know, I was working in a different area.'

'Within a month of me going down, he was in the ground. In the fucking ground! The video at the garage went public and everybody could see it was him. They assumed he'd been let off for grassing.'

Charlie took an involuntary gulp of air. Although the risk of such an ending to Clegg had always existed, he didn't think for one moment that it would happen. Not in this neck of the woods.

'For God's sake, Tommy, he wasn't a snout! Nobody was......'

'He was my best mate. We were like brothers. I didn't want it to happen, but I couldn't stop it. I was inside and I'm way down the peckin' order, so my say doesn't count. Anyway, if he wasn't the grass, he died for nothing so it's all your fault anyway, isn't it? You bastard!'

'If the video went public, it must have come from your side. The police copy will still be under lock and key,' explained Charlie.

'Maybe, but so what? It got out and that's what matters. Doesn't matter who leaked it!' replied Tommy, angrily.

'Look, Tommy, you can't lay that on me. I mean what happened to Clegg!' said Charlie, desperate to deflect the blame.

'Like I say, it wasn't me, I was in Durham,' responded Tommy. 'I heard it was a hammer on the old nut then probably the usual concrete overcoat. Like I say, I'm way down the list and the main guys don't put up with grasses. They don't like botched jobs either, so I'm still in the bad books for messin' up, but I'll be okay if I do this right. They just want me to like ...... see you off.' He smirked.

'What? You can't be serious? You're no murderer!' pleaded Charlie.

'Yes, I am serious. I don't really want to do it but I'm going to. I don't have a choice, do I? It's you or me. If I don't do it then it's me that'll be getting measured up.'

'For God's sake, Tommy, what's happened has happened. It makes no sense you going back to prison,' pleaded Charlie again, suddenly realising that Tommy was not really after the name of the grass. This was revenge for disrupting lifestyles, his own and the rest of the gang's. Charlie was beginning to realise that, without a miracle, these might very well be his last minutes. And he hadn't finished his garden pond yet.

Tommy smiled. His teeth were not at their best. Some were missing, and some had discoloured at different rates. Mostly yellow with an occasional purple hue. He was not going to be a hit with the ladies.

'I'm alibied to the hilt. I'm in Cornwall and I'll have the fuel receipts and everything else you could think of. False plates on an identical motor. I even have somebody who looks like me, and who will leave my DNA everywhere. He's got my toothbrush, my hairs and all that kind of stuff and he'll smear it where he needs to. He'll stay far enough away from any CCTV, so that they can't tell the difference. This has been planned virtually from the day I went down.

'Tommy, be sensible,' Charlie pleaded. 'You know that cops push the boat out when one of their own gets topped. More than ninety percent of murders are detected in these parts, but a hundred per cent if it's a cop, so I think you're kidding yourself if you think they'll fall for the Cornwall crap. I still have a lot of mates on the job, in high places, and they won't rest until they've found you. They'll be trying their best for me.'

'I wouldn't be so sure, you're not as popular as you think, mate. You're yesterday's news. History! Anyway, it's a chance I'll have to take.'

He was probably right. When you're gone, you're gone. Charlie recalled that they had told him he was irreplaceable, but on the day he retired, they replaced him.

Layton then pointed his gun towards Charlie. Charlie could see that it looked like a Beretta 9mm, with which he was familiar. He had been firearms trained himself and knew that it was probably capable of firing nine or more bullets at a muzzle velocity of several hundred feet per second. Even if he missed altogether with the first couple of shots, or just nicked him, he had plenty of spare ammunition. It was not possible to see what ammunition he was using but either it would make a neat hole at the point of entry and a far bigger one on exit, or it would make a hole big enough to hit a tennis ball right through, without touching the sides. Either way, it was bad news.

Charlie frantically looked around for some inspiration. Beads of fear were beginning to form along his hairline, while his throat dried to a croak. Tommy was in no hurry. He was enjoying it. While keeping an eye on Charlie he slowly transferred the gun from his right hand into his left and, with his right hand, reached into his right jacket pocket. He struggled to release its contents, but his hand eventually emerged with a six-inch-long black dull metal tube. It was a silencer. That made sense, thought Charlie. There was no point in making any more noise than was necessary. If Tommy had only been out for a week, he had done remarkably well to get hold of such kit so soon, especially if he was acting alone. The likelihood was that it was waiting for him all along. Pre-arranged with some criminal underworld armourer. More bad news. It meant that there had been some degree of planning after all, and that the Cornwall alibi was probably true.

The purpose of the silencer is to dissipate muzzle gases into bafflers along the inside of the tube, causing less frontal discharge and, ultimately, less noise. If it was a clean shot, he wouldn't hear the noise, but that was of no consolation to Charlie. He would be just as dead.

There was no longer any expression on Tommy's face, no pity, no hatred. The smirk had gone and there was no need for any more small-talk, as much as he was enjoying it. He had a pint of lager waiting for him somewhere and the delay was keeping him from it. As he began to screw the silencer into the business end of the pistol barrel, it dawned on Charlie that Tommy was right-handed and his only chance would be to rush him while the gun was still in his left hand and he was not quite ready. The distance between them was now eight feet, as Charlie inched closer. It would take three steps to close that distance, but Charlie was no spring chicken.

While Charlie was still contemplating his move, his ears ringing, his brain frantically looking for inspiration, he failed to see the garden gate open slowly behind Tommy. A second later, Tommy's body violently lurched forward and his arms flew out in front of him, thrusting the gun, silencer still only partly engaged, in Charlie's direction. It fell two feet from Charlie's toes. Tommy's knees buckled, as the brain told them it had left the building, and he collapsed into an untidy heap in front of Charlie. He could not have gone down quicker if he had tried, a sure sign that he was dead before he had hit the ground. Charlie flinched, and drew back, not knowing what to expect. A garden fork, sticking in Tommy's back at a near ninety-degree angle, sprang into sight, rocked slightly, and eventually settled. It was now quite still.

Beyond that, Charlie's eyes focused on the blue dress of Julie, standing behind Tommy's body, with her hands clasped either side of her head, her mouth wide open in a silent scream. She had quadruple spiked him in the upper section of his back. The widest part. And, in doing so, had surely saved Charlie's life. Charlie fell to his knees and vomited.

FOUR

'Oh my God,' shrieked Julie, 'what have I done?' She stared at the body, hands still clasping either side of her face, aghast at what she saw. 'Is he dead?' She circled the body, never taking her eyes off it, until she stood beside Charlie. He got up, wiped his mouth with a sleeve then held her around the waist and rested his chin on her right shoulder, kissing her quickly on the neck.

'What do we do now?' she said, pushing him away.

'Is the gate shut properly?' said Charlie quickly, ignoring her question. He was safe, for now, but his first instinct was to prevent anyone else from stumbling across the scene.

'No, it's just pulled to,' replied Julie, 'I didn't want to make a noise in case he heard me.'

Charlie darted over to the gate and engaged the latch, followed by the heavy-duty bolt, but not before peering outside to see if there was anyone around. If anyone did approach, it would be easier to explain the security overkill than the dead body with a garden fork sticking out of its back.

'I didn't see you come in. You were very quiet.'

'I kept out of your sight in case you gave the game away. If he'd seen both of us, God knows what would have happened.'

'You've saved my life, Julie. He was going to kill me. He *would* have killed me, that's for certain. It'll be justifiable homicide. You had no choice.' Charlie moved towards her and again hugged her tightly. 'What great timing, you saved my life, girl,' he managed eventually, aware that he was repeating himself.

'Are you going to report it?' said Julie, again pushing him away, clearly alarmed at his *justifiable homicide* comment.

'Of course! Why not, you've done nothing wrong!' replied Charlie, reassuringly.

'What about that poor man who was killed because they thought he was a grass? What about the others? Won't they come after you?'

The thought had already occurred to Charlie. She had a point. This was far from over. It was, if he knew anything about these people, just the beginning.

'How much did you hear?' he asked Julie.

'Everything. He's only a small cog in a big wheel, and all that. What if they're involved? They must have been involved in the planning of this..........' She made a wide sweeping gesture with her right arm over the grisly scene. For all Charlie had seen many dead bodies and she, probably none, he had never seen one die in such a way or so suddenly, in front of him, or one with a garden fork sticking out of his back. That kind of thing only happened in movies.

'What made you come back?' Charlie said, sidestepping her comments but knowing deep down that she was probably right. She was an intelligent woman, Julie. She could work things out for herself.

'I'd just left here and, as I was driving along the road, I saw this big black jeep thing, indicating to turn right. The only place it could have been going to was here. He was going too slow for the next turn off. His window was down and I saw his face. Didn't recognise him at first, but after about a minute, I realised it was one of those men you arrested for that big robbery a few years back. I was clearing out some rubbish the other day and came across your newspaper cuttings of the trial. His face was there, so I came back. I didn't know what to expect, but it's just as well, isn't it? But not for me. Not for me....' Her voice trailed away as she shook her head and looked for somewhere to sit. She was close to collapse. She was shaking and her legs buckled. She felt around for the driftwood bench and lowered herself slowly onto it, steadying herself with the armrest.

'If we aren't going to call it in, what are you suggesting – getting rid of the body and saying nothing?' asked Charlie. That option had crossed his mind also.

'As long as nobody saw him come here, as long as we give the place a thorough clean and as long as we hide him where he can't be found, it should be okay. Shouldn't it?' she said, shocking herself that she could be so devious.

Charlie thought for a few moments.

'Let's see if he had any back-up. Come with me, I'm not leaving you here, in case someone turns up while I'm gone. First things first, I'll have to straighten the body before rigor mortis sets in, otherwise it will be harder to shift later.' He knew that rigor mortis usually starts two to six hours after death when the body, depleted of oxygen, stops producing the adenosine triphosphate that aids muscle relaxation. Outside, in cooler weather, it takes a little longer.

'I'll need to get it under cover so that no one looking over the fence, or flying over in a helicopter, can see it. You phone your sisters and tell them you've got a headache or something. Be quick, I've got stuff to do here'.

'Helicopters?'

'Well probably not, but you know how my mind works. Just looking at all the possibilities. Covering all the bases. We're near the airport. And there's the drones.'

'What drones?'

'God knows how many kids got them for Christmas. Those little helicopter things with cameras. All it needs is for some little sprog to have a nose into our garden.'

Julie summoned the strength to get up from the bench and walk into the house. When she was out of sight, Charlie pulled the fork out of Tommy's back. It was well jammed and made sucking and crunching sounds as he rocked it back and forth, to prise it from the sinew and bone. The noises were sickening and he winced at the thought of the internal injuries and the damage he would be doing, if Tommy was still alive.

The fork had sunk in around 5 inches. The force used was surprisingly excessive, almost vicious, and certainly out of character for someone with Julie's temperate nature. She had to have severed his spinal cord in an instant, as it was difficult to imagine anyone going down that quickly, merely with punctured organs. The fork handle would have been wrenched from Julie's hands as Layton fell. Even with holes in the heart and lungs, he would deflate rather than drop at such a rate. Charlie had seen enough autopsies and worked with many Home Office Pathologists, so he had a fair idea of how the body works. He was mildly disappointed that he was never going to find out whether his diagnosis was correct.

Thankfully, none of the prongs had come out of the other side, or the blood would have saturated the ground beneath him. Nevertheless, he realised that Julie must have used considerable force, probably the exact words a Home Office Pathologist would use, if one ever got the chance to examine Tommy. Because death would have been fairly instant, even when Charlie removed the fork, and it took some force to do so, there was no spurting of blood. There was hardly a trace around the four neat holes in his jacket, just around the jagged perimeters, as the prongs wiped themselves almost clean as they were extracted.

Charlie moved the rubber pool liner to where it would do most good and dragged Tommy's body onto it, feet first, turning the sides of the sheet over so that it could not be seen.

He picked up the gun carefully and examined it. It was, indeed, a Beretta 9mm Compact. If Tommy did have back-up, they would be tooled up and Charlie needed to even the odds. He quickly checked it and released the magazine. It contained fifteen rounds and one in the spout. More than he had calculated. He disengaged the silencer so that it was easier to conceal. Pieced together, it measured close to thirteen inches, but separately, they were no more than seven.

He then unbolted the gate, and having made sure that no one was about, quickly examined the black Jeep Cherokee in the drive. It would be just about visible from the road, but the likelihood of its being seen was low. The postman had been, and most people on the estate moved around in their cars. Dog walkers were a risk, though, especially if the dog decides to cock its leg in the gateway.

As an afterthought, he put on some rubber gloves from the kitchen and took care not to touch or breathe on anything. DNA had come a long way and it was possible to identify someone by minute droplets of breath or sweat from finger smudges. It was a hire vehicle and the hire papers were in the glove compartment. They were in Tommy's name. The receipt was attached and payment had been made in cash. There was no receipt for a deposit, an indication that Tommy was, perhaps, known to the lessor, or that someone else had picked up the tab for that part of the transaction. It was due back at 9am on Thursday. The keys were still in the ignition. He removed them and put them into his pocket. Charlie's clothes were all going into the incinerator, so forensic transfer wasn't an issue.

A plan was already forming in his head. He padlocked the gate and he and Julie walked to her red Audi, which she had left twenty metres from the gateway, on the road, so as not to make a noise as she freewheeled towards the house. *Good girl*, thought Charlie, pleased that Julie had the presence of mind to approach quietly. They checked all roads within a half a mile radius. There was nothing that looked remotely like back-up. No one waiting in side roads, no cars, no pedestrians, absolutely nothing. He dared to hope that Tommy had gone it alone after all, that the Cornwall alibi was just a figment of his imagination, that after all this time, the gang had expelled him, shunned him, that he was a nobody, and that no one else knew what he had planned. Most of all, that he would not be missed. But Charlie could not take that chance. He was preparing for every eventuality.

Returning home, he parked the Audi just behind the Cherokee then drove the Cherokee further up the drive so that it could not be seen without actually entering the plot. The chances of that happening were slim to nil. He unlocked the padlock and they both went through the gate into the back garden. He bolted and padlocked the gate behind them. Entering the kitchen, Julie made for the heavy oak chair and sat at the even heavier oak kitchen table, head in hands, crying softly to herself. No doubt, she had done a terrible thing, but a jury, if it got that far, would see that she had no alternative. *Her husband was surely going to be murdered by this desperate convict, and her timely intervention saved his life. What else could she have done?*

'I know what you're thinking,' she said, finally, through her tears, 'report it and I'll get off with it. Two things wrong with that. Yes, I might get off with it but only after a trial and publicity that will ruin both of us. I couldn't stand a trial. It's alright for you, you've been to court hundreds of times. It won't bother you, you know what to do and say. But what about his cronies? They'll come after us, I know they will. They don't bother with what's right and wrong. If they're as bad as you say they are, we're dead. Oh my God!' she paused before starting up again.

'Even if we are in prison. And I couldn't stand that either. If we get rid of the body, I mean really get rid of it so that it's never found and there are no, what do you call them … forensics, to connect us, surely we stand a good chance of getting away with it?'

Charlie could not remember the last time she had said as much in one go. She was rambling but making sense, nevertheless.

As an investigator, Charlie had always tried to think like the criminal. He would ask himself what could possibly go wrong, then take appropriate steps to ensure that it did not. He had always tried to close down any conceivable avenue of escape, which is why his cases invariably resulted in conviction. He was never surprised by twists and turns. He had usually already anticipated them and was ready with an answer. Not once had he ever been caught out.

'I'm not saying I'm going along with it, but let me think out loud for a moment. Feel free to jump in. We have to assume that others are involved and I'm sorry to have to admit it, but whether we tell the police what happened or whether we dispose of the body and pretend nothing's happened, sooner or later, somebody will wonder where he is. Either way, we are in deep shit, or at least I am. You'll be alright, no one will ever know you were here and, if the worst comes to the worst, I'll say it was me. You were miles away. If they come at me again, I can handle it. We'll dump the body, then go on holiday for a while. Our CCTV will show us whether there are any callers to the house while we're away and we can take it from there. First, we'll wrap the body in the pool liner and put it out of sight until tomorrow. I'll get rid of the fork and buy another one. Through the night, we'll take the Cherokee back to the hire company and put the keys through the letter box. They will just think it's been returned early. Obviously, we'll make sure no forensics are

51

left. We will go a route where there is no CCTV. You will not follow me, but you will meet me about half a mile away from the drop off and bring me home. Tomorrow, I'll take the body to Amble and take the boat out. I'll transfer the body into the coffin and drag it on board.'

The 'coffin' was their pet name for their fishing tackle box on board Stormy Monday. Because of its size, it had a six-inch diameter retractable dolly wheel at each corner to help manoeuvre it along the floating dock and the gangway. Usually, it was a one-man operation, but it was easier with two, especially when lowering it down to the deck. It had no brakes and, uncontrolled, it could cause damage, albeit superficial.

'I've done that dozens of times so no problem there. I'll take it out as far as I dare, further than the eye can see, to where the water is the least tidal, where there is no interest to divers or fishermen. I think I know just the spot where there is a depression and where no one ever goes diving or trawling.' He was now the one rambling, but he wanted Julie to know that he'd thought of everything.

'I'll weigh the body down so that it can't float to the surface. The first three days will be the most crucial, as body gases develop and tend to give it buoyancy. I'll have to puncture the stomach.'

'Too much information!' interrupted Julie.

'You need to know these things! I'll remove the rubber sheet to allow decomposition and the crabs to dispose of it quickly. Torn to shreds and weighed down, there's little chance the tide will bring it in. I'll come back here and burn any clothing we were wearing during the entire operation, along with the pool liner, and take the ashes and anything else to separate council tips, about fifty miles away, ones that don't have CCTV. Any flaws, so far?'

'What then?' asked Julie. She needed further convincing.

'We crack open a bottle of champagne, and go on holiday!' said Charlie, smiling.

'You can't be serious? It sounds too simple! What if it goes wrong?'

'The risky bit is transferring the body into the coffin, but I can manage that. He's only about eleven stone. I won't do it until I'm a hundred per cent certain that the coast is clear. No one will see me dump the body in the sea, I'll make sure of that. The only other thing is, if they do find the body, they might eventually make the connection. You know, who has boats and who knew Tommy? I would become a suspect, but it's only circumstantial. Not good enough to convict. They might ask around our neighbourhood and someone might have seen the Cherokee, but it's unlikely. Even if it does backfire, at some stage we might have to admit the whole thing. In that case, we tell the whole truth. No one could possibly convict us of murder. They're bound to know that Tommy's presence here wasn't a social event. At most, it would be concealment of a body and depriving the coroner. One other possibility is that his family report him missing and someone might just mention he was coming to see me. We've just got to hope that they don't delve too deeply. If it does happen, though, we know nothing about it, right? At least unless the game's totally up. For that to happen, they need to find a body, and then they need to prove he was here, but if we do this properly, they won't do either.'

'Yes, but his pals don't need evidence, do they? You are still, as he said, unfinished business.'

'Don't make assumptions, we don't know that they will come after me. Tommy was the one with the gripe, it was all water under the bridge as far as the rest of them were concerned. They've moved on. They've had ten years to do something but they didn't. Anyway, if the CCTV shows any unwanted visitors, I can tell the police that it might be linked to threats made by Tommy when I put him away, and that I heard he'd got out recently.'

'You make it all sound so fucking simple, don't you?' she said surprisingly angrily. She wasn't usually given to swearing. 'But I suppose it's the years of dealing with low life. Their depravity has rubbed off on you. You think like them. You're too enthusiastic about it all. You're bloody enjoying this, aren't you!'

'I'm not enjoying it, but I'll take the rest of it as a compliment', Charlie replied, with a half-smile, not at all put out by her remarks, even her swearing, which was a rarity. It was also quite sexy, he thought, coming from a bird with a posh finishing school accent. 'It might just save us a lot of hassle.'

Back in the garden, Charlie sat on the bench beside Tommy's covered body. If he was wrong about his being a loner, both Julie and he were in a world of trouble. For Charlie's part, he had no one to blame but himself. But Julie did not deserve any of this. Whatever he was planning, it had to be perfect. He glanced around him to convince himself that no one could see what was going on. It was unlikely, such was their isolation. Satisfied that there was no danger, at least for the time being, Charlie searched Tommy's clothing. He did not know why, but he irreverently transferred Tommy's NY baseball cap to his own head, after giving it a couple of slaps on his thigh to shake off any debris. His greatest fear was that Tommy had been planning this for years, as he claimed, and that others were in on it. *But why was he alone?* It did not make sense. *Where was the back up? Why did they wait until now? Is it because they wanted Tommy to have the satisfaction of offing him?* If others were in the know and wanted Charlie dead as badly as he did, it would only be a matter of time before they made their next move.

The body search revealed a squashed packet of cigarettes, only five left in the packet, a red plastic disposable lighter, £60 in notes in a folding black leather wallet containing an old photograph of a small boy, probably aged around eight years old, behind a plastic window, and a little over £3 in loose change. There were two credit cards, one a Barclays Visa and the other a Marks and Spencer Mastercard. Both had expired seven or eight years ago. They had expired while he was in prison and there was probably no point in his renewing them while he was inside. Charlie didn't suppose a credit card would be much use there, even if he could get one. He could be potless, with no backers, or he could just be waiting for his new cards to arrive. His family would, more than likely, have kept up the dodgy car dealing business, so they might have kept his legend alive. In that case, getting a new credit card probably would not be so difficult. The boy in the photograph could well be around twenty by now, and that was not good. Certainly not if he was of his dad's persuasion.

The phone was a vital find, an obviously new pay-as-you-go Samsung. It was live and switched on, but he could not take the risk of activating it to access its information as, with cell-site analysis and triangulation, the authorities can tell, within a few metres, where and when it was last used. That may not be helpful if this all blew up in his face. But it was vital that he saw its history, just not here. Hopefully, it would not need a passcode to access the phone book or call log. He had not kept up with technology, and who knows what they can do these days. He went back inside to explain the situation to Julie.

'If Tommy has set up an alibi for Cornwall, it's logical that any activation would occur down there or on the way there and back. This kind of science is moving on at a pace and I don't know whether it's possible to pinpoint where it's been.'

'Where what's been?' Interrupted Julie.

'The phone. Keep up with me, Jules. One thing certain, I daren't risk accessing its memory here. To be on the safe side it's best if I drive down to somewhere on the route back, maybe the Manchester area. Ideally, I can get the vehicle registration number seen on CCTV, and if he does have an alibi, this will either support it or throw them in another direction entirely. If I go now, via minor roads, and come back via motorways, I can have the vehicle back at the depot for, say, 4am. Can you meet me at Hobson Way in South Shields, just off the Newcastle Road?'

'I don't understand. Why do you have to go to all that trouble?'

'I don't know if the phone will send a signal when I activate its memory. You know what I'm like with technology and I can't take the chance of activating it around here. I must see what's on his phone, see who he's called, see who's called him, text messages and suchlike. Also, if he's used it near here. It could indicate that we are in no danger or confirm the worst. At least we'll be able to prepare better. We'll stand a better chance. I'll have to act before the battery runs out, otherwise I'll need to buy charger.'

'I'm thinking we should just report it and take our chances,' said Julie, 'it seems like a lot of trouble and we might make things worse.'

Charlie sympathetically looked into her eyes and saw the unmistakable fear. If only he could make it all go away. She didn't need any of this but he owed his life to her, and whatever he did had to be for her benefit. He wasn't so sure which way to go himself, but it was she who could face any charges, or at least a grilling. No doubt, the verdict would be justifiable homicide but there are no guarantees and it could take up to a year for a result, by which time she would be a gibbering wreck.

He, on the other hand could take the blame. He could say that he seized the moment and stuck the fork in Tommy's back, but he knew how these things work. A re-enactment demonstrated or directed by the accused in a packed court, in front of a jury, will mostly backfire if the circumstances do not fit. He recalled one case where the jury was in fits of laughter as the accused tried to demonstrate why the angle of the stab wounds were so. He would have had to have six-foot arms with three elbow joints in each. He basically made a clown of himself and his barrister had little option but to throw in the towel. Charlie was sure that, in this case, he would be able to make a better job of it but, if it backfired, they were both in trouble and Julie would break down. Then they could both face a perverting the course of justice charge with a possible four-year sentence, possibly even consecutive to whatever else lay in store. On balance, it was too risky, and he shared his thoughts with her. Thankfully for Charlie, she agreed it would be foolish to attempt.

'Julie, it's your choice. You know I've been involved in lots of high-profile cases and you know what I'm capable of. I can find evidence, but I can also make it disappear. Even if Tommy's body is found, there is no way they will be able to physically put him here. He was in Cornwall, remember? There is no way they can prove that he died here, or that one of us killed him. Take my word for that. All you have to do is say you don't know anything about him and that he never came here, to your knowledge. Stick to that line, and nothing can go wrong. But if we are going to report it, we have to do it now while he is still fresh. We would have to explain any delay and that might be difficult.'

'No, let's get rid of it. You're right. If all I have to keep saying is, he wasn't here, I can hardly fluff my lines. By the way, it'll all be on the CCTV hard drive, best wipe it.'

'Let's take no chances,' said Charlie, 'let's replace it altogether. I'll smash it up and dispose of it. In the meantime, you go into town and buy something. The receipts will give you an alibi. Maybe still meet the girls?'

'Yes, to the receipts,' agreed Julie. 'But *no* to the girls. I couldn't carry it off. They would know something wasn't right.'

'Okay, then,' said Charlie, 'get a move on. Remember to meet me later. I won't be able to phone you while I'm on the road, so this is it until then, okay?'

'Can't you phone me when you are half an hour away?' she suggested.

'Not really. If they get hold of my phone, they might wonder why I was phoning you from Scotch Corner at 3.30am,' replied Charlie.

Julie nodded, got into the Audi, and drove off for the second time.

FIVE

Before Charlie set off for the M60, he checked the mileage against the hire documents. Since the start of the hire, almost five hundred miles had been driven. In the driver's door pocket he found a cash receipt for fuel from a service station in Toxteth, Liverpool. He tried to imagine why Tommy would want to go there. It contained its fair share of dens of iniquity, so that was no surprise. In any event, he would worry about that later.

He then siphoned as much diesel as he would need from his own BMW X5, and topped up the Cherokee. It took almost two gallons, but Charlie took another six gallons with him, in two five-gallon containers, just enough to top up the tank before returning the vehicle to South Shields. There was no point in having to fuel up at a filling station and risk being spotted on CCTV. Not that it would matter much, as any CCTV footage would be wiped clean long before it became an issue in the search for Tommy. It could be days before Tommy was reported missing, weeks before they became concerned and years, if ever, before his remains would come to light. The probation service would just assume he had done a runner, and list him as missing. The CCTV footage would probably be overwritten within thirty days but, as ever, Charlie was leaving nothing to chance. He also made sure he had Tommy's phone with him. The Beretta and silencer, he left hidden on a high shelf in the potting shed. In the event that the place would be searched, it would not be for several days at the earliest and, if he was prepared to leave the body in the potting shed, there was little point in making a special effort to hide the gun. He had considered taking the body with him and disposing of it

59

somewhere, hundreds of miles away, perhaps even Cornwall, but he didn't know the terrain as well as he knew his home territory. There were too many other ponderables like, *should he leave the Jeep there? Wouldn't that raise questions? How would he get home?* He was safer with plan A.

The journey was uneventful, but it took almost four hours to reach a point on the M6 that, otherwise, would have taken two and a half. He declined to use the satellite navigation system. He had no idea of its capability, but assumed that the vehicle's progress could be charted and that would have been too risky. Besides, a little extra mileage by taking the long way around and a few wrong turns could actually be helpful in confusing the police. If anyone suspected the truth and it all blew up in his face, it could be used to ask him awkward questions. He wore Tommy's baseball cap, pulled down as far as he could without obstructing his vision. It was uncomfortable. Charlie didn't like wearing headgear of any sort, but this time it was necessary.

Tommy's phone was still live. It required no pass code. Its data answered a few questions. There were eight names and numbers on the contacts list other than taxi firms and fast food outlets and, that morning, there were three messages, two from Tommy and one from a contact on the list. Tommy had the presence of mind to wipe all messages bar those three. He would have wiped those in due course, but he had not reckoned on hitting the snooze button so soon.

The first read, *Done yet?* from Vin. The second, from Tommy, in reply, read, *On the way.* The reply from Vin read, *You can join the party after Cornwall ha ha!* They were all made no more than an hour before his arrival at Charlie's house. Not good. A clear indication that there was a correlation between the texts and his visit. *So, Tommy was not on his own after all.* At least one character called Vin was in on it. No one with that name readily sprung to mind. Charlie disconnected the battery but decided to keep the phone well-hidden. It would come in handy one day. He also wrote down the contact names and numbers on an old lottery ticket, a non-winner from months ago. He had a few hours driving to mull over whether he should be honest with Julie about the phone but, in the end, he thought that the less she knew, the better. He emptied both containers into the tank and discarded them into a field, divested of any forensic links, when he stopped for a toilet break.

Now, for home.

The rendezvous with Julie and the return of the vehicle had gone to plan. She had done exactly as he asked. They had less than an hour of darkness left, but neither of them could sleep when they arrived home. They went over and over the plan until they were in danger of over-rehearsal. They were exhausted and they had another heavy day in front of them. Julie eventually turned in, beyond exhausted, but Charlie still had jobs to do. A trip to Amble with Tommy, to start with.

The body was easy enough to handle. Rigor mortis was full on and he had to drop the back seats of the X5 to accommodate it. He drove with the window partially opened as, although Tommy wasn't yet beginning to go off to any degree, cold meat has a certain aroma pleasant only to carnivores. He arrived at the marina just after 7.00am, time enough to do the business before it became busy. There were no other cars on site. The ideal situation. Once he was through the obstacle course of locks and barriers, for which he had keys and security cards, he parked as close as he could get to the berthing master's office. A final check of windows to see if there was anything incriminating on show gave him the satisfaction that the dark security glass had been worth the investment after all. One of the few indulgences Julie had allowed him.

The clanking of the steel rigging against two hundred aluminium masts, and the incessant whistling as the wind raced through a thousand braced wires was to be expected whenever there was even the mildest breeze, but this time, their protest seemed louder, as if to point an accusing finger at Charlie. It unnerved him to the extent that he became ultra-sensitive to every sound, but curbed his instinct to glance around him, conscious that he was now on camera, albeit not much more than a dot. He had to look like a regular berth holder going about his business, and any unusual activity could draw unwanted attention. Not that the closed-circuit television cameras were being manually operated at that time in the morning, but if the police ever had need to view the footage, they would seek an explanation for any overt furtiveness.

Happy that everything was fine and there was no need to panic, he walked down the gangway and along the floating dock, sheltered between the bund and the steep embankment, towards Stormy Monday. High tide was due at 9.49am, giving a depth of just over 4 metres. Still a way to go, but it was already deep enough to make way if he needed to.

On board, Charlie carried out a quick check to see that everything was as it should be then, satisfied that it was, he unlocked the padlock on the chain that secured the coffin and began to remove most of its contents to make room for Tommy. It needed to be as light as possible because of the gangway's steep gradient. Having removed most of the heavy items, he then began to haul it along the jetty towards his car. The jetty rose and fell gently with the ripples of the incoming tide but the passage was relatively easy compared with the gangway.

Almost at the top, a flicker of bright light in the corner of his eye made him stop and take the strain to prevent the coffin from rolling back down. He stood upright and looked towards the light source. It was a vehicle that had turned off the A1068, past the braid and towards the yacht club. Not a problem as such, he thought, it was too far away for the driver to see anything other than what they might expect to see. As a member, Charlie had every right to be there and the sight of him moving the coffin in this way was no big deal. He continued to haul the coffin up the ramp and onto the dock, occasionally glancing in the direction of the lights, which were no longer visible. A tidal surge slewed the gangway and forced him to hold on even tighter, the rough rope biting into his hands, causing him to wince. In hindsight, he reminded himself, he should have worn his gloves. He would correct that omission on the return trip, with the pair in the glove compartment. He would have to be careful. The last thing he needed was the coffin sliding into the sea with Tommy's body in it. That situation would take some rescuing.

Back at the X5, he opened the coffin, then the car boot, before taking one final nonchalant look around. The car that had just entered the yacht club car park was now visible, minus its lights. It was probably just someone doing some dry-dock maintenance, he persuaded himself. At a distance of two-hundred metres, there was little chance of his being disturbed. As Charlie turned to take hold of Tommy's rubber shroud, a voice suddenly cried out from no more than twenty feet behind him.

'Here, let me give you a hand with that, Charlie!'

Charlie drew back sharply, hurriedly pulled down the tailgate and turned to face the intruder.

'For Christ's sake, Cyril, you nearly gave me a heart attack! I didn't hear you above that flaming racket. What brings you here so early?'

'The hull needs a bit of attention. It's taking some doing so I thought I'd put a full day in,' replied Cyril Ridley, a jolly figure of a retired headmaster, with a handlebar moustache that interlocked with his outsized, bushy sideburns. Following his national service, he had joined the regulars and rose to the rank of captain, where he acquired his whiskers, before retiring to enter the teaching profession.

'That looks heavy,' he added, pointing to the large bulge in the boot.

'This?' said Charlie pointing a thumb over his shoulder in the general direction of the X5. 'No, I'm taking a few bits and bobs home. Too much to carry in one trip. I'm not going out today.'

'Aren't you? The forecast is good, you know?'

'I know,' agreed Charlie, but I have too much to do, hence the early start. Thanks anyway.'

Charlie made a point of removing the life jackets and other odds and ends from the coffin, then throwing them on top of the body to disguise the shape.

'I've just put the kettle on and I'm going to fry some bacon if you're interested?' continued Cyril.

'Would love to but, like I say, I've got a heavy day. Some other time maybe, Cyril?'

'Some other time it is,' replied Cyril, clearly disappointed. He had lost his wife two years earlier and always relished company. He was an ever present in Coquet Yacht Club and would always insist on buying the drinks. Charlie enjoyed his company and they often swapped tales of their escapades, each vowing that the other had the harder job.

'At least I can get hold of the bastards, unlike you, Cyril. I wouldn't have your job for all the tea in China!'

'At least my little bastards didn't often fight back,' he would reply. It was a ritual that gave them both a great deal of satisfaction, especially since they were now both able to put it all behind them.

Cyril turned and left, whistling a shrill version of the 'Have you ever caught your bollocks in a rat-trap' marching tune as he headed back towards the clubhouse. Charlie's eyes followed him until he was out of sight, regretting that he didn't have the time to humour Cyril with a few more minutes of his time. On his next visit to the marina, he thought to himself, he would make a special effort to seek Cyril out and spend some time with him.

More lights appeared to be heading his way from the direction of the town. Charlie tutted and cursed. He had left it too late to take Tommy out to sea and he had no choice but to abandon his plan. On reflection, it was like this most mornings and he wondered why he had even considered the plan in the first place. Sheer desperation of the situation, he supposed. He quietly cursed himself again then quickly returned the life jackets to the coffin, locked the car and returned the coffin to Stormy Monday. This time, using the gloves. It would be pointless, he conceded, to give it another go, but Tommy would be on the turn soon and a plan B was called for. He didn't have one. There had been no need, and if it hadn't been for Cyril's untimely intervention, he would be almost home and dry. But that was no longer the case and it was pointless dwelling on the missed opportunity.

On the way home, Charlie reflected on his failed plan. Perhaps it was for the best. If his plan had succeeded, and if Tommy was ever found, he knew that one limb of the enquiry would centre on boat owners. With the known connection between the two, that would have put Charlie right in the frame. Why he hadn't ruled that out earlier brought home the reality that he was fallible after all. From now on, he had to start thinking straight. If Cyril was quizzed, he would recall their unusual early morning meeting and the coffin-sized box alongside Charlie's car on a date to coincide with Tommy's disappearance. The connection, the golden nugget they always look for, would be made. Still only circumstantial, but too close for comfort. No, he had to dispose of the body in a way that would be more difficult to connect to him. Old Cyril had done him a favour.

In his childhood, Charlie had been taken by a friend to an old mine shaft near Shincliffe village, in Durham. Shincliffe had been a colliery village until the 1870s or 1880s, when it was closed. Its safety record was abysmal, not that that would have anything to do with the closure as, in those days, workers were expendable and death in the mines was regarded as an acceptable hazard of the job, at least to some mine owners. Closure was probably down to its being too uneconomical to mine. He was aware of at least one deep vertical ventilation shaft which, certainly the last time he was there in the seventies, had not been filled in or made safe other than to set a heavy-duty grill into some stone work at the opening. The miners and the owners lived in the hope that the mine would become workable once more and it would be cheaper to fit a grill and leave the shaft intact rather than to have to sink a new shaft later. Over the decades, it had been out of sight and, therefore, out of mind.

Children would drop stones into the darkness and wait for them to hit the bottom, probably no more than a few seconds later although, to Charlie, it had seemed like minutes. To his knowledge, it was still there, although the last time Charlie had visited the area was for his friend's funeral some six years ago. In the months leading to his death from pancreatic cancer, Charlie and he would talk about the old days. As far as Charlie knew, the situation was still the same. Mining had not returned, and the grate had been forgotten about. These days, kids did not go looking for outside adventure, they had everything they needed on the doorstep and never ventured far from the sight of their own front door. They shunned the outdoor life for computers, tablets and games consoles. Sad, but a sign of the times. Hopefully, on this occasion, that situation would work to Charlie's advantage.

The grill, as Charlie remembered it, was in disrepair and was coming away from the stonework. A sharp tug, he imagined, would dislodge it altogether. There was only one way to find out.

SIX

Back home, Julie was asleep in bed. He would explain the change in plan later but, for now, he needed to work quickly. Tommy's face was now purple, almost black in parts. Hypostasis, where the blood settles to the body's lowest point, and the head containing a lot of blood had seen to that. Charlie had lain him just as he fell, on his face, to keep the holes in his body uppermost so that blood would not seep out. There would be blood in his mouth from the perforated lungs, but that couldn't be helped. By now it would have coagulated and dried. Crusty, in parts.

Later, Julie would be booking the holiday, virtually two weeks touring their favourite parts of Scotland, but it was hardly going to be a holiday. They would jump whenever the phone rang, watch the news for any developments and, overall, have a pretty miserable time. Still, they wanted to make themselves scarce to earn some breathing space and to watch developments from afar. The CCTV footage of visitors to the house, relayed to Charlie's mobile phone whenever the CCTV was activated by the passive infra-red detectors, would tell them whether there was anything to be concerned about. And, of course, they could ignore their mobile phones if any unrecognisable number rang them. The numbers of virtually everyone they knew was programmed into their mobiles, and numbers appearing on their screens without names would be ignored. They could research unknown numbers later and respond if they needed to.

It would be the day after next, for their first hotel date, the Balmoral Hotel, just off Princes Street in Auld Reekie, a fine hotel, which was always their first stop whenever they ventured north. At least if they were going to be miserable, they were going to do it in style.

Charlie had plenty of time to dispose of the body and any other physical evidence, and replace the CCTV recorder. The body was the tricky bit. Unloading it was straightforward but he was not to know if the Shincliffe shaft was still accessible. He took a metal cable tow rope in case it needed a little persuasion.

Shincliffe had changed. It had undergone some modest development but, thankfully, the location of the shaft had not. Charlie took four sacks of quick drying concrete post mix that had been left over from the fence repairs earlier that month, and a 5 gallon can of water to set it and make good any damage. And a four-pack of natural yoghurt. The yoghurt would be spread onto the quick-drying concrete and, after a few days, the bacteria would do its work and it would take on the appearance of an aged structure, something he learned from a stonemason contact of his. A trick of the trade to blend new stonework with old.

The wooden gate leading to the field in which the shaft was situated, was secured with a rusted thumb latch, but the gate was not locked. The track into the field was overgrown and had not seen much traffic, if any, for months. He closed the gate behind him. The BMW all-wheel drive made it up the long slope with ease.

The shaft and the surrounding area had received no attention for years. Grass and weeds had permeated the dwarf stonework wall, which would be virtually invisible if it wasn't know that it was there. The immediate area was lush with long grass and varied vegetation that had not seen visitors in a long time. It had not seen a blade, and there was no sign of animal waste. In effect, the land was clearly of no use to anyone.

It was a school day. The area was attractive enough, but not particularly noted for its being a place of outstanding natural beauty so, all in all, it was little wonder that not a soul could be seen. The birds, apart from a pair of sparrows, were noticeable by their absence. Unused to visitors, they watched in silent curiosity, until the intruder had gone and situation normal had returned. The grate was still loose, but nevertheless secure. Before fixing the metal tow rope between the grill and the vehicle, Charlie gave it an almighty heave to gauge what force would be needed. It came away at the first attempt and Charlie ended up on his backside. No time to waste. A quick look around ... still no one in sight. In went Tommy's body, slipping from its pool liner shroud. Charlie had never worked so quickly and the fear of being seen by some busybody, as deserted as the place seemed to be, was overwhelming.

He replaced the grate into its vacated grooves. It only took one bag of concrete post ready mix, sprinkled with the correct amount of water to set it and make good the damage. Then the yoghurt. The concrete would be fairly solid in a matter of minutes, and would cure within a few days. In three weeks, it would be as hard as it was ever going to get. In a couple of days, the vegetation, flattened by his tyres, would right itself and there would be no evidence that a vehicle had been anywhere near. The thin, almost invisible mud track at the gated entrance was dry and compacted so hard that there was no chance of a mechanical match with his tyres in the mud. In hindsight, he wished he had used the hired Cherokee rather than put his own vehicle at the scene, but it was an afterthought. Not for the first time, he was doubting his own judgement. In any event, all in all, things were going well and there was no real need for concern. On the way home, it struck him that he had not waited to see how many seconds it took Tommy to hit the bottom.

Dumping the pool liner, the garden fork and anything that Charlie or Julie had worn since Tommy came on the scene, was next. Again, he gambled that any CCTV coverage at the council tips would be overwritten long before Tommy was discovered, or that he and Julie were in the frame. Normally, when a search for a body, a missing person or an article is required, it radiates outward from any point of interest to the inquiry. Not thirty or forty miles away, and certainly not without a link to those places. All in all, and given that council tips are a high turnover business, Charlie was satisfied that there was absolutely no chance of anyone linking either Julie or him, physically, to Tommy's death or disappearance. The tips at Romanway in Bishop Auckland and Tudhoe in Spennymoor were perfect for his plan. The skips were already near full and their contents would be recycled or taken to land-fill, within days, if not hours.

That evening, having washed and thoroughly vacuumed the BMW and ensured the new CCTV recorder was working, Charlie sat back to a bottle of fine Rioja, Faustino Grand Reserve. Julie had already taken the top off an hour earlier to let it breathe. He poured himself a glass and left it to settle and mellow for a few minutes more. He was only half way down the glass when Julie called him in for dinner. He carried the glass in with him, cupping the bowl in the warmth of his hand and holding the neck of the bottle in the other. He was going to see it off, then probably start on another.

Julie was uncharacteristically chirpy, considering the events of the past thirty-six hours. He assured her, without going into detail, that everything was taken care of. He kept quiet about the aborted Amble plan, and plan B. The less she knew, the better. He had not been seen, and any evidence to connect them was being, or had already been, destroyed or recycled. They spoke no more about it and the conversation turned to how well the property empire was doing, especially plans to build a new granny farm and to acquire more. Charlie confessed not to know or even care much about the siting of retirement homes, but gave the opinion that they could do worse than being sited near a Waitrose or a post office. Old people, he continued, like the comfort of reliability and convenience. Julie smiled and thanked him for this pearl of wisdom. Of course, this was how her family had been conducting business for many years, but she humoured him all the same.

After dinner and having exhausted their discussions, they briefly pored over the internet hotel brochures and wondered how they would fill their days until, at last, sleep beckoned. They had had none for nearly forty hours. Charlie would have an uneasy sleep that night, his mind was on the day's actions. Cracks had appeared in his plan. Not for the last time would he remind himself that retirement had caused him to take his eye off the ball. For Julie's sake, if for no other reason, he needed to be on his game.

Following a final fifteen minutes of watching the television news, interspersed with yawns on both sides, they climbed the stairs to bed. With the lights finally out, Charlie turned to Julie and took her hand in his, giving it a light squeeze.

'You okay, love?' he said, softly.

'Yes, thanks, and you?' she returned, in a hushed voice.

'Yes, fine, thanks.' Charlie leant towards her, found her forehead in the darkness and planted a gentle, warm kiss.

'Goodnight,' responded Julie.

The next morning would be a lazy start as it was pointless getting to their first hotel, a two-and a half hour drive at best, much before 2pm.

SEVEN

Their holiday in Scotland had been superb, considering all that had gone on before. It was as if, subconsciously, they regarded it as their last, should things turn awkward, so they put a lot of time and effort into enjoying themselves. Their journey had taken them via Edinburgh to Inverness, then back down the North side of Loch Ness, over to Skye and, finally, to Loch Lomond. This was the highlight for Charlie. His favourite hotel was Cameron House, on a magnificent estate on the banks of Loch Lomond where gillies would tend to their needs, even take them shooting. Charlie's prowess with a shotgun was evident, and so it should be. He had developed the knack of being almost as accurate from the hip as he was from the shoulder. He was also pleasantly surprised when Julie acquired the hang of it quite quickly. It crossed his mind, more than once, that Julie's ability to handle a gun might, one day soon, come in handy. It wasn't a healthy thought. He tried to put it out of his head but there was never any chance of that. Their lives had changed for good.

They spent five days at Cameron House and both indulged in virtually every activity the hotel had to offer. Charlie even persuaded Julie to take a thirty-minute flight in the seaplane moored on the jetty outside the hotel. The views over the house, the loch and the surrounding countryside were breath-taking. With the exception of a lone white cloud in the distance, the sky was blue, the loch's surface was as smooth as a mirror, except for the wake left by small boats, and the surrounding countryside was in full bloom. Purple blankets of heather shrouded the higher slopes turning to shades of green, brown and yellow as they descended to the loch. This was God's country, a touch of heaven. Charlie had absolutely no Scottish ancestry, no bloodlines above Hadrian's Wall, but he felt the pride nevertheless. And only half a day's drive from home.

Landing on water was the smoothest, quietest landing either of them had ever experienced. The engine had all but cut out as the plane glided slowly and quietly, and the floats threw up spray onto the Perspex windows as they engaged the still water. The engine reluctantly burst into life again to taxi them to their mooring, spluttering as it was deliberately starved of fuel by the pilot. When the aircraft eventually came to rest, both passengers unbuckled their seat belts, thanked the pilot for a wonderful experience then climbed down from the cabin. Their wide grins were confirmation, if ever it was needed, that they had had a wonderful time.

With the exception of two days, Charlie's phone bleeped once a day between 10am and 11am as the CCTV was activated by the postman. The drives on Darras Hall were too long for most leaflet and junk mail drops and there were no parcel deliveries or other visitors. All of their friends and family knew how long they would be away, so visits would be pointless. Charlie enthused over the fact that there had been no come-back, so far, but Julie would take some convincing. After all, it had only been a couple of weeks. And now it was time to go home. Time to face up to whatever would come next.

The journey home was an awkward one, certainly for Charlie. He made every effort to engage Julie in conversation and each time he opened his mouth she let out a little grunt until, patience exhausted, she finally turned to him.

'Look, Charlie, I appreciate what you're trying to do, but please give it a rest, okay? You're doing my head in. I know the situation as well as you do, so just leave it, if you don't mind.

Wait until we see what happens next and, hopefully, I'll be in a better frame of mind.'

'Okay', replied Charlie, not at all hurt or, for that matter, surprised. She was new to living under constant fear and the threat of a life-changing situation. For Julie's part, she wished she could turn back the clock and come clean about what she had done. She was sure, as Charlie had said, that the police or any jury would have seen things her way. As regards the likelihood of a backlash from Tommy Layton's friends, it may have meant moving to a secret location, somewhere like California or New Zealand. With their resources, citizenship and lifestyle would be no problem. Her silence was a natural reaction, thought Charlie, and he confined himself to rhetoric about the beautiful scenery and the incompetence of other drivers. It worked. Julie eventually came around and responded, not always favourably and not always without sarcasm, but at least she was talking.

After a whole lifetime of living on the edge, Charlie was more excited than anxious about confronting what lay in store for him. He enjoyed a challenge. Even danger. They had received no phone calls other than on the day they returned home, from friends or relatives who were just catching up. Julie had enthused about their break, a sure sign that, despite her situation, she really had enjoyed herself. And there had been nothing in the news about Tommy. This did not surprise Charlie. His experience was that criminals and their families rarely call the police for anything, unless it involves missing children. It was likely that Tommy and his wife had grown apart while he was away and that someone else would be seeing to her worldly needs. That was often the case. It was also possible that Tommy's son was not too concerned either. He was not used to having his dad around and he hardly knew him. It was unlikely that he was brimming with pride. Maybe he was not really looking forward to the homecoming and things were fine as they were. His dad's reappearance would result in a few changes, not all good. It was an even bet that Tommy's lad would be happy with the status quo.

It was also highly unlikely that anyone would tell the police that Tommy was last seen on his way to murder Charlie Payne. The longer they left reporting him missing, the colder the trail would get. There was no accounting for what the police would do when the Probation Service reported his no-show, but the likelihood was that Tommy's mugshot would simply join the hundreds of others in the national missing or wanted bulletins. Bulletins that few people read and to which fewer paid any attention.

If things remained quiet, Julie would eventually persuade herself that none of it had happened. If foul play was ever suspected, the police would always start with family, friends and associates. If the trail eventually led to Charlie, they would come to a dead end, certainly if Julie held her cool and denied all knowledge of Tommy or where he could be.

An option not be ignored by the police is that when criminals fall out, it occasionally results in summary executions. Charlie was aware of several such executions, all of them undetected. Because the police, understandably, don't put their hearts into it unless they have a definite lead they can't ignore, it is often a case of going through the motions. The James Clegg example was a case in point. Clegg, if Tommy was to be believed, had been in the ground for virtually ten years, but he had not heard of any missing person report, even while he was still in the job. And because Clegg was so closely connected to the team that Charlie had put away, it was more than likely that Charlie would have at least heard something. In the event that the Police asked him to speculate about the disappearance, he would decline. His disappearance was regrettable, but it was none of his business, is about as far as he would go.

As soon as they entered the house through the rear door, as always, Charlie and Julie made a dash for the CCTV recorder. They already knew the results from the link between the CCTV and the mobile-phone, but they preferred to rely on the hard-wired system rather than the wi-fi. As hoped for, there was nothing other than the regular postal service, just as the phone had shown. There were no messages on their home answer phone, but a number of missed calls. From the telephone number prefixes, they guessed that all calls were from cold-calling businesses trying to get them to update their broadband, change energy suppliers or PPI investigators.

The relief on Julie's face was evident. She sang to herself as she unpacked her suitcase and filled the washing machine. She switched on the kitchen radio and sang along and hummed to any songs she knew, then poured them both a large malt whisky, a reminder of their holiday routine, and set about preparing dinner from freezer ingredients. Grocery shopping could wait until tomorrow. Charlie could only stand and admire the change. He was glad for her. And somewhat relieved.

That night, Julie and Charlie made love for the first time since Tommy's fateful visit. Julie was tender and thoughtful. She was beginning to regain her confidence and enthusiasm for life. Charlie would have loved the Tommy saga to be over for her, but he was a pragmatist and knew, somehow, that this wasn't the end. Not even close.

EIGHT

Two weeks after Tommy Layton's disappearance, the driveway to Ray Morrison's house in Boldon was full. Eight cars in all, including Morrison's own two-tone silver and blue Bentley coupe. None was more than two years old, and all either BMW, Audi or Mercedes. The house itself was a 1930s mock Tudor mansion in superlative condition, with beautifully manicured lawns to the front. Not a weed in the gravelled drive and borders full of colour. The garden had been expertly planted by local celebrity gardener, Rosie Horden, so that colour appeared all year long. Unfortunately, there were some severe style errors with lions, horses, statues and gargoyles appearing wherever there was a space, but that was not Rosie's fault. Architectural styles were inappropriately mixed and the only person who couldn't see it was Morrison. He may have had the money, but he was without class.

All were gathered in the large sitting room when the maid brought in a tray of teas and coffees. She was Eastern European and either didn't know or didn't care that her boss was a gangster. Besides, it was a living and at least she, herself, was doing no harm. She had taken the drinks orders as the guests arrived. They amused themselves by inspecting the internal décor which echoed the external, a mishmash of styles and periods.

Pride of place was an oil painting of himself, by a self-taught portrait artist from the Armstrong Bridge Sunday arts and crafts market. For something that looked like a painting by numbers kit, colours laid boldly on the canvas with little or no subtlety, it had its appeal. Certainly to Morrison, and it took

78

pride of place in the centre of some fancy decorative plasterwork made specifically to frame the masterpiece, above the white marble fireplace strewn with urns, photographs and silk flowers.

In the centre of the mantle was a large, gold coloured ormolu clock with finials that gained height toward the centre and appeared to point and draw the eyes upwards towards the painting as if to say, *Look at me, look at me!* The furniture was a mishmash of mahogany, oak and glass, with various coverings and with little thought about whether the pieces complimented each other. The sideboard, glass-fronted display cabinet and at least four occasional tables, one of them with two additional tables nested below, were full of ornaments. Crown Derby and Coalport figurines, ornamental plates, cut glass, stoneware and electroplated nickel silver trinketry.

To cap it all, the twelve-seater mahogany dining table was permanently set for a three-course dinner, with two huge candelabra marking the third way points. They had seen no lavish entertainment, no dinner evenings. Mrs. Morrison's culinary skills extended to microwave meals and, if all chairs were occupied, the first diner would have finished their meal almost an hour before the last diner was served. It was a Victorian house in concept, if not in style, to display the trappings of his wealth. To his friends, he was a joke, but none dared say so.

Morrison waited until the last man had sat down before making his entry. No one stood up. They weren't familiar with the time-honoured protocol of standing up when a senior person enters. Respect, in fact, was thin on the ground for Morrison. He had no real friends, just employees and associates who surrounded him because they either feared or loathed him. And he paid reasonably well. Always in cash.

'You can finish for the day, Lettie. See you tomorrow, same time?' Morrison said to the maid.

'That's very kind of you Mr. Morrison,' she replied in her heavy accent. 'Same time tomorrow, then.' He waited until she had put on her coat and left. When she was halfway up the garden path he turned to the assembly.

'Any news? Anybody? It's been a while!' He addressed no one in particular but looked around the room at each face to see who would answer first.

'Not from me, boss,' replied the one they called Splash, so called because of his loose-fitting lips and his tendency to spray saliva when he talked. With the exception of one, they all shook their heads or shrugged.

The exception, Gary Thornton, offered, 'He must have gone. He's not the sort to bottle it. Even if he had bottled it, he would have gotten word to us. I think something's happened to him.'

Thornton was a short, wiry man who always wore light grey or brown double-breasted suits, always fastened, with wide lapels. He slicked his almost black hair back, resembling a twenties spiv, whether he intended that look or not. Only the white spats were missing. He was the thinker of the team and Morrison valued his common sense and measured responses. The rest of the team weren't so kind. They nicknamed him *Lighthouse*, after one of their number had said to him, following a skirmish in which Thornton had mysteriously disappeared only to reappear when the fuss died down, 'You're like a lighthouse in a desert, you are. Very bright but absolutely fucking useless!' The name stuck.

'When?' asked Morrison.

'Can't say,' responded Thornton, 'but he took the Jeep back, so it must have been afterwards.'

'How do you know *he* took it back? Could have been somebody else,' challenged Morrison.

'Could have been, but who?'

'Payne himself?' speculated Morrison.

'How's that?'

'Could have turned him over, Gaz. Payne might be getting on a bit, but Tommy's no specimen, is he?'

'What, and Tommy's somewhere licking his wounds?'

'Possibly,' replied Morrison. 'Alternatively, ...'. Morrison cocked his head to one side and raised both eyebrows.

The group looked at him, waiting for the alternative.

Joe Tailford broke the silence. He was the exact opposite of Thornton. Large, brash, bald through choice. His black suit hugged his entire body, leaving little room to expand further.

'What? You mean topped him? Took the shooter off him and topped him?'

'Well it's not out of the question, is it?' posed Morrison, 'I mean these things happen. As you know.'

The group remained silent, deep in thought. Tailford's thoughts took him back to the night of Jimmy Clegg's disappearance. It was shortly after the trial, ten years ago. The verdict had come as no surprise. There was no getting away from the fact that it was Tommy and Pritch's faces on video. But so was Clegg's.

Clegg knew this and, sensibly, remained at home throughout the trial, a two up, two down terraced house in South Shields. He had already had to answer some awkward questions from his colleagues and his presence at court would not have helped. Had the video been shown in court, those watching and who already weren't aware of the situation, may have put two and two together and formed a few questions of their own. So, he missed it. Not that he was any safer.

It had been a dark, foggy Sunday evening, shortly after the trial, when the knock came. Clegg did not get out much these days, he couldn't seem to find anyone who would drink with him. He knew that they all thought he had been given a bye for turning Queen's, because they had intimated as much. He was no snitch. Whoever set them up, it was not him, but only *he* seemed to know that. Nothing he could say or do would persuade them otherwise. He knew he was finished, as far as their trust was concerned, and it was unlikely that he would ever work with them again. His situation was hopeless. He wished he had been caught along with the others. At least he would be out after serving maybe six or seven years, whereas being labelled a grass was a life sentence.

He edged the door open slowly and peered cautiously out of the widening gap. Immediately, a hefty shove caused the door to open sharply inwards and connect heavily with his forehead, forcing him backwards and off balance. His right hand went instinctively to the site of the rising weal as he steadied himself against the wall. Joe Tailford stood in the doorway, the light behind him framing his menacing bulk. He stepped into the hall and gently closed the door behind him. There was no need to rouse the neighbours any more than was necessary. Clegg took a step backwards then retreated into the living room, followed closely by Tailford. He sensed the danger, but he was in no position to do anything about it. The heating had been converted to electricity some years ago and there was no familiar fireside iron poker to grab in self-defence. He braced himself for the inevitable beating.

The thunderous expression on Joe's face said it all. He could only hope that the beating would not be too severe, just a token gesture. He could not have been more wrong. In one swift, overarm circular movement, Tailford dropped a ball-pane hammer from the right sleeve of his overcoat and swung it, hitting Clegg right of centre to the top of his head, with such force that it jarred his shoulder when its journey was halted and could travel no further. The ball entered Clegg's skull and knocked him senseless as it drove sharp, bony splinters deep into his brain. With no time to protest or fend off the blow, he took the full force and dropped to the floor in an untidy heap. Mercifully, he could not feel the three further, equally vicious, blows, any one of which would have ended his life. Only after the final blow was delivered did Tailford utter a sound.

'For Tommy and Pritch, you heap of shit!' he hissed.

He stood upright and took a step backwards to survey his handy-work. It was a mess. Blood everywhere. On his trousers, up his sleeve, on his face, on the rug, on the settee, even up the walls, resembling a Jackson Pollock. Up to that point, he'd had no idea that he was capable of inflicting such carnage. It frightened even him. Shooting was so much more impersonal, but maybe too noisy for this neighbourhood. Besides, the team armourer was otherwise disposed when the decision was made.

After a few moments of silent meditation as he stared at his lifeless victim, Tailford leapt to the front door, grabbed the handle and pulled it open. He looked both ways to see if there was anyone about, then beckoned to the two darkly clad occupants of a blue Ford Transit van that had parked at the end of the terrace no more than thirty feet away. They started the engine and trundled as quietly as they could, to a point directly outside the front door. Gary Thornton and Vince Fletcher then entered the house without a sound, taking care not to cause neighbouring curtains to twitch. They brought with them a large heavy-duty cardboard box that had once, according to the printing on the side, contained a Zanussi washing machine. They closed the door gently behind them.

'How did it go, Joe?' asked Thornton, in a low voice. 'Did you have any bother?'

'None,' answered Tailford. 'It was quick. Didn't make a sound.'

'Good. Hopefully the neighbours heard nothing. Was anybody mooching around when you arrived?' continued Thornton.

'Didn't see anybody!' came the answer.

'Okay, let's get him into the box,' ordered Thornton. What he meant was, *You get him into the box!* They both looked at Clegg's head, a red pulped mess oozing thick blackened clots of blood. Fletcher drew back sharply and grimaced when he saw the mess. He studied the body, looking for the safest place to take hold of the blood saturated clothing without getting any on himself. It was impossible and he resigned himself to the inevitability that his own clothes were probably safer in the wash.

'Christ Almighty, Joe! You done him good and proper! This is going to take some cleaning up!' said Thornton.

'I know. Let me know if you need a hand.'

'Me? How's that?' protested Thornton.

'I've done the hard bit,' replied Tailford. 'You've got all night, once we've got Cleggie out of the way!'

Thornton knew his objections were futile. He had been allocated the clean-up by Morrison, fair enough, but he had not reckoned with such a mess. This was going to take some doing, if they wanted to avoid forensics. If heads rolled because he hadn't done his job properly, he would be next. If it took all night, he would make sure that nothing was left for the police to find. If they ever came looking.

Tailford duly helped Vince Fletcher to tip Clegg's body unceremoniously into the washing machine box. The cardboard was layered and thick enough to prevent seepage. As well as blood, the bowel and bladder muscles would soon relax and enable their contents to flow. The legs went in first, followed by the torso and head, which was, by now, triple-bagged in assorted give-away plastic shopping bags. Job done, they upended the box and, as the body settled, it let out a groan. Fletcher sprang back.

'He's still alive! Give him another whack!' he said in a panic.

'He's dead, you daft shite! It's just air in his lungs. It does that when the chest is compressed.'

'But I heard him say something!' protested Fletcher.

'The air travels through his voice box, you muppet. He's definitely brown bread!' Thornton smiled a smug smile and gestured towards both men to continue. He went to the door, opened it and peered out. Without taking his eyes off the street, constantly glancing in both directions and watching for curtain movement, he beckoned the two men to bring out the box. When they were immediately behind him, he darted towards the rear van doors and opened them wide, standing aside to let them slide the box in. It was an awkward size, top heavy and an uneven weight but they managed the heave it onto the lip. Then, with an almighty shove, they pushed it clear of the doors. They gently closed the doors to keep the noise down. Twelve seconds is all it took to complete the operation.

'It couldn't topple over, could it?' asked a concerned Fletcher.

'No, it's settled nicely but drive carefully, just in case,' replied Tailford.

'Gary,' he continued, 'you're going to have to work fast, mate. Give us a call when you need to be picked up. We'll not come into the street in case we wake anyone up, okay? Try not to make any noise. We'll park up in the unit, then it's over to the others to do their bit, okay?'

Thornton obliged. It would be pointless trying to clean the rug, it was too heavily stained. It would have to go. The vinyl floor and painted walls were fairly easy. A sponge and a cloth would do the trick, but it would need several treatments. The settee coverings were a problem. They would have to be washed before the blood dried. Thankfully, all of the cushions had removable covers. He would remove the thick of the blood, then put them into bin liners. He would worry about what to do with them later, but he had multiple choices. Either a trip to the laundrette, launder them at home or simply burn them. Clegg didn't get many visitors and it could be weeks or months before anyone missed him. Or the cushion covers. Thornton had enough time to work out all the moves. Nevertheless, within three hours, the house was spotless. Certainly, to the naked eye. The rug had been bagged then disposed of in a furnace, and the cushion covers were drying on Thornton's clothes drier next to the living room radiator. Refitting them would be no fun, given that they would have shrunk, but who cared? And, of course, the body of James Clegg was already encased in the concrete foundations of a new industrial estate. Hopefully, the unusual pink flecks would go unnoticed. By morning, it would be a solid block and ready for the first few courses of breeze blocks. The shelf life of the factory units was expected to be a minimum of fifty years. The perps would all be dead themselves by then, so discovery of the body at that time would be of no consequence.

Tailford's thoughts returned to the present. 'Yes, but how are we going to find out for definite?' he asked.

'We ask him,' said Morrison.

'How do we do that, Ray? Won't that be like a confession?'

'Not us, you clown, somebody from out of town!'

'When you say *ask*, what do you mean?' continued Tailford.

'You don't need to know,' came Morrison's reply. His lip curled in a snarl. He knew what he meant. They, on the other hand, didn't need to know.

There was unease among the group. Some shuffled uncomfortably in their seats, and they all looked at one another to gauge the strength of support. This was the murder of a *cop*, he was talking about. Albeit a retired one, but one with a reputation, one who had lots of loyal friends and commanded respect. Even the villains had a certain toleration of him.

Vin Fletcher, another of Tailford's ilk, remained silent throughout. Like Tailford, he wore the now customary black from head to toe. Image was everything to him and he was constantly brushing himself down. If he was nowhere near a brush, he would pick off individual specks of dust and hold them at arm's length between finger and thumb, and let them float off in the wind. When there were no specks, he would imagine them and perform the same ritual. It was a ritual that hadn't escaped the attention of his comrades who, every Christmas, bought him a clothes brush. Pink, if they could find one.

Morrison sensed the awkward mood.

'Look,' he explained, 'nothing can come back on any of us. We'll all alibi each other. This guy comes highly recommended. He's the best. No clues, nothing. He'll be in and out. I guarantee Payne will give him the answers.'

'Payne's no pushover, Ray. What if he doesn't cooperate?' asked Tailford.

'What if he knows nothing?' threw in Thornton.

'Then our man will know what to do. Don't forget why Tommy went in the first place. Look on this as a continuation of the status quo.' *A big word and some Latin in one sentence. That was impressive,* he thought. 'You were all happy about Tommy doing it so why not this other guy?'

They all looked around at one another again.

'Tommy was a mistake, Ray,' continued Thornton. 'He's rusty. He might have had the motive but his head wasn't straight. It was too soon.'

'Look, let's put it this way. Was Tommy ever going to be useful to us again?' ask Morrison, looking around the room for a reaction. None came.

'I mean, after ten years in the chokey? It changes a man. We wouldn't be able to rely on him. Who would work with him?' he added.

'Are you saying he was expendable?' ask Tailford, not looking at Morrison, but at the faces of the others.

'Aren't we all?' relied Morrison, looking directly at Tailford. He was sensing dissent, perhaps even a takeover.

'Look, if you don't like the way I do things, maybe you should take over for a bit. How about we put it to the vote?' he said, menacingly.

Tailford realised he had overstepped the mark. 'No, of course not, Ray, you're the gaffer, always will be. I just like to be clear on why you do things the way you do. I'm learning from you. I mean, say we get picked up for something heavy and we give different answers. It pays to be singing from the same whatsit. That's all. Like you say, Tommy won't be missed.'

Morrison thought for a moment. If he needed to whack Joe, none of his current gang would take the job on. Besides, he was too well liked and they might turn on him instead. It would have to be an out of towner. Perhaps even the same one who was commissioned for Charlie Payne. Hopefully, he would never have to make that decision.

'Well, I'm glad we've got that sorted. Look, the plan is no different, it's just another guy. A specialist. Tommy wasn't really cut out for stuff like this. A learning curve for me. It's going to be okay. Okay?'

'Suppose so, Ray. No dramas from me. Anybody else?' said Tailford, looking at each in turn.

Again, there was little response other than shrugs.

'There you go, Ray. Unanimous!' finished Tailford, triumphantly. And a little relieved that he had rescued himself from an awkward situation.

'Thought it might be,' replied Morrison, sarcastically. 'Look, keep your heads down and I'll let you know when it's all over. There's no hurry, it'll take time,' he finished. One by one they slowly left their seats and bade their farewells. All except, Tailford. Now that Morrison had lost his audience, he plucked up the courage to make his point.

'Ray, tell me to mind my own business, but are you really going to risk everything for something that happened ten years ago? It doesn't make sense. It's history and you weren't even involved. I know you say there's no comeback but you can't guarantee that. I mean, Tommy's finished. Like you say, he's weak. And his pal paid the ultimate ... you know, ... penalty. I can't believe you are going to this trouble for them. I mean, apart from that little setback with Tommy going down, which was nothing really, Payne has never crossed you.'

'It's not about Tommy, Joe. Tommy would have got caught anyway and he would take the rap on his own. We can rely on him not to talk. It was his idea, his revenge. We just sort of encouraged it. Or at least we didn't try to talk him out of it. No, Joe, not a word to anyone, mind. I trust you more than I trust that bunch of wankers. This is about Simpa.'

'Freddie? Freddie Simpson? Where does he come into it?'

'He'll get life if Charlie Payne testifies.'

'Fuck me, Ray, Freddie wants him *dead*? Tommy was going to oblige?'

'Yes, but he doesn't know the real reason.'

'What if Tommy cocked up?'

'There was always a plan B. The guy from out of town would take over. To be on the safe side, Tommy would come to a bad end as well.'

'Bloody hell, Ray! Better not let on to the others that Tommy is just a sacrifice. No telling what they might do. You don't want them walking out on you.'

'Walk out on me? I don't think so. They know which side their bread's buttered.'

'Look, it's a win, win situation,' he continued unopposed. 'If it comes off, Freddie has a chance. We'll merge and become the undisputed kingpins. At least up here. If Freddie goes down, I'll be taking over anyway. You see?'

'Not without bloodshed,' commented Tailford.

'No, that's why I would prefer a merger. There's plenty for all of us to make a living. Besides, I'll be taking over anyway,' explained Morrison, 'I know a lot of stuff you don't know, you see.' Morrison grinned broadly.

'Okay, Ray, I'll bow to your superior intellect. Just hope it goes your way.'

'It will,' ended Morrison, 'I'm sure of it'.

NINE

Another week had gone by without a whisper. Everything was back to normal apart from the obvious dread lurking in the background, but even that was diminishing with every day that passed. Charlie and Julie had had a lovely day at Newcastle Races and had just about broken even. The last winner had made up for the five losers. Par for the course. Their friends, Patsie and Kevin, whom Julie had known since her university days, had lost, but not too heavily to dissuade them from going back for more. None of them were racegoers as such, just when the mood took them. No more than once or twice a year. Both couples arrived and left in their own taxis.

The taxi stopped just outside the gates to their house. Julie pointed the fob at the closed gates and they slowly slid to the sides behind the manicured leylandii to allow the taxi access. Following the Tommy saga, they had had heavy, eight-foot tall electric double gates fitted. So heavy, they needed metal runners for support. No fancy scrolls, just black, vertical iron bars, with pointed finials to deter would-be intruders. There were plenty of easier ways into the property if the trouble was taken to look for them, but at least the gates looked the part.

The gravel made a satisfying crunching noise as the car came to a halt in a mild skid. As usual, they made their approach via the rear gate, through the lavender Wisteria arch. Charlie inserted his key into the door and unlocked it. Once inside, he turned to his left to key in the alarm code before it could activate and register at the alarm monitoring switchboard. It was inactive. Not for the first time, and probably not for the last, he had forgotten to turn it on when they left the house. He shook his head, hoped Julie hadn't witnessed yet another of his careless omissions, and smiled before turning towards the bench and the kettle, unaware of the dark figure sitting in his favourite leather wing-backed chair. Until he saw Julie's startled, wide-eyed stare at the space where Charlie would normally sit, her mouth agape.

Charlie heard the shots before he saw the gun.

Phut, phut!

Two muffled shots close together. Julie dropped to the stone floor, her knees connecting first, her face last, with a sickening thud, blood spraying from her nose on the impact and from the bullet hole to her face.

Her head rolled to the left, exposing the spurting bullet wound. One bullet had entered one inch below her right eye and slightly to the right of her nose, but it was her stare that startled Charlie most. Her eyes were fixed open towards Charlie as if to say, *This is all your fault!* And it was his fault, although he didn't know it just yet. The wound to her body was hidden, although the puddle forming in the area of the mid-section and racing to join the puddle from her head indicated that it was somewhere just above the navel. Had *he* been the assassin at close quarters, it would have been the same. One, perhaps two to the body and one to the head. At least that was his training, as he recalled. The assassin was similarly trained. The mark of a professional.

Charlie turned to see the gunman sitting in his chair, handgun still pointing in the direction of Julie. Ignoring the danger, in three strides Charlie was on his knees beside her. His mouth opened but there came no sound. He had not experienced such shock or grief. Or guilt. He had seen enough dead bodies to know that Julie was gone from him forever. The fact that it was soon to be his turn had escaped him. It was of no concern. For now.

The gunman left the seat and sprang towards Charlie, whipping his right temple with the barrel of the gun. It got Charlie's attention and although the blow had intended to hurt, strangely, it did not. A hand squeezed the back of Charlie's neck and forced him to turn to his right, where his eyes met the barrel of a long gun. It was a handgun with a silencer, total length about fourteen inches. Charlie did not attempt to identify the weapon. It was obviously deadly and in working order.

'Where's fucking Tommy?' demanded the voice, loudly.

'Tommy fucking who?' Charlie replied, equally loudly, angry and defiant. All that earned him was a jab in the face with the barrel, leaving a circular imprint in the area of his right cheekbone.

'Listen, mate, you can see I don't mess about, now where the fuck is Tommy?' he screamed.

Charlie saw his chance and, in one swift movement, immediately grabbed the barrel of the gun with his left hand and held tight as he pushed it away at full arm's length from his face. At the same time, Charlie instinctively found the assassin's testicles with a fierce and probably the best right uppercut he had ever delivered. The gunman let off three shots and, although the barrel and discharged gases were burning his hand, Charlie held on tightly. The alternative was even less attractive.

The blow to his scrotum took the wind out of the assassin's sails and, momentarily, Charlie had the upper hand. He wrestled the gun out of his hand, forcing it in an impossible direction and, in doing so, breaking the assassin's finger, trapped in the trigger guard. The man screamed and withdrew his hand as fast as he could, cradling it under his left arm while his left hand cradled his injured balls. For the first time, Charlie saw the face of his wife's killer. Angled features, piercing blue eyes, close cropped hair and clean shaven. Several scars were clearly visible through his hair, ranging from one to ten centimetres. Not a fighter's scars. This man had seen action, probably ex-military and maybe even Special Forces, making a crust from his stock-in-trade, now that he was on the wrong side of forty, Charlie guessed. He wore combat trousers and air-soled boots, and was powerfully built underneath his black lightweight Berghaus jacket.

He attempted to hide his fear, but his now watery blue eyes gave him away. The gun he had used to murder Charlie's wife was now pointing at him, and he knew Charlie would be dangerous. He would soon find out just *how* dangerous.

'Who sent you?' Charlie said, calmly.

'Fuck off!' he replied, bravely, but unconvincingly.

Charlie circled him until he found the angle he was looking for.

'Phut!'

The gun retorted, as a quarter ounce of lead entered his left knee at the base of the patella, disrupting sinew and shattering bone. Even if he lived through this, he would never again walk without a limp.

His mouth and eyes opened wide with the initial shock, then shut tightly as he struggled to cope with the excruciating pain. His breathing became short and rapid, as he let out sharp low cries of anguish, before regaining what composure he could. He managed an even less convincing, *Fuck off!* much quieter than the first.

'Who sent you?' Charlie repeated calmly. 'If you don't tell me I *will* kill you. If you know anything about me, you know I will. Don't you?'

The pain was preventing him from forming any kind of coherent reply and Charlie knew the gunman would be wondering whether he had it in him to finish the job. Charlie could have spared him that thought, because his mind was already made up. This man was going down, regardless.

'I'll give you a moment to gather your thoughts, then you will answer the question or suffer the consequences,' he threatened. The words were spoken softly and slowly, for effect.

'I don't know his name', he managed at last. 'They don't tell you. The middle man is Joey. Number's in my phone.' He fumbled around in his pocket for his mobile phone, watched carefully by Charlie, who stepped backwards and jabbed the gun towards his head. His injured hand emerged from his pocket, holding a blood-soaked mobile phone, which he thrust forward. Charlie motioned with the gun for him to put it on the floor. He complied.

'Does it need a password to get in?' Charlie asked, being careful how he handled it.

'Yes, it's nineteen, sixteen. I want protection for this. They don't like cock-ups.' He curled up, he straightened up, he curled up again. There was no comfortable position. He retched with the pain, but his stomach refused to give up its contents.

Charlie tapped in the code, selected the telephone icon, then the letter 'J'. Joey was second on a list of five names beginning with 'J', but there was no surname, only a mobile number.

'This Tommy guy, why was he so important?' barked Charlie.

'I don't know if he was. I don't know him, but he was important enough for them to want you out of the way.'

'Tommy said it was revenge. I put him away for a fifteen stretch. You saying somebody else was pushing his buttons?'

'Joey never said. He was interested in what happened to Tommy, but the main topic was you. As the mark. What happened to him?'

'Tommy? He's with Jesus. He was out of his depth. A bit like you.'

The gunman's head dropped.

Charlie thought for a moment. He had been threatened many times but the fact that this time it was for real, sent a shiver down his spine. He knew that it would never be over until there were no players left.

'You ex-army?' enquired Charlie.

'SAS', he responded, still cradling his painful knee and injured finger, although the body's natural pain suppressors were beginning to kick in to provide some relief.

'You've lost your touch. Did you ever hear of a Steve Payne? Probably a bit before your time?' Charlie was fishing.

'Name rings a bell. Yes, before my time. You related?'

'Will he know you?' continued Charlie, ignoring the question, although it wouldn't have mattered had he answered.

'Wouldn't have thought so. Before my time. I think he was SBS, wasn't he? Anyway, I kept the code.'

'What does that mean?'

'I never yapped.'

'About what?'

'Anything.'

The conversation was going nowhere, and time was of the essence.

'Can you stand up?' said Charlie, pushing a dining chair in his direction with his foot. Charlie watched him struggle to his feet. He was eventually able to stand on his good left leg while supporting himself on the back of the chair with his damaged right hand, the broken index finger protruding at an impossible angle.

'Where's your motor?' continued Charlie.

'Next street towards the village, about a quarter of a mile.'

'The keys?'

He again fumbled in his right jacket pocket with his injured hand, a difficult operation that caused him to wince, and handed Charlie the keys.

'Yours or hired?'

'Hired', he replied.

'How much was in it for you?'

'Sure you want to know how much you are worth to them?' The pain was becoming slightly more bearable.

'Yes, how much?'

'Twenty grand, five up-front. Not much for a life, is it?'

Charlie was unfazed. The amount was irrelevant. Besides, it wasn't bad for a day's work if you weren't bothered about ending people's lives. As a trained killer, trained by the government no less, killing really was all in a day's work.

'Where's the five grand?' he asked.'

'In my safe in a safe house.'

'How were you going to collect the balance?'

'They would get it to me through a third party.'

'Who?'

'Don't know. I would just be delivered to me back home.'

'By someone you know?'

'I don't know. Possibly.'

'Do you trust them?'

'Nobody's failed me yet. They would get nobody to do their work if they pulled stunts like that. People like me don't grow on trees. Besides, I'm not one to be messed with.' He immediately regretted that last remark. Charlie resisted the temptation to make an unflattering jibe.

'So, there are others involved?'

'Come on, you know better than that.'

Charlie then sized him up.

'Lean forward a bit,' he asked, gently. The gunman returned a puzzled, distrusting look, but he was in no position to argue. He bowed slowly, keeping his eyes on Charlie.'

'You had all the time in the world. Julie was no threat, but you shot her all the same. I would really like to break every bone in your body but that would mean extending your miserable life for a few minutes longer.'

The gunman looked up in just time to see Charlie raise the gun and point it with intent toward the middle of his torso.

'Say hello to Tommy for me.'

With that, he shot him in the centre of the chest from a distance of no more than four feet.

Phut!

Charlie instinctively sidestepped the body as it sped to the floor. The cold stone was as unkind to his face as it had been to Julie's. A quick check of his vital signs confirmed that he was dead. There was no apparent exit wound, a sure sign that the bullet had hit something solid as it parted muscle and organs.

Charlie had to work quickly before telephoning the police. Making sure there was no obvious blood staining on him or his clothing, Charlie locked the door then walked to where the dead man said his motor was, at a normal pace so as not to draw attention. Occasionally, he wiped the tears from his eyes as he fought the urge to scream out at the thought of Julie lying dead alongside her killer on the cold stone floor. Typically, there was no one about.

In the lane where the killer suggested it would be, was a lone black Range Rover. It bore a Liverpool registration number. Charlie recognized this from his days in dealing with their regional crime squad. He pinged the fob and the lights flashed several times, indicating that the alarm was now disabled. He quickly looked into the cabin. Nothing. In the boot, he found what he was hoping for. He checked the contents of a short, slim, varnished wooden case. It was a rifle, a .22 judging from the narrow bore, broken in two, to be reassembled with a little more than a twist and a click. The sights were almost as long as the rifle. This was no ordinary weapon. He then noticed the boxes of .22 calibre ammunition, four in all, one of them part used, if the appearance of the box was anything to go by. Potentially three to four hundred rounds, enough for a long siege. Satisfied that he had found everything he had hoped for, and more, he lifted the wooden case out and closed the boot, again ensuring he'd left no evidence of contact. He locked the Range Rover.

Charlie returned to the house, holding the case close to him so that any passer-by may not notice he was carrying something, but before doing so, he slid the case and the ammunition into the dense Leylandii hedge bordering a neighbour's garden. It took more force than he was expecting, but he managed, and smoothed over the ruffled, feathery foliage to camouflage the gap it had left. It was probably within the police search parameters, but at least if the police found it, it could not be directly linked to Charlie. It was just as likely that the assassin had placed it there.

Back in the house, he picked up the house telephone and dialled 999. He asked for the police, then told the operator what had happened and how he had managed to disarm the intruder and shoot him in self-defence. With only a few minor adjustments, Charlie then laid out the scene as he would expect to find it as an investigator, if his version was to be believed. He moved the furniture so that the body was where it should be in those circumstances. The car keys were put back into his pocket, minus any evidence of contact with Charlie. He then found a notepad and quickly wrote down the names and telephone numbers from the contacts list, before sellotaping it to a virtually inaccessible plastic panel within the dashboard of the red Audi, and returning the phone to the dead man's pocket. The search team was unlikely to carry out a search for deep concealment of evidence. Because the indentations on the next few pages could have given him away, he tore them out and stuffed them into the Rayburn, which heralded its latest meal with flashes of red and yellow flares. The CCTV system, thankfully, had not been switched on when he and Julie had left the house earlier that day. Another omission, for which he was grateful.

Most importantly, the chest wound was at the angle of entry that it should be, if the story of a violent struggle and two shots towards an attacker advancing at speed, was to be believed.

The case of his wife's murder was one that Charlie was going to have to solve on his own. He would have to do his own detective work to find the motive and whoever was behind the killing. He had little confidence in the police to put in the required effort on his behalf. Besides, he could not let them in on his plans. Hopefully, they would be satisfied that the murder of Julie and the death of her killer were both solved. The motive was not so important to them, although he hoped that they would settle for one of revenge. Of interest, yes, but both cases could be closed off without having to go to the expense or the use of valuable resources. He could have done with some help, but at least, this time, he would not be constrained by the rule book. There would be no rules.

Satisfied with his work, Charlie knelt down beside Julie. She was still warm, but cooling fast. She had stopped bleeding, but the blood was beginning to coagulate. Her face was white, both from death and the fact that she was all bled out. He broke down. He had not felt pain like it. The only thing that gave him strength was his steely determination that anyone and everyone who had had anything to do with her death was going to pay with their own lives. It was that resolve, and the adrenalin coursing through his heart, that kept him going. Tommy's gun, now concealed miles away, and the sniper's rifle hidden nearby, were going to see to that.

TEN

Still kneeling by Julie's side, Charlie heard the sound of cars turning into and approaching the front of the house on the gravel drive. He had left the gates open for them. Soon after, the back door opened and in walked two uniformed policemen, followed by a third who was carrying a box of one-size-fits-all blue elasticated shoe covers and a handful of brown paper exhibit bags tucked under his left arm.

'Put these on before you go any further,' he suggested to the pair, handing each of them two covers. They donned the covers, which was an awkward manoeuvre without touching anything to steady themselves, then they silently surveyed the scene.

'Sir, are you the person who called us?' asked one.

'Yes,' Charlie replied. 'This is my wife, and this is the man who shot her.'

'What happened?' he continued.

'We'd just got home and came in through the back door like we normally do. I was first in and went over to switch the alarm off, then he shot Julie. He came over to me and held the gun to my head. I took my chance, forced it out of his hand and pushed him back. He came at me, so I fired two shots at him.'

The officer could read the pain and grief etched on Charlie's face.

'I know this is hard, sir, but would you mind moving away from your wife? I understand you are ex-job, so you'll understand?'

Charlie understood, and indicated so.

'You'll want my clothes and suchlike. If you let me have some of those bags, please, I'll undress.'

The third officer handed him half of the bags, and laid the others on the kitchen table. They were the sort with window strips so that, once sealed, they didn't have to be opened to see what was in them. Charlie began to undress, shoes first then from the top down. He inserted each item into separate bags and handed them to the officer for him to write on the bags, the details of what they contained.

'Best not seal them just yet. One or two items might have blood on them, so you'll need to let them dry,' Charlie advised. He eventually stood naked apart from his socks and underpants, waiting for the next instruction. In the meantime, the third officer had left the house and returned with a white paper suit, which he handed to Charlie. He put it on. He had worn them before at murder scenes, and knew the drill. Legs in first, then hike it right into the crotch, to allow room to manoeuvre the arms in. He then zipped it up, taking care not to catch the hairs on his stomach and chest.

'I know you'll have to remove me while forensics do their work, so is there anything you want to know before we go to the nick?'

'No, sir', said the only one of the three to speak so far, appreciating the co-operation. 'It'll be a long job and I'm sure they'll still be here long after you've made your statement. You won't be able to come back here for maybe up to a few days, though. Do you have anywhere you can go when we're done?'

'Yes, I have a brother who lives in Whickham. Can I give him a call?'

'Yes, no problem. Not your landline, though, use your mobile if you have one, if you don't mind. Before that, though, you said the man came over ... came over from where?'

'From that armchair,' Charlie pointed. 'He was sitting there, obviously waiting for me.'

'Why you?'

'Well, he couldn't have had any interest in Julie and I used to put myself about a bit with people like him. I'm assuming he was doing someone a favour.'

'Like who?'

'Any number of villains. The favourite, in my book, is Freddie Simpson, probably. I'm just about to get him a life sentence for drugs offences. The trial's a few weeks away.'

The officer nodded. 'Okay, Mr. Payne, you can make that call now.'

Charlie called Steve and told him what had happened. Steve was devastated. His long silence was followed by muffled cries of disbelief. He quickly regained his composure, and agreed to give it a couple of hours, then come and wait for Charlie in the foyer of the police station.

Charlie confirmed with the officers that it would be Etal Lane police station.

'If I give you a list of everyone who needs to know,' Charlie said to the officers, not addressing anyone in particular, 'can you get the family liaison officer to make the calls? I don't feel up to it, and I don't think my brother will be capable, either. Julie and he were close.'

'Yes sir, we will be happy to oblige.'

An officer then invited him to take a seat in the back of the police vehicle, and opened the door by way of an indication. Charlie took the hint and obliged. Two officers accompanied him to the police station, both sitting in the front seats. It was a good sign. Had he been a suspect, he would be handcuffed and one of them would have sat in the back beside him. As they drove through the gates, he looked back towards his house then broke down, sobbing quietly. The officers left him to his grief. Nothing they could say would help.

Within minutes, the party arrived at the back door of the police station and Charlie was whisked into the nearest interview room. Beige walls, a wooden table and two wooden benches, all bolted to the floor so that they could not be used as missiles. No one had witnessed his arrival. Every spare cop was policing the aftermath of the big match in the town centre, which was a blessing to Charlie. No doubt, word would have spread already and he did not relish drowning in a sea of sympathy.

He did not have to wait long for his interview, which was undertaken by two detectives, neither of whom was known to him. One was a sergeant whose face was vaguely familiar, and the other a constable, probably just on attachment while serving his probationary period. He smiled and they shook hands. They were very sympathetic and understanding, as Charlie expected they would be. He gave his account as it happened. More or less. The name of Tommy Layton did not feature. They were going to have to work damned hard to get anywhere close to the truth, and Charlie wasn't going to give them any help.

The sergeant told Charlie that they had discovered a broken window at the rear of the house. They described the room and its contents and Charlie confirmed that it was a little used storeroom which was never locked because they had lost the key. This was the apparent point of entry. The sergeant also told him that forensics would need to hold on to the house for at least three days and that it would be guarded while it was in their hands. They would give the entry point priority, then repair the window at the earliest opportunity.

In answer to the question about why the alarm didn't activate, he repeated that he is generally forgetful and is always forgetting to set it, much to the annoyance of Julie. This much was true. The CCTV system wasn't mentioned but, if it had been, the answer would be identical.

As a matter of courtesy and common practice, Charlie was visited in the interview room by the senior investigating officer, an old buddy of his, Detective Superintendent David Lamb, who promised him that every stone would be turned to find the bastard who had ordered the killing. Lamb was an astute Glaswegian. He had started off life as a copper in the Metropolitan Police and had transferred to Northumbria Police for a promotion. As proud as he was of his heritage, he had made his life in England, had an English wife and English kids and would never go back *home* except to visit family. He would always support Scotland against England in any sport, and would never applaud England for any sporting achievements, but that was par for the course. Unlike some ex-colleagues, Charlie trusted him, but hoped that this was one investigation that would fail, and he would be left with the revenge theory.

The detective superintendent openly agreed that Charlie was the likely target and that Julie had been in the wrong place at the wrong time. Either that, or she was shot first just to shut her up before she screamed the place down. He shared the view that Charlie had upset many villains in his time, as had most *thief-takers*, and it wasn't beyond the bounds of possibility that one of them wanted to take the matter further. He would now focus on who that might be. Before they parted company, Lamb gestured to Charlie to stand up and come towards him and, without notice, he put both arms around Charlie and gave him a long hug. It brought more tears to Charlie's eyes.

'Thanks, Davy. That means a lot. We'll have a pint sometime, eh?'

'Too true, Charlie,' came the reply. Both meant it.

Almost six hours later, at 12.30am, Charlie was handed over to his brother, Steve, for some tea and sympathy, still in his white paper suit. When they met, they hugged and held the clinch for a full minute while each reassured the other. Steve seemed to be taking it worse than Charlie, but much of Charlie's crying had been done. He was devastated and angry, but he had to keep his wits about him. He was now implicit in the deaths of two men. And that was only the start.

Back at Steve's house in Whickham, a three-bedroomed stone-fronted terrace on Front Street, Charlie telephoned Julie's sister, Sue. It was late, but she was waiting for his call, whatever the time. He would have preferred to phone Jenny first, as they were more like buddies, but protocol dictated that he spoke to Sue first, as she was the elder. Jen had gone to Sue's house when the news was broken to them simultaneously by uniformed police officers. They were now coming to Steve's to see Charlie. He could have done without that.

With the telephone call now finished, Steve offered Charlie some tea, or something stronger. He chose coffee.

'Are you going to tell me what it was about, then?' asked Steve.

'Well, obviously, I was the target,' he started. 'He didn't need to kill Julie. I suppose he would have done anyway because she was a witness, but why her first?'

'To make you suffer?

'Probably.'

'But why, Charlie, what had you done to bring this on?'

'Revenge for putting his mates in prison?'

'Really? It doesn't sound like you're convinced either. What are your plans now? I take it you're not just going to let it lie?'

'What can I do? Best let the police crack on with it.'

'I don't think so, do you? Even if they get somebody for it, they won't even do ten years. Get me the names and you won't have any more trouble from them. Ever!'

That was the last thing that Charlie wanted, an alcohol-sodden, lovable loser, making matters worse.

'No thanks, Steve, I'll do it by the book but thanks for the offer. You can do one thing for me, though. I want you to hide something for me in your allotment. Buried deep but available at short notice.'

Steve grinned. 'I knew you wouldn't let it lie. Count me in.'

'It's not what you think. I can't explain yet, but will you do it for me?'

'Of course, but for God's sake, if you're planning anything, let me in. I've got skills that'll come in handy.'

'I appreciate that, Steve, and if I change my mind, you'll be the first to know. I'll bring it up tomorrow.'

Sue and Jenny arrived ninety minutes later. They talked and talked, and when the conversation dried up, they talked some more, going over old ground. They did not leave until after 6am. Charlie recounted, over and over again, what he wanted them to know, and why he was still wearing a paper suit. He answered all of their questions, at least the ones he had the answers to. Both sisters, although they would not say it outright, felt that their beloved sister had died because of Charlie's profession. Their hugs, when they parted, were not as intense and warm as they had been earlier. Charlie noticed the change, and it unsettled him. Things would probably never again be the same between them, he thought, and no one could blame them.

That morning Charlie slept in an armchair, covered by a blanket supplied by Steve. There was a bed for him upstairs, but now that he was dozing and quite settled, Steve would not disturb him. How the tables had turned. It wasn't so long ago that Charlie was caring for *him*, through his own difficulties.

Charlie slowly drifted into a deep sleep as his brain eventually shut down.

At lunch time, following a breakfast of poached eggs on toast, Steve handed Charlie the clothes bought for him that morning while he slept. A hot shower later, and with a new outfit, Charlie was ready to face the world again. Steve was not to be congratulated for his choices. Stone-washed dusky pink chinos, a navy and purple checked shirt and blue and white deck shoes would not have been Charlie's choice, but they were the right sizes and, strangely, they matched. Not exactly fitting for the most recent widower but they would do, for now.

Later that day, alone and under the cover of darkness, Charlie retrieved the rifle case. The longer it was left in the hedge, the greater the chance of its being found. He sealed it inside several heavy-duty black rubble sacks with gaffer tape before handing it to Steve, with strict instructions to bury it, unopened, at the first opportunity. Steve already had a place in mind for it. Under the shed. The base was supported by heavy duty fence posts placed parallel with each other, raising it from the ground to keep it dry. The gap was sufficient to slide the parcel in lengthways, with another piece of fence post cut to size and pushed into the gap to conceal it. Access could be gained in an instant. It was also deniable. With minimal effort the allotment was accessible, and anyone could use it to hide things. Besides, he had not long owned the allotment and there was no telling who else knew of its secrets. Charlie approved of the idea.

To Charlie's surprise, Steve showed no interest in the contents of the rubble sacks. Steve instinctively knew what it was by the size, shape and weight but, just to be on the safe side, he would also be taking a furtive peek after Charlie had gone. Charlie knew that his brother would do exactly that. It was probably just as well that he knew what he was harbouring.

Exactly one week later, the house was released back into Charlie's care. Things had gone too smoothly, in his mind, and he scoured the house for any cameras or listening devices. His paranoia for detail had saved him from awkward situations more than once, during his career. Without any detection technology to hand, he had not thought he would ever need it, his search took two whole hours. He knew how deeply bugs could be concealed.

Search over, he was satisfied that there was nothing to be concerned about, either inside or out. The list of phone numbers from the assassin's phone was still in its hiding place. The search had not been as thorough as it would have been for a suspect's house. A quick look at the numbers told him that at least one of them was familiar with a number from Tommy Layton's phone but that could wait. Right now, he needed a period of time to get used to the empty house and to plan his next move. His main concern was Julie's funeral, whenever that would be. The coroner would have to be happy to release the body before any firm arrangements could be made. It would also have to be agreed by the coroner that Julie's murderer was the man whom Charlie had killed, otherwise cremation could be ruled out. The accused is entitled to request a second autopsy and cremation, therefore, would deny that opportunity. Since there was no dispute about who killed whom, it was not going to be a problem.

In the meantime, Charlie arranged for the house to be professionally cleaned. The whole house, not just the kitchen, had been treated as a murder scene and the fine aluminium fingerprint dust was everywhere. Difficult to shift, so the cost would be reflected in the task, although that was of little consequence.

Charlie collected the local newspaper every morning, on foot, a half-mile-walk each way, which took him past the hedge where the sniper rifle had been hidden. In case the police weren't quite finished with him just yet, he resolved to adopt subtle counter-surveillance tactics with his every move. This is how he would live his life from now on.

ELEVEN

The day of the funeral arrived, 7th June, a day he would never forget. Charlie's phone alarm had been set for 6am but it was redundant. He woke from his broken sleep almost two hours earlier and was already showered, shaved and dressed, when the alarm went off.

It was a dreary day, for reasons other than the sad occasion. The weather was bleak and promised little more than a damp mist, not at all typical for June. Worse, he would have to contend with people. Lots of people. People he didn't necessarily like. People wanting to shake his hand and offer condolences, some sincere and some not so. Apart from the hangers on, who might eventually need a prod to remind them that Charlie wanted to be left alone, he would not see the back of them until at least two or three hours after the service. Charlie did not like crowds and he certainly did not like to be the centre of attention. He hoped that brother Steve, and Julie's sisters, would take some of the heat. They were certainly all capable of holding attention.

The service at St Mary The Virgin church was timed at 10am, which meant that the cortège would arrive at his house some thirty minutes beforehand. Sue and Jen arrived at 9am with Sue's husband and children, although, as teenagers, they were hardly children. Steve arrived five minutes later and Wendy, after another five. Wendy and Julie had been friends and the situation with Steve did not alter that, although contact had grown less frequent. She was dressed for the occasion, all in black. It was the same outfit she had worn for Paul's funeral. Julie was not one for taking sides but, if made to choose, she would have picked Steve. She'd had a soft spot for Steve, for the trials and tribulations he had endured, albeit entirely of his own making.

Apart from the usual polite greetings and predictable words of condolence, there was little conversation that morning. It was not the time to discuss the circumstances of Julie's death and it would have been inconsiderate for anyone to have raised the subject at such a time. Tea and coffee were offered. There were few takers, they had all fuelled up before leaving home, not knowing when they might next get the opportunity to eat.

At 9.30am the cars arrived. Three black limousines and a black hearse. The wreaths had been sent direct to the funeral directors and the coffin, a plain beech veneered box with brass coloured handles, was already dressed.

Charlie offered the man who was clearly in charge of the operation, and the six pall bearers, a stiff drink before pointing out within earshot, and for the benefit of the assembly, the seating arrangements for the cars. He did not want to have to repeat himself too often. It would be Charlie, Steve, Sue and Jenny in the lead car and the rest could make their own arrangements, taking what seats were left in the other cars. There were enough to go around so no one would be left behind.

The pall-bearers took several gentle sips then all drained their glasses before making an exit toward the cars.

It was now 9.50am and Charlie asked the mourners to make their way outside. As they emerged, they gave the coffin a respectful glance and dutifully took their places without fuss. Charlie helped both sisters into the back seat of the lead car and sat between them, with an arm around each. Finally, Steve got into the middle seat on his own. Glancing around, he saw that all three had tears in their eyes. It was only the second time he had seen his brother like this, and he hoped it would be the last. He had always thought that Charlie was impervious to anything, and seeing him like this was unnerving. Not like Charlie at all, although understandable in the circumstances. For all the church was only five minutes away, it was going to be a long journey. Steve faced the front and said nothing. He stared into the distance, trying to hold it together.

At the church, dozens of people lined the pavement and dozens more congregated outside. None stepped forward to speak to Charlie as he and his party climbed out of the cars. Instead, they just stared, mostly without expression apart from a group of Julie's ex-employees, who collectively sobbed and held handkerchiefs to their noses. Charlie recognised some old colleagues and nodded towards them. They had turned up to give him support. That was nice, he thought.

The funeral party stood to one side while the pall bearers wheeled the coffin onto a gurney. The vicar, looking suitably solemn, and although he'd never met Julie, took the opportunity to seek Charlie out and quickly shake his hand, before resuming his position at the head of the procession. When everything and everyone was in position, he began.

'I am the resurrection and the life ....' his voice trailed, off as he turned his back to the party and began to walk slowly through the porch towards the aisle. The coffin and pall bearers followed, with Charlie close behind. The pews eventually filled up to the sound of 'Unforgettable', sung by Nat King Cole. Charlie's choice. He and Julie had not given that depth of thought to their respective funeral arrangements as they assumed their time was a long way off. The song finished long before everyone had taken their seats. There were many faces that Charlie did not recognise, but there were also many that he did. Extended family, some of whom had travelled from Australia, and colleagues going back many years. Charlie was grateful that his best girl was going to be given a good send off. He stifled a sob. Steve noticed his brother's uncharacteristic public show of grief and gently squeezed his right elbow. 'Stick with me, bruv, you'll be okay.' Charlie could not help but smile. *Steve looking after me?*

The funeral went according to plan. Charlie allowed the vicar to give the eulogy that they had carefully scripted between them. Charlie would have loved to have stood up to deliver it himself, but he was no public speaker at the best of times, let alone when he was under such intense pressure and scrutiny. The vicar was magnificent. He had the congregation laughing and crying, and Charlie was satisfied that he had hit the right notes.

Now, for the tedious bit. The vicar had helped by introducing Sue and Jen to the congregation, and instead of Charlie and the sisters forming a line at the exit, they all moved outside and split up, inviting three queues instead of one. It worked to some degree because the church emptied far more quickly than it would otherwise have done, but most still made a bee-line for Charlie. After close to ten minutes, when Charlie felt his right hand was going to suffer paralysis at any minute, he held both hands up and announced: 'Folks, if you don't mind can we continue this in the Seven Stars? people are waiting for me there as well. Thanks, I'll see you all shortly'.

He then linked Sue and Jen, and followed Steve to the Seven Stars, a short walking distance away. The stragglers followed.

The function room was crowded. More than half of the mourners, around one hundred, had taken up the offer of refreshments. Aided by Steve, who did not leave his side for a moment, it was less arduous than he had thought it would be. He made a point of speaking to everyone. There was even room for the occasional joke and fond reminiscence.

After thirty minutes, out of the corner of his eye he spied his old friend, Gavin Wright, now an assistant chief constable. He was talking to Davy lamb and a few others of senior rank. Judging by the returned glances, Gavin, a beanpole of man at 6'4" tall and weighing far less than Charlie, wanted a word. He was always immaculately dressed and his grey hair, still plentiful, was perfectly coiffured. No ten quid barbers for him. For all he looked as if he'd worked from behind a desk all his life, nothing could be further from the truth. He was from the same mould as Charlie except his self- preservation senses were better developed, and he knew when to keep his mouth shut. Charlie had a lot of time for him.

He seized the moment and took Charlie to one side, away from his chaperone.

'It's a funny old world we live in these days, mate, isn't it?' he began.

'I suppose so, Gav,' responded Charlie. 'You never know what's around the corner, do you? One minute you're on top of the world, next minute some bastard pulls the rug.'

'Indeed,' he agreed. 'Occasionally, there are game-changing turns of event and no one can do anything about it.'

'I know,' agreed Charlie, 'tell me about it.'

'For instance, and forgive me for raising it here, you'll see why in a minute, leads have to be followed that you wouldn't have dreamt of in the old days.'

'I suppose so,' agreed Charlie, sensing that the conversation was about to take a twist.

'Charlie, there have been no real developments in the hunt for the contract and, as you know, these things have a habit of taking strange turns. Nothing surprises me these days so don't get upset if things start happening that you don't expect.'

'Like what?' Charlie's tone changed.

'Well, like I say, mate, things aren't adding up and some people think you might have more to give.'

'I've told them all I can. It was in self-defence. I mean, what else can I say? I've still got the scar where he whipped me with the gun. I was going to be next, so I thought *shit or bust*, and came out on top. Daft bugger came at me.'

'That's the problem. If he had just killed Julie and you now had the gun, why would he risk going for you? These are things you need to think about.'

'The same reason I risked going for him! It was me or him! He had just killed my wife, so he probably realised I would be capable of anything.'

'Yes, but he was a wrong 'un. You were the good guy. With values. He probably didn't expect you to shoot him.'

'Which is why he had a go, surely? I was the good guy and he wouldn't expect me to shoot him. Surely they can see that?' argued Charlie.

'Yes, but it's never been put to you that way, has it? I mean, formally?'

'You're not saying I'm a suspect, are you?' Charlie replied, a little edgy. He could do without the aggravation.

'No, of course not, but they have to explore every avenue and they may ask some awkward questions at some stage in the future. That's all I can say. One thing, Charlie, this conversation never took place, okay? If you do get a knock, act surprised.'

'Okay, Gav, thanks for the heads up. I can't think what else I can tell them, though. By the way, thanks for coming, I'm really surprised that a lot of the gang turned up. Some of them, I haven't spoken to in years'.

'We do that a lot don't we, turn up for funerals. Julie was well liked, as you know', he replied. He then shook Charlie's hand and caught the eye of his driver to indicate that he was ready to leave.

As soon as Wright had left, Davy Lamb stepped forward.

'What was that all about, Charlie?'

'Oh, nothing, just reminiscing,' he lied.

'A word of warning, mate, believe nowt he says, or at least take it with a pinch of salt. Certainly, never buy anything off him, know what I mean?'

'Gav's okay, we go back a long way,' said Charlie in his defence.

'Maybe, but be careful, is all I'm saying. I wanted to put this to bed but, for some reason someone is sticking their nose in. It's a waste of time, if you ask me, but just go along with it and it'll soon be over,' he ended, before walking away.

'Davy!' Charlie called after him.

'Yes, Charlie?'

'Who's pushing the buttons, is it Gavin?'

'No, Mick Redman has persuaded him that some loose ends need tying up and I've been told not to get in the way. Me! The senior investigating officer! I've told him I won't be undermined so we've agreed that my retirement date is the end of July!'

'That's outrageous, Davy, don't go on my behalf!'

'I've had enough anyway, Charlie. I was thinking of going in September, but this has made my mind up for me. They've done me a favour. It's no big deal. One final word of warning, don't trust Redman. There's just something about him that I can't put my finger on. Be careful, right? Anyway, who am I talking to – I've never seen anybody get one over on you! Take care! Oh, and I'll let you know when my retirement party is, okay?'

'Okay, Davy, keep a hold, mate!'

Davy left the pub. They would not meet again.

Charlie's thoughts that night were about what Redman could possibly come at him with. Nevertheless, he was grateful for the tip-off. And puzzled by Davy Lamb's remarks. He could not rule out sour grapes, because Gavin Wright and Davy Lamb had been promotion rivals until Gavin took off while Davy stuck. He had not had Davy down for the jealous type.

By now, the killer should have been identified. They should have confirmed that he was a hit-man from out of town. They would realise that Charlie was the target, not Julie, and that she had surprised him, so he pulled the trigger on her. They had on record the photographic evidence of the linear abrasion on the side of his head where he was pistol-whipped, and the circular mark on his face where he was jabbed with the business end of the barrel. The damaged trigger finger of the killer, where Charlie had disarmed him by force, completed the picture. But would they have found the connection between the hit-man and Tommy? Charlie had, because of the matching telephone numbers, and it was likely that the police would make the connection eventually, if they had not already done so.

Two days later, he would find out.

TWELVE

It was eight in the morning, two days after the funeral, when the front doorbell rang. Charlie, who had been studying the news pages on his iPad, put it to one side, got out of bed, walked to the window, moved the bedroom curtain to one side and looked out onto the drive. What appeared to be an unmarked police car was waiting outside, but the occupants were hidden by the porch roof. He had forgotten to close the security gates yet again. So much for his lie in. *Why so early? What's the urgency?*

Charlie put on his dressing gown and went downstairs. He shouted towards the door, 'Hang on a minute,' while he punched the disarm code into the alarm system. In the doorway stood his old colleague, Detective Chief Inspector Mick Redman with his sidekick, another ex-colleague, Sergeant 'Angel' Gallagher. Her real name was Anne but, for some reason, everyone called her Angel. This is the call he had been warned about.

Both were smiling, which is always a good sign, although when Mick smiled, you knew he either had wind or he was about to slip a stiletto knife between your ribs. He was not to be trusted. Charlie already knew that without having to be told by Davy Lamb or anyone else.

Mick had red hair and a face like a Margarita pizza. He was slightly heavier than he should be for a little under six foot, but he was always immaculately turned out, wore designer suits, mostly light colours, and highly polished brown brogues. His shirts had no cuff buttons and always required cufflinks. He had dozens of pairs. Renowned for them. Skills-wise, he was average at best, and Charlie always felt he must have had a backer to get as far as he did. A bit of a nonentity, really. He never ate with his colleagues as he always had an errand to run at lunchtimes, and would never drink with the team after shift, preferring to disappear on his own somewhere. Not at all a team player.

'Come in,' Charlie said. 'Tea or coffee?'

'Neither,' said Redman, as he stepped through the door into the hall. 'We just need to ask you some questions to clarify a few things.'

Charlie feigned a puzzled look and stepped backwards to let them both through to the living room, gesturing towards two armchairs in front of and either side of the unmade fire. The fire was mainly for effect and would only be lit for special occasions. Redman's words had been short, and delivered coldly. The smile was a mere front. His arrival heralded a bad day.

'You don't mind if I do?' said Charlie, gathering his thoughts. 'I've just got up and my mouth is as dry as the proverbial.'

'No, help yourself,' replied Redman, 'can I talk while you do it?'

'Fire away,' he replied, all ears.

'The guy who shot Julie was from the Liverpool area. Ex para called Craig Collins. Ever heard of him?'

Charlie thought for a moment. 'Can't say I have. What's his background?'

'Like I say, ex para. SAS, I believe. Knocks around with some heavy people. Believed to be a hired gun, these days. No credited hits, though, so it might just be bullshit.'

'Unlikely, though. He was pretty cool. No panic when he shot Julie then turned on me.'

'Well, as you can gather, it looks, on the face of it, as if someone has it in for you. Your poor wife was just in the way, God rest her soul'.

'Yes, I gathered that, but why?' agreed Charlie. 'I mean, villains know the score. If they get caught, they take it on the chin, there's no need to take it out on the cop who put them away.'

'I agree, but there's more to it this time. I'm afraid I'm going to have to continue this conversation under caution, do you understand?' Charlie was not expecting this but switched to attack mode.

'I understand the caution alright. It means you suspect me of something, something that could end up on a charge sheet and, to keep any conversation within the rules of admissibility, you have to administer the caution, right?'

'Yes. Look, you're not suspected but we have to follow protocol, you see?'

'Okay, but you do realise that Julie's funeral was only a couple of days ago and I'm still not at my best?'

There was no reply.

Angel was decidedly uncomfortable, and it showed. Her smile had gone and she looked alarmed, as if even *she* did not know what was coming next. With Mick Redman, that was no surprise to Charlie, he was too gung-ho for his own good.

'Go on, then', Charlie goaded.

'What?' Redman replied.

'Caution me. If you can remember it'.

Redman did so, hesitantly. It was not perfect, but it contained the gist, so it would be acceptable in court.

Charlie stared at him, silently.

'When did you last see Tommy Layton?' continued Redman.

Charlie did not flinch. He knew there was the possibility that he would, one day, be asked that question. He was well prepared.

'Tommy Layton? Now there's a blast from the past. I suppose it would be the day he went down?'

'Haven't you seen him since?'

'No, he's in prison, isn't he? He'll have only done ten of his fifteen. He's not the kind to knuckle down and score for his full discount.'

'I think this is going to take some time, best we record it down the nick,' said Redman, getting to his feet.

Angel was clearly agitated. She looked at Redman pleadingly, but he was having none of it. Charlie decided that if the game was up, and that was far from certain, Redman was going to have to put a full shift in to get anywhere close.

'Can I get dressed and showered first?' asked Charlie.

'Twenty minutes long enough for you?' came the reply.

'Yes, help yourselves to tea and coffee. Won't be long'.

At least they had given him the courtesy of allowing him to be presentable, thought Charlie. Others may not have been accorded that privilege or, at least, they would have been chaperoned to prevent escape.

It took just under twenty minutes. He did not bother with the shave. They had made themselves some tea and were sitting in the fireside armchairs.

'Okay,' Charlie said, 'ready when you are.'

They got up, carried their cups through to the kitchen and put them on the kitchen bench then returned to the living room and walked towards and through the doorway to the hall. Charlie remained in the doorway to the kitchen. The front door opened, and Redman took a few steps outside. Charlie remained still. Moments later, Redman reappeared in the hall doorway and looked quizzically at Charlie.

Charlie spoke first. 'Haven't you forgotten something?'

'Like what?' responded Redman.

'You have to tell me why I'm being arrested, surely?'

Redman smiled, 'No, there's no need for that, Charlie, it's just voluntary.'

'You need a volunteer for that. I'm not volunteering.'

Charlie's face was expressionless. He was going to take Redman on. And he was looking forward to it.

'Come on, there's no need for that, is there, Charlie? We just want to clear a few things up, but it would be best if it was taped and under caution.'

In that case,' said Charlie, 'it's either an arrest or bring the tape recorder here'.

Redman deliberated for a few moments.

'Charlie, please don't make me do this. It's only routine.'

'If all you want is a taped conversation then bring the tape here. I'll tell you everything I can.'

'No, Charlie, and remember I didn't want it this way. You're now under arrest!' He had made his play and had no option other than to go through with it.

'For what?' Charlie replied.

Redman thought again. 'For being implicit in the murder of your wife or perverting the course of justice. Something like that. Don't make it any more difficult than it is, Charlie. I really don't want to do this, but you aren't helping matters. You leave me no choice.'

'Let's see, now,' said Charlie, 'ten grand for the wrongful arrest and ten grand for each hour or part thereof. That's next year's round the world cruise sorted, thank you.'

Angel was beside herself. This obviously was not in the plan.

There was stony silence throughout the ten-minute car journey. At the police station, Redman decided he would cite the reason for arrest as Charlie's complicity in the death of his wife, the supporting evidence being inconsistencies in his account of what had happened. The custody officer, old Baz, was persuaded that there were sufficient grounds for the arrest. At least they sounded convincing, although he didn't believe them for a moment, but he was in no position to openly challenge Redman. Charlie Payne was a far better man than that. They had nothing on him.

Baz had been a bit of a lad in his day. His bent nose betrayed his pugilistic tendencies and he had come to Charlie's rescue more than once. For all he could still mix it with the best, his beer swilling led to the loss of his place in the CID and his being confined to uniform, indoors. It didn't stop him, though.

'Still enjoy the odd cup of tea, Baz?' said Charlie, with a wink and a smile. Charlie was referring to Baz's habit of filling his tea pot with beer to have during his tea break, then sucking a mint if the sergeant or inspector walked in. He would always offer them a cup and if they said yes, he would say that the pot was now clay cold and he would make a fresh brew. They only accepted his offer once, so Baz was forced to make a fresh brew, and they suspected nothing.

'Yes, actually, would you like some?' Baz returned the wink and the smile after glancing towards Redman and waiting for him to look away. 'It's cold now so I'll have to make a fresh brew.'

'Not yet, thanks, too early for me. Might have some later when it's fresh out of the pump. I mean pot? He tapped the side of his nose.

Baz smiled again.

Charlie was searched, and his belt and brown leather slip-on shoes were removed from him. This was standard procedure and he had no issues with it. The search wasn't as thorough as it would have been for a regular villain, and they missed the iPod Nano in his shirt pocket, which had been recording every sound since Charlie had come down from his shower. He was offered a solicitor, but he declined, on the grounds that he had no need of one, and told them so. He did not want Redman to constrain himself in the presence of a solicitor. The more Redman would say, the more Charlie would learn. He could read Redman. Old Baz then placed him into a cell and closed the door as quietly as he could. The clunking sound as the heavy metal door met the heavy metal frame momentarily unnerved Charlie. He had heard it many times, but not from the inside.

'Sorry, boss!' he heard old Baz say, apologetically, through the tiny hatch. 'He's full of shit! I'm sure you'll be out shortly.' he added, quietly.

Charlie had seen the inside of that cell many times, but always with the door open. About eight feet by six, beige featureless walls, a wooden bench and thin plastic covered mattress for a bed. It made the cleaning of bodily fluids, excrement and blood, a lot easier. And, of course a stainless-steel toilet bowl without a seat. No toilet paper, you had to ask for that, alerting other cell occupants that you needed a bowel movement. All part of the humiliation and resistance breaking process. Attempts had been made with inferior paint to cover the graffiti and initials of its many former occupants, but some of the detail could still be made out. Some names he recognised, others, he didn't. He resisted the temptation to add his own name. Besides, his only scratch-worthy tool was his i-pod, which would have been a waste.

Forty-five minutes later, after trying to match up the initials to villains Charlie had known, he was led back to the custody office by old Baz. He was soon met by Mick Redman and taken into an interview room, where Angel was already waiting. The recording machine was switched on immediately, with the usual protocols and introductions being observed. He was again cautioned. This time, Redman got it right. He was reading it from a card.

Redman did the talking, but Charlie was watching Angel. She was easier on the eye. He detected moisture in her eyes, and she gave Charlie a look that told him she obviously did not want to be there. But he was glad she was.

'You have given an account of what happened to your wife, but there are consistencies I want to explore,' began Redman, putting on a posh accent for the record. 'For example, why would he shoot her first, if you were first through the door?'

'I don't know,' replied Charlie.

'In your statement, you say that you entered the kitchen then turned left to deal with the alarm. He must have had a good few seconds to see you.'

'I agree, but maybe he saw Julie as an unwanted distraction and decided to deal with her before me.'

'How do you mean 'unwanted distraction'?'

'Well, women have a tendency to panic and scream the place down. Maybe he didn't fancy taking that risk.'

'Or he wanted to talk to you about something and let you know he meant business?' said Redman.

'Talk to me about what? We didn't know each other.'

'Why did he not kill you first? You were the threat, not your wife. What did he say to you?

'That's two questions, which answer do you want first?'

'Why did he not kill you first?' replied Redman.

'How can you expect me to answer that? I don't even know why he was there!' Charlie responded.

'He must have said something?'

'I would have thought so, too. Maybe he was thinking about what to say when he got too close to me and I took the gun from him.'

'It doesn't stack up, Charlie, there's something you're not telling us. The circumstances of your wife's death are extremely suspicious,' ventured Redman.

'That's twice you have referred to Julie as my wife. You know her name and I think it's discourteous that you don't use it. You have met her several times. You've even had dinner with us, so please do me a favour and refer to her by name. Secondly, he never got the chance to say anything. As soon as he put the gun to my head, I saw my chance to take it from him. By all accounts, I was going to die so I had nothing to lose. It paid off. Thirdly, you have gone about this the wrong way. You have totally pissed me off with your attitude. There's a time to be soft and a time to be hard. What have I always said?'

Redman gave Charlie a puzzled look.

'Wasn't it 'eat shit if you have to, but get the result?' In other words, *softly, softly!* But, of course, you know better. I've got nothing more to tell you and before you give me the warning about what a jury may infer from my silence, you have to get this case before a jury. There is no case. I've done nothing. There can be no charges, no trial, no jury, therefore if I choose to remain silent it will be irrelevant'. It was Charlie's turn to play to the tape.

Rant over, Angel smiled through her moist eyes and made a face, putting a hand up so that Redman could not see her obvious delight.

'It doesn't add up,' said Redman, undeterred. 'Why didn't he kill you straight off if that's what he'd come to do? You were first through the door! He must have said something! He wanted something from you. What was it?'

'You have my statement', replied Charlie, 'I would really like to give you more, but I can't elaborate any further.'

'There are a number of options as well as the obvious. You know, as a detective, that you have to keep an open mind and rule nothing out. In that case, how about he and Julie were lovers and that either you disturbed them or lured them and topped them both?' suggested Redman. 'I'm not saying that happened, but you have to agree, it's an option?'

That remark ought to have angered Charlie, but it had the opposite effect. Redman clearly had nothing. He was out of his depth, clutching at straws. Charlie sat back in his chair and smiled, saying nothing, while shaking his head. Redman knew that the killer was a professional hit-man. He had nothing usable. He was trying to goad Charlie into saying something that might give him an opening. *But why would he do that? Was there another agenda? Did he suspect the truth? What evidence did he have?*

Redman continued. 'The bullet wounds were very accurate. The one in his knee looks like a carefully aimed knee-capping designed to cause pain, and the chest wound is dead centre, not at all like a spur of the moment panic shooting'.

'Pure coincidence. How can you say the bullet wounds were very accurate? Define accurate as opposed to inaccurate! I'm no novice I'll grant you that so, even in a panic, I'll fare better than the man in the street,' Charlie offered, 'but this was a split-second reaction!'

'According to our records you were a marksman throughout your firearms days, only dropping to first class on one occasion'.

Charlie smiled and shrugged. 'Fifteen years ago. I'm an old man now.'

'Come off it with the old man bit. You're only fifty or so. You never lose it, Charlie. The speed probably goes first but you never lose the instinct. That makes it possible you tortured him before shooting him dead on purpose'.

'Why are you talking to me like this? The guy shot my wife and was going to shoot me. He made that clear. I took it off him and got him first!'

'So, you say! It sounds too good to be true. *You're* too good to be true!' He took a moment before changing tack.

'I understand that Tommy Layton came to your house? Rumour has it that you took the gun off him, topped him and that was the gun you used to kill the two lovers'.

At last, Redman was getting to the point.

'For God's sake, Mick, get a grip! Do you know what you sound like? You've lost the plot! What on earth would make you say Tommy Layton came to my house? There's something about this that stinks!'

Charlie looked at Angel. Angel shrugged. It was the first she'd heard of the Tommy Layton connection.

'Look,' Charlie continued, 'ballistics will have shown that the bullets in his body were fired from the same gun as the bullets that killed Julie! Tell me I'm wrong! Go on, tell me I'm wrong!'

'Yes,' responded Redman, 'but who's to say he brought a gun? Who's to say it wasn't the gun you took off Tommy?'

'What the fuck are you on about? What's this with Tommy's gun? What gun? Am I missing something here?' The temptation to raise his voice was almost overwhelming, but he didn't want to appear rattled.

He continued. 'I'm sure you will have found Collins' DNA and prints all over the gun. How do you explain that? How do you explain the injury to his trigger finger?' demanded Charlie. 'The damage to my head and face?'

Tommy Layton had been mentioned several times. This was about Tommy, nothing else. Something was nagging at Charlie. He knew that there had to be a hidden agenda for bringing him in, but he couldn't quite put his finger on it. He suspected that someone was pulling Redman's strings. But Redman wasn't clever enough or brave enough to declare his hand without some backing. He was saying anything, anything at all controversial, just to provoke a response. He was trying to goad Charlie into saying something usable, to open up a can of worms. Collins may not have turned up had Tommy not disappeared. But Charlie was already one step ahead and waited for the next question.

'What was he doing there in the first place, Charlie?'

'Who?'

'Tommy.'

'Doing where?'

'Your house?'

'What? Tommy's been to my house? When was that?'

'Clever guy, eh?' responded Redman, who could think of nothing better to say.

'Look, Mr. Redman, I've told you all I know. There's nothing more, believe me. Now charge me or let me go!'

'I'll release you when I'm good and ready!'

'You're wasting everybody's time, Redman. It is like I said in my statement, and I'm not going to repeat myself. We're in for a long night, so fetch me a cup of tea, there's a good chap. Better still, ask Angel to do it. I don't want you to hockle into it.'

Redman clenched his fists.

'Now, now, Mr. Redman, I see you're getting ready to punch me. If you do, I'll defend myself and punch you back, and you know you are no match for me, as big as you are.' Charlie realised that Redman needed one more little push to take him over the top.

'All those years in my shadow and you learned nothing, did you? I'm so disappointed in you. Oppression evidenced on tape? Tut, tut. Keep going like that and we'll start talking about your child porn. Does your team know they have a pervert leading them?'

'My fucking what?'

'Your team?'

'No, what did you say about porn?'

'Don't deny it. I've seen it in your drawer. I'll expose you for what you are. A nonce!'

Redman's hands were slammed flat to the table in order to gain height and propel himself closer to his intended victim but, in forgetting the laws of anatomical physics, his face thrust forward, presenting his chin. Charlie needed no invitation and duly obliged with a fierce straight right, rocking Redman's incandescent face and sending him back to his bench-seat. It hurt, but drew no blood. He was not expecting that. He had no answer for it. He slid from the seat and stumbled towards the door, steadying himself with his right hand while the left probed for any missing teeth. There were none, but that's not what it felt like. He flew out of the interview room, slamming the door behind him. The pair listened and waited for the balloon to go up. It remained deathly quiet.

'What was that about?' enquired a smiling Angel, unfazed by the unexpected turn of events.

Charlie nodded silently towards the recorder. Angel, knowing what that meant, made the usual closure statement and switched it off. Charlie did likewise with his iPod while her head was turned towards the recorder.

'Having a bit of fun, Angel. Allegations like that are easy to make but hard to prove. They are even harder to disprove, but once it's out there it stays there. At least a little piece will stick. Serves him right. I only chinned him because he was coming at me.'

'I take it it's not true then, the child porn?'

'Probably not. Not to my knowledge, anyway. But I am prepared to say I've seen it in his drawer while he was working for me. I can cover my back if asked why I didn't do something about it. I'll say he was working on a porn case around that time, I believe. I know he has done in the past.'

'I like your style,' she said, 'he had it coming.'

'What will you say if he alleges assault?'

'Self-defence, Charlie, a pre-emptive strike. I'm not afraid of him and he knows that. Anyway, the record will pick up the tension and the escalation. It's a non-starter.'

'Angel, there's something not right about him. It's as if he's out to get me. I can't explain why but I think someone is pulling his strings. What do you think?'

'I'll keep my ear to the ground. You might have something. You're not the only one to have their concerns about him, but I didn't say that, okay?'

'I mean, what has Tommy Layton got to do with anything? I'm totally lost off,' continued Charlie.

'No idea,' said Angel, 'we didn't discuss the interview plan beforehand. It's all his own work.'

She got up, opened the door and looked along the cell block corridor. Redman was nowhere to be seen or heard but she could hear voices in gentle conversation in the background. She recognized old Baz's laugh. Redman had not pressed the attack-alarm, the long black rubber strip that runs the length of the cell block. She sat back down, leaving the door slightly ajar so that she would be able to hear approaching footsteps. Then, with both hands, she warmly took hold of Charlie's left hand and began squeezing and caressing it. It was reassuring, if surprising, and very welcome.

After a lengthy pause, she continued, her voice much lower and softer. 'Do you know how I got the name Angel?' she asked.

'No idea,' replied Charlie, who genuinely had no idea.

'When I started working for you seven years ago, you were so nice to me and you made me feel welcome. The team noticed it,' she giggled, 'and they started calling me 'Charlie's angel' and the name stuck. Didn't you know that?'

Charlie remembered the day she started work. Very pretty and recently divorced, so he understood her situation. She was in need of some slack whenever she was late or when she fouled up. He had made allowances. It had not taken her long to toughen up and show she was worthy of her place in the squad. She was soft, and hard as nails in the same measure, and trustworthy. Above all, she had fabulous breasts. Had it not been for his love of Julie, and the fact that workplace relationships invariably end in disaster, he may even have been tempted to try his luck. Her farewell kiss and cuddle on his retirement was also something special, he recalled. But it was a message he ignored.

'I thought they always called you Angel?' said Charlie, smiling at the revelation.

'No, it was Anne only until after the first week', she smiled. 'Something else you should know,' she continued, 'I fell in love with you.' She looked at Charlie for a reaction. He looked at her awkwardly, not knowing what to say.

'And now?' he asked, unsure of what he wanted to hear. He regretted the question almost immediately, and bit his bottom lip.

'Oh, still in love with you', she said, trying to sound matter-of-fact, and briefly looking away before finding the courage to look him in the eye again. She continued, taking away Charlie's opportunity to reply. 'I hope we can meet up for a coffee or something?'

'I would love that, Angel. Just to set the record straight and while we're being honest, I fancied you as well but, apart from being married and in love with my wife, I didn't agree with office romances. So many problems, so many wrecked marriages. A recipe for disaster. Obviously, that's no longer a problem but remember, I'm still hurting.'

'How about after work? No strings?' she asked, not wishing to lose the momentum.

'Tonight?'

She nodded.

'Okay, but make it after seven. I've got stuff to do before then. And if you're sure they aren't watching the house. Fraternising with the enemy could cost you your career.' Charlie said it jokingly, but he was also deadly serious. It's what he would have done if he was on the case, even if it was just with a covert camera with motion sensor to catch any comings and goings.

His motive for allowing her visit was twofold. He would enjoy her company, although he was far from ready for anything more than that, and he needed to know where these latest developments were leading to. Or where they were coming from. The possibility had not escaped him that she may be involved in the conspiracy up to her neck, and that her motive was to get him to drop his guard and give something away. He thought that unlikely. On balance, Angel was to be trusted.

'After seven, then,' she agreed with a smile.

She then led Charlie back to his cell and followed him inside, pulling the door not quite closed behind her. She put her arms around his neck, pulled him tightly towards her and kissed him briefly on the lips, not seductively but in a sisterly way. Charlie needed some affection. It was good. If she was play-acting, it was an award-winning performance.

Although it seemed unlikely that he would, neither knew whether Redman would make an allegation of assault, so they remained in the cell for five minutes before Angel led him to the custody suite. It was clear that Redman did not relish drawing attention to himself this way. Besides, Charlie was capable of making such an allegation believable. Either way, he was nowhere to be seen, and Angel asked old Baz to release Charlie without bail. She would defend her decision to do so if Redman made something of it. She might have to mention the child porn allegation and, in fact, would relish the opportunity to do so, if pushed.

Baz duly obliged, with another wink and a smile. He had the utmost respect for Charlie, a former boss, but little or none for Redman.

'Hope everything turns out okay for you, boss,' he said, as Charlie filled his pockets with what had been taken from him during the booking in procedure. 'We're all gutted for you. Not sure what that wanker's thinking about but I won't be accepting you in here again, not without something cast in iron.'

'Cheers, Baz, but don't risk your job because of me. I can look after myself.' He returned the wink, and walked out. Angel mouthed a *see you later* as she held open the door for him.

THIRTEEN

At one-minute past seven, Angel arrived in her silver Mercedes SLK convertible. Charlie had already done his best to sweep the area for cameras and devices and, unless there was some new, sophisticated gear on the market which was difficult to detect, he was reasonably happy that the house was sterile, and he was not being watched. At least from within the immediate vicinity. Trees and hedgerows played their part in obscuring his house from neighbours whose houses could be potentially used for long-range photography.

Charlie met her at the front door. Taking her through the murder scene near the back door, even though it was now nipping clean, would, perhaps, have spoiled the moment. He greeted her with a smile and a peck on the cheek. She responded with a hug that drew him close to her. He recognised her perfume. Chanel No. 5, one of his favourites. She had changed her clothing from a business-like suit to blue skin-tight jeans, short elegant brown leather boots and a blue checked shirt with a Levi label on the breast pocket. She looked as if she was ready for a hoe-down. All that was missing was the Stetson. Her hair was short, almost black, and her make-up almost non-existent, just some dark eye shadow to compliment her hazel eyes, and a light brushing of glossy red lipstick. Her skin was virtually flawless, requiring little help. She looked gorgeous and, even though sex was out of the question as far as Charlie was concerned, he felt she had come prepared. Just in case. It was a compliment.

Charlie had also showered and shaved and put on his latest Yves Saint Laurent after-shave. Even though nothing was going to happen, he felt that the effort was called for. It was a compliment in return.

'Are you over your ordeal?' she enquired.

'Officially, no, I'm distraught and traumatised, and Mick Redman will pay the price, or at least the Force will. A fair few grand, my solicitor reckons'. He was bluffing. Suing the police wasn't his style.

'Poor Baz,' threw in Angel. He's only got three months before he retires, go easy on him.'

'Baz will be fine. He was professional and had no other option but to take Redman's word. I'll make sure he comes out of it smelling of roses. I probably won't go ahead with it anyway. I was just angry, but thinking back, I quite enjoyed it.'

'Watch Redman, Charlie, he's seething, so expect some follow up. We nearly came to blows when I challenged his behaviour. How dare he do that without letting me in on the game-plan! It's most unprofessional. Do you know he's not well liked?'

'You kind of hinted at that earlier. I can't imagine why,' Charlie responded sarcastically. 'Anyway, isn't he off his patch? I thought he was serving at South Tyneside these days?'

'He is, but they reckon he knows some of the names being bandied about, so he's handy for local knowledge.'

That remark was worthy of further exploration, but he decided not to pursue it in case it raised suspicion. Nevertheless, he wanted to know.

'Come on, I'll get some drinks then we can have a chat about it. I'm having a Jack Daniels, what would you like?'

'Just coffee, please, if I have anything stronger, you never know what might happen. Anyway, I have to drive home to Jesmond.'

'Jesmond?' said Charlie, ignoring the 'you never know what might happen' and sub-consciously looking for an address.

'Osborne Road area, handy for the pubs and restaurants. I only have a two-hundred-yard walk to Scalini's and Osborne's. It's brilliant.'

'It's a couple of years since I've been to either of them,' Charlie responded. 'Does Osborne's still have a button you press to see whether you get your drinks for nothing or two for one?'

'They do. I was there last week, and I got lucky. One round for free. It's a good night in there. It's where you go to pull, not that I go there for that, but it's good just watching them. Most men haven't a clue. They just want to talk themselves up.'

'How should they behave, then?'

'Just be themselves. Talk, but not about themselves, unless asked. No football, no rude jokes, no over the top compliments. Don't try too hard, but be attentive, genuinely interested. Take it slowly.'

'Do you know, I'd forgotten about all that. My last two relationships were started by the women. I didn't have to do anything.'

'A bit like now?' She smiled.

'It's looking that way,' Charlie replied. 'I'm enjoying the attention. Believe me, I like your company. Just being with you is enough.'

Angel smiled. Charlie led her into the sitting room and she chose a red leather wing-backed chair. Sitting in a sofa may have given out an awkward *join me* message and Charlie had already warned her that his body was off limits. Not that she was planning anything, she would know that it was far too soon. He returned to the kitchen to make the coffee, leaving her to inspect her surroundings.

'Julie certainly knew how to dress a room, didn't she?' she shouted through. 'I mean it's like something out of Ideal Homes. Are they all antiques?'

'Pretty much,' Charlie answered. 'Sometimes, antiques cost less but they tend to keep their money. That little Georgian Pembroke table, for example, the one with the white vase on it, cost £400 when we bought it but it's now two to three grand. Just makes sense.'

He brought the drinks and sat on the seat closest to her, just close enough to clink his glass against her coffee cup. Anywhere else in that vast room would be almost too far away to have any conversation at all.

'This is a Ponteland death,' he said, swiftly changing the subject. 'What's the South Tyneside connection?'

'Well, you know he mentioned a Tommy Layton during the interview? He's from South Tyneside, and he's disappeared from the face of the Earth. According to a snout, he was coming to see you for old times' sake. I think he had a score to settle.'

'Who told you that?'

'Redman, after I challenged him about it.'

'Who told him that?'

'Beats me!'

'Very strange,' remarked Charlie, putting the glass to his lips.'

'Redman isn't letting it go, you know? He's on a mission or something. I think he has his own agenda, because the local police certainly aren't bothered. His family haven't reported him missing. Some think Redman's too close to the crims for his own good, and some even think he's on the take. I'm not sure if he's gone that far but I wouldn't want to be associated with him.'

'Have you got his mobile phone number?' asked Charlie.

'You're not going to have it out with him, are you?'

'Why would I do that, you daft clot? No, just curious. If I hear anything, I'll give him a call. I want this cleared up just as much as he does.'

'Yes, hang on, have you got anything to write it down on?' she said, taking out her own mobile phone from her right jeans pocket.

Charlie reached over to the Pembroke table and, from the drawer, took out a pen and a sheet of paper. As soon as she began to read it out, he recognised that it was one of the numbers on either Tommy's or the assassin's phone. *But which one, or is it both?* That would make a huge difference. He was careful not to let on that the number was significant. Comparison with the phone lists would wait until she was gone.

That was enough casework chat, and Charlie changed the subject deliberately. The remainder of the evening was spent on *where are they now?* and *what became of?* updates and reminiscences. Of which there were many. When the grandfather clock struck ten, it signalled time for Angel to leave. Her choice. What could have been an awkward moment, passed without incident, to their relief and probably with a little regret.

Before she left, she warned him again about Redman.

'I can't stress this enough, Charlie, just don't mix it with Redman. He's dangerous. I have to work with him, but you keep your distance, okay? I don't want to see you get hurt.'

'Okay, I won't,' Charlie promised. Redman had nothing on him but, if he continued to make trouble, that would be a different matter.

Angel drove off, watched by Charlie, who did not close the door until the headlights had faded into the distance. Just in case she changed her mind. His resolve was beginning to weaken.

When the coast was clear, Charlie checked Mick Redman's mobile number against those of the lists of Tommy and the assassin. There was a match with Tommy's but not with the assassin's. The entry *MR* related to Mick Redman's telephone number. He sat and thought of how that could be. Redman had a fair few informants, some of whom were properly registered and some who were not. Villains, even major league, were known to snitch on rivals, both to gain favour and to disrupt the competition. Tommy would have been one such grass, he was the type, but he'd hardly been out of prison long enough to be cultivated. Unless, of course, the cultivation started while Tommy was still inside. Or even before he was sent down all those years ago. On its own, that information could not be developed without drawing attention to Charlie, but it was worth knowing, all the same. He now knew of a positive connection between Redman and Tommy Layton even though the connection was not quite clear. He certainly could not reveal it to anyone. Had Redman's number been in the assassin's phone, that would have been an entirely different matter. Copper or not, his name would have made the *to do* list.

FOURTEEN

It was the first Tuesday of July, Charlie's day to meet the usual suspects at The Bacchus for an evening of swapping war stories and to talk about who was on God's waiting list. He had worked out the connections between the phone numbers and there were still some gaps, but that was for another time. Tonight was going to be a night off. They had been meeting there for as long as he could remember. Some of them were long retired, others more recently, others still serving, but counting the days. They all agreed that the job is not what it was, and the age-weary saying, 'The job's fucked', was mentioned more than once.

To avoid having to repeat himself, Charlie waited until most of the group were gathered and gave an update of his circumstances. He needn't have bothered. Six times, in all, he had to repeat himself to the stragglers. Condolences were quickly exhausted and thereafter the subject was given a wide berth. It was like they pretended that none of it happened. That suited them all. Besides, one of their number, Andy McLaren, had just broken the news that he was recently diagnosed with prostate cancer. It was early days but both parents and his brother had all died from cancer, none of it smoking related, so it didn't bode well for him. There was hope, because he was told that it was still in the early, treatable stage, so it wasn't all bad news. It put a damper on the evening, nevertheless, but they still managed a joke or two. Naturally, the topic of erectile dysfunction was mentioned more than once in the jokes that followed, but that possibility was the least of Andy's problems. For now, anyway.

It was Charlie's round. He gathered up the empty glasses from the table and carried them to the bar, putting them down heavily to attract the barmaid's attention. It worked, and she smiled without looking in his direction.

'Be with you in a minute, darling,' she announced, as she finished serving another customer. When she became free, she slinked to the part of the counter where Charlie was standing, ensuring that he noticed her. She smiled and looked over his left shoulder towards his company. 'Three John Smiths, two Fosters and a Guinness, is it?' Charlie was impressed.

'Well done, great memory!' he complimented her.

'And a soda water with a slice of lime for the lady?'

Charlie's eyes narrowed. There had been no lady in the company. He turned towards the group and, sure enough, they had been joined by Denise, Andy's wife, who drinks nothing but soda with a slice of lime when she's in public. Andy was one of those lucky few whose wives who don't mind running around after their husbands. He supposed that it was to prevent their menfolk from making fools of themselves, getting into trouble or rolling in drunk at all hours. Julie would do this on occasions, but she would warn Charlie not to make a habit of it or take advantage of her good will. Charlie turned back to the bar. 'Yes, that would be nice, thank you. I'm amazed that you can remember these things.'

'Years of practice. It's quite easy, really.' In actual fact, this particular barmaid saw all women of her age group as potential rivals and subconsciously memorised their hair, clothing, jewellery and make-up. And their husbands.

While she was pulling the Guinness, Charlie felt his right arm being lightly gripped. He turned to see that Denise had joined him at the bar. It was good timing as he could have done with a hand to help him with the drinks. She then threw her arms around his neck and gave him a lingering, tight embrace, unconcerned that such intimacy was exposing the delightful secrets of her shapely contour. For all she must have been at least fifty, she still had it all.

'How've you been?' she said at last, gently kissing him on the cheek. Denise was the highlight of the evening, so far. Although he dared not show it, he could have stayed in that position for ever. There was something about a cuddle from a woman, pretty much any woman, that Charlie liked, but he knew there was nothing in it from Denise's point of view. He appreciated her concern.

'Well, you know, the usual. Good days and bad, I suppose. It's going to take a while.'

'I know. I don't pretend to know what you're going through, but I lost my sister two years ago and I was devastated. It does get better over time, you'll see. You never forget, but the pain becomes more bearable. You will find happiness again, believe me. I know now's maybe not the time but if you ever want to chat, just call me.'

With that, she gave Charlie another, even tighter hug. Fortunately, she pulled away before the tightness in his pants was shared with her. Her offer was genuine, he felt, and although having someone to talk to about his grief would have been an immense help, he knew he would never take her up on it. If he was seen in her company, tongues would wag, and he was not prepared to add any new complications to his life. Besides, Andy was a good mate and, in his condition, more bad news, even a hint of it, was the last thing he needed.

Back at the table, Charlie put two drinks down and returned to the counter for the remaining three. Denise had already taken her soda and two of the pints. She had occupied Charlie's vacant chair so those on the leatherette bench seat bunched up to make room for him. Denise had changed the dynamics of the group and its discussions, and the evening passed more quickly.

It was now approaching 8.40pm and Charlie had had enough of the company for now. He was going to try pastures new. Others with trains to catch or had other engagements had already left. Andy and Denise had only just left, and others who lived nearby had declined a lift. It was a little too early for them. Charlie bade goodnight to the three remaining soaks and left, following the usual handshakes. He preferred to walk the half a mile to take a taxi from the Central Station, maybe dropping into one or two bars on the way, rather than use the much closer taxi rank in Grey Street. He liked walking and it would give him the opportunity to clear his head, maybe sober up a little.

His route took him via Highbridge, a relatively quiet narrow lane, especially at that time on a Tuesday. On the opposite side to the comedy club, about fifteen yards away, he saw the figure of a man wearing a grey coloured hoodie. It was clean and new, maybe brand new. He was leaning against the wall, right foot planted firmly on the pavement and the other with the sole of his left foot resting at an angle against the wall behind him. He was talking to someone on his mobile phone while glancing around as if he was waiting to be joined, although Charlie could not hear what was being said.

As Charlie neared, the hoodie heard his footsteps and looked in Charlie's direction. His left leg came down swiftly and he pushed himself gently away from the wall, as if to ready himself for action. He muttered something into his phone, pressed a button to end the call, then put it into the left pocket of his hoodie. Although Charlie still could not hear what was said, he distinctly got the impression that he had said something like, 'Got to go now'. Charlie's instincts told him that he was the centre of attention and that something unpleasant was about to happen. Maybe he was about to be robbed. Everything about the situation pointed towards a bad day. He kept walking towards the hoodie, but he had a plan. He always had a plan. Whenever he went into Newcastle for a night out without Julie, he carried the brass knuckleduster that he had confiscated from a scrote almost twenty-five years earlier. It was beautifully machined, and his limited research had convinced him that it was a relic from the First World War, carried by Tommies in case they were involved in hand to hand fighting in the trenches. Its origin and history had not been confirmed, but he believed it anyway. It is likely that there had been a dagger at one end and a short skull-shattering pommel or spike at the other, but these had long been sawn off and filed down. Even if he was wrong about the impending attack, it was comforting to know that anyone who attacked him would leave an abundance of DNA material behind, and might require stitches. In all that time, not once had he needed to use it, and he was often tempted to ditch it. He was glad that he hadn't. Charlie's instinct was right. As he passed in front of the hoodie, he could see that the eyes were firmly fixed on him. The right eye bore the marks and yellowing of a week-old violent encounter, but he was still up for it, it seemed.

With his right hand, the hoodie suddenly whipped an eight-inch blade from out of his left sleeve and growled, 'Give us your fucking...'

That was all he had time to say. Charlie's metal-clad punch landed on the cleft of his chin and snapped it clean in two. The hoodie's eyes opened wide in complete shock, as he staggered backwards. The second punch, dealt with equal vigour, fractured his left cheekbone. Charlie heard the unmistakable popping sound. The third was delivered as the hoodie was on his way to the ground. It landed in the area of his left temple, and the noise again told Charlie that he had, in all likelihood, fractured his skull, or at least caused a continuation of the fracture to his cheekbone and eye socket. Either way, Charlie had undoubtedly spoiled his evening. If not his whole year. The mugger's eyes closed. He was unconscious. It could take him hours to come around, if ever. As he lay on the ground, Charlie could see that this was no ordinary mugger. Wrong age, for a start. He was near forty and athletically built. Street robbers are usually much younger, thinner, and they generally rob to feed a habit. The knife was a sporting knife, top end of the market, Charlie guessed, a man's prized possession, not the usual kitchen knife favoured by low-life smack-rats who would rather spend their coin on dope. There was a familiarity about his face. Charlie had seen him before, but could not place him. It crossed his mind that this may have been no mugging after all.

There was still the unresolved Tommy situation, and Charlie was also the chief witness in the trial of a very heavy villain. His death could have positive results all round. He felt his blood run cold. Charlie left the knife in the mugger's grip but retrieved the mobile phone from his left pocket. There was no time to look at it now, to see who he had been speaking to.

The whole incident had taken less than ten seconds, and a quick glance around told him that there were no obvious witnesses. If anything, the hoodie could be mistaken for a beggar, and ignored. He took his chance and left the scene unnoticed. He could have summoned assistance or called the police, but something in the back of his mind told him that it would be better to escape, then regroup to collect his thoughts.

He switched his own phone off. If he ever did become a suspect an activated mobile phone could be used to plot his movements. Charlie was not too well up on the technology. He was working from knowledge he had gained years earlier, unaware that, to certain people, particularly those responsible for the security of the country, nothing was impossible. He knew that switching his phone off guaranteed nothing, because his Bacchus friends could inadvertently drop him in it if the police made an appeal for anyone in the area at the time, to come forward. Nevertheless, it would make the task of tracking his movements so much harder. He was not going to make the task any easier for the investigators.

He then ran to the end of the alley where it joined the Bigg Market, and followed the crowd, walking in the same direction to reduce the chance of on-comers seeing his face. He wended his way to the Central Station Taxi rank, all the while paying attention to any sirens or blue lights. There was no queue and he was able to grab the first cab in the rank, a black Skoda Fabia. He directed the cabbie to take him to Osbourne's in Jesmond.

There, he found himself a table in a dimly lit corner with relative ease. It was quiet. Angel was nowhere to be seen. He had not expected to see her, it was a long shot, but he was disappointed nevertheless. With nothing else to do, he began to write down all the names and numbers contained in the phone's memory. Already, there was a familiarity with some of the numbers. He also looked at the messages. There was only one of interest. It read, 'Bacus, high bridge, station. Just if alone.' Charlie swallowed hard. This was confirmation, if ever he needed any, that he had been set up for a hit. He made a note of the number it had come from. Again, it was familiar.

The last call had been made to someone called Joey. A pattern was emerging. After one pint, which he made to last forty minutes in the forlorn hope that Angel would walk in, he left the pub and took a black cab back to the city centre, The Star pub in Westgate Road, which was even less busy. He washed the phone in the gents' toilet wash basin to remove any forensic evidence then had one final pint. It was purely for effect, as he was having to force himself to drink it. Besides, he had things on his mind. He left a little over half of it, before heading back on foot towards the taxi rank outside the Central

Station. En-route, he made a slight detour up Fenkle Street and deposited the phone down a drain. Charlie knew that the more complicated his movements were in town, the easier it would be to muddy the waters. It would only matter if he ever became a suspect. If not, no harm done, just a longer night out than planned.

There was only one other person in the queue, but the cabs were plentiful, and both scored a ride within seconds. The roads were clear, and the journey home took a little over twenty minutes. Speed limits were ignored, the driver pressing to get back as soon as possible. This was a quiet night for taxis, and drivers wanted to cram as many fares as they could into the next couple of hours.

Throughout the journey, Charlie strained his ears to listen to the radio traffic. Nothing of interest. Descriptions of suspects were often circulated to taxi drivers when the police were looking for someone, but there was no such circulation while he was in the cab, and nothing to indicate that it had already been circulated. Escape is often by taxi, so it made sense for the police to ask taxi offices to help in this way. The taxi driver acted naturally and gave out no coded messages. He was not at all uncomfortable with the man sitting to his rear. All was fine. The incident had not yet gone public, although Charlie knew that the unconscious man should have been found by now, by a passer-by. Maybe he had been collected by a back-up team waiting around the corner. But he would have been unable to speak. He would have to have been taken to hospital. He needed more than just home rest for the injuries he had sustained. His face was a sack of broken bones. He was going to be sore.

There was no point in Charlie's going to great trouble to disguise the fact that he had been into town, or even that he had taken the route he did. If he was identified by the man he had laid out, at least he had a reason for doing so, although the knuckleduster would be difficult to explain. He could say that, given his recent experiences, he feared for his life and carried it for use only in the event that he felt his life was under threat. That was more believable, especially given the presence of the knife. Especially, also, that this was no ordinary mugger. Charlie felt sure he belonged to an organised crime syndicate. This was either related to the Tommy Layton situation or to the Freddie Simpson trial.

The taxi stopped outside of Charlie's gates. He had now taken to closing them to prevent unwanted guests from wandering in, except for the odd occasion when he was expecting someone. And when he forgot to close them. Which was more often than he would have liked. Unscheduled visitors would have to ring the bell and wait outside. The gates incorporated a letter box, but parcel post was given no special dispensation. The delivery driver would either have to ring the bell or leave a card and return the parcel to the depot. Fortunately, Charlie, unlike Julie, was not one for internet shopping. He preferred traditional methods for the little shopping he did.

Back in his kitchen, Charlie took off his clothes to inspect them for traces of blood. He felt there should be none since, although he had obviously broken bones, judging by the grotesque sounds the mugger's face had made, he did not think he had broken the skin. There was nothing apparent but, bar the leather jacket, his clothing went into the washing machine on a short wash. It would be washed, dried, ironed and worn again within two hours. Even if his assailant had regained consciousness and named Charlie within minutes of it happening, it would take the police at least two hours to make sense of it and respond. That was highly unlikely. The mugger would not be able to speak for hours, if not days. Time was on Charlie's side, but he was not taking any chances. While the washing machine was doing its work, he vigorously brushed the leather jacket for any incriminating fibres and sponged it clean, drying any lingering damp patches with a hair dryer.

Within the two hours that Charlie had previously set himself, he was wearing the same clothes again. If the police did call and he was wearing a different set of clothes to what the witnesses would describe, it might have raised questions. But the clothes he was wearing would have no forensic evidence on them.

Having thought long and hard about the situation he decided that he would not deny being in Highbridge at the time in question. Nor would he deny punching the mugger. But he would deny the knuckleduster and would deny hitting him more than once. If the victim was severely injured and had any property missing it must have been someone else coming along afterwards, taking advantage of the circumstances.

Satisfied that he had his story straight, he turned up the heating a notch and settled to watch television with a large Jack Daniels and Coke in his hand. On ice, of course. And in the usual lead crystal tumbler given to him as a retirement present.

2am came and went. There was no news coverage about the incident on either the radio or the television. No one had rung the gate bell. It was time to go to bed.

Getting to sleep was difficult, though, as the endless possibilities churned in his mind. Was it just a mugging after all or was it really an intended *hit*? He ruled out the mugging because of the telephone connections. But the hit did make sense. That bothered him a lot. Not one, but two failed attempts on his life. The attempts would continue until whoever wanted him dead achieved their goal. Perhaps it was time to man up and pick up the gauntlet. It was either him or them. He decided it was going to be them. His wife was gone, he had no kids, his brother had become a nobody, probably still dabbling in drugs, and there was no one left to shame. His colleagues would understand why he'd done it, perhaps even respect him for it. The prospect of prison was not too bad. Simple food, but plentiful, and many books to read. Segregation was a likelihood given his past, and what he was about to do, so the chances of being cut to pieces or being buggered senseless were extremely low.

For now, he had other things on his mind. He had weapons and ammunition. Fifteen rounds for the Beretta 9mm and hundreds of rounds for the Ruger .22 rifle. He also had the knowhow to escape capture or conviction. All he had to do was identify the names behind it all. In the morning, he would take himself somewhere remote, where I could think straight and take a serious look at what clues he had. Stormy Monday. She was long overdue a run out.

FIFTEEN

It was a calm day when Charlie visited the marina early on the July morning, following his unfortunate encounter with Molloy. He was an early riser on boat days, in order to make the most of the day, and had arrived just as rush hour traffic was gathering pace. Stormy Monday was in fine condition, thanks to a monthly visit to turn over the Perkins diesel engine, a touch up here and there and to keep abreast of marina news. All that was needed was a decent hosing down and a swabbing to freshen it up. But, first of all, he would test the kettle and the frying pan to make sure they were still working. A cup of tea and a bacon sandwich was the usual start to his marina day.

The marina was quite deserted, and he saw only two other people, a regular whom he knew only as Benny, a large, rounded man probably a few years older than Charlie and, of course, the ever-present Cyril.

'Morning, gents,' shouted Charlie, 'Nice day for trip out?'

Cyril was the first to respond. 'Morning, Charlie, fancy a snifter? What about you, Benny?'

'Why not!' responded Benny, who was always easily tempted. Charlie could think of no valid excuse to decline, other than it was only breakfast time, besides he owed Cyril, for snubbing him earlier. He reluctantly nodded approval and gave the thumbs up. His other business had waited long enough, and could wait a little longer. He made his way towards the yacht club and climbed the stairs to the main entrance. Benny and Cyril had been closer to the club and were now standing at the bar.

'A bit soon for this, isn't it, Cyril?' remarked Charlie, jokingly.

'Not a bit, it's nearly 9 o'clock! You don't mind, do you, Tom?' he said to the barman who was still doing his pre-opening chores.

'No problem, but I can't take pay until eleven. It's the licence, you see.'

'We're good for it. Rack them up, then!' replied Cyril, 'Double Glenmorangie's all 'round!'

'Single for me,' interjected Charlie, 'and I'm paying or I'm leaving!'

'Suit yourself,' replied Cyril, 'No argument from me.'

'Likewise, Charlie,' added Benny with a smile.

They picked up their drinks, clinked glasses, and picked a table near the window with a panoramic view over the marina. Some of the early cloud was beginning to clear and rays of light broke on the white hulls of the boats bobbing up and down on the incoming tide. There was no objection from the boats as, although they were built for all weathers, they much preferred to bask in the sun.

'Life doesn't get better than this does it?' said Cyril, falling heavily into an armchair. 'I hope I've got another ten years of this left in me before I'm carted off to the crumblies' farm. Or worse,' he chuckled. 'No complaints from me.'

Benny was embarrassed. He opened his mouth in preparation to remind Cyril that he had forgotten about Charlie's misfortune. Charlie noticed his hesitation and headed him off by agreeing with Cyril, raising his glass again to emphasise the point. He winked at Benny as if to say, *let it go*. There was little point in embarrassing the old chap. It wasn't his fault. Besides, it was really of no consequence. Benny was visibly relieved, but remained quiet throughout, only adding to the conversation when they brought him into it with a question.

The talk inevitably turned to the state of the education system. Cyril took centre stage as education was within his comfort zone. He hadn't a clue about football and knew even less about rugby, Union or League. Three drinks later, and now bored to distraction, Charlie drained his glass and stood up to go. 'If I have any more, I won't be able to take her out,' he said, 'It's been great chatting, but I'm off now.'

'Okay,' replied Cyril, 'but don't leave it so long next time. I haven't seen you for nearly a year!'

'No,' said Charlie, 'I was only here ......' He stopped. Cyril didn't remember their chance meeting the day he'd brought Tommy's body to the marina. 'You're right Cyril. Must have been last Summer. I think I'll be coming more often now that I'm on my own.' The comment was lost on Cyril. But not on Benny, who patted Charlie on the back.

'Sorry for that, mate, you did well,' said Benny. 'See you next time.'

Charlie put a £20 and a £10 note on the bar. It was still too early to ring it in.

'Keep the change if there's any, Tom. Cheers!'

Charlie walked off towards the door. He heard the two continue the conversation behind him in low voices. When Cyril, clearly alarmed, let out, 'Oh, my God, I'd forgotten!' Charlie grinned from ear to ear and continued to walk without turning around. The old duffer was in no position to testify. Not that he had any weight to add to any police enquiry, but it was convenient, and a relief, nevertheless.

On board, Charlie cooked a late breakfast of bacon and eggs, then completed his checks and called the coast guard to inform them that he was taking Stormy Monday out, no more than five miles and to the south by south-east. Estimated time of arrival back at port was between 1400 and 1430 hours. The Coast guard had no weather warnings to give out. In fact, it was going to be ideal sailing weather, with a good breeze and little swell. 'Roger that, Charlie, have a good 'un,' came the closing reply.

After allowing the plug to warm up, the engine started first time. He left it idling while he unhitched the moorings then returned to the wheelhouse. The marina, was now becoming a hive of activity as, one after one, owners and fishermen began to arrive. No need to delay for the exchange of pleasantries. A smile and a wave as he passed, would suffice. Within minutes, he was out into the open sea, sails now gently billowing, but never out of sight of land. Charlie guided the boat to where he wanted it to be, about a mile east of Coquet Island. Its lighthouse, a square limestone tower painted white, was clearly visible. The island was now uninhabited, except for sea birds and an occasional seal, basking in the elusive sun, the resident keeper having vacated it some years ago when the lighthouse became automated. Now it was home to about 36,000 puffins and a number or terns, gulls and kittiwakes. It was a pity there was no viable market for bird shit, thought Charlie.

The sails taken in and the boat now calmed, he took out his pieces of paper, laid them out on the galley table, and held them down with anything heavy. The breeze, although now light, was still apt to blow the pieces of paper off the table, or out of the boat altogether. He had gone over it all before, but another look wouldn't hurt. He might find something he missed the last time.

There were eighteen numbers taken from Tommy's phone and a similar number listed on Collins' phone. Neither phone contained the other's number but one of the numbers *did* match. They had a mutual acquaintance. One was a South Shields villain and one was from Liverpool. *Why would they have a matched number? Were they working for the same man?* It would make sense if they were. In Tommy's phone, the name listed was *Ray*. In the other it was listed simply as *RM*. It had to be Ray Morrison.

Tommy's phone also contained the number of Chief Inspector Mick Redman. It also contained the number of a Tony, whom Charlie had identified more than a week earlier, as Tony Molloy. His would-be mugger-cum-murderer.

Molloy's phone contained Tommy's number and the matching numbers from the two phones. The entry was under *Ray M*. It was Morrison, alright. The same number was now in all three phones. Joey featured in Collins' and in the mugger's phone. Morrison and Joey were either pulling the strings, or they could lead Charlie to the man who was.

A number of questions had to be considered. *Was Tommy really working for Morrison when Charlie got him sent down? Who were his associates and where are they now? Who did he meet up with when he came out of prison? How was he going to find any of the answers without showing his hand? Did he really need to know these things if he already knew that Morrison was the answer to everything?* He would need to take his time and give it some thought. One thing for sure, he could not do anything soon because tomorrow, he had something big planned which required his full attention. Molloy was coming out of hospital and Charlie had planned a surprise reception for him. Then a few weeks later, it was the start of the Freddie Simpson trial.

SIXTEEN

August was proving to be a busy month. Molloy had been cleanly dispatched and the day of the long-awaited trial had arrived. Charlie's very last trial. Hopefully. He had felt this way many times before, excited but cautious, and full of trepidation. He knew the defence would focus on him and his handling of the investigation

He went over and over his account and asked himself what could possibly go wrong. He put himself in the shoes of the defence barrister, as he always did, and asked all the difficult questions he or she could ask. He could see no real weaknesses and the case was seemingly watertight. Why, then, were they pleading not guilty? They could only attack his integrity, make him look unreliable. Even bent. There was no entrapment, no agent provocateur, the interviews were all kosher and recorded. Admissions had not been slipped in to replace denials. There were no inducements, no threats, veiled or otherwise, to his family. Nothing. No one had been allowed to walk away for turning *Queens*. There would be no leniency for pleading guilty, the only realistic sentence was life. Perhaps he was going through the motions and a guilty plea would be entered at the last minute? In his heart of hearts, Charlie thought that unlikely. Freddie was a fighter, not the type to roll over.

Court One was in the same place it had always been since it moved from Kenton Bar and The Moot Hall, the second floor of the Newcastle Crown Court on Newcastle's quayside. A fabulous location, on the doorstep of one of the city's many evening destinations, with numerous bars, restaurants and nightclubs,

Very handy for court result celebrations and commiserations alike. The Tyne was literally a stone's throw away for jumpers. The height would not kill them unless they chose the eighty-foot drop from the Tyne Bridge, in which case it was a fifty-fifty. Unless they misjudged it and hit the quay rather than the water, which was sometimes the case, especially in the dark. A head with femurs for earrings was not a pretty sight.

Court security officers were on their game, and searched barristers and police officers, even those who were regulars, just as thoroughly as they would a visitor or an obvious prig. For the first time in twenty or so years, Charlie was entering court with no baggage, only his own statement and a copy of his policy book, which explained the reasons behind his decisions and which he had taken care to copy before he left the police service for good. Everything else was brought by other members of the investigation team. Apart from the actual drugs, as that would have presented a major security issue given their street value of £1 million plus. Photographs and analysts' statements were sufficient to prove their existence. The defence team was not making an issue of it.

Detective Sergeant Ron Harding had replaced Charlie as the senior investigating officer since his retirement, mainly just to do the running around that precedes a trial. Nevertheless, it was likely that Charlie would take the brunt in the witness box as the direction and decision-making during the entire investigation had been his. Certainly, if he was working for the defence, he would exploit the fact that the retired detective was probably still in holiday mode and a little rusty. He would be giving him a hard time. Charlie expected no less.

Ron Harding was not much better placed. He had been foisted on Charlie as a career move, a tick in the box, but he was never a detective in the true sense. Everything was by the book and he would cut no corners, take no chances. He worked his allotted hours, no more, sometimes less, and none of his own cases were difficult, as Charlie recalled. He was a makeweight that needed the prefix *detective* on his curriculum vitae, and to give him kudos in his circle of family and friends. Potentially, senior officer material, Charlie thought. He had not given evidence before, not even in Magistrates Court. As every detective knows, following a redneck into the witness box could be a nightmare. You had no way of knowing whether they would stick to the script, whether they would deviate or whether they were strong enough to withstand cross-examination. A good indication that something had gone terribly wrong would be for the first officer to be sent to the cells after giving evidence so that there could be no communication with officers following him into the witness box. It had happened to three of his colleagues over the years, but never to Charlie. God forbid that it was his turn now.

As usual, Harding's evidence was uncontentious. He only did as he was told, made no decisions for himself and was Charlie's second man during the interviews. Charlie did not recall him opening his mouth except to introduce himself and say *no* when Charlie asked him if he would like to ask any questions of his own. There was no guarantee that he had even been listening during the interview. In effect, he was just a bag carrier but, no doubt, he would dine out on this case as his very own for many years. Charlie did not mind, it was no longer of any concern to him. His time was over. Ron was a nice enough bloke and would not harm anyone, unless it was to save his own skin. He was quite academic, knew the law and had all the right answers for the interview board. He would go places. Unless, of course, he cocked up along the way, which was unlikely since he was risk-averse.

Harding barely got out a 'Hello, Charlie', before he was whisked away into a consultation room by McLeod, Queen's

Counsel for the prosecution. Charlie looked on, puzzled. *Why had he not been invited? Was there a problem?* In the meantime, Charlie sat in the public seating area, mixing with victims, witnesses, criminals and their families and interested parties or random public that had nothing better to do.

Almost fifteen minutes went by, during which time he read and re-read his statement and policy book. He was now at saturation point and just wanted to get in, do his bit, then get out. The way things were going, he would be lucky to get in before lunch.

McLeod was not one of his favourites. An imposing figure of six feet three inches, made even taller by his wig, and a contrived, plummy accent interspersed with the occasional Geordie slip. It was the first time he had been on Charlie's side, not representing defendants, and there was a lot of history between them, none of it friendly. Still, he was onside now. *Wasn't he?*

It was now almost 11am when, into the waiting area walked a group of eight people. Charlie's jaw dropped. Among the group was Charlie himself as a seventeen-year old youth. A young Charlie! The more he stared at the youth, the more intrigued he became. After a few seconds, one of the group, a forty something female, took the youth by the arm and sat him beside her, with their backs to Charlie. She obviously had not seen him. The female was unmistakably Jane Elliot, a former girlfriend for several years until eighteen years ago when she ditched him, supposedly because of the hours he kept. Julie, who was not so bothered about his hours, because she worked long hours herself, snared him on the rebound. He had been miffed at being dumped, not so much that he loved Jane and could not bear to be without her, but he had never been dumped before, and his pride hurt more than his heart ached. Still, he might have married her and, although he was contemplating a proposal around about then, she took away that decision from him.

Oh, God, this isn't happening! He stood up and walked towards the panoramic window so that no one could detect his discomfort. Still reeling from the discovery that he might have a son, the public-address system broke his concentration with a call:

'*Would all parties in the case of the Crown versus Simpson, please go to Court One.*' The group got up as one and entered Court One. It had suddenly got worse. *Were they somehow involved with Simpson?* They had not been present when Charlie had searched Simpson's home, so no connection had been made. Nor did the connection come out during the investigation. As a witness, Charlie was not allowed into the court until he was called, so it could be some time before he would know the situation, one way or the other. At the same time, Detective Sergeant Harding emerged from the consultation room with McLeod, and while McLeod went straight into court, Harding crossed over to Charlie and spoke.

'McLeod thinks it best if we aren't seen together until after we've both given our evidence. I'm afraid you are going to have to stay here'.

'Any problems, Ron?' Charlie responded, seeing the final chance for a rehearsal going down the tubes.

'Not really, the evidence is good. We don't know how they're going to play it'.

'Okay, maybe see you later'. It was Charlie's fault that he had not been included. He was the supposed expert, and should have insisted on a conference well before the court date.

'Yes, sorry we haven't had time to go over things, but it seems pretty straightforward. If they don't plead, God knows how they are going to come at us. I'd better go. See you later'. He disappeared through a security door and along the corridor to the police room. For the first time, as far as his career was concerned, Charlie felt isolated. This is not how things were done in his time.

Just as he had felt all along, there was going to be no rollover. The case was opened with a five-minute speech by McLeod and the statements of the officers who had discovered and analysed the drugs went unchallenged. The undercover officer used in the investigation was not called. His evidence was not contested. It was soon to be Charlie's turn, and if Jane hadn't already seen him, she could not possibly miss him now. He could have done without such complications but, on the plus side, he drew strength from the thought that he might actually have a son.

When the call came from the usher, '*Detective Inspector Payne?*' Charlie sprang to his feet, straightened his tie and took a few gulps of air. He walked through the darkened airlock and into the court, sensing that all eyes were on him. Which, of course, they were. To his right were the public seats, every one of them taken by, he presumed, Simpson's family and supporters, including Jane Elliot and the young man he assumed to be her son. Possibly *his* son. There was no reaction from Jane. If she was indeed with the Simpson family, she would already know the name of the officer in the case. She may even have read the depositions. She would have made the connection already. The thought briefly occurred to him that she may have passed on some information about his private life that he would rather had stayed under wraps. Then again, he could think of nothing that she knew that could hurt him.

The public sat facing the witness box and the judge's bench, of which they had an unobstructed view, but most court officials, the jury and the defendant were separated from them by a wood and glass partition. Two other faces were immediately recognisable, both males, although Charlie could not readily put names to them. Other than, perhaps, one was called Glen. They were both criminals whom he'd helped put away about ten years earlier for drugs offences. They would only have served five. Their names would come to him eventually.

It was unusual to find criminals, certainly of this calibre, in the public gallery. Defence barristers would prefer their clients' supporters to look respectable, preferably female, vulnerable and motherly. Besides, being in court gives most criminals the willies, so being there voluntarily was strange. There had to be a purpose to it.

Freddie Simpson sat in the dock, flanked by two prison officers. What they could have done if Freddie kicked off, Charlie could not have imagined. One was probably only ten stone wet through, and the other, although twice the size, was all belly and lard. Probably lightning fast over two yards, after which he would fall over. In contrast, Freddie was six-foot of mostly solid muscle, all 16 stone of it. His head was bald through choice and the swallow tattoos on his neck, inflicted when he was seventeen, were fading, but still noticeable. He wore a white long-sleeved shirt, probably to cover up the other tattoos on the advice of his barrister but it was cheap and thin, probably bought in haste for the trial by someone who didn't think he was worth wasting the money on. It did not disguise the fact that he was an out and out thug. He obviously hadn't had much sleep, judging by the bags under his eyes, and his attempt at a menacing stare in Charlie's direction was not missed by the jury. *Bring it on, mate, the jury's got the measure of you already!*

A security officer stood by the door, ready to deal with any rowdies, on a nod from the judge. He was of the knuckle-dragging variety, big and powerful, the type that would work the doors in his spare time.

The usher did not have to tell Charlie where the witness box was, although he insisted on doing so. He had been there so many times before that he wondered whether there was a brass plaque with an inscription to his memory. There was not. The usher did not have to tell him to take the bible in his right hand and read the oath from the card, but he insisted on doing so.

Charlie introduced himself as 'Detective Inspector Charles Payne, retired'. McLeod accorded him his *new* status, referring to him as Mr. Payne throughout the proceedings. He was an accomplished barrister and led Charlie through the evidence with ease. Charlie had been the officer in charge of the case. An undercover officer from another part of the country had been used to infiltrate the lower reaches of the criminal organisation, and after six months of skilful manipulation, was an established fringe member. In time, and having been involved in many deals himself in order to get himself established, he was able to provide the time, date and location of the next big deal where most of the main players would be involved. There had been eight main targets on the wanted list and the police would have settled for three or four, but they got five. A great result, they thought, especially since the haul included the main man, Simpson. Four had pleaded guilty, and a week earlier, they had been sentenced to between eight and fifteen years.

The interviews were not challenged, they had all been recorded and the wording, intonation and general conduct could not be disputed or challenged. There was no oppression, badgering or raised voices. That's not the way Charlie worked. He preferred the Columbo style – playing dim-witted before finally delivering the bombshell. That, too, would come through on the recordings should anyone wish to hear them. But they did not.

Although Simpson had declined to answer any questions, the interviews had been read in their entirety so that the jury would begin to get a feel for the defendant's integrity, or lack of it. Not answering questions could be just as incriminating as answering questions, and the judge would be entitled to invite the jury to ask themselves why the defendant would not wish to answer them. Indeed, that's what he would later do, during his summing up.

Then came the turn of defence counsel, Robert Ashley. Unlike McLeod, Ashley was a diminutive figure with pinched features and gold rimmed spectacles that perched on the end of his nose.

'*Here we go,*' Charlie thought, as he flexed his leg, arm and neck muscles like a fighter preparing for round one. It was a routine, subconscious, but a routine nevertheless. He was preparing for another marathon in the witness box. His record stood at three and a half days. *Surely that record is not in any danger?* He hoped that anyone watching this little performance would not misread his non-verbal communications for something they were not.

There followed almost thirty seconds of silence during which Ashley looked at Charlie, then his notes, then at the judge, then at Charlie again. It was as if he wanted Charlie to say something. Charlie had used the same tactic on many occasions, and he was determined not to be the first to break silence.

'Mr. Payne', started Ashley, accentuating the *Mr.* as if it was calculated to insult, 'how well do you know the defendant?'

Charlie was not sure what he meant. He did not know him well, and their paths had crossed no more than a dozen times in thirty years. He knew he could not answer that question truthfully without giving away the fact that he was a known criminal, something the jury is not usually allowed to know, although there was no mistaking the fact that he was an unpleasant looking individual. He had also been a short-term informant of Charlie many years ago. He looked at the judge for inspiration and guidance.

His Lordship, Judge Herbert Conroy, a rotund gentleman with a ruddy complexion to match his scarlet and purple robes, explained to Charlie that the court was already aware of the defendant's criminal background, and that he should feel free to answer the question truthfully. Charlie nodded and smiled.

'I have arrested Mr. Simpson on two occasions that I can recall. The first, for robbery, and the second, about twelve years ago, for dealing in cocaine. Both resulted in prison sentences.' Charlie's confidence was up. That is all it took, one answer to get back into the swing.

'Have you known him in any other capacity?'

'He's never been a friend or an acquaintance if that's what you mean'.

'Has he ever provided you information about the criminal activities of others?'

'You know I can't answer that,' he replied, looking at the judge again.

His Lordship stepped in. 'Mr. Ashley, what is the purpose of this line of questioning?'

'Perhaps I should explain, my Lord. My client freely admits that he has supplied information to Mr. Payne. He was a one-time informant. I am trying to demonstrate that there is more to Mr. Payne than meets the eye, and it is a question of the officer's integrity here.'

'I think we need to discuss this in chambers, Mr. Ashley'. The judge then turned to the jury. 'Members of the jury, for the moment, you will disregard this line of questioning until I instruct you further. This court is in recession and we shall return for 2pm prompt.'

The clerk of the court sprang to his feet, as if awoken abruptly from his slumber. 'Court, rise!' Everyone stood up and waited for the judge to bow and leave his throne before they dispersed after returning their bows, the legal teams to the judge's chambers, the jury to their room, and the remainder to wherever they wished.

Charlie left before the public did. He considered taking Jane to one side but knew it would not be appropriate, certainly not at that time, certainly not if she was linked to Simpson in some way, and certainly not in front of the thugs who appeared to be in her company. He would have to bide his time, but the situation would need to be resolved, one way or the other. Having a son could be a life-changing experience, for good or for bad, but he had to know. That night, he would raid the family photo archive and put a collection of photographs together of himself as a teenager and carry them around with him until the opportunity presented itself to speak to her.

Throughout the evening, Charlie reflected on the day's proceedings. Sure, Simpson had been an informant for Charlie many years ago, but everything was properly recorded. There was no informant in this case, or covert human intelligence source as they were now referred to, other than the undercover officer. *What was he up to?*

The session resumed at exactly 2pm, the following day, and Ashley resumed his line of questioning.

'Has my client ever provided you with information about the criminal activities of others?'

Charlie again looked at the judge, who nodded approval. He chose his words carefully.

'Yes, twice, but it was years ago. I don't recall specific details, but it was all recorded. The records can be retrieved if needed.' At least Charlie hoped they could, given the department's recent upheaval through redundancies and relocation.

'There will be no need for that,' responded Ashley. 'Besides, I doubt whether there will be any record of the transaction I have in mind.' He paused, looked at the judge and waited for him to scribble his notes.

'Do you recall a meeting with my client in June 1998, when you propositioned him to gain intelligence on a gentleman called Mason? He declined, and you threatened to see to it that he would get his comeuppance someday. No matter how long it takes?' A further pause while he made sure the judge was writing it all down. Charlie knew not to interrupt, as much as he wanted to.

'And isn't today, the day of reckoning?'

This was a granny, a rather poor one. Charlie looked at Ashley, but otherwise remained expressionless. It had never happened. It was a desperate measure from a drowning man who had run out of straws. If that's all they had, he could bat off questions of this nature all day long.

'Mr. Ashley, that's a lie. I did not go to your client on any such matter. He provided me with information on two other people, but that was long before 1998.'

'You see, Mr. Payne, the reason I ask is that my client says you offered him £5,000 of public money to be split two ways, half for him, the other half for you?'

Charlie could not help but crack a smile. 'That is a ridiculous suggestion. I am not corrupt, and I have a good track record. Besides, I wouldn't betray my profession for any amount, let alone a paltry sum like that.'

'A paltry sum, Mr. Payne?'

'Yes. It's quite insulting, really!' Charlie looked at the jury. He knew how to play them.

'Oh, then, what is your price?'

Charlie shook his head and smiled but declined to answer. McLeod rose, to object.

'Mr. Ashley!' said His Lordship, loudly, anticipating McLeod's objection. Ashley was undeterred. He would keep going until told to shut up. The wad of Simpson's £50 notes in his pocket, sufficient to choke a donkey, was worth the risk.

'In fact, you have been after Mr. Simpson ever since, haven't you, and you will stop at nothing to get him?'

'Objection!' shouted McLeod, looking daggers at Ashley.

'Sustained,' responded the judge, 'Mr. Ashley, no more of that, please, it is not in line with what we discussed in chambers,' he said peering over the top of his reading spectacles.

'No, my Lord,' acknowledged Ashley with a faint smirk. But he had already accomplished his aim, to plant in the minds of the jury that Charlie could possibly be bent. His acceptance of the judge's comment without protest, was evidence of that. But if only one juror believed it, others could be persuaded to follow, and the outcome would be far from certain.

'Mr. Payne', he continued, 'I understand that you were arrested quite recently for shooting a man dead in your house in extremely dubious....'

'Objection!' virtually screamed McLeod, before Ashley could finish his sentence.

'Sustained!' agreed the judge. 'My chambers, please.' He continued, as he rose, 'Members of the jury, you will disregard this line of questioning until I speak further on the matter'.

'Court, rise!' announced the clerk, rising to his feet. Everyone stood. More ceremonial bowing after which the judge left, visibly annoyed, and crimson-faced. McLeod stared at Ashley in disbelief.

Twenty minutes elapsed before McLeod sought Charlie out and took him to a consultation room. No doubt he had been in chambers discussing the rules of engagement. At his request, Charlie gave him as much detail as he could about his personal circumstances, about his former dealings with Simpson and the circumstances of his shooting of the Julie's killer. In due course, everyone was called back to court and took their places. Ashley was first to rise.

'No further questions, my Lord,' he said, before taking his seat. Charlie was right, he'd made his point and did not want to press the matter in case his tactics fell apart. He was saving the rest for his final speech when it was too late for objections from the prosecution.

McLeod rose, turned to the jury to make sure he had their undivided attention, then gestured to them to look towards the judge.

When the room finally fell silent, His Lordship began.

'Members of the jury, before we adjourned, you heard Defence Counsel make reference to Detective Inspector Payne's shooting dead a man in his house. I want to explain this to you, then you should put it from your minds altogether. This was reported in the newspapers some months ago, and I have those reports in front of me. I don't often rely on the press, except, perhaps, for the racing results, but it seems that a hired assassin went to the home of Mr. Payne in order to kill him, for reasons known only to him, and one can only assume that the unfortunate Mrs. Payne, somehow, got in the way and was killed instead. Mr. Payne, fearing that he was next, after all, he was the reason for the assassin's being there, one might assume, seized his moment, disarmed the man and fatally wounded him. You might say he acted in self-defence. You might even think the assassin had it coming. Certainly, the police had a duty to get to the bottom of what happened, and Mr. Payne did spend some time with them, but he was released without charge. It is neither relevant to this case nor does it have any detriment to Mr. Payne's character. Please continue Mr. McLeod.'

'My Lord, if it please the court, I know you have explained to the jury what happened in the Payne household, but I would like Mr. Payne, himself, to explain what happened that terrible day,' pleaded McLeod.

Judge Conroy indicated approval with a wave of his hand.

'I'm obliged, my Lord.'

'Mr. Payne', said McLeod, turning to Charlie, 'You were married, were you not, to your wife, Julie, now sadly deceased, at the hands of someone who was sent to kill you?'

'That is correct. She was murdered in June of this year,' he replied, looking directly at the jury. 'Shot in the face and body by a paid hit man.' He jabbed his right forefinger into his face at a point to coincide with where the bullet had entered.

The jury looked uncomfortable. Most of them held his gaze but others looked away. The courtroom went silent. Freddie Simson smirked. It didn't go unnoticed.

'And did you shoot the gunman dead?'

'I did. While I knelt by my wife's side trying to revive her, he put the gun against my head. I instinctively grabbed it and wrenched it from his hand. He was going to kill me anyway, so I had nothing to lose by having a go. I shot him twice in quick succession as he tried to get the gun back, hitting him once in the chest and once in the leg.'

'Do you have any regrets about what you did?'

'No. I feared for my life. He was a professional hit man, I believed, although I didn't know that at the time. Had there been any malice on my part, I would have emptied the magazine into him. But there wasn't. I was too distraught, and I just wanted to incapacitate him.'

'Do you have any idea why he would want to kill you or your wife?'

'None, other than I have been instrumental in sending a lot of big names in the criminal fraternity to jail.'

'Why were you arrested?'

'I had just killed a man. It is standard procedure and I accept that without question, but I was released without charge because it was clear that it was in self-defence.'

McLeod waited for that information to sink in and make its mark before he continued.

'Mr. Payne,' he continued,' would you mind explaining your circumstances, as discussed earlier?'

Charlie took a deep breath and looked directly at the jury. All eyes were on him. It's what he wanted because he needed them to understand what he was about.

'My wife had her own business when I met her in 1996. A string of hairdressing shops. She was quite wealthy in her own right but when her parents died, she inherited a third share of a huge property empire. We were multi-millionaires as long ago as 1997. We lived a fairly simple lifestyle, we weren't flashy, rarely holidayed abroad and had no children. Our situation just kept getting better. Until she was murdered.'

The jury were hanging on to his every word and waited for more, loving every minute of it. He was done, for now.

'Mr. Payne, I understand you have standing orders to certain charities, Barnardo's and NSPCC?''

'I do.'

'When did your standing orders to those charities begin?'

'I believe it was around 1990. They are charities close to my heart. I was brought up in a Barnardo's home. I was giving a bit to each and it gradually increased to what it is now.'

'And how much is it now, if you do don't mind my asking?'

'£800 per month.'

The jury gasped.

'How much was it back in 1998?'

'I would need to check my records, but between £300 and £400 per month, I think.'

'So, £2,500 in those days, your supposed share of the informant money, would amount to around 6 to 8 months charity money.'

'It would.'

'But you were a millionaire, even then, so that kind of money, please don't take this the wrong way, it was really of little consequence in the circumstances?'

'I suppose so. That's why I kept upping it. And they're each down for a million in my will.'

A member of the jury had to stop himself from leading a round of applause. Some glanced in Simpson's direction to see what he was making of it all. He sat motionless, although he was beginning to accept that his ruse had backfired. Ashley was unfazed. It was matter-less to him whether Simpson was acquitted. He had already been paid in readies.

'What would you do if you suddenly came into another £2,500, even in 1998?'

'Give it to charity. I already had an obscene amount of money by then. In the late nineties, I won an all-expenses paid holiday to Florida in a charity auction, but I gave it away to a colleague who needed a holiday more than me. It was worth at least £3,000, they said, even in those days. I could have sold it, but I didn't.'

'How much was your bid?'

'I paid over the odds, £3,800, I think, but it was for a good cause.'

'Which charity was it?'

'Marie Curie.'

'You paid more than it was worth, but gave it away?'

'Yes, but it was for a good cause.'

'These are hardly the actions of a man who would debase his public office and integrity for a mere £2,500, would you agree?'

'I would.'

'Mr. Payne, I'm sure that everyone is dying to know why, when you have been so comfortable for many years, did you continue to work in a high pressure, stressful and often dangerous job?'

'A sense of public duty and something exciting to do. And catching people who make their living by causing misery to others. I found the property business boring.' It won more smiles from the jurors.

McLeod turned to the judge, trying to conceal his delight.

'No more questions, my Lord'. He remained on his feet, anticipating that His Lordship would adjourn for the day. He had anticipated well.

The prosecution and defence speeches, and the judge's summing up, would take place the following day, in that order, before the jury retired to consider their verdict. The defence had been threadbare and the little ploy to discredit Charlie had backfired in style. The guilty verdict was virtually assured, although such things don't always go to plan, as Charlie recalled. But, aside from the professional pride aspect, it no longer mattered. He was released as a witness and there was no need for him to await the verdict in court. But he would. He wanted the satisfaction of seeing Ashley's face, probably more than Simpson's face, as his client was taken away. He also wanted to see Jane Elliot. And her son. Possibly *his* son.

SEVENTEEN

The wait was long, but as a trained sniper, he was used to that. No one would see him enter his observation post and set up his equipment. He would enter the site around 0330 hours, during the hours of darkness and probably while the local constabulary were taking time out from their patrols, after their breaks, to do paperwork. He wore the best camouflage suit Her Majesty's Forces could provide, and intertwined it with foliage from his surroundings. A passer-by would fall over him before seeing him. But that was unlikely, because no one ever went there except for the annual service visit by the local authority gardener, and that was not due for a couple of months. The long wait was nothing to him. In the summer heat, it would be quite pleasant. He had waited far longer in 40-degree heat and minus 5, so this was a walk in the park, by comparison.

His rifle, a Ruger rim fire .22 calibre, was equally invisible, with only the lens and muzzle free from camouflage. Any smoke from the discharge would be long gone by the time they realised where the shot had come from. They would eventually trace the path of the bullet but not for several hours, by which time he would be miles away. The autopsy, at least four hours away and probably eight or more, would reveal the likely angle of the trajectory and all suspected sites would be forensically searched in daylight when the autopsy revelations were known, probably not until the following day.

Afterwards, he would slowly crawl unnoticed to a point where no one would see him break down and pack the dismantled sniper rifle, camouflage suit and food and drink packaging, into a small sports holdall. This was a relatively short stay so there would be no need for hot drinks or a bag to collect his body waste. He had already cleared his bowels and would use an empty one litre plastic bottle to collect the three pees he might need to take during that period. He would leave nothing behind, no trace except a disturbed patch of foliage which may never be found. Even if he was caught, no matter. He was prepared for it. Part of him even hoped for it so that he could set the record straight, claim the credit for ridding the world of a louse, but the longer he could stay undetected, the longer his mission would continue.

His target was Glen Harrison, a known drug dealer who always managed to stay clear of trouble while his lieutenants invariably took any fall if it went wrong. He had it coming. He was long overdue.

EIGHTEEN

Later that day, Charlie attended court bright and early. For at least five minutes he was the only person around. With luck, there would be the chance to speak to Jane Elliot. He was prepared for a rebuff, hostility even, depending on her relationship with Simpson. And the verdict. A life sentence was probable and, if she was romantically linked with Simpson, it was inconceivable that she would stick with him. Once his meal ticket status ended, he would not see her for dust.

McLeod's closing speech was quite short, little more than 15 minutes. He did not have to try hard to convince the jury. He outlined the overwhelming evidence and the defence's clumsy attempt to discredit Charlie. He made a great play on how Ashley was only working on the instructions of Simpson. And, to Charlie's surprise, he said that in all the years he had known Charlie, he was an officer of impeccable character even though, at times, they had been on opposing sides. He piled on the praise to such an extent that Charlie was at the point of nausea. He was no saint.

Ashley went through the motions. He knew the game was up and was probably relieved that Simpson would go down for a very long time. He had done his best with what little he had to go on, and no one could fault him for his efforts. His reputation with cash-paying clients would still be intact, enhanced even, thanks to his double rebuke from the judge. This was a man who would take risks for his clients. Afterwards, he would shake Charlie's hand and give him a wink and a smile. It was the nearest Charlie would get to an apology. But he knew Ashley was saying, 'Sorry, but I'm only doing what I am paid to do'. Charlie got that. He expected no more, no less.

It took the jury no more than forty-five minutes to return a guilty verdict. The vote and the decision itself would take no more than a couple of minutes and the tea ritual and farewells would take up the rest. Besides, they are advised not to return in indecent haste otherwise it would look as if they had not weighed up both arguments. Even though the judge could have passed sentence immediately because of the likely life sentence, he adjourned for reports.

Charlie stayed behind to talk to McLeod. He wanted to thank him, but he was also interested to know what issues the judge would be considering before making his recommendation as to time to be served before consideration for parole. It was at that point Charlie saw Ashley talking to Jane Elliot on the very same subject, the two thugs hanging onto his every word. Jane was clearly the next of kin. Her son, on the other hand, appeared to be disinterested in the fate of his father. With luck, his *surrogate* father.

They eventually all left the court together, the two thugs leading the way, obviously anxious to use their mobile phones and be the first with the bad news to whoever was interested. It gave Charlie a chance to catch Jane's eye.

'We need to talk,' Charlie whispered. She looked at him after first glancing around her to make sure that no one else was watching.

'Not here, not yet,' she whispered back. He handed her a piece of paper onto which he'd already written his mobile phone number. She took it, which was better than he had hoped for. Jane had worn well considering that she was closing in on fifty and lived in fear, not knowing whether each knock at the door was the police, or a bitter rival of Freddie's. But Charlie no longer felt anything for her other than she was a friend from the past. Any flame he'd held for her had long been extinguished.

She quickened her walk, ostensibly to catch up with the others in her party, and Charlie hung about, waiting to catch the eye of Detective Sergeant Harding and take him for the customary drink and a gloat. He could do that much for him, but the *little shit* was nowhere to be seen. Lucky escape, Charlie thought. That's one tradition he did not mind breaking with.

The time was now a little after 4pm and Newcastle Crown Court was nearing the end of its business for the day. Countless times the doors had burst open followed by a group of people whose demeanour said it all. Jovial and pleasantly animated meant the case was going well, or they had won. Downcast, argumentative or unpleasantly animated meant that it was going badly, or they had lost. Anything else could mean it was still in the balance.

Harrison emerged first, face like thunder, mobile phone to his left ear. There was no mistaking this ugly bastard. He turned left toward the Pitcher and Piano pub, and hesitated while he listened to what the person on the other end had to say.

His face now filled 50% of the lens, with the crossed threads settling just above his left ear. This was it. The pressure had already been on the trigger for that last five seconds and it just required the final squeeze to send the projectile on its way. The bullet finally released, the target's face disappeared from the view of the telescopic sight, replaced by a blood and tissue spattered wall several feet beyond. Skull and brain fragments adhered to the rough surface, while heavier particles raced to the pavement at varying rates.

The sniper looked away from the gun-sight momentarily, to take in the full scene. Another man, just as big and as ugly, had gone to the aid of the fallen man and was leaning over him, calling his name. The sniper smiled as he recognised him.

Gotcha, he mouthed. The shot, more hastily delivered than the first, found its mark in the throat, as the face turned to search for the spot from where the first shot was fired. It was equally fatal, and fragments of his spinal cord joined his friend's brains, decorating the same wall and pavement.

Having done this kind of work for his unit in Iraq, with private work on the side, the assassin remained still for a few seconds so as not to give away his position to searching eyes, then slowly and calmly, he backed away to behind a large shrub, dismantled the weapon and disrobed. He then loaded his gear into the holdall and carried it towards his car, placing it into the boot. He had taken care to avoid any route or car park covered by CCTV and he would leave via the same route. By doing so, he had given himself further to walk and drive, but if that's what he had to do to avoid detection, so be it. Nothing could be considered too much trouble. Not if he had unfinished business. He was only just getting started. An hour later, the weapon and his camouflage would be back in their hiding place and he would be showered and changed.

After waiting for around five minutes Charlie went to the lift and pressed the down button. Nothing happened. Court business was still going on so it can't have been switched off for the day, he thought. On his way down the stairs he was met by a security officer coming up at speed.

'I'm sorry, sir,' he said, 'but there's been an incident outside, and the exit is being cordoned off. I'll have to take your details and let you out the back way.'

'What kind of incident?' Charlie asked.

'A shooting, I think. Looks like they're dead so you can imagine the circus.'

Charlie looked out of the window and towards the ground. Sure enough, there were blue lights, the faint sound of competing sirens and lots of people running in all directions.

'Man or woman?' he asked, realising that Jane could be right in the middle of it, if not a victim. She had left at about the right time.

'Definitely a man. So, they say. There might be more than one.'

Charlie gave him his contact details and he led him down the back stairs and out into the court car park.

'Someone will probably want to speak to you, eventually,' he said. 'Seemingly, the dead guy had been in the public gallery, court one.'

'Court One? What did he look like?'

'No idea, mate. Never seen him. Just going off what I've heard, really.'

If the victim had been in court one, it guaranteed that Charlie would be interviewed by the police, eventually, but probably not that night. At least, on this occasion, he would not be a suspect. For one, he was in the building when it happened. They would also have difficulty pinning a motive on him since he had nothing to gain by the deaths.

Charlie decided that it was a power struggle. A rival outfit taking out the remaining faces to ensure little resistance when they took over. If it was the heavies who went to the court with Jane, he was glad. Good riddance to them, he thought. It was always good when villains fell out. It saved time and effort.

The streets either side of the courts were cordoned off and Charlie was pointed towards a footpath that would lead him north, up the hill toward the city centre. He decided he had cause to celebrate. One villain going to his *nanna's* for the rest of his natch, and at least one for the incinerator. His ties with the police were now severed and he had some celebrating to do. He would go and surprise his brother, Steve, whom he had not seen for a few days. Steve had been a bit morose lately as it neared the anniversary of Paul's death and, like Charlie, he could probably do with some company.

That night, Charlie stayed at Steve's house. Steve was his usual quiet, pensive self and not much company, only perking up when Charlie told him of the trial and the drama outside the court afterwards. He switched on the television and found the BBC news channel. A shooting outside a Crown Court following a high-profile trial was bound to make the national news. Sure enough, it had, and they both sat in silence as they watched the coverage. It lasted for ten minutes, during which several eye witnesses and a police spokesperson were interviewed by the press.

There was also speculation about where the shot had come from, with close-ups of a bank of foliage on the Gateshead side of the Tyne and mugshots of the two victims. These were the two who had been in Jane Elliot's company. They were named as Jimmy Hargreaves and Glen Harrison. There was no mention of Elliot and the press speculated, now that a local drugs baron was out of the picture, it could be the start of a turf war. Charlie had already made up his mind that it had to be just that, but if it was, it was a huge risk to do it so publicly and so soon. He would have expected them to bide their time and do it up a back alley.

'I'll bet I'm interviewed about this,' Charlie said at last. 'Both these guys were in the public gallery in my court, and if plod has anything off, they'll want to look at everything.'

'Suppose so,' said Steve. 'Fancy a can?'

'Don't mind if I do,' replied Charlie. It was the start of a full-on session, and Steve had to go out to the off-licence to replenish his stocks. Charlie gave him a couple of twenties.

'Get a decent whisky or bourbon, if they've got any, and a bag of ice. Maybe some crisps and nuts?'

Steve took the money. His own tenner wouldn't have gone very far. It felt good to see Charlie in a good mood these days, and the pair of them hadn't had a session since the night of Paul's funeral. It was long overdue.

NINETEEN

The following morning Charlie woke up in a strange bed, to the sound of Strange Brew, his mobile phone ring tone. He opened one eye and squinted at his watch. It was light outside, but dark behind the heavy curtains. By the time he was able to focus and tell the time, the caller had rung off. It was just after ten. He sank back into his bed to catch a few more winks and the phone rang again. This time he snatched the phone and looked at the caller ID. It was Angel.

'Charlie, remember me, it's Angel?'

'Hello, Angel, of course I remember you, how could I forget?' He lay back into a comfortable position and managed a smile.

'Charlie, I need to come and see you about the shooting outside of court yesterday. Are you free?'

'You're not going to lock me up again, are you?' he joked.

'Course not, this is just routine. Are you free now?'

'Yes, come along, I'll put the kettle on when I see the whites of your eyes. By the way, I'm at my brother's house in Whickham. Give me an hour or so to get home. How about around twelve?' Twelve was fine.

'Steve?' shouted Charlie, 'are you awake? I've got the fuzz coming to see me about that court shooting. She'll be here in ten.'

'What, you've brought them here? To my gaff?'

'Yes, what's wrong with that? I'm not in any trouble. You're not keeping any hoisty gear, are you?'

'Course not, what do you take me for? You jump in the shower and I'll clear up downstairs. They won't want to see me, will they?'

186

'Don't worry, you get first shower and I'll make breakfast. I'm seeing her at my house at twelve. I wouldn't bring her to this dump. Got any bacon?'

'New pack top shelf of the fridge. No butter for me, just brown sauce, thanks. What dump?' he said, as an afterthought.

Charlie obliged. Steve had come back down to his usual self, following the highs of last evening. The drink had loosened his tongue and they had had a right old catch-up. But now he had the daddy of all hangovers. Charlie had also gotten around to offer to help Steve set up in business. Steve didn't seem keen to go it alone, whether he lacked the confidence or was just stuck in a rut, but he hinted that he might get involved with Charlie, if Charlie ran the show. This brought the conversation to a halt, as Charlie wasn't in the market for another job. He was retired, full stop, apart from the monthly board meetings with Sue and Jen which, for all the good he was, he might as well have not been there. But he would be prepared to come out of retirement if someone came up with a no-brainer that required little effort from him. Financial backing – no problem, but actual work other than, maybe, consultancy, was not in his plans. Drink sampler or food critic, he thought, but that was about it.

Charlie was looking forward to Angel's visit. Firstly, he liked her, probably a bit more than he should. Secondly, he needed an update on how things were progressing with the other matters. He went over some of the questions he needed to ask her and rehearsed, in his mind, what he would say. It was vital that he did not say anything to contradict what he had already said, or to give rise to further questions from her.

Charlie was already in the kitchen when he heard the wheels of her car turn into the driveway. He had opened the gates for her in readiness. He looked out of the kitchen window.

Good, he thought, she's on her own. She parked her car, a silver Mondeo job car, and locked it with her remote. She carried a black leather handbag large enough to hide a kitchen sink, and a slim leather briefcase, also in black. He opened the front door and invited her in, but before he had fully closed the door behind her, she put both bags down and put her arms around his neck, hugging him tightly.

'I'm sorry for what happened the last time', she said. 'That bastard's out of control.' She kissed Charlie on the left cheek and held him tightly for a further few seconds, during which Charlie felt that the gentlemanly thing to do would be to reciprocate. To show there were no hard feelings, if nothing else. She relaxed her grip and pulled her head back so that their noses were no more than four inches apart. She looked into his eyes, then at his lips, then into his eyes again. He knew what was expected of him. They kissed gently, at first, then more deeply and passionately. After a few seconds, she disengaged. She straightened her clothes.

'You have no idea how long I've waited for this moment,' she whispered, 'I'm in love with you, as I explained, but I can wait. Have been from the moment we met. Does that put you in an awkward position?'

'It doesn't. Not now', Charlie whispered back. 'But I think we should keep the situation under wraps for now or it might complicate things.'

'In what way?'

'Well, they say that less than a year is a bit, you know, premature. Also, I don't think the police are finished with me. They might even have me under surveillance. I know how things work, remember? And then there's the possibility of someone coming to finish the job.'

'Do you really think so? I mean, you're the victim. What you did was reasonable in the circumstances. The coroner delivered a self-defence and justifiable homicide verdict. As for the others, you just don't know. Chances are, it's over.'

'I know, but I have a feeling there is more to this than meets the eye. Redman was full of venom in his attack on me. I know he lacks grace and eloquence sometimes, but this was different. I think there is a hidden agenda.'

Angel thought for a moment. 'What kind of agenda?'

'I think someone is pulling his strings?'

'Well, anyway, let's not spoil the moment talking about him. Now that I've told you how I feel about you, how do you feel about me?' she asked. Her eyes were moist and fearful. She hoped for a favourable answer.

'This is awkward. I feel very deeply for you, always have done, but I am the loyal type so nothing materialised while we were working together. And now.... well I'm still in mourning. Kind of. I'm not ready to take up with anyone else just yet but when I am, I would like it to be with you. I love your company and I couldn't wish for a better pal. I hope you'll understand that?'

'I do', she replied. 'It's probably too soon, and I'm sorry for putting you in this position.'

'You don't see me struggling to break free, do you?' Charlie replied with a smile, pulling her tightly to his developing bulge.

'You're giving me mixed messages here, Charlie. Your voice is telling me one thing but down there seems to be saying exactly the opposite.'

Charlie could think of nothing to say in reply. He wanted her, but convention and his perception of what was decent, were forcing him to at least make a gesture of resistance.

She eventually broke the silence. 'That seems like a nasty swelling you have down there, would you like me to tend to it?'

Charlie's embarrassment eventually gave way and all he could think of to say was, 'That would be very nice, if you think you have any remedies?'

She did have. And she applied them.

They lay, still coupled, for several minutes, continuing to kiss passionately.

'I love you,' she whispered into his left ear.

'And I love you,' Charlie replied immediately, not knowing whether he meant it. But his life had suddenly taken a turn for the better. Julie was dead, and she was not coming back, but here was a woman who wanted to be with him. She had loved Charlie from a distance for many years and had kept herself for him. It was time to give something back, but it would be another few months before he would dare go public. There were some, in particular – Julie's sisters, who would be horrified. They would not expect him to take up with anyone ever again. Well, they were going to be disappointed, because Charlie had no intention of becoming celibate.

'So, where do we go from here?' she teased with a smile.

'Ideally, you would move in with me and we would thumb our noses at anyone who disapproves. But I think it would cause you difficulties at work and, as I say, I still don't think they're finished with me. There's more to come. If you do move in, we should play it low key until things on the work front run their course. What do you think?'

'As you say, I think I'll stay where I am for the moment and see how things develop. If everything's okay, I'll lease my own house out and move in here, if that's okay? But can I see you every day, or at least as often as you can?'

'Sounds like a good plan. Listen, if there *is* something going on, you might hear rumours about me. Don't believe what you hear but if you have any concerns, come to me. Of course, you won't hear anything if they know you've thrown your lot in with me, hence the caution. Do you understand what I'm saying?'

'Of course, I'm not daft. What rumours do you think I might hear about you?'

At that point, their bodies disengaged, and she turned Charlie onto his back, straddling him. She pinned his hands to the back of the sofa, with outstretched arms. She went nose to nose and smiled, awaiting his answer.

'Well,' he started, 'from what Redman was saying they seem to think I had something to do with the disappearance of Tommy Layton, and that I executed the bloke who shot Julie. Stuff like that.'

'Yea, well, they were the rantings of a man who is under the microscope himself. He's not flavour of the month, at the moment, but please don't repeat that. If you do, it could come back on me and I won't be able to confide in you ever again.' Her tone was serious.

'Angel, I would never compromise you. I'm probably just being paranoid.' He gently broke free from her hold and pulled her towards him. 'You've been a life changer for me. I can't wait to go public and show you off, but it's too soon.'

He had already declared his love for her, but once was enough for now. He didn't want to over-egg it and things were moving quicker in that direction than he wanted. He was enjoying it, but caution was needed, or things could backfire.

Her smile returned. 'Neither can I, Charlie Payne. But for now, I need to get back to work. Can I take a statement from you about what happened at court?'

'Yes, of course. How about dinner tonight?'

'That would be nice. How about Horton Grange, if they can take us a short notice?'

'Great choice, I'll book it for seven thirty and pick you up at seven? If there's a problem, I'll come back to you. Listen, there's obviously going to be a lot of contact between us. Better that I get us two 'pay as you' go phones that aren't traceable. All calls should be made or taken in the open air, and we should have code words for our meeting places.'

'Fine by me. Sounds like you know what you're talking about. It also sounds like you've done this before, I'm not sure if I can trust you now,' she said seriously, breaking into a smile. 'I'll only use the job phone if it's to do with work.'

They both visited the bathroom, Charlie, the master bedroom en-suite and she, the main bathroom, and took care of business. A final check in the mirror to ensure things were as they should be, then they met downstairs and she took his statement. He could have written it himself, but his version would have contained his agenda and been, perhaps, too long-winded where there was no need. Her version would suit the enquiry and be more succinct.

In essence, he described the two thugs in the public gallery, their demeanour when they left, and gave no opinion as to why they should have been there. No conjecture as to what led to their deaths. He had things to do. Bad things. Certainly, in the eyes of most, especially the law, and the sooner his profile was lowered, the sooner he could go about his plan.

TWENTY

Three weeks to the day of the court killings, during which there had been much publicity but little information, Charlie was at home, waiting in front of the television for the 6pm news, as was his routine. His spaghetti Bolognese dish was in the dishwasher and he was about to start on his mug of tea. No sugar but with the customary ginger snap. He leant forward and as he turned up the volume, the mugshots of Harrison and Hargreaves loom into view.

'The police have revealed today, that the killings of gang members James Hargreaves and Glen Harrison outside Newcastle Crown Court on 28th August, are linked to the killing of Tony Molloy outside his home in South Shields almost two months earlier. Ballistics experts have confirmed that all bullets were fired from the same gun. Although they won't commit to any theory, all the deceased are believed to belong to the same criminal faction, in which case it appears likely that a rival gang is involved. Members of the public are not thought to be at risk, although the discharge of firearms in public places is always a danger to the public.'

Charlie went purple as the realisation struck.

'The bastard!' he screamed. 'The bastard! What the fuck's he playing at? He picked up his mobile phone and couldn't dial Steve's number quick enough.

Steve answered.

'Have you seen the fucking news?' he shouted.

'Yes, I've seen the news. Why weren't you honest with me?' shouted Steve back.

'Are you at home? I'm coming over.'

'Yes, I'm home. Stop at the offy on your way over. And none of your shit mind, you've been no better! If you'd levelled with me none of this would have happened! Well it would have, but not like this!'

Charlie pressed the end call button and grabbed some cans from his supply in the pantry. Beer for him, lager for Steve, although he felt they might end up throwing them at one another rather than drinking them.

The drive to Whickham was surreal, and he almost caused a collision at the edge of his estate. Horns blared and he was forced to mouth an apology. It galvanised his mind and he drove carefully for the remainder of the journey.

Steve would not have known about the rifle's history until the news broke about the bullets coming from the same barrel. He was not sure whether he should be pleased or angry. But why would Steve shoot these two guys? Certainly not to do Charlie a favour, he thought. They were nothing to him, not even in the same gang he was looking at. On the plus side, if Charlie was alibied for the court killings then it was unlikely that he would be fingered for the Malloy shooting. He was looking forward to Steve's explanation.

He arrived at Whickham twenty-five minutes later, the car hissing and clicking as the hard-pushed engine panted for breath.

'Explanation!' demanded Charlie as he pushed past Steve in the doorway.

'Charlie,' began Steve, 'no apologies, mind, those guys were responsible for Paul's habit. They killed him. I've been biding my time but when you hid the rifle on my allotment, it gave me an idea. I couldn't believe my luck. You know I'm a trained sniper so what did you expect? The cops haven't a clue about me, they're chasing the shite. Anyway, who are you to talk? It must've been you who saw that Molloy bloke off, if my calculations are right?'

'Are you finished?'

'For now.'

'You could have compromised me, Steve!'

'Bullshit! If anything, I've made the investigation more complicated. Let's see them pick the bones out of that!'

After ten seconds, Charlie responded. 'Is there any chance this could come back on you? Is it known you had a grudge?'

'I don't see how. We didn't actually have a big fall out, or anything, and it was years ago. They won't find the gun and even if they do, they can't put me to it. I'm moving it tonight. Got a better place. I don't think they'll find an association between me and them and, anyway, I dropped off the radar a couple of years ago. I'm cool with it, how about your job on that Molloy kid?'

'That's different!'

'Different? How?'

'He tried to kill me, Steve. Made it look like a robbery but I got the first one in. He was mixed up with the people who killed Julie. I was the target and Molloy had the contract. I got his phone. The links are all there. I decided enough was enough, and he was the first.'

'The first? Who was the second?' enquired Steve, beginning to see a new side to his brother.

'Hasn't happened yet. Still trying to identify them.'

'So, more to come, then?'

'Steve, they ruined my life when they killed Julie. I've only got you left, which isn't much.'

'Thanks a bunch, big brother!'

'I'm going after the lot. I'll keep going 'till they're all gone, or I get caught.'

'Need a hand, bruv?'

'What?' barked Charlie, looking up at his brother. 'From you?'

'Who better? Don't forget I've got the t-shirt. I'm better than you at this. Trained for years. Got a number of credits to my name. And, some they don't know about. This lot are vermin. No qualms, mate. Besides, it's the first time I've enjoyed myself since I punched that singer twat.'

'Steve, it's not fun, it's cold blooded murder even if it's a good cause. Treat it as fun and you'll get caught. You have to do everything I say, okay?'

'Does that mean I'm in?' replied Steve, grinning.

'Let me think about it. I don't want to get you into trouble. Prison will be hell for the likes of us.'

'You don't want *me* to get into trouble? If anybody gets caught it'll be you! If we box clever, take our time and give nothing away, how could we go wrong? With your knowledge and my skills, we could go on for years. I could do with a more high-powered rifle, though. Yours isn't much good beyond 200 yards, for pinpoint accuracy.'

'No new ironware. Anything new will provide a trail, and we wouldn't last five minutes. We'll lie low for a few months. Nothing spoiling. In the meantime, I want you to tell me every last detail of how you did the quayside job, and I'll tell you about mine with Molloy. Hopefully, you'll learn something, okay?'

'Fine by me. And that's rich, me learning from you? Maybe you'll learn from me! It was my stock-in-trade, remember? Me to go first?'

'I'll go first, Steve. I'm going to tell you stuff which will show me in a different light. As a brother, I am trusting you with my life, okay? You'll never do anything to hurt me?'

'Take it as read, bruv. Don't know why you have to ask.'

Charlie told him about the visit of Tommy Layton, his death and the disposal of his body. The torture and execution of the hit man, Craig Collins. The strange treatment of him by ex-colleague, Mick Redman. The beating and subsequent execution of Tony Molloy. The possibility of his having a son to the girlfriend of Freddie Simpson, who was linked to the two thugs Steve had shot. His developing relationship with Angel Gallagher and, finally, his plans for Ray Morrison and anyone who has anything to do with him.

Steve stopped him dead. 'Ray Morrison? He employed the bastards I slotted outside the courts!'

'No, they were Simpson's men, surely?' replied Charlie, not sure of what to make of Steve's claim.

'Well I know they had connections with Morrison a few years ago. Have they changed sides, then?'

'I'm not sure. Maybe both teams have linked up? It happens.'

'Anyway, I want Morrison badly.'

'Not this one, Steve, he's mine. He might have been indirectly involved in Paul's death, but he was directly responsible for Julie's. I want him to feel the fear. I want to see the bastard beg for his life. If you do it, he'll not see it coming.'

'Fair enough, bruv, as long as you can guarantee it. Fuck me, you've been busy! You, a mass fucking murderer? And no one suspects anything?'

'That's the problem. I think the police believe Tommy Layton came to see me, then disappeared without trace. I denied it, of course, but they are still digging. They seem to accept there was a contract out on me. Still is, probably.'

'Digging? Do they think you've buried him, like?'

'Not that kind of digging, muppet! Nosing around!'

'I know that, you plum. What's the chances of them being able to pin anything on you?'

'Nothing on what I've done up to now. No forensics, no links to the weapons, nothing. I've kept everything tight. Only you know anything. The only thing they could get me on is if I'm followed and I lead them to the weapons, or you lead them to the weapons and provide the connection to me.'

'How likely is that?' queried Steve.

'Unlikely, if we leave the weapons alone for a while. It might even pay to move them again, as you say. Because I have to work without taking anyone else into my confidence, it's all taking time. I've got all the time in the world, so there's no real hurry. Lots of pieces to put together before the next move.'

'Okay,' replied Steve, 'I'm in no hurry either. Do you want to tell me everything you've found out up to now?'

Charlie told him about the mobile phone links between Layton, Morrison, Redman and Collins. He was almost there, but needed to plug a few more gaps. He didn't know how significant Redman's involvement was, because it wasn't unusual for senior police officers to have the phone numbers of their snitches, and many of the major villains were snitches. Redman's involvement may be something, or it may be nothing, but it required further investigation.

'How do you plan to take Morrison out?' enquired Steve.

'Not sure, but I need to get him alone, out of public view. Maybe even with others, if it comes to that. I'll be masked up and have enough ammo for maybe ten or twelve of them. Not relevant at the moment, though. I need to think about it.'

'Will you include me in your plans?' asked Steve, afraid he might be written out of any plan that Charlie was hatching. He was desperate to be involved. Looking after Charlie was now his *raison d'etre*.

'It's possible. I might need you to watch my back.'

'Good, I have a vested interest and if you miss, I won't. Incidentally, that .22 sniper rifle is a little gem for short distance stuff, although I prefer a fifty-calibre round. It allows you to shoot accurately for more than a thousand yards, but with this, if I measure the distance right, I can put one through the eye at 200 yards. It gets a bit vague after that, but I can still get a three-inch cluster up to about three hundred yards. The guy you got it off must have known his stuff?'

'SAS before he was demobbed, I think. Went over to the dark side. He'd heard of you. Vaguely. Said some strange stuff.'

'Strange, like what?'

'Like he'd never met you, he kept the code, stuff like that.'

'Anyway, cool! Mustn't be that good, though, if he got rolled by an old twat like you!'

'Watch it! You're still not too old to get a good spanking!'

'Do you wanna try it?' asked Steve as he leapt from his seat and pinned Charlie to his, before jumping around to the back of the chair, with Charlie in a loose headlock, and taking him gently to the ground.

'Do you wanna try it?' he repeated.

'Okay, skinshies,' said Charlie, hanging onto the forearm across his throat. Steve brought Charlie back to an upright position, still sitting in his chair.

'Okay, then, maybe not a spanking but, remember, you have to sleep sometime,' he warned, grinning, drawing his thumb across his throat in a cutting motion.

'Charlie, I have to confess, I've never felt more alive than I do now. Working with you, something worthwhile to do, doing what I love. The adrenalin- rush! It doesn't get much better, does it?'

'Not so fast, bruv. We have to take our time. See how far the police get with the others. Another one so soon might just tip the balance in their favour. Also, Morrison will be running scared and we need him to drop his guard and relax a bit. Then *bang*, he's gone. Okay?' enthused Charlie with a swift punch to the palm of his hand.

'Okay, then. What is it you say, *softly, softly*?'

'Exactly. Let's get away with what we've done so far, then crank it up again.'

'Can I just say, Charlie, please, please run every move past me. This is my territory and I'll keep you right. By the way, how are you getting on with that Angel lass? Seen any more of her lately?'

This was awkward for Charlie.

'I've seen her a couple of times, Steve, for a coffee and a chat. She's nice. I can talk to her and she's a good listener. Besides, she knows stuff.'

'What stuff?'

'She's going to keep me posted on any developments. She doesn't like Redman. Hates him, in fact.'

'How much does she know?'

'Nothing. Absolutely nothing,' replied Charlie, truthfully.

'Okay, bruv, but don't rush into anything. Know what I mean? It might not go down too well with Julie's family and friends. Or yours for that matter. You need to chill out for a bit longer. At least a year,' advised Steve. 'It's only been a few months. Too soon to have lady friends, okay?'

'Yes, I know, mate. I'm keeping my distance, but I think we'll be getting together in the long term.'

'Well, the longer you can keep it quiet, the better, eh?'

'I know,' agreed Charlie, whose thoughts momentarily turned to Angel. He had given her hope for their relationship and did not want to disappoint her. She did not deserve to be treated shabbily, but her own common sense and convention would tell her that there was nothing doing for at least a year. She would understand.

The two continued their discussions, going over old ground in detail. They were looking for fault in the way each of them had done things in order to improve their future performance. Neither could find any real fault with the other's game, which was tremendously satisfying. They understood one another and thought that, perhaps, they would make a good, close team after all. A few beers later, and Charlie nodded off on the sofa. Before climbing the stairs to bed, Steve removed a throw from the matching chair and placed it over Charlie, before kissing him gently on the forehead.

'Goodnight, bruv,' he whispered, 'things will get better, you'll see.'

'You too,' whispered Charlie back, smiling. 'I hope so.'

TWENTY-ONE

Look at these photographs and tell me what you see,' invited Charlie, passing three photographs of himself as a seventeen-year-old, to Jane Elliot. She had called him one week after their meeting, and they had arranged to meet in The Diamond, by the river in Ponteland. Jane had made an effort, something she always did, but the cigarettes, late nights, the occasional slap and years of worry, had taken their toll. She had had her blond hair done professionally for the occasion, a short bob.

It was years since she had been for a night out in a pub without a chaperone, or the fear that something might go wrong, so it was a rare occasion for her and she was going to give it her best shot. Her face was lined and her blue eyes more deep-set than he remembered, but her make-up was subtle. She was still attractive, but the two of them had both moved on. That book was closed and conversation, other than about Mark, was difficult.

One photograph was with a group of friends, not posed for, one was a cheesy pose for the camera and the other was with an old school girlfriend.

'My God!' she said, 'I see what you mean.' She continued to look at the photographs before venturing, 'I often suspected as much, you know. He was born about three weeks too early for it to have been Freddie's, and he went full term. He looks nothing like him, but I didn't really notice the resemblance with you until he was fifteen. There was just a faint similarity. But then I didn't know what you looked like at that age. Freddie would kill me if he found out Mark wasn't his. Mind you, they don't get on, but Freddie would flip if he thought he'd brought up somebody else's kid. Especially a copper's kid. I did love him because he was sometimes fun to be with, but I know what he did for a living, although we never talked about it. He's a wrong 'un, but you know that already. It's Mark who I feel sorry for. He's a good lad and he's always been embarrassed about his dad's line of business. Did I tell you he's studying law? Wants to become a barrister but his dad wants him to work for the firm? He won't let him go to university. Says it's a waste of time. Poor kid's at his wits' end. He needs to be applying for a place now ahead of his A levels or he'll miss the boat.'

'Tell him to apply. I'll back him, but he doesn't need to know that unless you want to tell him. Freddie's line of work isn't for him. He'll end up the same way as Freddie, and you wouldn't want that. Incidentally, I'm up for a DNA paternity test if you are. If you don't want to go that far, have a look at the middle finger of each hand. If they are bent and lean towards the pinky, he has the Payne family characteristics. Charlie held up his own hands to demonstrate what he had just described. *Quod erat demonstrandum!*'

'Quod what?'

'Its Latin. It means something like *what will be demonstrated.* I was showing you the family trait.'

'Oh, I see,' she said, still not certain about what he meant.

'He might also be flat footed,' continued Charlie.

'He's flat footed alright, but I've never noticed his fingers. I'll have a look tonight. How am I going to broach the subject of you maybe being his dad? He might not like the idea.'

'That may well be the case, but the truth's always best. I can give him a better chance in life, a chance to hold his head up. My money's honest and legit, which is more than can be said for Freddie's. Incidentally, I hope you realise the financial investigation guys will have most of it off him in due course. I understand his accounts are frozen while the investigation takes place?'

'Yes, I'm living on cash he hid away. It'll run out in a year. Do you really think they'll take everything he's got?'

'Very likely. They have awesome powers, the courts.'

'What happens to me?'

'Nothing. You haven't done anything.'

'No, I mean what am I going to live on?'

'Benefits, I suppose. Unless you've got a job. I'll give you a couple of ton a month to help you get by, at least while Mark's at uni. I'll see him okay throughout uni, and until he gets started in work. I've done okay in life.'

'Yes, I heard. I'm really sorry about Julie. Neither of you deserved that.'

'Incidentally, something I've been meaning to ask for years. Why did you leave me? I mean, I was going to propose, did you know that?'

'I had an idea you might and that's why I left you. I didn't want to be a copper's wife. The hours, no money, the worry.'

'I could have got a desk job.'

'You wouldn't have done. You would have gone crazy. You needed the action.'

'I suppose so,' conceded Charlie, honestly.

'Mind you, Freddie was just as bad. I hardly ever saw him until he wanted something. A good provider, though.'

'Well it's history now, no point in going back. But I'm serious about Mark. If he's my son I want to do right by him. He'll want for nothing, regardless of whether he wants me in his life. How does he feel about coppers?'

'Much to the annoyance of his dad, I mean Freddie, he seems to be okay with them. He used to get on well with the policemen that visit his school for safety talks and suchlike. I don't think it would be a huge issue. It could screw with his head, though, I mean thinking that his dad is a no-good lag but he's really a copper. A well-off copper! '

'What's he like at school? I mean, is he bright?'

'They expect him to get at least three A grades and possibly a fourth,' she said, proudly.

'Who does he get that from? It certainly isn't me. I was mostly Bs and Cs,' admitted Charlie.

'Likewise,' agreed Jane.

'Anyway, let me know how things progress, will you?'

'Yes, can I reach you on the same number?'

'Yes, write it down where you won't lose it. Don't put it in your phone memory, and every time we have a conversation, best wipe it. If you can, whenever you can, would you arrange for us to meet? I mean, once he knows the truth?'

'I'll try.'

'One other thing, were you around when those two guys got shot outside the court?' asked Charlie.

'I was still inside the entrance, but saw the melee. It was awful. Those poor men.'

'Who were those guys, friends of yours?' he pressed.

'Not really,' said Jane, shaking her head.

'Freddie's?'

'They know him, but they work for somebody else. They were more interested in you.'

'Me?' said Charlie, looking at her quizzically.

'Well, they kept talking about you.'

'What did they say?'

'I don't remember. Nothing, really, but they kept mentioning you by name.'

'So, they weren't there for Freddie?'

'I don't think so.'

'But you looked as if you were all together?'

'Coincidence. They were just hanging around.'

'Do you even know their names?'

'I think one was called Glen because they mentioned each other's names. Not sure about the other one. Jimmy, maybe?'

'Have you heard of Ray Morrison?' Charlie was now treading on thin ice by declaring an interest, but it was a risk he was prepared to take.

'Who hasn't, around these parts?'

'Were they working for him?'

'I've no idea, pet. I might be married to the shit, but I have no interest in what he or his kind get up to. It would be too dangerous to take an interest. They're all paranoid about being grassed up.'

With nothing else forthcoming, Charlie left her at the pub, to phone for her own taxi. He gave her £60 to cover both journeys. She still hadn't finished her drink and was in no rush to down it. Besides, the £60 was generous and there would be enough change for another couple of drinks. He wouldn't normally leave a date on her own, but Jane was capable of looking after herself. They had grown apart, and although they considered whether a peck on the cheek would be the thing to do, they settled for a handshake instead. She was the first to offer her hand, and Charlie took it, grateful that she expected no more. He was also grateful that she was not putting obstacles in his way to prevent him from seeing his son. In fact, she seemed pleased with the potential outcome, the fact that her son was being offered a chance in life. Charlie felt a mixture of trepidation and relief. Mostly relief.

Within forty-eight hours, Jane contacted Charlie.

'I've told him about you. He seemed to take it well, but went to his room and didn't speak for hours. He knows you were the cop who put Freddie away. Given the situation, I don't think he's too bothered about that. He saw Freddie hit me a couple of times, so there's no love lost. He even hit Mark when he came to my rescue, poor kid.'

'Have you mentioned meeting up?'

'Yes, he's up for it. Soon as you like.'

'That's great, Jane, thanks for doing that.'

'He has the fingers!'

'Pardon?'

'He has your fingers. I told him about yours and made him hold up his hands. They are bent, just like yours. He's not totally convinced, but I think the photos might do it.'

'I'll show them to him when we meet. How about I take him for a meal when he finishes school? Does he like pizza?'

'He loves pizza, especially Marco Polo in Dean Street. Shall I tell him six o'clock tomorrow? It'll give him a chance to change. You know what kids are like for being seen in school uniform in public.'

'Marco Polo, for six tomorrow, sounds fine.'

'I'll come back to you if it's not okay. No alcohol, mind!'

'No problem. I'll look after him, put him in a taxi and suchlike.'

The phone clicked. Charlie stared at his mobile for a few seconds, as if it was going to be of assistance. *What the hell do you say to a seventeen-year old son you haven't met?* The answer came to him when they met two days later. All of the other rehearsed versions went out of the window.

Mark had made an effort. A comb had been run through his hair, and these weren't his after-school mufti for lounging around. He wore navy and white deck shoes, spotless white chinos and a navy-blue dress shirt. He would have looked the part on board Stormy Monday. The thought crossed Charlie's mind, but now wasn't the time to dwell on such images.

'Hello, Mark, how are you?' Charlie started, taking the initiative.

'Well, thanks. And you?' Mark replied, equally confidently.

This kid has presence. A young man who, if he is shy, certainly isn't showing it.

'A bit nervous to be honest,' replied Charlie, truthfully.

'Yeah, me too.'

There was an awkward silence until Mark broke it. 'Hold out your hands, face down,' he ordered, with a smile.

Charlie obliged. Mark held out his, in mirror-fashion, his fingers touching Charlie's at the middle finger tips. 'I suppose there is a resemblance,' he said as he traced the bend in both left hands with the index finger of his right hand. 'So, you never knew, until a few weeks ago, that you might have a son?'

'That's right, I saw you in court. I was looking at *me* as a seventeen-year old.'

'Mum says you have some photos?'

Charlie reached to his inside jacket pocket and drew out a brown envelope. 'They're a bit tattered around the edges, but they're still sharp enough. Don't laugh at the fashions.'

Mark took them out of the envelope and studied them before finally saying, 'Blimey!' He said no more than that, but Charlie detected a faint smile.

'What do you reckon?'

'Rupert the bear trousers? Purple jacket? And your generation has the cheek to call mine?' He was smiling. That meant a lot to Charlie. It meant a whole lot.

'Pretty conclusive, put together with the other stuff, I would say.'

'Yes, but how do you feel?' asked Charlie, still anxious that Mark wouldn't accept the situation.

'Okay, I suppose. I just have to get over the fact that Freddie isn't my dad.' He thought for a few moments. 'Mind you, it won't take long, he had no time for me and mum.'

Charlie smiled.

'It's not funny, you know!' Mark scowled.

'You know, I would love to have a son. I thought the chance had passed me by but when I saw you in court, that was, well, life changing for me. I'm your biological dad, but I'll also be your real dad if you'll let me.'

'Yes, but how do you feel about that? I mean, it's a life-changer, isn't it? For both of us?'

'I don't really know. My wife was my life, did you know about her?'

'I did, yes, I'm sorry. I heard it in court.'

'Everybody needs to have a reason to get up in the morning, something or someone to help give their life some focus. I have my brother, but he's getting his life sorted so I wouldn't mind focussing some attention on you. Would you mind that?'

'I suppose not.' He shrugged. Mark was a teenager and Charlie was going to get no more than that.

'Anyway, have you applied for university yet?'

'Not yet.'

'Do it tomorrow. Aim high, Oxbridge if you can. They might have already allocated the places. I will pay for your lodgings and expences, you won't be left short. You won't need a student loan and I'll settle the fees so that you're clear of debt when you're finished. You'll be able to hold your head up. You don't have to say your dad was a copper, because I know that could cause you difficulties. Just say I'm a partner in a property empire. Here's my card with the company name on it. I'll write my address on the back. You can say that it's your home address, if you like. It might open doors and smooth your way through the selection process.'

'Are you a snob?' said Mark, smiling. He smiled a lot.

'No, but *they* might be. Your choice, I just think you should use every trick in the book.'

'What if I don't even get an interview?'

'I will contact them and offer some kind of sponsorship with strings attached. Money talks with that lot.'

'You would do all that for me? Without concrete evidence?'

'One day, you might have kids, and *then* you'll understand. Most parents will go to the ends of the Earth for their kids. Even if they've never met.'

'Don't you want to be certain before you blow your money? Like a paternity test?'

'If you like. Do you want me to arrange it with your mam?'

'Yeah, it makes sense. What if it goes badly wrong and I'm not yours?'

'I've taken a liking to you, so I'll support you for the sheer hell of it anyway. Wouldn't want to wreck your dreams. Like I say, I need a focus in life. In the meantime, how are you for pocket money?'

'I get twenty quid a week over and above dinner money, but I have to work for it. Housework and suchlike.'

'The paternity test could take a few weeks, but I don't want you to delay applying for uni. Positive or negative I want to support you anyway so I'm going to give you a couple of hundred to get yourself an interview suit and some proper shoes. Nothing daft, mind, but you have to impress some fuddy-duddies, grey men in grey suits.'

'It's not like that, these days!' said Mark, grinning. 'Where have you been? My God, Charlie!'

'Isn't it? Get one anyway. Another few quid for shoes.' Charlie peeled off £250 from a wad of £500. 'Use it wisely, don't be tempted to blow it on other stuff. Know what I mean?' He looked around to see if anyone was watching. An older man paying such attention to a younger man and handing over money, a stranger at that, had other unwelcome connotations.

'Yeah, thanks.'

The pizzas were ordered. A Peroni for Charlie and a coke for Mark, with a jug of water. Conversation, in the main, was about Mark's life to date. Charlie's appetite to understand and get to know more about his newfound son and heir was insatiable. But Charlie also knew the dangers of getting carried away. It was going to be *softly, softly* for now. He dismissed the taxi idea and dropped Mark near, but out of sight of, his home, and they shook hands. He had one burning question left.

'Before we go our separate ways, did Freddie ever talk about me?

'Not really. He would never talk business in front of me. When he got arrested, he was whisked away and I didn't get to see him until the trial. To be honest, I wasn't bothered. I was allowed to. I say *allowed*, what I meant was *dragged* to see him in his cell, with mum. You got a mention then.' He smiled.

'Come on, then, what did he say?'

'You sure you want to know?' he replied, again with a smile.

'Yes, go on!'

'Well, let's say you're not flavour of the month. He used a few choice words. He reckons you set him up and you were going to get yours when his QC went for your throat. We all know how that went. What a dickhead! Any doubts I had up to then just disappeared. He is nothing to me. To be honest, I'm chuffed he's not my real dad and I won't be visiting him.'

Charlie could not help but smile, all the way home.

One week later, the results were confirmed. Charlie had a son.

Charlie, Mark and Jane all agreed to keep the news a secret. At some stage, though, they were going to have to tell Freddie.

They would do this through solicitors, when the time was right. Probably at the same time as she filed for divorce, and probably in time for Mark receiving his degree.

Mark would not need to change his name to Payne, although Charlie would be delighted if he did, but that would be Mark's choice. There could be trouble when Freddie found out, but that was a long way off, maybe three or four years. It would be up to Jane to make excuses for Mark's absence during visiting hour, but she, at least, would have to visit to ensure that she had a roof over her head and that her money supply didn't dry up. At least until she could fend for herself. Right now, though, it didn't matter.

Two months later, 7th November, Freddie Simpson's mother died. Mark's nan. She had fallen down the stairs at home, broken her right tibia, and died in hospital of a pulmonary embolism. The break had caused her blood to clot, and a huge one caused a blockage in her lung. That was the end of her. Both Mark and Freddie took it badly, but not so much Jane. The two didn't get on, but Jane always did her duty by her, lending a hand with occasional housework and shopping. Even keeping her company one evening a week.

She would not miss the old battle axe, but she was sad for Mark and Freddie. For all Freddie was a nasty piece of work, he was a devoted son to his mother and would drop everything for her. Jane knew the suddenness of her death would hit him hard. And although, as it turns out, she was no more Mark's nan than the Queen, Mark could not undo the love that had grown between them over his seventeen years. It was not her fault that she was no longer his nan, and no one would have been more hurt than she, had she known the truth.

Nan was only in her early seventies, and had hardly a day's illness in her lifetime. Her husband had left her, never to be heard of again, when Freddie was eight years old, and she'd had to bring him up alone. Times were hard, but she managed. She had grown thick-skinned and uncompromising, as Jane knew all too well. Freddie thought that she would last forever. It was bad enough his being in prison, but it haunted him that he was not around for her during her last days. A son owed that much to his mother.

TWENTY-TWO

The day of Nan Simpson's funeral arrived, a cold, bleak November Thursday morning, with a mist that was not destined to clear up until well into the afternoon. Freddie arrived in a white prison van, flanked by two police cars containing drivers and two pairs of armed police officers. They made no secret of the fact that they were armed, holding their Heckler and Koch MP5 assault rifles at the ready. The guns weren't just for show, they were meant to deter anyone from trying to spring him and, whereas their orders weren't to shoot to kill, in spite of the media's liking for the phrase, they would aim for the largest target, the torso. Death was the likely outcome, but an unhappy coincidence rather than the intention.

This was a service reserved for dangerous criminals with dangerous friends. The police would always be more heavily armed than the enemy, and they would be far better shots. In any fire-fight, they had to win. It was the rule.

Freddie had been allowed to wear his own dark grey suit, one that Jane had brought to him in the prison. It was a tight fit around the waist. He had put weight on. The prison food was plentiful but lacked the input of a dietician who really cared what the prisoners ate. Either that or someone was creaming off the top.

Freddie was also lazy and did not exercise as often as he should. He had shaved, but had nicked himself in several places and his hair was no longer the traditional number one cut. It was different lengths, different colours dominated by grey. He had only been away for a few months and already, he was losing his self-esteem. His allies were all dead or serving time, and his lukewarm friends had deserted him, pledging their allegiances elsewhere. By the time he was due to be considered for parole, if ever, he would be in his seventies and no match for the opposition. His visitors dwindled, eventually leaving only Jane. She was there under sufferance and he knew it. The visits were becoming shorter and, in time, they would dry up altogether.

There was an air of resignation about him. Jane was already standing by the chapel entrance, waiting. As he got closer, she took two steps towards him, but the barrel of a rifle barred her way.

'It's me wife, guys, howay man,' Simpson pleaded softly, without his usual barb. 'I've got these bracelets on,' he said, lifting them up for show. 'What do you think I'm going to do? Give us a break, man.'

The rifle barrel was withdrawn and Jane threw her arms around his waist, squeezing him tightly.

'I'm sorry, pet,' she said, looking up into his eyes. 'You don't deserve this. You've got enough on your plate.'

'Where's Mark?' he asked, avoiding eye contact. He had noticed that her warmth was cooling with each visit, and sensed the insincerity. Rather than let it eat him during the long nights when he had little else to think about, he had persuaded himself that the feeling was mutual. It helped him cope better with the loss. Mark, on the other hand, was a different matter but he was nowhere to be seen. Freddie's heart sank. He craned his neck to search for him in the small crowd, but drew another blank. There were only twenty or so mourners, no pals, no one he recognised, mostly parishioners who were doing their duty. It had crossed his mind that he was at the wrong funeral.

On the periphery were dozens of rubber-neckers. Paparazzi with an array of cameras, and commentators. The passing of a public enemy's mother was newsworthy, and these predators were there to witness his mourning.

'You know how much he loved his nan,' Jane started. 'He was too distraught, so he begged to be left at home in case he made a fool of himself. Poor lad, he'll grieve in his own way,' she explained. Freddie nodded and made no comment. He was disappointed, a little angry even, but he understood. He had missed his own nan's funeral for the same reason when he was a teenager. Freddie himself was none too keen to be there either but it was his duty to see the old girl off.

Mark was upset alright, but two hundred and sixty miles away in Oxford, preparing for his first term exam. Besides, he could not face Freddie. Freddie was now a distant, painful memory.

The short service and interment over, the prison officers turned Freddie around and walked him slowly back towards the prison van. Both were still handcuffed to Freddie, but one would eventually have to free himself in order to drive the van back to the prison. The other would travel with Freddie in the back, both in separate compartments.

As the driver was searching his pocket for the handcuff keys, Freddie's legs suddenly buckled, and he fell backwards to the ground, dragging both officers with him. He was a dead weight. He was dead. With a single bullet hole to the back of his head. A split second later, what sounded like the crack of a whip could be heard over the silence. There was no exit wound and the cause of his fall was not immediately obvious. Perhaps he had fainted? After all, it wasn't uncommon. The warden closest to him cradled the back of his head while trying to work out the best method of resuscitation. His hand suddenly felt warm and sticky and a fingertip accidentally entered the bullet hole.

'Jesus!' he shouted, thrusting Freddie's head away from him in disgust. 'He's been shot! Get him off me! Get the fucker off me!' he screamed. Both were aware of the high risk of HIV infection from people in prisons and having the blood of a lifer all over you was not a thought to be relished. Besides, if there was a gunman, he might not be finished. There might be more to come. Without a thought for the victim, they struggled to free themselves from Freddie, allowing the parts of his body that were being supported to fall unceremoniously onto the gravel, with a customary thud. The blood-soaked warden could only stare in horror, while the other tried frantically to beckon over the police escort who were some yards away, oblivious to what had happened.

The paparazzi saw it all. A shoal of frenzied piranha feasting on a stricken corpse. They captured every frame of Freddie's last moments and the news coverage that night would be spectacular. The camera crew could not believe their luck. A real scoop. An assassination right before their eyes. It was what every journalist would give their right arm for.

The assassin, unseen, sloped away, happy with his work. He had made his shot from a little under 100 yards away, hidden in some dense laurel bushes on a grassy mound. The mist had not unduly affected his line of sight and there had been no need for camouflage, or lying in wait, as he knew the precise timings. He had been there when news of the funeral leaked, and had correctly guessed where the prison van would have to park. Ninety-seven yards, give or take a yard, and the sights were already calibrated and ready. A yard shorter or longer made no difference, the bullet would still find its target, albeit slightly higher or lower to the tune of an inch or so. Top, middle or bottom of the head, all the same, it would be fatal.

The rifle spent no more than five seconds in the raised position then, within three seconds, it was broken down into two parts, to fit neatly inside the assassin's Barbour jacket. All he would do then is back away, then walk the thirty yards to his parked car. The number plates had been cloned with an identical car, to avoid capture on any CCTV or paparazzi cameras, then driven to a secluded lane to swap the number plates back. A thirty second job. Then home for tea. Via the rifle's hiding place.

The news coverage reached the number one slot, all channels showing it over and over again, some in slow motion. They analysed the jerking of the head, the moment the bullet entered and the confusion and the panic of the prison officers. The BBC concentrated on the eye-witness accounts while Sky News, albeit as interested in what people had to say, were equally interested in the angle of trajectory, what kind of weapon had been used and where the bullet came from. The cameras panned the area and, whereas they must have at least swept past the gunman's location, he would be long gone, taking the single empty cartridge case with him. They were safe in presuming that the killer was male. There was no known precedent for a woman committing a murder like this. At least not in these parts.

Everyone saw the news. It was repeated so often that it would have been difficult to dodge. Ray Morrison, as puzzled as anyone, called a summit meeting at his house. It was the only place he was confident was not bugged. Everyone who entered his house was patted down and he would regularly have the entire house swept for spyware. Like Charlie, he was not one for taking unnecessary chances.

Freddie's death was unexpected. The general consensus was that it was also unnecessary. He was inside and had no one left on the outside to command. He no longer had any business interests. Those interests that the police knew of, he was about to lose through process of law, and those that the police weren't aware of had been taken from him by other interested parties.

So, what was the point of it? It didn't make sense. But in the absence of a plausible explanation, the press speculation was, once again, that it was related to gangland rivalry. The police were non-committal, as usual. They already had enough egg on their faces without making matters worse by speculating. They had three unsolved murders and a fourth was more than they could handle without bits falling off. The official line was that they were keeping an open mind and refused to link it to the other deaths without evidence. Privately, though, it was a different matter. It had to be linked. At least, they would hope it was, then they would have one enquiry but with multiple scenes.

Morrison's team did not know what to make of it, either.

'Any ideas, Ray?' asked Joe Tailford.

'Not one, Joe. It's a mystery. He was out of the game, unless it's one of his own.'

'Yes, but who? Most of them are inside, two are dead. It only leaves that gimp with the foreign sounding name and a few muppets. They haven't the bottle or the nous for that, surely?' ventured Tailford.

'Probably not. Limpy Luca certainly hasn't. Maybe he's upset somebody inside? You know what it's like for fall-outs.'

'Well, they've gone to a lot of trouble, whoever they are. Something like that takes a lot of setting up. A total waste of money,' continued Tailford.

'Unless it was the same joker who slotted the lads outside the court?'

'Well, whoever it was, Ray, it's got to be good news for us, hasn't it? I mean, if there was going to be any resistance it's all gone now.'

Morrison smiled. Tailford noticed.

'Unless, of course, you arranged it?' added Tailford, reading a sinister interpretation into the smile.

'No point. Why take the risk? He was already out of the way. No, I'm not involved in any way. God's honest truth, Joey. Yes, it benefits us, but it was all going to be ours anyway. He was all washed up.'

'I suppose so, but I don't want any shocks, Ray. If you are hiding something, it'll backfire if we aren't kept in the loop. Our stories have to match.'

'Don't worry, Joey, none of us have anything to fear. Let's just wait and see what happens. I'm surprised the cops haven't been sniffing around. Usually that means they suspect us or else they want our help. If they don't want our help, it means they are on to something.'

He could not have been further from the truth.

Like everyone else, Charlie did not know what to make of the shooting. He was pleased that they no longer had to break the news to Simpson that Mark was Charlie's son. It was also good that the police had a different murder to concentrate on, and provide Charlie with some breathing space. Police resources would be stretched to breaking point.

The feeling did not last. Two weeks after the shooting, Charlie was alone at home when the midday radio news stunned him.

'Police have today confirmed that the bullet that killed Freddie Simpson while attending his mother's funeral, was fired from the same gun that killed Glen Harrison, James Hargreaves and Tony Molloy. It is believed that all four men were connected, and it now appears that this is a turf war, possibly with outside connections. The police remain tight lipped about the shootings and will neither confirm nor deny this possibility, but a press conference has been arranged for 6pm this evening'.

Charlie threw his half coffee mug into the kitchen sink, sending coffee up the walls, curtains and blind. The mug did not survive. He would leave the mess for his cleaner, Anna, newly appointed not two weeks earlier. After uttering every profanity he had learned over the decades, he sat on a kitchen chair at the table and put his head in his hands, tugging at the hair above his ears, to a point where it was beginning to hurt. As quickly as he had erupted, he calmed down, took out his mobile phone and dialled his brother's number.

'That you, Steve?'

'Yes.'

'Heard the latest?

'What?'

'The bullet that killed Freddie came from the same gun that killed all the others.'

'I can explain....'

'I'll bet you can,' interrupted Charlie, 'I'm coming over, stay there!'

Charlie was disappointed in Steve. What was he thinking? He was a maverick, a loose cannon, a liability. The gun would have to be taken from him before the damage became terminal. If it wasn't already.

Steve opened the front door and stepped aside to allow Charlie past. He stared straight ahead, avoiding eye contact. No words were spoken until they sat down in the living room.

'Beer?' suggested Steve as a peace offering.

'No, thanks,' Charlie replied, curtly, 'I told you about the dangers of doing stuff without consulting me! I appreciate that you did it for me but do realise you've put me right behind the eight ball?'

'In what way?' responded Steve, slightly perplexed.

'Motive. The police will be looking for a motive. Simpson was already out of the game. His gang are all inside and his empire was being divided up. No one could have done anything about it. It would be pointless to take him out. No, the only one with a conceivable motive was *me*. I've taken over his son, his pride and joy, his heir and successor! Don't you remember? If I didn't get him first, he would get me, that's the way they would look at it. Then, of course, his bullet links me to the other shootings. Getting evidence from scratch without a name is difficult, but it's a lot easier when you have a suspect. Things fall into place and they could make a strong circumstantial case. If I was on the case, I think I would find it a doddle to prove. You might have fucked me over this time, bro. And yourself!'

Steve thought for a moment. Charlie had a point. He'd been a bit hasty, but he wasn't going to admit it. 'Can you remember where you were at the moment Simpson was shot?' he asked.

'In the house. Alone. No alibi,' fired back Charlie.

'Apart from your CCTV and mobile. Just make sure the footage isn't overwritten.'

'Can they do that with mobile phones?'

'Of course! Where've you been?'

If you're telling me the truth about being at home, you're in the clear.'

'I could have set it up, though.'

'Yes, but you didn't, and proving that you did would be a hell of a job. You're in the clear.'

'Where's the guns?'

'Well hidden. No connections to either of us. No forensics.'

'All the same, you need to stop making decisions. For both our sakes!'

'Okay, no skin off my nose.'

'Look, I think I'm going to move things forward. I would hate to get caught before the job's finished. Maybe Jane and

Mark can keep their mouths shut long enough. In the meantime, I need the guns off you. I need to put them where you can't get your hands on them.'

'Why?' enquired Steve.

'It's the only way I can guarantee you won't do anything stupid again.'

'Okay,' conceded Steve, 'I'll get them tonight.'

'No, I want them now, please. Both guns, all the ammo, everything. Get your coat on.'

'Charlie, you're taking a risk by moving them. Leave them where they are, I guarantee they'll never be found. The more you handle them the bigger the risk. I mean, what if you have an accident while you're moving them? No, mate, just leave them, I know what I'm doing.'

Charlie thought for a moment, then nodded. Steve was right. 'Okay, but for the last time, do nothing without my knowledge or you'll sink us both. We'll get life with no prospect of parole. In different prisons. No visitors, no contact with each other. Do you want that?'

'No, but remember I told you I could sort it with no trace of the bodies. All I needed was a list of the names and my old unit would have taken them out. You're the problem here, you're stubborn!'

'Steve, man, get in the real world!'

'Suit yourself,' ended Steve. He had meant every word, but Charlie wasn't having any of it. Still, they were doing alright as they were, and having some fun along the way.

TWENTY-THREE

The police were drawing blanks on all accounts. Tony Molloy had been beaten up, judging from his injuries. He had been found by a passer-by who called the police and ambulance services. He was unconscious all night, and when he eventually did come around, the doctors advised the police against disturbing him. No approach was made to speak to him for two days, at which time he refused to say what had happened, or to make a complaint. The police were aware of the knife which was found in his hand, and they could prove it was his. They knew his background, and it was likely that he had bitten off more than he could chew in that alleyway. Because Molloy refused to help, they assumed that he had been up to no good and had picked on someone bigger than himself. There were no witnesses.

As far as his shooting was concerned, although it was probably linked to his beating, there was no evidence. They correctly pinpointed from where the shot had come, but that was all. No one saw the killer and there was no forensic evidence other than the striations on the bullet as it travelled along the barrel, but they would have to have the rifle before that was of any use. Molloy had many enemies, but none stood out as firm suspects. There was nothing much to go on.

The Morrison firm could have pointed the police in the direction of Charlie Payne, at least for the beating, but that would have pointed the finger at themselves. They were, therefore, on strict orders from Morrison not to give anything away. Besides, it never entered his head that Charlie was capable of beating up Molloy, let alone shooting him in cold blood.

Detective Chief Inspector Redman knew of the link between Tommy Layton and Charlie Payne and, by inference, with all of the deceased, but it was too far-fetched to consider Charlie as a suspect for the murders. It would have been out of character. He might be capable of some rough stuff, even a bit of violence occasionally, but killing in cold blood was different. Collins' death was another matter. Even if he had been executed, Redman knew deep down that Charlie was just doing what most men would have done in the same circumstances.

Redman had stuck his neck out once too often, and nearly come a cropper. Charlie's suggestion that he was into child porn, which he wasn't, had irked him, unnerved him even, and made him see how vulnerable he was, certainly around Charlie. He was going to keep his head below the parapet from now on and get through the remainder of his service relatively unscathed.

None of the Morrison team had visited Molloy in hospital, so they were in the dark about who had attacked him. They wanted to distance themselves from him in case the police got too close to them. Molloy would understand. They would wait until he was released from hospital, then they would hold a party for him. He would then reveal the gory details of his beating. Or so they had hoped.

The police had just as little information or idea on the shootings of Glen Harrison and James Hargreaves. Their intelligence suggested that the pair had had a foot in the camps of both Simpson and Morrison, who had mutual respect for one another. Sometimes even did business together. They had the bullets linking all four deaths, but still no idea of the motives or suspects. They knew of no one in their force area capable of such organisation, or the capacity to kill on such a scale, and had sought assistance from other police areas and, in particular, the Serious Organised Crime Office. They were working on a few theories, but nothing had come of them yet. It was only a matter of time. Or so they hoped.

Freddie Simpson's murder was equally mystifying. He was going nowhere. He was a shadow of his former self. He no longer had any allies to speak of. His killing was spiteful, certainly not strategic. There was nothing to be gained.

These murders were their biggest crisis since the hunt for the Yorkshire Ripper. Multiple killings, and not a clue as to who was responsible for them.

Charlie Payne was doing exactly what they were doing, but in reverse. He listed the weak points in his defences. There were many. Firstly, love him or not, he had an errant brother who had become a liability. Then there were the four linked killings. The gun that fired the bullets was well hidden and cleaned to within an inch of its life, but if it ever came to light and the connection was made, the pair of them were in trouble. Hopefully, Steve had done enough to ensure that that would never happen.

Then there was Freddie's son, effectively taken away from him by Charlie. While Freddie was alive, Charlie would always be looking over his shoulder. The motive was obvious. If ever that came out, Charlie could be propelled into the spotlight, and God knows what else the police might find. Even though there were no forensics, and everything else was circumstantial, sometimes, circumstantial evidence is enough. It wasn't a good situation to be in. As Steve had pointed out, he was alibied for the actual shooting, but he could have been involved in the arrangement and planning. Charlie would have preferred that Freddie Simpson was still alive.

TWENTY-FOUR

It was a shade after seven on the evening of 28th November, when Charlie's phone rang. The display lit up the name *Steve*. Charlie accepted the call and put the phone to his left ear.

'Fancy a pint, bro?' Charlie could have put money on that being Steve's opening words. 'I'll drive, I'm just going to have a couple.'

Charlie hadn't been out for a week, and was becoming stir crazy. 'Okay, then. Where?'

'It's years since I've been to the Beamish Mary. I was reading about it in the paper. It's one of these CAMRA places and it's just won another award.'

'Steve, there and back twice, it's going to be sixty miles for you!''

'I don't mind, Charlie, give me the fuel money if it makes you any happier.'

'Fine,' said Charlie, 'but I'm in the process of cooking some sweet and sour chicken. There's enough for two if you're interested.'

'Not sure about that, mate, your culinary skills ain't the best, I've heard.'

'I've had to learn,' retorted Charlie, 'besides, it isn't rocket science.'

'Just a taster, then,' returned Steve. He could not remember the last time his big brother cooked for him. It was something to look forward to.

Steve turned up thirty minutes later. The table was already set and they both sat down to sweet and sour chicken with rice. Tinned and boil-in-the-bag, but tasty nevertheless.

'Your cooking's come a long way, mate, I might come here more often,' remarked Steve after clearing his plate.

'Thank you, mate, you're cooking the next one. You're not so bad yourself, I hear?'

'It's a deal,' replied Steve. He smiled to himself. Microwave rice and hob-heated chicken curry on a medium heat for five minutes wasn't difficult. But the point was, he and Charlie were bonding. If only he could stop disappointing Charlie they could become best of friends.

Dishes in the dishwasher, probably another two weeks before it would be full enough to switch on, they finally set off in Steve's Mondeo. Thirty-five minutes later, they came to a turn-off sign-posted *No Place*.

'I might have known you would drink in a place with a name like that!' remarked Charlie.

Steve smiled. 'I've only ever been here once, about ten years ago, but it's got a good reputation. I think you'll like it.' He parked right outside the front door. His was the only car there. Anyone inside the pub must have walked, such was the bus service.

The room was dimly lit, which created a warmth about the place. For all it was the last week in November, the Christmas decorations were already up and it all looked very festive. The open log fire was burning away, sending out sparks from the latest addition of aged, dried timber. A waitress, dressed all in black apart from a white apron, was clearing away the last of the place settings. They would not be required until lunch time the next day, as they did not do breakfasts. No call for them. She heard Charlie and Steve walk in.

'I'm afraid the kitchen's closed if you want food, but I could rustle you up a sandwich if you like?'

'Not for us, thanks,' replied Charlie with smile. He would come to regret that. His was a face that was memorable, especially to a middle-aged, not unattractive, no rings on her fingers, probably divorced, looking for a man, waitress. It was a popular eatery, but went quiet after the rush, except for weekends. But this was Wednesday. Those remaining were mostly couples, at least in the lounge area, talking quietly to one another. In fact, the only non-couple there was Steve and Charlie. They kept their voices down because, occasionally, they would refer to their deeds of the past few months, and to what lay ahead, although not in enough detail to pose a risk.

In contrast, the bar area was not so quiet. Raucous laughter could be heard from no more than three or four voices. It was jovial at first but the mood changed quickly and the dialogue became less than friendly. Hostile, in fact. The barman, who was serving in both the bar and lounge areas connected with an open door, looked decidedly worried. He knew the signs when it was about to kick off. One of the locals, an elderly man in a burgundy pullover and olive corduroys, who addressed the barman by his first name, spoke.

'Is everything okay in there, Sean?'

Sean said nothing, but raised his eyebrows and mouthed a few silent words back.

'Who, Billy the Bull?' replied the elderly gentleman, quietly.

'Shush, Ed, not so loud or he'll know we're talking about him,' replied the barman, who looked back through the door to the bar area, checking to see if Billy had heard him. He wiped his brow in mock relief for the benefit of Ed. The noise suddenly grew louder. Sean disappeared from sight and could be heard pleading, 'Come on, Billy, there's no need for that. Billy, stop it, man. Enough is enough!'

'Mind your own fucking business!' came the curt reply. 'Bitch has crossed me for the last time!' he added. A loud slapping noise was heard, instantly followed by a woman's scream and the sound of a chair falling over. A few more slaps were heard, each followed by a scream and desperate pleas, 'Don't, Billy, stop it, please!' But Billy didn't stop. More slaps followed.

It was too much for Steve to bear. He shot out of his chair and ran towards the door leading into the bar area. Charlie rolled his eyes in a *here we go* submission, and followed him, but not before he had taken one more gulp from his pint. If it was going to have to say goodbye to it, he wanted one last slurp.

Billy, surname McDonald, heard the door go with a bang, and turned to face the intruder.

'Who the fuck are you?' he spat.

'I'm the attitude adjuster!'

'The fucking what? You want some as well?' shouted McDonald.

'That's the idea, you thick fuck!' replied Steve. Launching himself at McDonald without warning, he threw a powerful straight right to his unshaven jaw, the speed and audacity of which caught him off guard. It connected perfectly and down he went, landing hard on his backside. Steve stood back to allow him to get back up. He wasn't finished just yet. McDonald, not used to such generosity, smiled and obliged.

'You're dead!'

For Steve, actions spoke louder than words. Not having to think of something clever to say bought him time to weigh up his opponent, and the next move. McDonald was big, much bigger than Steve in every respect, and about ten years younger. It should have been a mismatch, but Steve had spent years fighting and killing people who were trying to do the same to him. Not women and non-combatants, and he did not like bullies. This one was going to get the fright of his life.

Charlie was ready to step in and help his brother, but he had a sneaking feeling that Steve would come out on top. It was unlikely, he thought, that McDonald would have experienced the intense fitness and fighting regime of the Royal Marines, and whereas that was a long time ago, Steve was no shadow of his former self. His speed, strength and knowhow we're still there. Or at least Charlie hoped they were.

McDonald saw Charlie and turned toward him. 'One at a time or both together?' he jibed.

'Just me, you fat fuck!' threw in Steve before Charlie could answer.

Charlie shrugged, but readied himself for action in case he was needed. He wasn't going to let his brother take a beating.

McDonald moved forward and within range, planting his leading right foot no more than eighteen inches from Steve's own leading left foot. That was a mistake. In a flash, Steve shifted his weight onto his left foot and shot out his right foot, the side of the heel creating a sharp edge, delivering a fierce blow to the centre of McDonald's right shin. The bone splintered, and McDonald let out a shrill scream and stumbled forward, shifting the weight from his injured leg to his good leg. Another mistake. Steve side-stepped the stumbling body and instantly followed up with a fierce kick, this time toe first, to the good leg, doubling McDonald's pain and causing him to fall to the floor, writhing and clutching at his two useless legs.

'Not so big now, eh?' taunted Steve, whose words could hardly be heard above McDonald's din. He followed up with a hefty kick to the jaw, his teeth splitting his tongue. The sheer force switched off his lights.

'C'mon, let's leave it,' pleaded Charlie. Steve had made his point, he thought, so why hang about.

'In a minute,' replied Steve. He then prised McDonald's right hand open and lay it on the floor, palm down, as flat as it would go. He stood on McDonald's wrist to make sure he couldn't pull it away, then picked up an overturned bar stool and crashed it down onto the back of his hand, several times. Although

McDonald was oblivious to the latest trauma, his body recognised it was under attack and flinched with each blow, his knees jerking sharply.

'He'll not be hitting anybody for a long time,' said Steve.

He then began to lay out the other hand to repeat the operation. This time, Charlie intervened.

'That's enough, you've made your point,' he said, taking Steve by the arm and pulling him away. 'We need to go.'

He then rolled the injured man onto his side, into the recovery position. Breaking a bully's hands is one thing, but allowing him to choke on his own blood or his tongue could be manslaughter, if not murder. That would change the game altogether. Not that he cared about McDonald, but the detection rate for murder was over ninety per cent but far less for assault, so why take the chance. As things stood, McDonald may not even want to make a complaint. It was a no-brainer.

He was careful not to mention Steve by name. He then told Steve, quietly so that no one else would hear, to get in the car and drive up the road and out of sight. 'I'll join you in a minute, I'll explain then. Hurry!'

Steve did as he was asked, without question. Charlie and the barman helped the distressed woman to her feet, still sobbing.

'Thanks for that,' she cried, 'he had it coming. I hope the bastard doesn't wake up.' Charlie prayed for the opposite. Another death at this stage would be inconvenient. She lunged at the unconscious man and gave him a half-hearted kick to his right thigh. Charlie tugged her away gently. She had had enough rough treatment, judging by her red, swollen face. Once she was seated, Charlie turned his attention to McDonald. He was breathing and showing signs of recovery. His moans grew louder as the pain began to register, then he let out a loud scream when his fully recovered pain receptors knew the score. He was now almost fully conscious and aware of his injuries.

His right hand was a puffy, painful sack of broken bones. As he moved his legs to try to get to his feet, the piercing pain from his splintered shin bones told him he was going nowhere, except in an ambulance. His lower jaw, broken at least in one place, added to his woes and made it difficult for him to utter anything intelligible. Charlie took the opportunity and made his exit, quickly checking for any CCTV cameras. There were none. That was good, he thought, just reluctant, unreliable witnesses. That should not be a problem.

He was followed out by the barman and one of the couples from the lounge area, who had decided that they had had enough excitement for one night. The police would be coming, and they did not want to hang about and be witnesses. The barman, Charlie hoped, would just give a vague description of the two strangers, and declare that he would not be able to identify them again. The others, he hoped, would do likewise.

Unfortunately, the waitress had seen his face and was unlikely to forget it. Charlie could only hope that she would turn a blind eye. Not that he had done anything to warrant a charge sheet, but that was little consolation and his brother might not be so lucky. McDonald was probably the local bully who terrorised the village and, with a bit of luck, no one would want his assailant brought to justice.

The police, in all likelihood, would be just as pleased. They did not mind it when his kind were on the receiving end.

There was no one else outside and Steve's car was now a hundred yards up the road, steam and smoke coming from the exhaust, and lights blazing. The registration number could not be seen from that distance and, as long as no one else had noticed it or sneaked out to take a peak, there would be little chance of its being identified. Charlie jogged up the road to the waiting car and climbed into the front passenger seat.

'Put your foot down, just in case somebody decides to follow,' he barked. Steve obliged, pedal to the floor. The tyres screeched at first, but found their grip, and the car sped up the road. To avoid any oncoming Durham police cars, he took the Hill Top route to Sunniside, then to Whickham. Within two minutes he would be out of the Durham Constabulary area and into the Northumbria Police area.

'You know why I asked you to leave?' said Charlie.

'Yeah, mate, the registration plate. I'm not daft. Do you think anybody saw it?'

'Don't think so. They were glued to their seats, keeping their heads down. I think you've done everybody a favour,' he reluctantly conceded. 'As you say, he won't be hitting anybody, any time soon. If ever. His hand was mashed up and even if it heals, he'll always have problems with it.'

'At least I've left him one good hand to wipe his arse with,' joked Steve.

After a few moments, Charlie started up again. 'You shouldn't have done it, you know. You're drawing attention to yourself unnecessarily. We've managed to get away with everything so far and we don't need to take risks like that in front of witnesses.'

'But you said the witnesses wouldn't want to know, and nobody saw the plate,' replied Steve in protest.

'That's just my guess, but you never know. It was a risk all the same.'

'Was I right to stop that bloke from hitting the woman?'

'Yes, but doing the right thing isn't always the smartest move. You should have left once you'd dumped him on his arse. You'd made your point.'

'Anyway, how could that compromise us for the other stuff?'

'Suppose we are brought in,' explained Charlie, 'any plod worth his salt would do background checks. There's you with a military background, a mercenary, an ex-druggie with connections to some dead bad guys. There's me, known killer of a bad guy with connections to *your* dead bad guys. I also had a motive for offing Simpson. My face was all over the newspapers not so long ago. If the penny drops, we're in the frame for some pretty heavy stuff. Just don't do it, okay?'

'Yes, but I just beat you to it. I saw you clench your fists, and don't deny that you were on the point of getting up yourself.'

'Yes, but I didn't, and that's the difference.'

'You didn't stop me from smashing his hand. You could see what I was going to do.'

'My attention was distracted by the woman,' lied Charlie.

'Yeah, right!' mocked Steve.

'Anyway, keep your head down from now on, Steve, okay?'

'Okay.'

Steve dropped Charlie off outside the electric gates. He did not want to go in for a nightcap as he was already on what he thought was his limit. Charlie did not argue. He was tired and looking forward to his bed. He failed to perform his usual routine of checking the news. It was not important anyway, and it could wait until tomorrow.

Tomorrow arrived sooner than he had hoped. His mobile phone rang at 3am. Charlie was in a deep sleep and did not hear it the first time around. It rang again, this time causing Charlie to stir. Again, it ran out of rings. By the third attempt, Charlie was awake, wondering whether he had imagined the phone ringing. It rang again. He picked it up. The screen read *Steve*. He looked at his watch. Not good. Something was up.

'Steve?' he said, into the microphone.

'Just listen, Charlie, I'm at Stanley police station. They have arrested me for an assault in the Beamish Mary. I didn't do it.

236

Just letting you know. I might not be able to keep our appointment tomorrow. I'll let you know when I'm released.'

'Don't ring off, just answer yes or no, can they hear me?' asked Charlie, frantically.

'No.'

'Do they know about me?'

'No.'

'Are you going to tell them?'

'No.'

'Is there anything incriminating in the house?'

'Maybe. Not sure.'

'Guns or ammo?'

'Not sure.'

'Fuck! Are they searching it?'

'No.'

'Right, I'll sort it, just sit tight and let it take its course. Admit nothing, let them prove it. They'll lose the will.'

Charlie ended the call. Someone must have seen the registration number. The whys and wherefores were not important, but it was vital that he remove anything incriminating from Steve's house. Fortunately, it was small and he had few possessions, so the search should not take too long. He quickly got dressed and grabbed his car and house keys. Steve had given him a key to the doors, which Charlie had attached to his own bunch of house keys, and there was no burglar alarm to negotiate.

En-route, he thought about what the police were likely to do. The injured man was probably sedated in hospital and it was unlikely that the police would have taken a statement from him so soon after the event, given his condition. There was no guarantee that he would ever make a statement. His kind often prefer to seek their own retribution. It was unlikely that, other than a brief first interview about whether he did it or where he

237

had been, Steve would be properly interviewed until after 9am. He was entitled to 8 hours rest, whether he needed it or not. Such a serious crime would probably be left to the CID. It may be lunch time before they got around to speaking to him. And why would they search his gaff? The weapon was a bar stool, still in the bar, and the only other piece of physical evidence would be Steve's clothing. They had probably already taken that. And why would they let him use his mobile phone to make his phone call? Maybe they were just going through the motions, not taking it too seriously? Still, he could take no chances, the place had to be cleaned of anything that could connect either of them to the other matters.

Charlie parked his car one street away and approached Steve's house on foot. It was in darkness. Steve's car was still outside. The police should have taken it. They could impound it because it had been used to get away from the scene of a crime. It was comforting that they hadn't. A cat was lying underneath it, enjoying the dying heat from the engine before it finally went cold. Which would be about now. It would look for another in due course. Car lights entering a street were always a welcome sight for cats at this time of year.

Charlie stepped through the front door and closed it quietly behind him, making sure that it was locked. It was bitterly cold outside and not much warmer inside. Steve wasn't one for wasting money on heating when a jumper and a blanket would do.

'Hello?' he called out. It was just habit. He was not expecting a reply. No response. He immediately went to the back door. If the police called and he had to make a quick exit, he didn't want to be wrestling with locks and bolts. He turned the key in the Chubb lock to open it, and unbolted the door in two places. He stepped outside into the yard and undid the single bolt to the gate. He peered outside and formed his escape plan. If

238

disturbed, he would turn left. The distance to the cut was much shorter that way, and cover was marginally better. He returned to the house, turning the key in the lock but leaving the bolts undone. He didn't want anyone walking in on him and, at the same time, wanted to be able to leave quickly without having to wrestle with too much door furniture. He then climbed the stairs, two at a time for the first three strides, at which point his body reminded him that such exertion wasn't a good idea at his age. He entered the main bedroom and switched on the light. The bulb was no more than 40 watts and there was no shade. Steve didn't see the point of unnecessary frills that served little purpose. The bed covers were turned back as if someone had left its warmth in a hurry. The chair over which Steve would normally put his clothes, was empty. He had probably put on the same clothes he had worn at the pub.

Charlie started with the bedside cabinet and scored immediately in the top drawer. A box of .22 rifle cartridges.

'Christ', muttered Charlie. 'What a tosser!' He left it where it was and continued the search. If the police called at that very moment the ammunition was better in Steve's drawer than in Charlie's pocket. In another drawer he found newspaper cuttings of the crown court slayings.

'God, what a tosser!' he mumbled again, under his breath. The rest of the house was clean. At least, of incriminating evidence. Before he left, twenty minutes later, he checked that Steve had taken the coat he had been wearing at the pub. It was nowhere to be seen. There should be no need for the police to come back to the house. He burnt the newspaper cuttings there and then, in the bathroom washbasin, making sure that nothing was left. The brief burst of heat was welcome. He opened the bathroom window to allow the smoke and burning smell to escape, then turned on the tap to douse the flames, leaving soggy, black ash. He cleaned up then resumed the search.

He found nothing else incriminating. Satisfied that his search had been thorough, and using rubber gloves he had found in the kitchen, Charlie put the ammunition into a polythene bin bag. He would take it home and hide it until he could reunite it with the rifle. He was at risk of being stopped by a patrol car but, as long as he drove within the speed limits, there was little likelihood of that. The drive would be uncomfortable, nevertheless. He closed the bedroom window then returned downstairs and reset the back-door bolts.

Finally, he peered outside. Nothing stirring. He locked the front door behind him and made his way back to the car. Again, no movement, just the same cat watching him approach the car. It refused to give ground until the engine sprang into life, at which point it crawled from under the car and gave Charlie a look of indignation. Charlie gave it the fingers and a smile as he left and turned for home. The ammunition stayed on the front passenger seat in case he had to jettison it quickly.

It was now approaching 4 am. There were no cars in the road and nothing parked up any of the side roads on his approach to home. No one was waiting for him. Almost at once, he buried the ammunition under a tuft of lawn at the rear of the house, using a trowel from the potting shed. The repair to the lawn was virtually invisible. It was only temporary, and the ammunition would be moved during daylight.

Charlie returned to bed. The sheets were cold and he kept his shirt on to lessen the chilly effect. Surprisingly for Charlie, who tended to overthink situations, he fell asleep almost immediately and did not wake until shortly before midday. It was now almost winter and the heating would stay on all day, so leaving his warm bed was no big deal. He showered and selected his clean clothes from his well-stocked wardrobe. Julie had always bought his clothes. She just needed his collar, chest, waist and inside leg measurements, which had not changed for eight years. Charlie was not particularly fashion conscious and the clothes he owned would probably last him the rest of his life. At least he hoped they would. He wasn't fond of shopping. He did insist on having a say on what jackets and shoes she would buy for him, but that was about the extent of his involvement.

It was now 3.30pm, and his mobile phone rang. It was Steve.

'Hi, Bro, fancy a pint?'

'Where are you, Steve?'

'At home. Will I come to yours?'

'Okay, then. What happened?'

'Released without charge. The big guy wouldn't make a statement. Probably because he doesn't want it to get out that a little guy creamed him. Half an hour.' Steve rang off.

Charlie was relieved. First of all, his brother would not be going to prison and, more importantly, neither of them had been compromised as far as he could tell. But he was going to have to beat some more sense into him about covering his back.

The half hour dragged. Finally, Steve's Mondeo turned into the drive. Charlie had opened the gates in readiness for him. He walked through the side gate and in through the back door. Unusually for Charlie, he stood up to meet him. Not as a mark of respect, but with every intention of punching him. Two things prevented him from doing that. His love for his brother and the fact that Steve might hit him back. Charlie could usually handle himself, but Steve was something else.

'What the fuck possessed you to keep ammo in the house? And the newspaper cuttings? Even Clouseau would have made the connection.'

'Sorry about that, I'd been cleaning the gun and I thought I'd put everything back. The papers, yes it was stupid, sorry.'

'What? You brought the rifle to the house?'

'Well yes, but that's before we started all this business.'

'Steve, what am I going to do with you? Somebody might have seen you. There might be gun oil on your furniture and fittings. The ammo, the cuttings. You're going to finish us both!'

'You're over-reacting.'

'I'm not! How the hell do you think major crimes are detected. It's little, almost invisible stuff, like that! Steve, one last time, take nothing home that can drop you in it.'

'Okay, point taken.'

'And burn your furniture. I'll replace it all!'

The silence lasted a full minute while Charlie started to empty the dishwasher.

'What happened at the nick?' he asked, breaking the silence as he placed a coffee mug on its rack.

'They interviewed me but I denied being there. I said I didn't know what they were talking about. Even the guy who got my number got some of the letters mixed up. I don't think the other witnesses would come forward. I did them a favour, after all. Anyway, it turns out the guy didn't want to press charges. Apparently, he's going to sort me out himself so the cops have told me to watch myself. He knows a lot of heavy types and he's a bit of a lad himself. Maybe I should have done the other hand as well. Maybe I should take him out altogether when the dust settles. What do you think?'

'Definitely not,' replied Charlie quickly, 'now that there's a direct link.'

'I know, only joking.'

'Yes, but someone came forward with your number. To be on the safe side, you should assume that the guy will change his mind and that he will bully the others to testify. Trust no one. Believe that the whole world's on your case, and ready to drop you in.'

'Okay, can we change the subject, I'm getting bored.'

'Okay, but just one more thing. What happens if the guy does change his mind? What happens if he smells compensation? No chance of that, if he doesn't support a prosecution.'

'What do you advise?' asked Steve.

'He has to identify you, the witnesses have to identify you. Grow a beard, shave your head, put weight on, get rid of your jacket.'

'Seriously?'

'Yes. Get rid of your jacket, I'll give you the money for another one. Grow some stubble and get a haircut or change the style. If it's going to happen it'll likely be within the week.'

'Well, if you think so.'

'I do. Play it safe. Get used to covering your tracks. Get rid of any clothing you wore when you were handling the gun. I'll give you the money for new stuff. Do it sooner rather than later.'

'Even my Barbour that cost nearly £200?'

'Especially that. Get one of a different colour and make sure every thread of your old one is burned or ditched far away.'

Charlie switched on the television set and found the Sky Sports News channel. He took two cans of beer from the fridge and handed one to Steve. Business over, they could relax. They watched the football match updates. Again, Newcastle United had nothing to play for. No chance of Europe, little chance of relegation.

'Whose turn is it to beat the Toon today?' enquired Steve. For all they were brothers, Steve had always followed Sunderland.

'Liverpool, again,' conceded Charlie with an air of resignation.

'Shite, mate, sorry,' he said with a smirk.

They watched in silence. Steve picked up The Mail, which he bought from the newsagent on his way over. The holiday supplement fell to the floor and he picked it up.

'Fancy a holiday, Charlie?'

'What, with you?'

'Why not? Might be a laugh. I haven't been away since that time in Africa. I wasn't welcome. They shot me in the arse, so anywhere but Africa.'

Charlie thought for a moment.

'Okay, but not until I've finished business here.'

'What's the next move, then?'

'Morrison. He's the main guy, I don't think there's anybody above him.'

'How-about we take out the lot? Get them altogether then bam!' He spread his right hand from side to side pulling an imaginary trigger.

'It'll take some planning.'

'He's bound to have meetings with them now and again, let's watch him. Find out his routine.'

'Not a bad idea, Steve.'

'House or nightclub?'

'Probably the club. After Christmas, when it's dead. It would cause less of a stir, and we'll know that anybody else there is involved in the business and not just a visitor. Besides, the police will already be dealing with the usual Christmas murder, on top of the problems they've already got.'

'When?'

'Fairly soon. We need to watch the comings and goings for a while, identify the pattern then go for it.'

'How many are you hoping to get?'

'Three to five, maybe. I believe he goes nowhere without at least two flunkies with him.'

'Three to five? Do you know how difficult that can be, even with an Uzi? Are you up to it?' enquired Steve. Charlie's bottle was a little suspect, in Steve's book. He was too anal.

244

'I think so. I'm good enough to at least drop three or four before they know it's happening. It's a full magazine. Fifteen shots.'

'Killing at close range is different to long distance, you know. Face to face, especially in cold blood, isn't easy.'

'I know, I'll be okay. As you know, I've done it before. The skill is still there, and I would be letting Julie down if I gave up now. I've got what it takes.'

'If you want, I'll do it,' offered Steve, sincerely.

'No, it's my shout. The last few months I've been building up to this day, it'll go like clockwork, I'm sure.'

'If I do it, they will just disappear off the face of the earth. I can do things like that. Plod will be bamboozled.'

'Can you bollocks! No, Steve, it's my shout.'

'Okay, but I'm coming as back-up. You're not having all the fun!'

'I sincerely hope you are. I need you on the outside with a radio in case you need to warn me.'

'And the rifle in case you miss,' added Steve.

'Steve, I'm prepared to be caught but I don't expect you to take the same risks. For me, it's about honour.'

'I'm just as prepared for the chokey, Charlie,' replied Steve, 'Paul's death ended any chance of me having a proper life. Besides, we won't get caught.'

'Anyway, how are you getting on with your new son?' added Steve, changing the subject.

'It's a slow burner, mate. He's in his first term at Oxford so I haven't seen much of him. It's probably better that way, for now. Don't want to rush things.'

'It's Law, isn't it?'

'Yes. He nearly missed the boat. Freddie Simpson didn't want him to go.'

'I know. I did you a favour there.'

'He was no threat in prison.'

'I know, but it was a loose end. Better he's gone.'

'I suppose so, but it created its own loose ends, so don't make decisions like that without consulting me.'

'You would have said *no*.'

'I might not have. It had crossed my mind as well, you know.'

'Anyway, you don't have all the answers. It's done and dusted. He isn't missed and, hopefully, there'll be nobody coming after you.'

'Yes, well from now on, no more without discussing it first. I mean it, Steve, we have to do it my way.'

Steve tutted and rolled his eyes.

Once the football scores had been read out, the pair gave each other a hug and Steve left.

TWENTY-FIVE

It was December 13th, 7am, when the gate buzzer went. It did not register at first, but it became persistent and Charlie's brain eventually got into gear. He left the comfort of his bed, walked towards the window and moved the heavy curtain to one side. There was condensation on the window pane and he cleared a small circle to look through. Subconsciously, he wiped his wet hand on the curtain. On the other side of the gate was a single car, no logos or markings, with its headlights on. A tall, dark figure stood at the gate. *CID! That's all it could be.* He watched for a moment. *Yes, it must be CID!* It did not look like Angel. This was not good. Had Steve's blunders finally caught them both out?

He quickly found his spare pay-as-you-go phone and rang Steve. He answered immediately.

'Steve, Charlie here. The police are at my door!'

'My bell's been ringing as well. I'm just about to open up!'

'Listen, they will try to play one against the other. Believe nothing, say nothing. Don't refuse to answer questions, don't get clever, just deny all knowledge, okay? Ask for the duty solicitor but tell him nothing either - the consultation room might be bugged. Good luck!'

'Understood. Count on me.'

'They'll seize your phone and ask who it was who phoned you just now. Just say it was a wrong number, okay? Remember, don't tell lies, just give non-committal answers, okay?'

'Got it, hang on,...... I think they're breaking in ...' Steve's voice trailed away. The phone fell silent.

Charlie ran downstairs, carrying his dressing gown, and threw the pay-as-you-go phone into the grey embers of the solid fuel Rayburn, which sparked into life with the injection of oxygen and the prospect of a new meal. Within seconds there would be no trace of it. He threw in some more fuel.

He then switched on the lights, inside and out, found the gate fob and pressed the button. The gates slowly opened and in drove the car. There were only two occupants.

He donned his dressing gown and tightly fastened the belt. There was unlikely to be any physical stuff otherwise they would have come mob-handed but, just in case there was, he did not want to come apart and reveal all. Fortunately, the heating had already come on and the house was beginning to warm up. He opened the front door and met them head on.

He recognised neither of them. Both wore overcoats, one camel, the other, grey herringbone. The grey herringbone wore a red paisley tie and the camel wore a striped tie. The colours didn't exactly go together, but that was unimportant.

'What can I do for you, gents?' he asked, trying not to look concerned. It was bitterly cold with a chill breeze, and the dressing gown was failing to serve its purpose. He held the overlap in place. The grey herringbone replied.

'Mr. Payne, Charles Payne?'

'Yes?'

'I'm Detective Sergeant Ian Hughes and this is Detective Constable Trevor Peart. Can we come in?' They both flashed their warrant cards, which he immediately recognised as authentic. He had lived with one for thirty years and would be able to spot a forgery a mile off.

'Yes, come in, it's cold out here.'

They entered and waited for Charlie to close the door. 'I'm afraid we've been asked to bring you in on suspicion of a serious assault on Tony Molloy in Highbridge, Newcastle on 3rd

September.' He then cautioned Charlie. This was the day that Charlie had been dreading, but he was prepared for it. He had been preparing for it for months.

'Who's Tony Molloy?' responded Charlie, immediately.

'I'm afraid that's all I can tell you for now. Would you like to get dressed, please?' asked Hughes.

'Yes, but I haven't assaulted anybody. I don't know who you're talking about. Am I being arrested?'

'Yes,' came the curt answer.

Charlie went back upstairs, followed by the pair. It seemed to him that the assault on Tony Molloy was their strongest case, but the others would soon creep into the conversation. It was difficult to see how they could fail to mention them, since there was clear evidence, thanks to his brother, that they were connected. The only evidence they could have was from his friends from The Bacchus, whom he knew had given statements putting him within 100 yards of the assault, around the time it happened. There was no malice intended, they would not think for a moment that one of their number was a suspect.

Being in the vicinity was not enough without motive, forensic evidence or an identification at the scene. Hundreds of people would have been just as close, just as eligible. Provided they had not found the rifle, there was no possibility of forensic evidence that he shot Molloy. Besides, they could not link him to it, unless it could be somehow tied to Julie's killer.

It was likely that they would have made the Simpson connection, but they had no evidence other than an inference. So far, so good, but he hoped that Steve was giving his case the same logical thought and that he was up to the grilling that was coming his way. Their freedom depended on it.

Charlie was furious with himself for not sitting down with Steve to discuss a game plan for if ever they were arrested, but he hoped that his hurried warning over the phone would be just enough to do the trick. As they drove through the gates onto the road, he saw two white police carriers. Search officers, he thought, probably ten or more for a house of this size. A deep search could take two full days. They could cause a lot of damage, even take plaster off the walls. *But they won't find a mortal thing. Everything is safely tucked away elsewhere.*

Once again, he was at Etal lane Police Station. No sign of old Baz. The reason for the arrest was given as *assault on Anthony Malloy in Highbridge, Newcastle upon Tyne, earlier this year.*

The custody sergeant commenced the custody record. Charlie did not recognise him. No allies here, he thought. The sergeant went through the script and Charlie answered all questions respectfully. He declined medical attention, he wasn't in need of any, but agreed to a duty solicitor. Without being asked to do so, Charlie emptied his pockets, took off his belt and his shoes.

'Been here before, then?' asked the sergeant without looking up.

'Loads of times,' responded Charlie. There was no response, verbally or visually.

Detective Sergeant Hughes patted him down to make sure he had not missed anything, then nodded approval towards the custody sergeant. This time, Charlie had not brought his Nano-i-pod. He would be pushing his luck to think that he could get away with that twice.

He was led away to male cell number 5, a different one to the last time. It was furnished with a blanket, neatly folded, and a new toilet roll. The room had been prepared and reserved just for him, he thought.

'We will come and see you once you've had your consultation with the duty solicitor, okay?' said Hughes.

'Fine,' said Charlie, not that he had any choice in the matter.

Steve's arrest was altogether different. He just managed to get to the door before it came off its hinges.

'I hope you've got good insurance?' he started, 'these doors don't come cheap!'

The response was without humour. 'Steven Payne, I'm arresting you on suspicion of the murder of Glen Harrison and James Hargreaves.' Steve did not see who spoke, but a cold, black handgun was menacingly thrust in his face, before he was turned around forcibly and quickly lowered to the floor, face first. His arms were snatched by gloved hands, his hands covered with nylon bags and forced behind him, before being roughly handcuffed. He winced as the hard, angular metal bit into his wrists. Complaining would have resulted in the cuffs being tightened another notch or two. He did not complain.

'Are there any firearms in this house?' demanded a voice.

'Firearms?' asked Steve in feigned surprise. 'What would I want with firearms?'

He heard the sound of heavy boots running upstairs and cries of 'Armed police! Stay where you are!' as they went into in each room, followed by, 'Clear!' Steve could have told them that there was no one else in the house, but would they listen? He did not suppose they would.

Within what seemed like seconds, the hallway was crowded with armed police, some with Heckler and Koch pistols and at least one with something altogether bigger.

'All clear, sarge,' said one, 'do you want the search team in now?'

'Yes, Lee, bring them in as soon as we leave,' replied the sergeant.

Steve was gently helped to his feet, still cuffed.

'Sorry about that,' a dark figure spoke. 'With any arrest for firearms offences it has to be quick, you understand?'

Steve nodded and managed a weak smile. He noticed the man's epaulette bore a silver badge with three stripes.

'Is there anything in the house that shouldn't be here?' the voice continued. 'Only, we'll be searching it anyway and you will help yourself if you can tell us now.'

'There's nothing here, honest. I haven't a clue what you're on about, I've killed nobody!'

'Okay,' continued the voice, 'but we have to take you in for questioning, okay?' His tone was more conciliatory. His job was done, one arrest with no casualties. And a compliant subject. Top result.

Steve's house was clear of anything that would compromise him, he hoped. His brother had taken care of business, but had the police come a few weeks earlier it might have been a different story. He was placed into a cage in the back of the police van, still handcuffed, but one of the officers had rearranged them so that he was cuffed to the front. Presumably a safety measure for the journey. The cage was large enough to have a bench seat in it and to allow him to stretch his legs a little. He was alone with his thoughts, which turned to Charlie. *Had he been arrested too?* It was an assumption he had to make.

It was now 8.40am and Charlie's cell door was opened. The custody sergeant peered around the door and announced, 'Duty solicitor is here, a Mr. Harding. Do you know him?'

'Heard of him, but I've had no dealings with him,' replied Charlie, rising to his feet. He was led to an interview room where he found a smartly dressed, well-groomed man in his fifties. This was no runner, thought Charlie, this guy was the real deal.

Harding stood up and offered his hand, which Charlie took. ''I'm Mike Harding,' he said, 'from Harding and Harding law firm. I gather you asked to be represented?'

'Yes, but I'm not sure I need you. I asked for you as a precaution.'

'I understand. What have they told you so far?'

'Just that I've been arrested for assaulting Tony Malloy.'

'And did you?'

'No. I told them I didn't even know him but, on the way here, I suddenly remembered that he was the guy who got shot recently. That wasn't me either, by the way. I don't know him.'

'Have you any idea why they should think it was you? Could they have any evidence?'

'I don't think so. I mean they can't have, because I haven't assaulted him. Listen, I'd better fill you in about a few things. I think there's something unhealthy going on.' Charlie told him about his police service, the death of his wife at the hands of a paid killer and his subsequent shooting of the assassin. He continued with his arrest and questioning and about how Detective Chief Inspector Redman kept bringing Tommy Layton, a previous customer of Charlie's, into the line of questioning, making him believe that there was a hidden agenda. That was as much as he wanted to tell Harding, for now.

'I knew about the situation with your wife, it was headlines for a few weeks. I'm sorry. As regards what's going on now, we'll just have to wait and see. In the meantime, I have to give you some standard warnings. If you admit any wrongdoing to me but then tell lies to the police on that same point, I cannot continue to represent you. You will either have to tell the truth or decline to answer the questions. That, of course, carries its own risks...

'I know the drill, Mike,' interrupted Charlie, 'don't worry on that score.'

'Okay then, are you ready?'

'I am,' replied Charlie.

'In that case, I'll just fill in the legal aid forms then I'll let them know we're ready. If nothing else, it'll help to run down the clock. Unless they have something more than assault to talk about, they only have 24 hours. Which means, effectively, they have until midnight. Unless, of course, they arrest you for his murder as well.'

The two arresting officers were also the interviewers. They walked into the room and sat down, before setting up the recording equipment. They loaded the tapes, switched on the recording machine, introduced themselves, then invited Charlie and the solicitor to do likewise. Up to that point, not a word had been spoken.

Sergeant Hughes opened the interview.

'You've been arrested on suspicion of assaulting Tony Molloy on Tuesday, 3rd September. Did you know him?'

'No, I didn't,' replied Charlie. 'I've heard of him, though. On the way here, it dawned on me he was the bloke who got shot a while ago. Bit of a bad lad, I understand. I might have seen him around, but I've had no dealings with him.'

'Did you assault him?'

'No.'

'It was a vicious assault. He had a broken jaw, a fractured cheekbone and a fractured skull.'

'Look at me, sergeant, do you think I am physically capable of doing that?' invited Charlie. 'According to all the reports he was an ex-professional boxer!'

'According to the pathologist, some form of weapon was used.'

'I don't carry weapons. I was having a night out. Why would I need a weapon? Was anything found at the scene?'

Detective Sergeant Hughes looked at the notes he had brought in with him but offered no explanation of his own.

'Where were you that evening?'

'Well, if it was the first Tuesday of the month I will have been in The Bacchus with friends.'

'The Bacchus near Highbridge?'

'Yes.'

'That's only a few yards from where the assault took place.'

'Is it?'

'Yes, it took place in Highbridge. What time did you leave The Bacchus?'

'I'm not sure. I normally just go once most of them have left. It's nearly always before 10pm, though.'

'Where did you go from there?'

'To Osbornes, in Jesmond.'

'You're fairly precise about that?'

'Yes, the last twice I've been to The Bacchus on a Tuesday, I ended up in Osbornes.'

'How did you get there?'

'By taxi.'

'Where from?'

'Outside the Theatre Royal.'

'Can anyone confirm this?'

'I suppose it's a bit much to ask a taxi driver to remember me. Otherwise, no.'

'To get a taxi from there, you would naturally have to turn right out of the pub?'

'Yes.'

'But we have a statement from someone to say you turned left. Towards where the assault took place.'

'I sometimes go that way, but not always. This time and the time before, I went the other way.'

'How can you be sure?'

'Like I said, the last twice I've been to The Bacchus, I've gone to Osbornes afterwards. They've got CCTV, maybe they still have the footage?' Charlie knew that the footage would have been taped over by now. But it neither helped nor hindered his case. He was trying to show willing.

'We will,' replied Hughes. 'Why did you go to Osbornes?'

'I like it there. The beer's good, so is the atmosphere. Besides, most other places are quieter on a Tuesday.'

'Did you meet anyone there?'

'No.'

'Did you know anyone there?'

'No, just the regular faces.'

'Why would you go to a pub where you don't know anybody?'

'I will get to know them eventually, but it's going to take a while at the rate I'm going. I'll have to step up my visits.'

'Why would you leave convivial company to go to another pub where you'd be on your own?'

'The more convivial parties had left. I struggle to have a conversation with some of the others, besides, they were getting ready to leave as well. By the way, I presume that you've spoken to most, if not all of the crowd that gets in on a Tuesday? It doesn't surprise me that one of them said I turned left. I often do, but not on that night. It's an understandable mistake. Especially when you've had a drink. You said you had *a* statement. One *single* statement? I presume that the others couldn't remember which way I turned or else they say I turned right?'

The sergeant again dodged the question.

'Tony Molloy was shot outside his home around 4pm on 23rd September. Where were you on that day?'

'I think I was at home all day. I remember seeing it on the 6pm news.'

'Can anyone vouch for you being at home?'

'No, but if you check my e-mail account you will be able to see when I've opened or sent e-mails. I also have a CCTV system that keeps everything for 31 days, but I think you've just missed the boat on that one.'

'We'll check anyway.'

'Are you saying I'm a suspect for the shooting?'

'Not at this stage, but when a man suffers horrific injuries then a few weeks later, he's shot, we have to consider there might be a link, wouldn't you agree?'

'I suppose so. But I didn't assault anyone, much less shoot them. I mean, why would I? It doesn't make sense.'

'There is a school of thought that it is all linked to the shooting of your wife.'

'You've lost me there. I take it you know about what happened after my wife was shot?

'I do. Apparently, you were the target but it all went wrong?'

'Yes, Julie couldn't have been the target. I mean, how could she be?'

'Why were you a target?'

'Probably because I've made enemies along the way. Upset a few people. It's a hazard of the job. I also had a trial coming up. I was all that stood in between Freddie Simpson and a life sentence. Do you feel safe, yourself, at all times?'

The sergeant dodged the question yet again.

'I understand it had something to do with the disappearance of Tommy Layton?'

'Chief Inspector Redman said that as well,' replied Charlie. 'What is it with you guys? The last time I saw Tommy is when he was starting his fifteen-year prison sentence.'

'I don't believe for one minute that someone would want to kill you just for putting people in prison.'

'Some of these people aren't normal like you and me, but what other explanation is there? '

'So, you are saying that the last time you saw Tommy Layton was in court? About ten years ago?'

'Yes.'

'Are you absolutely certain about that, Charlie?' interjected Harding. 'You don't need to...'

'No, I want to, Mike. I've done nothing wrong and the sooner they can write me out of their enquiries the quicker they can go after the real bad guys.'

Hughes continued.

'I now want to talk to you about Freddie Simpson .....'

The solicitor again interjected.

'Are you happy to answer these questions, Charlie, they are talking about a man who was murdered. Do you need further consultation?

'I'm happy to continue,' replied Charlie, meeting the solicitor eye to eye, 'Like I say, I've done nothing.'

'I understand that you had a reason to want Freddie Simpson out of the way?' continued Hughes.

'Of course not. I suppose you're referring to the fact that I am the biological father of Mark Simpson who Freddie thought was his son?' From the line of questioning, Charlie knew that if they didn't already know by now, it was only a matter of time before they did, so honesty was the best policy.

'Yes.'

'And why do you think I would want him out of the way?'

'Well it was, to say the least, a dangerous situation, wasn't it? I mean Freddie wasn't known for his forgiving nature, was he?'

'Look, Jane Elliot was my girlfriend for years before she and Freddie met. She became pregnant shortly before we split, but she didn't let on. She left me because she knew I was about to propose, and she didn't like the hours I kept. She saw no future in it. It wasn't a case of me having an affair with a criminal's wife. That would be asking for trouble and I would deserve everything I got. I only found out about Mark at Freddie's trial. He looks like I did at that age.'

'That wouldn't have mattered to Freddie, though, would it?' replied Hughes. 'I mean, that it happened before he met her?'

'Possibly not, but Freddie got life, so there's not much he could have done. Also, he didn't have much in the way of influence or outside help anymore. I certainly didn't feel threatened. Besides, I don't think he even knew the situation. We would have told him at some stage, to make things official, but I still didn't see him as a threat.'

'I understand your brother, Steve, was a sniper in the Marines?

'Was he? I knew he was with special forces, but he never talks about it. Where is this going?'

'It may surprise you to know that he is also in custody and being questioned right now?'

'I can't think why. Those days are behind him.'

'Wasn't he a hired gun, a mercenary when he left the forces?'

'I know he went to Africa for some reason, but that's all history. Unless you tell me what this is about, I won't answer any more questions about him. I'll be happy to continue with questions about myself, but that's all.'

'Okay, we'll leave it for now. Interview suspended at 9.14am.'

Charlie stayed behind at the request of Harding. Once the detectives had left, Harding asked, 'What was that about, Charlie?'

'Well, it seems to me that they are trying to pin the shootings of Malloy and Simpson on me and my brother. It's ludicrous. They can't possibly have any evidence. Yes, I can see why they would think the way they do, but they're putting two and two together and coming up with five.' Charlie was careful not to give anything away. He knew that certain behaviour and comments would create interest, enough to make them, and Harding, feel they were on the right track. He had to play it as a total innocent. He could not display excited, anxious or angry behaviour. He knew that the paternity was an issue they could play on, but it did not amount to evidence. He knew that there was no hope of their linking him to Tommy's disappearance. The chances were, Tommy would not be found for years, if ever, and there was nothing to connect him or his house to Tommy, he was sure of that. He knew that a statement from a drunk friend, saying he had turned left and not right, could not be relied upon. He sometimes did, he sometimes didn't, and it would not be difficult to throw doubt on that version. If that was all they had, it was going nowhere. Only Steve could change that.

Steve had also opted for legal representation and he too was allowed a consultation with the next in line duty solicitor, Mark Raine. The police had decided not to use the same duty solicitor as they had for Charlie, in case he gave away information about what was being said. They would want to play one off against the other and once they had differing accounts, they would try every trick in the book to make those differences count. Steve knew that.

'What have you been arrested for?' Raine asked Steve.

'Murdering Glen Harrison and Jimmy Hargreaves.'

'And did you?'

'No way. God's honest truth.'

'Why do you think they've arrested you, then?'

'I knew them both, sort of worked for them.'

'Did you ever fall out with them?'

'No.'

'Is there anyone who would disagree with that statement?'

'I don't see how. I just left their employ when my son died. I had a breakdown and haven't really worked since. But I had no axe to grind with *them*. The verdict on Paul was misadventure. The police brought no evidence to suggest blame on anybody.'

'They are the men who were shot outside the Crown Court, were they not?'

'Yes.'

'I thought so, quite shocking, really.'

Steve agreed.

'Do you have an alibi?'

'Not really. I was in the house. My brother came there straight from court and told me about it.'

'Why would he do that?'

'He comes to mine a lot these days, since Julie died. He can get quite lonely, I think, and we see a lot of each other now. Like we've discovered each other again, if you know what I mean?'

'Is there anything else I should know? I mean, I'd rather know now than be surprised during the interview.'

'I don't know if it's relevant, but Charlie is a retired cop. He was in charge of a case in court that same day, the trial of Freddie Simpson. It was Charlie's last ever case, and he wanted to celebrate. Got life, I believe, not a bad one to finish on.'

'He came to yours straight after the trial?'

'Yes. Maybe they think there's a link, but it's just coincidence. Also, I was in the Marines and was a trained sniper. Also, when my time was up, I did some private work in Africa.'

'Private work?'

'Best way to describe it is a mercenary.'

'Ah, I see where they are coming from. You are a trained marksman, you had a connection, albeit tenuous, to an ongoing trial, and you are quite capable of such an act, given your background. Do you know if your brother has been arrested?'

'No idea.'

How to you think the police are going to come at you?

'Well, if they've done their homework, they'll probably mention everything I've just said.'

'What will you tell them?'

'The absolute truth. If they don't raise it, I will. I don't want to give them any ammunition to trip me up later. I want to put this to bed.'

'Good, it pays to be totally honest, if you've done nothing wrong. Have you had any refreshment? Would you like me to arrange for some?'

'No thanks, I'm okay.'

'In that case, I have some legal aid paperwork I need to complete, then I'll tell them we're ready. If I see you getting into difficulties, I'll ask for a break, then we can discuss how to handle it, okay?'

'Yes, no bother, Mr. Raine.'

It was now 10.15am. The door to the interview room opened and in walked one male and one female officer, both in plain clothes. The male carried a clip board containing some notes, and the female, some tape cases. She broke the seal on the wrappings, inserted two tapes into the machine and switched it on. The male spoke first.

'I'm Detective Sergeant Phil Brentwood, and with me is Detective Constable Holly Proctor. Would you mind identifying yourselves, please?'

Both Mark Raine and Steve obliged.

'You've been arrested on suspicion of the shootings of Glen Harrison and James Hargreaves outside Newcastle Crown Court on 28th August this year. What have you to say to that?'

'It wasn't me.'

'Did you know either of them?'

'Yes, I worked with them. It was a few years ago, though.'

'Doing what?'

'The doors.'

'How did you get along?'

'Fine. They were good with me and I always got paid on time. Decent bonuses, which is more than you can say for other outfits.'

'So, no hard feelings?

'No.'

'Did they ever deal drugs? I mean they're dead now so it's not as if you can do them any harm.'

'The truthful answer is, I don't know. Probably. They're all at it, aren't they? But I didn't see anything. I was mostly outside or just inside the entrances, looking out. Anyway, it pays not to ask questions. Best case, you get the sack. Worst case – who knows?'

'I understand your son, Paul, died around the time of your employment with them. Drugs overdose?'

'Yes, but it was prescribed drugs, not the recreational stuff. And whisky.'

'There is some suggestion that you blamed your employers for Paul's death.'

'I don't know why. I don't think they knew him, did they?'

'And that you bided your time?'

'Whoever is suggesting that has an overactive imagination. Even if they dealt in drugs, and I don't know that they did, I don't think Paul went to any of their pubs.'

'I understand you had a habit at one time?'

'Yes, but before I worked the doors for Glen and Jimmy. It was cocaine. I've been clean for years, by the way. I think I would have known if the guys were supplying that stuff. Anyway, as I said, Paul died of barbiturates and alcohol. A different ball-game.'

'Could it be that he had a habit, fuelled by Harrison and Hargreaves.'

'Everything is possible, but I wouldn't know. You are barking up the wrong tree.'

'Where were you on 28th August?'

'I was at home.'

'How do you remember that.'

'Because I saw my brother that day. He came to mine after the trial and told me about the shooting.'

'That was afterwards. Where were you between 3pm and 4.30pm?'

'Still at home. I'm on benefits so I don't go out much. I go to my allotment Mondays, Tuesdays and Fridays. Most other days I stay at home.'

Detective Constable Proctor interjected.

'But you own a car?'

'An old Mondeo. Had it since before I stopped working. I don't do many miles in it. Sometimes it never moves from the street.'

Proctor continued the interview.

'How do you pay for its maintenance.'

'Charlie helps out when I ask. Pays for services and suchlike. Sometimes he sees me alright for fuel. I don't make too many demands. I like my independence.'

'Apparently, your brother is loaded?'

'Yes, he is. His wife's family were wealthy. He keeps offering and I know if I want a new car, he'll be good for it, but I don't. I'm not one for material wealth. Neither is he, by the way.'

'Do you know he has a son?' continued Proctor.

'I do. Mark's his name. He only recently found out about it and he's delighted. He's always wanted kids. You see, me and him were brought up in a home, never knew what it was like to have real parents. He was disappointed when Julie couldn't have them. At least I think it was down to her, they never discussed stuff like that with me.'

'Do you know that a criminal, Freddie Simpson, brought Mark up thinking he was his?'

'Sort of, I don't know the details, but Charlie's good with that. It's not an issue. I mean it happened before Jane met Freddie. If anybody should be worried it should be Jane. She let Freddie think he was his for 17 years.'

'How close are you to Charlie?'

'These days, very close. Since his wife was murdered. At times like that, you need your family around you, don't you? Can I just say, and I don't mean to be rude or anything, but what's this got to do with the shooting of Glen and Jimmy?'

'There are some interesting relationships between a number of incidents that have happened over the past few months,' resumed Brentwood, 'and we are trying to piece them together.'

'Well, I'll help you all I can, but I don't think that'll amount to much. But fire away.'

'Do you own a .22 rifle?'

'No, my preferred calibre is 50mm.'

'Have you ever fired one?'

'A .22? No, they're just toys compared to the military hardware.'

'But good enough to kill from a few hundred yards?'

'A few hundred yards? You're definitely barking up the wrong tree, mate. Maybe with a bigger calibre. I think 200 yards would be the limit for a pea-shooter. What was the distance the shots came from?'

Brentwood ignored the question.

'There are police officers searching your allotment. What would you say if they found such a rifle?'

'They won't, unless somebody has put it there. I know every square inch of my allotment and unless one has been put there since the day before yesterday....'

'If there is anything there, they will find it,' added Brentwood.

'I don't doubt they will, but I think they're wasting their time. They have to do what they have to do, I suppose.'

'Did you know Tony Malloy?'

'No, I don't think so.'

'What about Freddie Simpson?'

'Again, no. Just what my brother told me about him.'

'What did he say?'

'That he was a loser, and that all his team had left him or died. Basically, he was a nobody.'

'Did he show any animosity towards him?'

'No, it's just a job to Charlie. I don't think he feels animosity towards anybody. With the exception of the guy who killed Julie. But that's sorted.'

'Does he have any suspicion as to who put Julie's killer up to it?'

'If he does, he's never said anything. I think he wants to put it all behind him and get on with his life.'

'I think we'll end it there for now, we'll come back and see you later. Interview terminated at 10.31am.

'What was all that about?' asked Raine after the officers had left.

'Well, it seems like there has been a lot of shit going on, and they suspect that maybe Charlie and I are involved.'

'And are you?'

'No way. It's all innuendo. They'll find nothing at the allotment except mostly cabbages and turnips. They'll dig them up before they're ready. I might be able to salvage a few.

There's nowt in the hut either, just a primus and stuff to make tea. Not even a girlie magazine.'

'What if they find something?'

'If? If my uncle had tits, he would be my auntie!'

'Be serious, please,' Raine scolded. 'The last thing you want to do is piss them off with wisecracks.'

'Sorry. I don't see how they can find anything, unless somebody has put something there.'

'Are you worried?'

'Not really. Not at all, in fact. If they find something it has been put there by someone else. They've made a huge mistake. I hope they don't take it out on me when they realise their mistake.'

'We'll cross that bridge when we come to it. What about your house? Is there anything there that could possibly cause a line of questioning?

'Absolutely nothing that I can think of. I lead a simple life, keeping myself to myself. I don't bother anyone, and no one bothers me. Correction, I was arrested about a month ago on suspicion of assaulting someone in a pub in No Place. The Beamish Mary? It came to nothing, but it was a hair-raising experience.'

'What were the circumstances?'

'I don't really know. Apparently, this bloke got a good hiding and they got the number of the car the man was driving. It was similar to mine, but that's all. I was in and out within a few hours.'

'Okay, we'll see if they raise it. Ready for a cuppa?'

'Okay then,' agreed Steve, 'Milk but no sugar, thanks.'

Mark Raine left the interview room, which had been left unlocked. He closed the door behind him. It then occurred to Steve to check for listening devices. It was the easiest place in the world to search. One wooden table, two wooden benches all fixed to the floor, plus a recording machine. He looked everywhere, which took him no more than a minute or so. There was nothing that looked remotely like a microphone, except the one in the recording equipment. In any event, anything they heard would be of no use.

It was again Charlie's turn. Hughes and Peart entered the room. There were no triumphant grins, no smirks, just straight faces. It was clear that they had still found nothing, after three hours. But, if Steve had done the job properly, there was nothing to find. Two new tapes were inserted into the recorder.

'Interview resumed at 10.25 am. You are still under caution. What were you wearing the night you were at The Bacchus? The night of the assault on Tony Molloy?'

'I normally wear my thick leather jacket. It should be hanging in the hallway on the coat hooks. There are two, a thick one and another one. It's dark brown. I think I will have been wearing my brown brogues, probably my dark blue Chinos. Not sure about my top.'

'Where did you go after Osbornes?'

'I think I went to The Star on Westgate Road?'

'Why?'

'I often call there before I get my taxi home from the Central Station. It's a decent music venue. Maybe not Tuesday nights but it's on my radar.'

'Why didn't you get a taxi home from Osbornes?'

'I wasn't ready to go home. It was still quite early, and I enjoy listening to the crack.'

'Do you ever join in with the crack?'

'No, but it's still entertaining. You never know what you might hear. It's an art that we older coppers developed. It's a pity it's discouraged these days. Besides, I live in a big, empty house. I rattle around inside.'

'Are you saying you were looking for company? Perhaps female company?'

'Do both of us a favour, don't make this personal, eh?' Charlie tried to conceal his distaste for that remark, and refrained from changing tack and being as awkward as he knew he could be. He knew that if he played games, he might enjoy them, but he could be there forever. The sergeant also knew it was a senseless, unhelpful remark.

'Sorry, there was no need for that,' he apologised. He was aware of Charlie's skills and didn't want to turn the interview into a sea of complications. It would get no one anywhere.

'How long did you stay at The Star?'

'About as long as it takes to drink a pint. I don't think I finished it, so maybe twenty to thirty minutes?'

'Does anyone there know you?'

'I doubt it. I maybe call in once every three months and have one pint.'

'And from there, you got a taxi home?'

'Yes, from the Central Station. I think there was no queue, so I got one immediately. The driver was Asian, and apart from saying, *Hello, where to?* nothing much else was said. He should remember me though, because he remarked about how the lights came on and the gates opened when I pressed the fob.'

Charlie knew from the line of questioning that the sergeant was struggling to find anything new to talk about. It was a delaying tactic, pending the results of the house search. Charlie knew that they would find nothing. Tommy's phone and the phone number lists were miles away, with no prospect of anyone finding them. The guns and ammunition were hidden likewise, or at least he hoped that Steve had done the business. In the unlikely event that they were found, there was no possible link to Charlie or Steve, forensically, mechanically or otherwise. Their only chance would be to break Steve and, up to that point, there was no sign of that happening.

'Okay, we'll take another break. Time now is 10.32am.'

Detective Constable Peart switched off the machine, took out the tapes and marked them up, while Hughes sat in silence. They then left the room. Within five minutes, Charlie was back in his cell. *So, it's going to be a long break? They've got nothing!*

Sergeant Brentwood again entered the room in which Steve was sitting with the solicitor, flanked by Detective Constable Proctor who was carrying a manila folder and two tape cases. Brentwood opened his folder while Proctor broke the seal on two tapes and inserted them into the machine. She flicked the switch.

'The time is now 11.13am, the interview with Steven Payne is resumed. The search of your house and allotment are still ongoing. In your house was found a book about guns. Do you still have an interest in guns even after all this time?'

'Yes, but much in the same way that you'll watch detective dramas on television long after you retire. No disrespect intended but you can't seriously read anything into that. You'll also find a book about dog breeding, but I've never owned a dog and I have no intention of breeding them. The gun book might have been interesting if a .22 calibre rifle has been ringed with a note saying, *use this one to shoot Glen and Jimmy.* Oops, I hope I haven't given you an idea!'

Brentwood did not bite.

'We also found some correspondence from Durham Constabulary relating to an assault,' continued Brentwood, 'What was that about?'

'I was arrested on suspicion of assaulting a man in the Beamish Mary pub. Somebody had written the number of the getaway car down and some of the letters matched mine. I was brought in but there was no further action.'

'We've spoken to the PC involved and he says it was definitely you, but the victim wanted no further action. He wouldn't make a complaint.'

'He would say that, wouldn't he? He's just covering up because he got the wrong man. I was in the house all night. They took a punt and made a mistake, that's all.'

'Well, so you say.'

'Yes, I do. It was a mistake. I'll be happy to stand on a parade if they want to take it further.'

'According to you, the police are making one mistake after another.'

'Look, it sometimes happens like that. Don't feel too bad about it. I'm not reading anything into it, but on everything you've spoken to me about so far, you've got it wrong. I hope you get the right guys for this, I really do, but there's nothing more I can help you with. I would like to get out as soon as possible. Have you considered a geophysical search of the allotment? It will save us all a lot of time.'

Brentwood ignored the suggestion.

'Like I say, the search is still going on, but it may take hours yet.'

'What happens to me in the meantime? I've done nothing wrong.'

'You're here until we are finished the search, and pending what further questions we have.'

'You talked about my brother earlier, is he here as well?'

'He is.'

'I've got to tell you, if you're talking to him about the same stuff you've got it all wrong.'

'We'll see. I understand that while you were in the military you were seconded to a unit undertaking something called 'dark ops'?' said Brentwood, changing the subject.

'Sorry, can't go there,' replied Steve curtly.

'Can't or won't?'

'Both. Neither. Take your pick.' Steve raised both eyebrows simultaneously in a challenge to Brentwood. He could legitimately decline to comment and gained some comfort from that.

'You do know the judge can comment on your refusal to answer?' insisted Brentwood.

'Yes, but he won't. It's not relevant to the case,' replied Steve, equally insistent.

'Is it to do with some code of honour?'

'Sorry, I'm not going to answer questions about what I did in Her Majesty's Forces.'

'You'd have to kill me? Is that it?'

Steve did not reply, although nothing would have given him greater pleasure than to watch Brentwood shit himself with fear in the knowledge that he only had seconds to live.

'Did you kill anyone while you were in the army?'

'We were trained to kill people. It's what the army does. I can get you a brochure if you like? They would have been disappointed if I didn't at least try, in the right circumstances.'

'And did you try? In the right circumstances?'

'What do you think?'

'Did you ever kill anyone for Queen and country?'

'Sorry, I'm not obliged to answer that.'

'Says who?'

'Says you. Didn't you say that at the start of the interview? Anyway, change the subject, or no more answers, mate.'

'Okay, just bear with me. It's up to you whether you answer but I have warned you about what a judge can do, okay?'

Steve said nothing.

'I understand you were known as 'Suicide Steve?' continued Brentwood.

'Was I?' asked Steve, knowing full well that he was.

'Something about throwing your parachute out of a plane then diving after it, hoping to catch up with it, strap it on and deploy it before you hit the ground?'

'Yes, you should try it sometime,' he suggested. 'It doesn't half clear out your tubes. Beats colonic irrigation.'

'Isn't that a bit crazy?' asked Brentwood, whose knees were quaking at the mere thought of it.

'Not so risky, really. I practiced wearing an emergency chute the first few times, and when I was comfortable with my timing I ditched the emergency one. Did the killer do that? Parachute down and slot them?'

'No.'

'Well it's irrelevant, then!' interrupted Steve.

'The point I am coming to is that you are a crack shot, an adrenaline junky, a risk taker. I mean, outside a court swarming with police? That's right up your street, isn't it?'

'It's not in my nature to kill people, believe it or not. Army training or not. It wasn't me. I was at home.' He sat back and folded his arms. That was the end of the answers as far as he was concerned. Brentwood had also reached an impasse. He had made his point and would take the matter no further, at least for the time being.

'I will continue this interview in due course. In the meantime, interview suspended at 11.17am.' The tapes were removed and marked up.

'Hang on,' interrupted Steve, 'are you going to tell my brother about this?'

'Of course. Doesn't he know?'

'No. I think I'm due a bollocking. He doesn't like me doing dangerous stuff.'

Brentwood and Proctor then left the room, with a smile on their faces, but no further forward than they had been earlier that morning.

When the door was closed, Raine said quietly, 'Look, I don't know whether you've done any of these things or not, but unless they find anything incriminating, or unless your brother implicates you in anything, I can see you sleeping in your own bed tonight. They are struggling, you can tell by the substance of their questions. Unless the searches run into tomorrow, in which case you're stuck here.'

'There's nothing for them to find, and Charlie couldn't possibly implicate me. I've done nothing. I'll be very surprised if he's done anything either. I mean he has a great alibi for Glen and Jimmy and he had no reason to see off that Freddie bloke. He hasn't got it in him.'

'Well, let's hope so. I can see where they're going with the circumstantial evidence. It's very interesting but they're going to need substantially more. Two thirds of the jigsaw are missing.'

As Raine got up to leave, he turned to Steve. 'Did you really jump out of a plane without a parachute?'

'Yes. Only half a dozen times though, there was a few of us..........' He didn't finish the sentence. Raine raised the palm of his left hand as if to say, 'No more, please.' He wobbled a little as he went through the door, shaking his head.

Steve smiled to himself. Those days were over. The thought of doing it again made him feel sick to the stomach. His deeds were not common knowledge. Someone in his old outfit must have had a loose mouth.

Apart from two microwaved chicken meals, exactly the same ingredients served at 1pm and 5.30pm, and two cardboard cups of tea, Charlie heard nor saw anything until 8.20pm, when his cell door was unlocked and opened by the custody officer, a different one to the one who had booked him in. His face was familiar, and Charlie smiled. He was sure the face had worked for him on a murder case some time ago. He became more sure when the face returned the smile. 'Hello, Boss, remember me? Graeme Prior? The Patrick Dent murder?'

'Of course, I remember you, Graeme, how are you these days?' replied Charlie, relieved that Graeme had reminded him of his name. Forgetting names was like letting people think they had not made an impression on you when you met them. Not good skills.

'I'm fine but this is a bit of a mess, though. The older guys are all rooting for you so good luck. You're going to be interviewed again, would you like to come this way?'

'Yes, no problem, Graeme. Any chance of a cuppa?'

'Of course, I'll bring your brief one as well, he's waiting for you. He's a good guy, this one, one of the straight ones.'

Charlie was shown into the same interview room where his previous interviews had taken place.

Sergeant Hughes wasted no time with pleasantries, and got straight into his stride. Once again, Peart did nothing but manage the tapes.

'Interview resumed at 8.32pm. Mr. Payne, the searches have now been concluded. Do you have anything to add to what you've already told us?'

'I presume you found nothing, then? No need to answer that, I know you couldn't have. No, as I say I would love to be able to help you, but I'm in the dark. I don't know anything. Is my brother still here?'

'He is. What do you know of his military service?'

'He was in the Marines. And maybe a parachute regiment, so I understand. Why?'

'The SBS, eventually. Your brother is very interesting. He has all the credentials for being a hit man. Trained sniper, fearless.'

'Fearless? Steve? You've got to be kidding. He's a pussy!'

'Would you throw your parachute out of an airplane at fifteen thousand feet and dive out after it a few seconds later, in the hope of catching it up? On a regular basis?'

Charlie's bottom jaw dropped and his eyes opened wide. He was visibly shocked and Hughes could see that the shock was genuine. He continued.

'Do you know he was involved in some dark ops towards the end of his career, things the government couldn't possibly admit to? Extremely high-risk stuff, possibly involving kidnap and assassination?'

Charlie picked up on the word *possibly*. So, they didn't actually know the details. It was supposition. Nevertheless, Charlie's shock continued. It explained a lot about Steve. He didn't really know his brother at all.

'Anyway,' resumed Hughes, 'on a brighter note, you are both being released. If you would like, we will take you to either his house or yours.'

'Okay. What happens next? Straight release? Bail?'

'You'll be bailed for further enquiries. We still have a lot to do and we might need to speak to you again.'

'Okay, no problem.' Charlie masked his relief.

The interview was terminated and the officers left after completing the sealing of the master recording, beckoning Charlie to follow them.

'Well, Charlie,' said Harding, 'they must have found nothing. I think they're clutching at straws. It wouldn't surprise me if you don't hear from them again. If you do, here's my card. Give me a call, okay?'

'Yes, no problem, Mike.'

'Do you want me to hang on until you leave the police station?'

Charlie chuckled. 'No thanks, I can handle it.'

In the custody suite, Charlie's property had already been laid out on the desk and he was invited to check it off against the record he had earlier signed. It was all there, including his house and car keys. He replaced his trouser belt but carried his shoes to the foyer with him. He would put them on while waiting for Steve.

Steve had undergone a similar final short interview and was led into the custody suite just as Charlie left via the door into the public foyer. Like Charlie, he was handed all of the property taken from him at the start of his custody, including his house, car and allotment keys.

'Is there much mess?' he asked.

'The house is fine, but we've given the allotment a good turnover. Sorry,' replied Brentwood. That was surely an admission that they had left it in one hell of a state. Still, ordeal over. For now.

'Okay, I suppose you've got to do your job.' He was then taken to the foyer, where Charlie stood up to greet him. They hugged.

'You okay, bruv?' asked Steve.

'Yes, and you?' replied Charlie.

'Fine. What was that all about?'

'Search me, mate. Can't wait for a soft chair and a decent cuppa. Are we going to yours or mine?'

'Can we go to yours?' asked Steve, knowing it was far more comfortable.

'Yes, no problem,' agreed Charlie. 'Then you can tell me about jumping out of airplanes without a parachute.'

'So, he did tell you, then? The snide bastard!'

Charlie shook his head in disbelief.

Both had been bailed to return to the same police station at 10am on 15th January. If the police found any evidence in the meantime, they would not wait until then to put the evidence to them. It would be an early morning raid when they least expected it.

TWENTY-SIX

The journey was quick, but quiet, with nothing spoken about their experiences. The police car pulled up outside the gates to Charlie's house and they thanked the driver, who was unknown to either of them. Probably just some young cop not involved on the case. Charlie opened the electric gates with his fob, and the outside security lights illuminated the driveway and much of the surrounding area. The police car drove away as quickly as it had arrived.

'Right,' said Charlie, 'listen carefully. Both of our houses and cars are bugged and tracked. Phones and possibly your allotment shed as well. Play the innocent but don't ham it or they'll know we're onto them, okay?'

'How do you know that?'

'They had nothing. The interviews were short and not very hard. They were just buying time to fit the devices.'

'I must admit,' replied Steve, 'if you add all mine up, they came to about a quarter of an hour. Not long for a suspected murderer.'

'Any hard questions?'

'Nothing hard, really. Like you say, they've got nothing.'

'Likewise. Remember, when we go in, no amateur dramatics, play it cool, okay? We'll have to talk about the arrests or it'll be unnatural, okay?'

'Yes, I know what you mean.'

Charlie held his keys to the light and selected the right one. He unlocked the door and they entered the house. He went straight for the kettle, filled it from the cold water tap and took two coffee mugs from the wall cupboard. 'Tea or coffee?' he asked.

'Tea for me, please.' The heating was already on, and the house was warm and cosy. They both took off their coats and hung them over kitchen chairs.

'What did they ask you about, Steve?'

'Me? They virtually accused me of shooting those two blokes outside of the court. You know, the one where that Freddie bloke's trial was at.'

'And did you?'

'What, you as well? Fuck off! What do you think I am?'

'Well I don't know where you were.'

'Charlie, why would I do that? I mean I had no issue with them. Come on, bruv, you don't think I'm capable of that do you?'

'Probably not,' said Charlie, motioning with his hands to discourage Steve from over-playing it. 'Anything else?'

'Yes, they virtually accused you of shooting Freddie at the cemetery. Did you?'

'Now, it's your turn to fuck off. Of course I didn't! Is that what you think of me?'

'Why do you think they suspected us?' continued Steve.

'Well I can see their point. Putting it all together there's a lot of unfortunate circumstantial. Wrong place, wrong time. Oh, and the little matter of you jumping out of airplanes with no parachute while on suicide missions. What was all that about?'

'Charlie, you know I'm not allowed to talk about certain things, so just leave it there, okay? And the parachute thing, that was personal, not Army training. I was a member of an elite club but it's all in the past.'

'Do you know they tried to suggest that you would make an ideal assassin with your background?'

'Yes,' said Steve, laughing 'if they only knew what a soft shite I really am. They even brought up that time I was wrongfully arrested for an assault in the Beamish Mary. They're way off the track.'

'I know,' agreed Charlie. 'I hope they get a breakthrough soon, then they'll be off our backs. After I've drunk this, I'm going to see what damage they've done. Then maybe a pint at The Diamond?'

'Sounds good to me. I'm just pleased that's all over.'

'I know, me too,' agreed Charlie.

Charlie's house was not in too bad a shape. There were signs that they had been everywhere, and little was in its right place, but there was no damage to speak of. The sitting room chairs had all been moved, judging from the tell-tale indentations in the carpet where the feet had once stood.

'I'll tidy it all up tomorrow,' he said. 'Do you fancy kipping here tonight then helping me tidy up then we can go to yours and do the same there?'

'It's a deal,' agreed Steve.

Within thirty minutes they were washed, refreshed and en-route to the pub, a fifteen-minute walk.

'Did you stick to what I told you at the nick? You didn't try to be clever or anything?' asked Charlie.

'Of course. Maybe one bit of cheek, though, I suggested they use a geophysical device to hurry the search up. They weren't amused.'

'Well, if that's all you said, no harm done. Anything else?'

'Not really. They tried to goad me about my military service, as you know, but I gave them nothing. Other than that, they didn't give me a hard time at all. It's not like you see on the telly.'

'They were buying time to install the bugs and stuff. They were just playing with us. It's a high-profile case and I'm sure the Home Secretary will have given them the authority. They've got nothing, so they need to hear us talking about it. Your military service is a problem though, Steve. You need to be straight with me. Every day another skeleton comes out of the cupboard. They didn't base Steven Seagal on you, did they? We are in it up to our necks and I need to know what can hurt us. In your own time, please, and be honest with me.'

'Well, I can't tell you everything, but I was part of a unit that sorted out problems when there was no diplomatic solution. Some characters you just can't negotiate with.'

'Go on,' invited Charlie.

'That's it, really.'

'Did you kill people?'

'Sometimes.'

'How many?'

'Between us or just me?'

'Just you.'

'From distance, eight or nine. I wasn't counting.'

'Targeted names?'

'Mostly.'

'And close quarters?'

'Few dozen, maybe. A couple with the blade, one with a crossbow, one or two with a broken neck and the rest with small arms fire.'

'Bloody hell, Steve! Who knows about it?'

'The unit. The prime minister of the day and probably the foreign secretary. Maybe one or two senior civil servants. Well, maybe they don't know about all of them.'

'You're kidding?'

'Nope! It's been going on for centuries. All deniable, of course.'

'What if you're caught?'

'You take it on the chin and hope they spring you.'

'Can any of this come back on you?'

'Theoretically, yes, but only if one of the unit sells his story. In practise, it ain't going to happen. Certainly not after the last two tried their luck. The stakes are too high. It would mean sudden death and the testimony would never get into court. They would be signing their own death warrants.'

'What do you mean?'

'They would be killed. Probably long before they got to court.'

'Is this some sort of discipline code?'

'Kind of. It's only been broken a couple of times that I know of and the perps just disappeared off the face of the Earth.'

'Who did they get to do the honours?'

Steve thought for a moment then stopped walking. Charlie stopped slightly ahead of him and turned around to face his brother.

'Me, Charlie. I was the fixer.'

Charlie momentarily froze.

'What?' he said, a little more loudly than he had intended. He caught up with Steve. 'Are you saying that not only are you a trained assassin with loads of notches, you execute colleagues who go over to the dark side?'

'Never from our own unit, but yep, someone has to do it. It was years ago and somebody else has that role now. There's not a witness programme in the world that could protect the person who exposes me. It ain't going to happen, so stop worrying about it. The cops didn't seem to know a lot, so I think the information came from someone who doesn't know much. Just reputation, just what they've heard. No harm done. If it develops into something nasty, one word from me and somebody will disappear.'

'You're not going to tell your pals, though?'

'Not yet. If the informant disappears, and by the way, they would never find his body, it could lead back to my door. No, we'll just wait and see what happens.'

'What would happen if your unit knew what you were up to with me.'

'Genuinely? They'd drop everything and be here within two hours. Give them the list and it's game over. They hate the bad guys just as much as we do. I told you that earlier, but you wouldn't believe me.'

Charlie still didn't know whether to believe his brother. After all, it was a bit far-fetched. But that was Steve. People never knew whether to take him seriously.

There then followed a long silence. These new revelations were worrying, but were not evidence as such, although it did unnerve Charlie. Steve, on the other hand, was unfazed.

At last, Charlie restarted the conversation.

'Did you say you can make people disappear?' he teased.

'My speciality,' replied Steve with a smile.

'I wish I'd known earlier. I might have saved myself some hassle. Anyway, if you're so good, how come you keep dropping bollocks?'

'I'm a bit rusty and some things were out of my control, like your failure to tell me what you were up to. You're not exactly perfect yourself.'

'Okay, listen. From now on, we do everything together, or at least let each other know what's going on, okay?'

'Of course.'

'And if one of us doesn't approve, within reason, it doesn't get done, right?'

'Fine by me.' Another silence until Steve started up again.

'You know we had a conversation about acquiring more weapons?'

'Yes?'

'I can get them from a different source. Untraceable. The unit has a huge selection. When you hand them back you have to declare what they've been used for. The same level of secrecy is applied. Same sanctions for snitches.'

'Let's hope we don't have to use the service, then,' ended Charlie.

They continued walking. The pub was within sight.

'We have to keep to our normal routine and act naturally,' resumed Charlie. 'Another thing, we have to get another motor to travel about in. Above all, we need to act fast and finish the job just in case we slip up and they get something on us before the mission is completed. I would hate to go down without getting the main man.'

'Okay, if you can get me a grand, I'll source the motor. What about surveillance?'

'Too expensive. They might keep it on for a couple of weeks but after two weeks of getting nothing from the devices, they'll have to withdraw. The honey pot will be limited and surveillance costs an arm and a leg. They might not even have any funds, but we have to assume they do. Keep your eyes peeled but don't make it obvious.'

'What am I looking for?' enquired Steve.

'If they're on foot, you may not see them. They're pretty good. They will adapt to the surroundings. If you're in a drinkers' pub it might be a couple of blokes hanging around. If you're in a family pub it might be a man and women. Maybe even with a rent-a-kid. You probably won't notice them.' Charlie broke off when he caught Steve grinning.

'What?' asked Charlie.

Steve continued to grin but said nothing.

'Have I just given a lecture to a man who knows more about surveillance than I'll ever know?'

'It's not your fault, Charlie, you weren't to know. Your head's too far up your own arse!'

'Smug bastard!' said Charlie, now grinning himself. He did not know whether to love or loathe the new Steve. On balance, he was enjoying it.

'I think I'm going to enjoy this, Charlie. It's a bit tame, though, not a bit like chasing your chute, shit running down your leg in case a gust of wind spoils your day.'

Charlie did not wish to be reminded of that again. The mere thought of it was shattering his nerves.

At the pub, they drank two pints each, Charlie was on beer and Steve on lager, then walked back to Charlie's house. A crisp frost was beginning to form, and their footsteps could be heard from a distance. They stopped occasionally, and listened. Silence, except for the occasional passing car.

Back at the house, they watched the news channel for half an hour, discussing only the news agenda. And then bed.

The following morning after showers and breakfasts, they tidied the house, keeping an eye out for any obvious spyware. There was none that they could see. Either they were well concealed, or Charlie was wrong. In any case, they could not take the chance. Charlie would have another look when he had the house to himself and he was pretending to do the housework. Found or not, any devices would stay there until they both responded to their bail then, as long as they hadn't given the police a reason to keep the devices where they were, they would be removed, just as secretly as they had been planted. Steve and he would be given further interviews, about nothing, or simply kept waiting to buy the police the time they needed to remove the devices.

Charlie did not have long to wait before he found one of the bugs. It was inside the antiqued brass ceiling rose of the large chandelier in the sitting room. At least he presumed it was a bug. There was nothing that looked remotely like a lens so, at least, it was not a camera. The 2mm diameter fine mesh matt black microphone face was virtually invisible, nestled inside one of the many dull black indentations. He realized that they must have taken the whole assembly down, drilled a tiny hole and inserted the microphone. A battery would not last long so they must have wired it into the mains. Ordinarily, it could remain undetected and working for the life of the chandelier. It was unlikely that the Home Secretary would allow it to go on that long.

A second device was concealed behind the kick board in his kitchen floor units, presumably also wired up to the mains supply. The colour matched the units, although it could not be seen without lying down on the kitchen floor, within three inches of its location. He found it by running his fingers along the length of the floor units. It felt like a small inset screw. It was where no screw head had any business being. He took a photograph with his mobile phone to confirm the find. These guys know their stuff, he thought. *But then so do I.*

He stopped looking. The chances were, they would only be in the locations where conversations took place and the police would find it hard to convince anyone that the more private areas needed to be monitored. Nevertheless, he would assume they were everywhere.

He telephoned Steve.

'Steve, just to let you know, I'm running late. I should be at yours in about half an hour, okay? Have you eaten yet?'

Steve was not expecting the call. They had had no arrangements, but he knew that Charlie was trying to tell him something.

'No bother, mate, I'll be waiting. See you then.' He put the phone down and took a quick shower. He had already shaved that morning and he did not mind a five o'clock shadow. In fact, he preferred it. Something to do with his image. He put on some cologne and his smartest casuals, jeans that hadn't been washed for a month, and a blue checked shirt. He wore his only pair of shoes, not counting trainers, and waited for the toot of the horn. It came five minutes later.

Charlie immediately got Steve's attention by putting a finger to his lips as he climbed up onto the front passenger seat, to remind him that the car was probably bugged.

'I've been thinking about that holiday, Steve. Fancy a few days away next weekend?'

'Just a few days?' replied Steve.

'For now, yes. I just need a break. I was thinking maybe Scotland?'

'Sounds good to me. Listen, have you heard anything more from the police?'

'Not a thing.'

'You knew these characters, have you got any theories of your own?'

'Not really. I mean I'm out of that game now, it's somebody else's turn to have the sleepless nights wondering where the breakthrough's going to come from.'

'For me, Charlie, it's shite on shite. They get greedy and want it all.'

'Look, let's not spoil the evening, I've had enough of that lot.'

'Okay,' agreed Steve, 'where are we going now?'

'I'll surprise you.' Charlie tapped Steve on the elbow and once again, put a finger to his lips. Steve nodded approval.

Three minutes later, Charlie turned into the car park of The Bay Horse, to the puzzlement of Steve.

'I thought we were going somewhere exotic?' he complained.

Again, Charlie's finger came up to the lips.

'What's wrong with this? I hear the beer's excellent? Food's decent, from all accounts.'

'I suppose so,' said Steve, sulking.

They got out of the BMW and Charlie stopped on the steps and turned around, taking notice of all the passing cars, hoping to spot any surveillance-type behaviour without making it obvious. It was unlikely that they would identify him. He was too far away from the road, and his figure was a virtual silhouette.

If the car did have a tracker, the police would already know where he was anyway.

That evening, the end game was planned for three Wednesdays hence. Charlie and Steve had watched Morrison's nightclub, aptly named *Morrisons*, in Ocean Road, South Shields, for a number of Wednesdays before their arrests, and a few other nights besides, to establish Morrison's routine. They had always travelled to South Shields in either Steve's or Charlie's car, but now that both cars were thought to have listening devices and trackers in them, they had no choice but to acquire a different car.

With money given to him by Charlie, Steve bought a Mercedes CLK saloon, an older, high mileage job with plenty of life left in it. Under a false name, of course, and from a second-hand dealer within a mile or so of York railway station. There would be no listening device or tracker in that. A little extra in the envelope made the dealer less cautious about following procedure to the letter. Steve would park it out of the way so that it would not attract undue attention. No one would associate him with it. When this mess was all over, he would ditch the Mondeo and run the Merc, this time legitimately and under his own name. He would even consider insuring it this time.

The routine was the same every Wednesday. Morrison would arrive early evening, with two henchmen, always the same two.

'This holiday in Scotland, it's also work. Boring work,' announced Charlie, suddenly, changing the subject.

'Come on then, spill the beans,' replied Steve, a little disappointed.

'We need an alibi for the time we do the business so what we are going to do is spend a few hours in a hotel room pretending that we are at home.'

'Eh?' uttered Steve.

'I have this device that will record continuously for up to eight hours. When we leave my place to do the business with you know who, we just switch it on and it'll play constantly. Best do at least six hours' worth in case we get delayed. We'll build into it a *goodnight* piece, okay?'

'Fine by me but what are we going to talk about for six hours?' replied Steve.

'We don't have to talk the whole time. We'll watch a DVD or two, complete with the usual inane comments you would get from people watching movies.'

'Sounds like a plan. Can I pick the DVDs?' asked Steve, starting to regain his enthusiasm.

'Yes, but nothing too outlandish,' warned Charlie. 'Maybe Bambi and Dumbo?'

'On your bike!' replied Steve, indignantly.

'Also, I'll be writing a sort of script. There are no lines to learn, just a list of topics for discussion and a list of dos and don'ts. We don't want to dry up or say the wrong thing. I'll be saying something like, *Do you fancy watching such and such a programme about to start in five minutes?* Something like The One Show or Corrie or whatever else is on the telly on a Wednesday, just to confirm that it *is* Wednesday, and you say, *No, I'd rather watch a DVD I've brought.* Understand?'

'Charlie, you're a devious so-and-so!'

'I know,' said Charlie with a chuckle, 'it might need a few takes to get it right, though.'

They had their meal, steak and chips, one rare, the other well done, then Charlie drove back to Steve's house, leaving for home after one more beer.

The next day, Charlie telephoned Steve to arrange a pick-up at his house for around 11am on Saturday. They were going to stay somewhere nice in Edinburgh, he promised. He had booked the hotel via the internet, as he did not want prying ears to hear which hotel he intended staying at. He wanted no one beating him to the hotel and placing more listening devices.

At 11am the following Saturday, Charlie picked up Steve as promised and they headed for Edinburgh. There, they stayed in his favourite hotel, The Balmoral. On arrival they took their small suitcases to their rooms and had a quick freshen-up before meeting, as agreed, in the lounge bar.

'I've got to say, bruv, I didn't think we'd actually be coming to Scotland. You threw me there. I know what you're like. I thought you would have gone in the opposite direction to throw them off the scent!'

'Well I considered it, but if my car has a tracker they'll know exactly where I am, and they'll be suspicious if I try to lay a false trail.'

'We should have come in the Merc,' offered Steve.

'No, I don't want to keep throwing them off the scent. I want them to surveille us. I want them to get sick of surveilling us, and finding nothing. I also want them to run out of money. They can't justify it for very long. They might be at their limit already.'

'Do they really do that?' asked Steve.

'I've had the rug pulled plenty of times. It's ruined a few cases but there's nothing you can do about it. The public purse can take only so much,' explained Charlie. 'Unless, of course, the team is willing to do it for time off, which is rare. Can't see that happening for the deaths of a handful of crap. They'd rather be out drinking.'

Charlie got up from his leather armchair and ordered two pints of bitter. Although Steve was a lager man, he did not like what was on offer. The barman insisted on taking his time to get it right. He was a master, a perfectionist. No overflow to make the mahogany bar wet, he would let the first pull settle before executing the next. The pair watched impatiently as their mouths became dryer with each pull. At last, the barman lovingly placed the glasses on the counter, side by side, same distance to the edge of the bar, logos to the front. It wasn't a moment too soon.

'How much?' exclaimed Steve, not meaning to be so loud, when he heard the barman ask Charlie for £12.60p.

'Sorry about my brother, Andrew,' apologized Charlie, 'Steve's only used to clip joints.' He passed the barman £30 and added, 'Same again, please and keep the change.'

The barman smiled. 'No problem, sir, and thank you. Will sir be dining with us tonight?'

'Better not, eh? Unless you have mince and tatties for Prince Charming, here.' He nodded towards Steve.

'No, but I can ask the chef to mince the fillet mignon.'

'In that case, no thanks,' replied Charlie.

'What was all that about?' asked Steve as Charlie placed the glass in front of him.

'Oh, nothing. Italian or Chinese later?'

'Italian, please, I get Chinese twice a week at home.'

Within seconds, both glasses were only half full.

In another thirty minutes they had drained their second glasses and were in George Street.

'Do you know any decent restaurants around here?' enquired Steve as they headed west.

'Yes, quite a few,' he responded. After walking for two minutes, the tantalizing waft of aromatic Indian spices being gently fried in a steamy kitchen somewhere nearby filled their nostrils. The aroma grew stronger as they continued walking. It was too good to pass up.

'Fancy Indian instead?' said Charlie.

'Why not. I'm starving,' replied Steve. Minutes later, they entered the Star of India restaurant and were greeted by a smiling diminutive twenty something waiter, wearing a tux. Probably the son of the owner, learning the trade of generations before him. His manners were impeccable, as were the tables, which were beautifully set with pristine white table cloths and matching napkins folded to look like swans, guarding over the silver and sparkling glassware. They had come to the right place, thought Charlie, but it should have been busier than it was. Only two of the tables were taken, one with four males aged between twenty-five and forty. This was a nice restaurant and, somehow, these people were out of place.

At another table were three young women in the same age range. The two parties were clearly unconnected. It was a pleasant enough atmosphere and the low conversations could not be heard above the piped Indian music, but something was not right. They took the seats offered, equidistant from both parties, and ordered their drinks followed by their choice of food. They already knew what they wanted. Popadums, no starters, a Balti, a Bhuna, one rice and one nan to share.

Within a few minutes, their drinks, pickles and popadums arrived and they tucked in. Between mouthfuls, Steve whispered to Charlie, 'What do you reckon to that lot?' nodding in the direction of the males.

'What do you mean?' replied Charlie.

'They seem to be taking an interest in us. They can't be surveillance because they were here before us and they had no idea we would come in here. My guess is they are local bad lads. Maybe that's why people are staying away?'

'You noticed that as well, did you? You might be right. Time will tell.'

They did their best to avoid the stares of one of the men in particular, the shortest of the four. Each stare was followed by hushed words to his friends.

The meal finished, Charlie pushed his plate away and returned the latest stare.

'What can I do for you, gentlemen?' he asked, forcing a smile.

'What do you men, pal?' asked the short one who had been doing most of the staring. Although the shortest of the four, he was still the size of Steve.

'It's just that you've been staring at us all night and I wondered if you knew us, or something.'

'Didn't mean to stare, pal, no offence intended.'

Charlie looked at Steve in silence. They knew intuitively that the matter was not ended. After a few more seconds, Charlie got up to go to the lavatory at the back of the restaurant, making enough noise about it so that the men would hear. As he disappeared through the door, the two larger of the men got up and made to go in the same direction. The taller looked the oldest of the group. He was bald, with tattoos peaking above his neckline and below his cuffs, and he wore a heavy brown leather jacket and jeans, with black Doc Martens. His friend was slightly shorter, but still gave Steve two inches, and wore similar clothing, the difference being his jacket was of denim.

Steve stood up and placed himself in their way. The babble coming from the table of women fell instantly silent. They, too, had sensed the tension.

'I wouldn't go in there,' said Steve with a grin.

'Why not?' responded the leather jacket.

'He's waiting for you. He's going to knock you out then shit in your mouth and piss in your pockets.'

'Is that right, pal,' said the leather jacket, menacingly.

'Sure is, and while he's doing that, I'll be slitting their throats,' added Steve, nodding towards the two who had remained seated. He then produced the empty beer bottle he was holding in his right hand and smashed it against the nearest table, leaving only the neck and a wicked, jagged, glistening shard.

A stifled 'Oh my God!' was heard from the women's table.

Steve moved aside to let the two men pass.

'Go on, then, off you go. Make sure you wash your hands, if you can,' he invited. He then made a dart for the two still sitting down, rounded the smallest, pulled his head back by the hair to expose his throat and carefully drew the jagged edge across the taut skin, producing small spots of blood where the tip of the broken bottle met any resistance. He looked up at the first two.

'Go on, then, what are you waiting for?'

'You're fucking mad, you are. You've nae idea what trouble you're in. This is Big Alby's place.'

'Ring him!'

'What?'

'Ring Big Alby and tell him some mad Englishman has just taken his place over. Go on! We'll wait here for him. Tell him he's going to need ballistic armour.' He patted the left side of his chest where a shoulder holster could have been.

The big man thought for a moment. He did not fancy having to explain to Big Alby why two middle aged Englishman had turned over his number one team, and yet not one drop of English blood had been spilled.

'Hey, pal, no need for any o' this, right? I mean, come on, let's have a wee dram and put it behind us, okay?'

Steve passed the broken bottle to his other hand and without warning, delivered a speedy, powerful straight right to the jaw of the other sitter, knocking him clean out. He had not been expecting it, and had no time to brace. His arms instantly fell to his side and his head lolled from side to side before coming to rest, staring at the space between his legs. Steve returned the broken bottle neck to his right hand.

'Take these arseholes with you and get out. We'll wait here for Big Alby.'

The two did not need telling twice, and went to the aid of the stricken man, taking care not to go within striking distance of Steve, while the man with the injured throat held a napkin to it, at the same time cursing and muttering to himself indecipherably in a strong local accent. They each placed a limp arm over their shoulder, grabbed their man around the waist and dragged him pigeon-toed towards the exit. It would be even money whether they phoned Big Alby first, or hailed a cab to take their unconscious colleague to hospital. Steve did not much care.

As the four were leaving, Steve turned to the tuxedo-clad waiter. 'Sorry about that. Are these guys much trouble?'

'Yes, sir, he replied. Much, much trouble. You see how bad is my business?' He gestured towards the empty seats.

'Tell them you are now doing business with the mad Englishman who is putting together an army to come back and take over his manor. I'm not really, but just tell them that. If they give you any trouble, give me a call and I will come back to sort them out, okay? That's a promise!'

'Okay, sir,' he managed, not sure what to make of the offer. Steve wrote his telephone number on an old betting slip he found in his pocket, and handed it to the dumbstruck waiter.

Seconds later, Charlie re-emerged from the lavatory and saw the empty table. Maybe his suspicions were unfounded after all.

'They've gone, then?' he asked Steve, surprised that things had not taken a turn for the worse.

'Yes,' replied Steve.

'Thank you, sir, very much. Please come again,' interjected the waiter, beaming with delight. 'This is on the house, with our deepest respect and gratitude.'

'No. we'll pay,' replied Steve quickly. 'We aren't like them. Charlie, pay the man, please.'

Charlie, a little nonplussed, coughed up eighty pounds, to include a generous tip that brought yet more smiles from the waiter. It wasn't so much the tip that pleased but the fact these people weren't out to put the bite on him. Charlie had questions, but he left them for outside.

As they walked past the table containing the three ladies, they stood up and Steve was treated to a round of applause, heightening Charlie's curiosity. The older of the women planted a kiss on his cheek. Charlie looked quizzically at Steve. Steve shrugged.

Outside, Steve told Charlie what had happened.

'I knew they were up to no good. You were right about one thing, though.' Charlie produced his brass knuckleduster. 'I had this in my hand ready to go. Not sure if I would have shit in their mouths, though. Best take a back-street route back to the hotel, just in case. I'm going to stop socialising with you, you cause trouble wherever you go.'

'Come on, you love it,' replied Steve, 'but let's go via the car. I want to sleep with the monkey-wrench.'

The following day, they rehearsed what little script there was and left it on the coffee table as an aide memoire. Charlie left the *Do not disturb* sign on the outer door handle. Surprisingly, the recording only needed one take. Both had performed well, and quite naturally. Charlie played excerpts back to check the sound quality and content. It was fine, but he would need to listen to the whole tape again at some stage to make sure that there were no glitches that could be picked up by the police. There should be no sirens, no doorbells, no room service. He was not looking forward to that, but it had to be done in case there was a problem with the recording. The police would analyse the recordings over and over again to try to hole the alibi, so it needed to be perfect or they would have to do it all over again.

The movies were well chosen by Steve, the first being The Godfather, the second being The Godfather Part Two. Had they enough time, they would probably have watched the third in the trilogy, but enough was enough. They had what they needed, and were becoming stir crazy. Once again, the bright lights of the city centre beckoned. This time, they would take a taxi to The Royal Mile and lie low in some upmarket pub with no bouncers. One night of excitement was enough for now.

TWENTY-SEVEN

The day of reckoning had arrived, 7th January, a dark Wednesday evening. Charlie and Steve had done their homework over a period of weeks and they had synchronized their recorded alibi with the television clock. It was all systems go.

The routine was always the same. Shortly after 6.30pm, Morrison would arrive at the front door of his nightclub and let himself in with a key. He would be the first in. The cleaners had long gone and the boiler had not long fired up. It was his paperwork night, such as his paperwork was, and he had about an hour before the staff started to arrive. He did not open for the afternoon session these days as the punters would not pay his prices. The pubs already had that business sewn up. But some of those pubs were his, so it made no difference.

He was always flanked by his two henchmen, Vince Fletcher and Joe Tailford. Their history with Morrison went back at least twenty years. They had all started out together on the same path, but Morrison emerged the king-pin. He had leadership skills, of a kind, and could make decisions. Often bad ones, but decisions, nevertheless.

Being a member of the golf club, charitable donations and fund-raising were all part of his game but, somehow, he had not yet managed to join the rotary club or the Freemasons. When he had made tentative noises about becoming a member he was always met with an embarrassed but diplomatic, *Best not, Ray, eh?* His business persona fooled no one, and he knew it. He was a proud man and would not risk the inevitable rebuff.

They all wore navy coloured Crombies, which had developed as their uniform. Morrison's, of course, was of pure cashmere wool, while the others were of a wool and man-made fibre mix. Probably from a lower end fashion store. They were on good money but, unlike Morrison's coat, theirs would occasionally have specks of blood and snot on them, hence the more workmanlike versions. Ditching a coat that cost around a ton was okay, but even the wealthy would baulk at having to throw away a coat that cost close to a grand.

As always, before they stepped through the door, they each looked to their left and then to their right. Strangely, they never looked behind them. Not these days. Their reputation was fearsome and woe betide anyone who fancied their chances. They had performed this routine thousands of times without incident. This time, to them, it was going to be no different. Why should it be? But they were wrong.

Taking advantage of their complacency, a black-clad figure had already emerged from the shadows of an adjacent doorway and his silent crepe-soled shoes had brought him to within five feet of the trio.

In the meantime, Steve had found himself an observation post on a single storey flat roof building with a dwarf wall on top. He had chosen it weeks earlier while he and Charlie were carrying out their recce. The roof led to nowhere in particular and gave no access to windows, which is why it was not heavily defended. And if the graffiti artists could find their way up there which, judging from the blaze of colours on the brickwork, they had, it would present no problem to Steve.

The felted roof was covered in swirling leaves which would eventually find their way to the pile against the wall, where they found shelter and huddled together. It was otherwise open to the elements but, for all it was cold, it was not raining. He was well wrapped up with weatherproofs and the two-foot wall provided some respite from the cold north easterly breeze, as well as some concealment.

The Ruger was wrapped in sackcloth so that it would not glint in the moonlight and give itself away. Not that there was much moonlight through the low cloud ceiling. The cloth was secured with string at points along the length of the weapon so that the loose folds would not hinder its operation. His black ski mask and dark green combats would ensure that even if he stuck his head above the wall, he would not be seen. His periscope would, hopefully, remove that necessity. In panoramic mode it gave him what he needed – sight of anyone approaching the venue. Zoomed in, it simplified identification.

His job, that night, was to protect Charlie's back, to warn him, via their two-way radios, of anyone approaching. So far, the system had been redundant.

Now, immediately behind them, Charlie tapped the rearmost of the trio, Tailford, on the right ear with his Beretta, silencer already engaged, hard enough to get his immediate attention. He flinched and a hand instinctively went up to the site of the pain, accompanied by a muffled protest.

'In!' Charlie said, forcefully, as he jabbed the silencer sharply into the same man's ribs as he turned to see who had dared to do this to him. The other two turned and saw the gun. Their hands instinctively went up in surrender. Tailford gingerly cradled his throbbing ear against the collar of his coat, his head tilted to one side.

'Do you know who I fucking am?' hissed Morrison, full of rage.

'Yes, actually, I do!' Charlie quickly tapped him solidly on the top of his head where his hair was thinnest, creating a two-inch weal which caused Morrison to wince and shield himself from further blows.

'It's because you are Ray Morrison that I'm here. Murderer, gangster, all round twat! Now move or I'll slot you right here!'

The three moved forward and Charlie kicked the door closed behind him. It shuddered when it hit the framework, but slowly swung back to leave an eight-inch gap.

'Office!' directed Charlie firmly, flicking his gun in the direction of where he imagined the office to be.

They walked towards a door which bore the engraved brass plaque, *Private*. Morrison turned and said, 'Key's in my pocket.'

Charlie replied, 'Go for it. I'm watching.' He stood to one side so that he could observe the hand movements and levelled the gun at Morrison's head.

Morrison's hand went into his right coat pocket. He took out a bunch of keys and selected one. He inserted it into the lock and turned it then looked towards Charlie for approval of his next move. It came with an impatient nod. Morrison opened the door, which led to a stairway up to the next floor, and pushed it fully open, letting go of the handle to reach around and switch on the light.

'Go up and wait at the top. No funny business, this thing has five for each one of you,' warned Charlie. They ascended in silence, one stair at a time. Each hoped the other would try nothing, in case the gunman turned his gun on all of them. He seemed mad enough to do so. At the top of the stairs, Charlie repeated his instruction, 'Office!'

The three walked ten feet along a corridor and Morrison hastily punched a four-figure code into the combi-lock of a heavy natural wooden door, made even heavier by the multiple coats of varnish it had received over the years. He grabbed the handle, turned it and pushed the door open before reaching inside to switch on the light. Charlie was watching him closely. He had no idea what could be hanging on the wall beside the light switch. Morrison then dropped his hands, empty, to his side, and walked in. The office was large, about thirty feet by twenty. In the middle was a large Edwardian polished mahogany table with ten chairs.

At the far end was a huge mahogany, leather-topped desk with the usual paraphernalia, a photograph frame, redundant blotting paper pad, pens and a single tea cup and saucer. Typical white canteen ware. Nothing fancy for Morrison in the workplace. Besides, he was too fond of throwing crockery at those who incurred his displeasure.

Charlie closed the door, inspected the underside of the table for hidden compartments and unpleasant nasties, then commanded them all to sit, waving the gun towards the table. They sat. Morrison, at the head of the table nearest the huge desk and the other two in chairs about as far away from Morrison as they could get. This was Morrison's problem, not theirs, and they wanted to keep some distance from him in case the gunman decided to let fly.

At that point, Charlie peeled up his ski mask to reveal his identity. He did not mind their knowing who they were dealing with. In fact, it was part of the plan. There was no turning back, he had already committed himself, and he was sure he had the right team, particularly Morrison. Even if the others had no active part in Julie's death, they were at least guilty by association.

'Well, well, it's Mr. Payne!' said Morrison with a nervous smile. 'To what do we owe this pleasure? You know the trouble you're in, I suppose?'

Charlie said nothing, but took out the mobile phone he had taken from Tommy Layton. He turned to Tailford.

'What's your name?'

'Joe Tailford,' he replied, unsure of the relevance. Charlie flicked through the phone's address book and found the entry for *Joey*. He pressed the button. Seconds later, a muffled ringtone could be heard. Tailford looked down at his left coat pocket then back at Charlie.

'Take it out, then,' ordered Charlie, impatiently.

Tailford took out the phone. It was still ringing.

'Answer it!' barked Charlie.

Tailford answered it. 'Hello?' he said nervously.

'Hello, Joey,' responded Charlie, 'nice to see the face behind the name.' He rang off. Tailford still held the phone to his ear, waiting for more orders.

'End call, then back in your pocket!' ordered Charlie. Tailford quickly did as he was told then took his hand back out of his pocket and stared at Charlie.

'You?' barked Charlie towards Fletcher. 'Name?'

'Vince Fletcher,' he replied, nervously. He knew that Joey's phone call meant something, but wasn't quite sure what.

'Let's see what this one does,' said Charlie, ignoring Fletcher and punching the contact, *Ray*, in the phone's memory.

About three seconds elapsed before he heard a muffled ringtone coming from the direction of Morrison.

'Answer it', said Charlie, calmly, eyes firmly clamped on Morrison's. Morrison took a mobile phone from his left pocket and looked at the screen. It read, *Tommy*.

'What's this?' enquired Morrison, bemused.

'You know what it is. You ordered me dead. Joey here was the middle man. My wife got in the way and got killed. You've had three goes but I'm still here. You just can't get the staff these days, can you?'

'The phone proves nothing. You've got nothing. You're fucking mad if you think you can get away with this! It'll never stick!'

Charlie ignored the comment then scrolled down to find the name, *Vin*. He raised the phone to his left ear. Three seconds later, Vince Fletcher's mobile rang. He fumbled nervously for the phone in his pocket and looked at the screen. He did not recognise the number. He lifted the phone to his left ear and managed a feeble *Hello.* His hand noticeably trembled.

'Got a case of the shakes have we, Vin?' teased Charlie, who ended the call and replaced the phone back into his coat pocket.

It was Charlie's turn to smile.

'I've got three kings, a good hand if I say so myself. What have you got?' He looked at them all individually. There was no reply.

'Why?' asked Charlie. There was pleading in his voice.

'Why what?' Morrison responded first, with a bit of edge to his voice.

'Yeah, what?' responded Tailford, with not quite so much edge. Fletcher remained silent. He had a feeling that the phone numbers meant something, but did not want to make matters worse by showing Charlie disrespect.

'You tried to kill me, all of you. You're all in it. Why?'

Joey spoke first and fast. He couldn't wait to point the finger. 'It's that mad bastard there!' he said, nodding towards Morrison. 'It was on his orders. We didn't want it but big mouth over there wouldn't listen. Threatened to do the lot of us if we didn't go through with it!'

Morrison, smiled and responded.

'Joey, Joey, Joey, you know that's not true.' He turned to Charlie, fighting for the words. 'It was nothing personal, you understand. Tommy just wouldn't let it lie. He wanted you dead for what you'd done to him. Ten years in the pokey can seriously damage somebody with Tommy's limited intelligence, you know. He's not the brightest. Time plays tricks with your memory. He probably talked himself into believing that he was innocent and that you fitted him up. When he never showed up, we thought he'd either bottled it or you'd got the better of him. Trouble is, Tommy's not the sort to bottle it so we assumed the other option. Then Craig Collins got the instruction from higher up to find out what happened to Tommy. Nobody told him to whack you.'

'Higher up?' responded Charlie, sharply.

'Can't say. Just higher up. You don't want to know.'

'I do.'

'Believe me, you don't, Charlie. You got your revenge in. Best leave it there,' said Morrison, hoping Charlie would do just that.

'He's talking shite, Mr. Payne. It was Freddie Simson who suggested it, and him there,' he pointed at Morrison, 'thought it was a great idea. You were going to testify against Freddie and both of them wanted you out of the way.'

This was news to Vince Fletcher, who looked quizzically at Tailford. He thought it better not to involve himself further. Things were bad enough already.

'Shut your fucking hole, you slag!' shouted Morrison, 'I'll deal with you later!' he threatened. Morrison needed to convince Charlie that there was still a threat and if he conceded that Simpson had ordered his death, the buck would have to stop right there. Besides, Simpson was no longer around to face the music.

'My money's on you, Morrison,' said Charlie. 'You're the common denominator. Your signature's all over this.'

'Charlie, this is a mess,' replied Morrison. 'A huge bloody mess. On your side, Julie's dead. On the other side, it's Tommy and Craig ....'

'And Tony Molloy,' added Charlie, 'don't forget poor Tony.'

'Tony Molloy? Was that you?'

'Afraid so. I thought you would have known that?'

'Fuck me, Charlie!' For the first time, Morrison was beginning to sense real danger

'And Simpson. And Hargreaves. And Harrison,' added Charlie, raising his eyebrows. 'They all had to go, but they're just the first batch.'

Morrison's head dropped. This was not what he was expecting. There was the distinct possibility that Charlie was planning the same end for him and he might have only minutes to live. His options were severely limited. It was either beg for mercy or blag it. He chose unwisely.

'For fuck's sake Charlie, do you know how much trouble you're in? They'll throw the key away!'

'No one can prove anything. There are no witnesses, and this isn't going to court,' replied Charlie.

'You don't get it, do you?' he continued. 'Perhaps a bad choice of words,' he added, mockingly. Without taking his eyes off Morrison, Charlie shot Tailford and Fletcher in the chest, both within a split second.

Phut, phut!

The muffled cracks from the well-oiled silencer, although relatively quiet, caused Morrison to flinch and put his hands out in front of him instinctively in defence. His mouth gaped open in horror. Both of his mortally wounded lieutenants slithered to the floor in slow motion as their life force drained away.

Fletcher died fairly instantly. The bullet had pierced his right ribcage and travelled through his chest, destroying everything in its path, through his heart and through the left ribcage, finally lodging itself in the wood-panelled wall behind him. He felt nothing.

Tailford was not so lucky. The bullet pierced his right ribcage and lung and exited through his rear left ribcage, missing the heart and spine. Without immediate medical attention he would die within a few minutes through shock and loss of blood. In the meantime, he would have a long, agonising, anguished wait, knowing that, very soon, his lights would go out for ever. And there was nothing anyone could do for him. But Charlie was not going to wait that long. He moved closer and, without taking his eyes off Morrison's, slowly lowered the gun and pointed it at Fletcher's head, within his peripheral vision.

Phut!

The Beretta barked again. If Fletcher wasn't already dead, thought Charlie, he certainly was now. His eyes rolled to the top of his head, signalling the very last moments of his life. The bullet had entered his right temple, exiting above his left ear, and wedged itself into the floorboard beneath his head.

Phut!

The Beretta barked once more. Tailford was also now dead. He'd still had enough life in him to be looking up pleadingly towards Charlie when he took *his* shot in the right eye. There was surprisingly little blood as his heart had already slowed to a virtual standstill.

Charlie did not blink.

'Is the mist beginning to clear?' he said to Morrison.

The mist had indeed cleared. Morrison experienced an involuntary, audible bowel movement, and his bladder emptied simultaneously.

'Oh dear! Squeaky bum time?' mocked Charlie. 'Don't worry, your time hasn't come yet...'

'What do you want?' pleaded Morrison, desperately. 'Just name it and it's yours!'

'How about my wife back?' responded Charlie. 'Sort that out and I'll consider we're quits.'

Morrison could not reply. He did not know what to say without making matters worse.

'Why, Morrison? WHY?'

'Charlie, I'm really sorry about Julie, I really am. If you hadn't shot Craig, I would have done – the fucking idiot. All he was meant to do was to find out what happened to Tommy. He must have panicked when Julie came into the room and he fired. Fucking bastard!'

'You know I've got Tommy's phone, so I don't need to draw you any pictures about what happened there. Why did you send Tommy to see me?'

'I didn't. Tommy took it bad when he went down. Prison life didn't suit him. Pritch even less. He died in the nick. Tommy always wondered who fingered him and Cleggie got the blame. You know how it is when people rat. He was dealt with. Trouble is, Tommy got to thinking, nearly ten years' worth of thinking, that it wasn't Cleggie after all, so he came after you to find out who it was .....'

'Tommy didn't ask me anything like that. Nothing. He just came to kill me. He was going to use this gun.' Charlie waved it then brought it back to bear on the centre of Morrison's chest.

'Look, I swear I didn't set you up, Charlie! Tommy did what he did by himself. Craig is, well, Craig. He didn't do his job, which was just to find out what happened to Tommy. It went badly wrong...'

'He didn't ask me anything either, your hit man, he just went for it and wasted my wife. Would have wasted me if I hadn't done him first. The buck stops with you. You're the top man. And you're contradicting yourself. I don't know which version to believe. If any!'

'You've got it all wrong, Charlie, it wasn't like that!' protested Morrison, whose discomfort in sitting in his own mess was plain to see. The foul odour merged with the smell of fear. He was in a desperate predicament.

'He'd already been paid five grand up front! You don't get that kind of money for just having a word!'

'Look, I want to make amends, Charlie. As I say, just name it!' he pleaded.

'What's the Simpson connection? Joey wouldn't have said that if it wasn't true, given the trouble he was in.'

'Figment of his imagination. Wishful thinking. I always suspected he was a Simpson man, poor schmuck.'

'Why is Detective Chief Inspector Mick Redman's number in Tommy's phone? Why is it in yours?' Charlie knew the number was in Tommy's phone but he was only speculating about it being in Morrison's. It was a bluff. But he was right.

'Me and the Detective Inspector go back a long way. We helped each other out from time to time...'

'Helped each other out? In what way?' interrupted Charlie.

'Well .... you know .... I would give him information and he would .... do me favours?' offered Morrison.

'What favours?'

Morrison hesitated. Charlie raised the gun to point directly at Morrison's face. 'Okay, okay, calm down. I would pay him.'

'He was on the take? That's why you've managed to stay clear for all these years?'

'Not just him', offered Morrison, who saw a glimmer of hope in this new interest, 'it goes much higher. All the way to the top, if you're interested. I'll do you a deal and help you put them away. I'll turn Queens. I have the proof...'

'What proof?' interrupted Charlie again.

'Diaries, meetings, amounts changing hands. Even camera footage. It'll blow your mind. It was my insurance.'

'Did they know about this stuff?' enquired Charlie.

'Course not.'

'What camera footage?'

'Here. This office.'

'Where are the cameras in this building? Where is the recording gubbins?'

'One on the entrance and each fire exit, about three in the corridor downstairs, one just outside this office and one in here. It's hidden in that smoke detector near the corner. Nothing in bars or dance areas, it would upset the punters.'

Charlie had noticed the smoke detector when he carried out a dynamic survey on entering the room. He did not need to look again for confirmation.

'Where's the recording equipment and the viewing screen?'

'In that corner,' replied Morrison, pointing towards a corner of the room behind Charlie.

'Show me,' said Charlie, gesturing towards the alcove with his gun. 'It goes without saying, no sudden movement or any funny business or I'll slot you.'

'You'll get no trouble from me, Charlie, I'm with you.'

Morrison carefully and slowly sidled towards the alcove, watched by Charlie, the muzzle still trained on Morrison's body mass. He moved aside a portable raffia screen with the flurry of a magician trying to convince the audience that there was nothing to hide ... no tricks up his sleeve.

The screen was live and the picture flickered from camera to camera.

'Show me the footage of what went on in this room when we all entered,' ordered Charlie.

Morrison studied the console for a few seconds, then pressed a few buttons. Instantly, the screen lit up as the office light went on and the group walked in.

'It operates on movement. Goes to sleep when nothing's happening. Saves memory that way,' offered Morrison, who then stood back to allow Charlie to watch. Charlie did not need to watch, he had already seen his work first hand and he needed no reminding of his destructive force. 'Where's your footage of the historical stuff?'

'I download the interesting stuff onto a separate external hard drive. I keep that in my safe and just take it out when I need to.'

'Where's the safe?'

'Over there,' said Morrison, pointing to the corner closest to his desk.

'Open it!' ordered Charlie.

Morrison walked slowly towards the safe. He had stopped looking at the gun, now that there appeared to be a glimmer of hope. Some bargaining tool that could save his wretched life. Something that could mean he was worth more to Charlie Payne alive than dead. He picked up a bunch of keys from his desk, selected one of them and inserted it into the lock. It turned with ease then stood upright from his stoop. 'Do you want me to take it out?'

'Yes, please,' replied Charlie sarcastically, craning to see if there was anything in the safe that could harm him. 'No tricks, or I'll shoot. But then you know that already, don't you?' he said pointedly.

Morrison said nothing. He slowly removed the contents of the safe and put them on top of his desk. A metal cash box came out first, about twelve inches by eight, and four deep. Next came some DVDs, notebooks and diaries. Finally, a personal computer portable hard drive, followed by two bundles of bank notes.

'The information about bent coppers, footage etc is all in there?' enquired Charlie.

'Yes, but you'll need me to go through it with you to make sense of it all. It's not obvious what all the stuff means, and how it goes together.' It was his trump card. 'Obviously, the money's yours. Twenty grand, I believe.'

'Have you got any screwdrivers?' asked Charlie, unimpressed.

'Screwdrivers? What for?' enquired Morrison.

'I want the memory out of that computer in the alcove. I don't want to leave any evidence of what's gone on tonight,' answered Charlie.

'Understood,' said Morrison, smiling. Perhaps he really *was* off the hook. He moved to the middle of his desk, selected another key from the bunch and turned it in the lock of the top drawer. He stood back, looked at Charlie and opened both palms towards the drawer in a *would you like me to open it?* gesture.

Charlie understood the gesture and nodded. Morrison opened the drawer and took out a small set of screwdrivers, little better than the kind you might get from a middle-of-the-range Christmas cracker.

'First of all, get tonight's footage on the screen and wipe it,' he ordered. Morrison worked the mouse to retrieve the footage.

'Now, wipe it.' Morrison did so.

'Now, play it again.' Morrison took it back to the time they had entered the building, and pressed *play*. There was no footage. It was blank. It had been successfully deleted. Charlie then beckoned to Morrison to move away from the computer. He switched the computer off at the plug and removed all connecting wires. He turned it on its back, unscrewed the cover then removed the internal hard drive, placed it on top of the desk and stood back. The operation had taken no more than two minutes. Charlie picked up the internal hard drive and placed it into his pocket. He would smash and burn it later.

'Is there a server or is it stand-alone?'

'Just stand-alone.'

'Okay, now what's this about police corruption at the top? Who's the main man?'

'The Assistant Chief..... Mr. Wright. I knew him when he was a simple dick, sorry, detective. He done well for himself. Even better with what I was feeding him.'

'What was his involvement with Layton, Collins and Molloy, the guy who tried to do me on the street and make it look like a mugging?'

'Nothing, really. He knew you were going to be spoken to, but he didn't make any of the running. Tommy and Craig were going against orders. They were out of control. The guy who mugged you got shot a few weeks later. Fuck, that was you, of course it was. I forgot. And the two outside of court. And Freddie.'

'Is there any footage of Wright on the tapes?'

'There will be. He came here a few times. He was even driven here by his chauffeur. God knows what he told *him*.'

'What about your records, does he get a mention in there? Any amounts of money beside his name?'

'Yes, it's my insurance policy, like I said earlier,' said Morrison, convinced that he was going to be of use to Charlie. Yes, he might have to lie low, maybe move away for a while, maybe even go to prison for a few years, but anything was better than a wooden overcoat.

'Show me where Wright and Redman get a mention in the books.' Morrison obliged. Charlie flicked through the pages and saw each name mentioned several times, with cash amounts alongside their names.

'Is there any footage of these transactions?'

'Yes, among that lot,' said Morrison, nodding towards the pile of DVDs and another external hard drive.

Charlie raised his eyebrows and forced a smile.

'Anyway, you've missed one, Morrison, haven't you?'

'Missed one?'

'Yes, the most important one of all.'

Morrison froze. He did not like the sound of that.

'I've got what I came for. More than I was expecting, actually,' said Charlie. 'Now for the finale.' He lifted up his gun to shoulder height and carefully took aim. This one is for sending Tommy after me.' Morrison's hands shot out in front of him in defence.

'Don't!' he pleaded. 'I'll get rid of the bodies and none of this happened!'

Phut!

The bullet entered Morrison's left wrist and travelled the length of his forearm, stopping only when it came to rest against the humerus, causing him to jump and give out a short, sharp, guttural scream. He instinctively twisted his body to shield the injured part from further danger.

'This one's for sending Collins after me.'

Phut!

The second bullet entered Morrison's right elbow joint from the rear, shattering the heel of the ulna. He collapsed to the floor, writhing in agony. No words would come. His mouth gaped open in a silent scream.   This one's for sending Molloy after me.'

Phut!

The bullet entered his groin area. The pain was absolute and without immediate medical treatment Morrison would die of shock within minutes.

Charlie knelt on his right knee beside Morrison's petrified, stinking body. He felt no pity, no guilt, no remorse. The job had to be finished.

'And this one is for killing my missus. You might as well have pulled the trigger yourself, you bastard!' He inserted the silencer muzzle into Morrison's mouth and pushed his jaw closed against the hard steel.

'Are you ready? ......One....two... THREE!' He paused a while to prolong the drama. Morrison shook uncontrollably with fear, his eyes wide open, looking pleading at Charlie. Charlie smiled then resumed the count slowly, finally pulling the trigger on *seven*. He wanted it to last longer but he was now tiring of the game.

Phut!

Morrison's head jerked backwards as the hollow-nosed bullet ripped through his throat and severed the spinal cord from his skull. He died instantly and dark red blood formed an expanding puddle below his head. His eyes remained open and stared at the ceiling, locked in complete surprise. The facial muscles would relax in time but, for now, his face would remain distorted.

Steve was still waiting patiently. Charlie was taking his time, or else he was in some kind of trouble. But there was no indication of any violent struggle. From his vantage point he could see little, and hear even less. The office light had gone on, as he would have expected, and there was no sign of any disturbance, no tell-tale muzzle flashes or noises.

He put the radio microphone to his lips and pressed the transmit button.

'Steve to Charlie,' he said, as loudly as he dared. He waited for a reply. Nothing. As he was about to climb down from his observation platform to investigate, he heard approaching footsteps. Putting his eye to the periscope, he could see a man and a women, their backs only, walking along the pedestrianised area towards the nightclub entrance.

He again depressed the transmit button of his radio. 'Male and female approaching, do you copy? Repeat, male and female approaching. Now entering, copy?'

Again, there was no reply. The male pushed open the door and entered. As the female followed, she stumbled when her heel buckled under her. She stopped, uttered a curse and said something inaudible to the male, who briefly turned, replied, and continued inside. The female took off her shoe and inspected it. Steve gave another frantic warning over the radio, again without reply, but it was now time for him to move.

By the time he had climbed down from the single storey roof, the female was out of sight. He assumed that she had followed the male inside.

Charlie stood up, taking a long last look at his victims. He was about to unscrew the silencer to make it easier to conceal on his way out, when the door to the office opened. In walked Redman, stopping in his tracks on seeing the carnage. And Charlie's gun. Charlie froze.

'Fuck me, Charlie, what have you done?' shouted Redman, genuinely horrified. He surveyed the scene, hardly believing his eyes.

Charlie knew the game was up and it would be pointless trying to wriggle out of it, given the evidence in front of him.

'Just taking care of business, Redman,' he said, indifferently. 'Wife murdered and several attempts on me. They weren't going to stop until they got me so it was either me or them, because you lot were no help. My so-called friends. No regrets, you understand? He had it coming and so did all the others. That includes you by the way, you bent bastard! You were on the take and you knew what they were up to. You didn't say a fucking word.'

Charlie raised the gun again and pointed it at Redman. He was not sure whether he could kill a copper, even this one, but he was going to buy time until he could figure out what to do next.

'See those books over there?' invited Charlie, nodding towards the pile. Redman looked in the direction of the desk.

'Those books contain details of transactions between you and this mob. You and a few more besides. You're finished! Morrison even filmed the transactions. You're fucked!'

Redman responded. 'What books, what records? I don't see any. This little lot will disappear. And you're under arrest for murder,' he said. 'Unless you're going to kill me as well. Are you? And what about Angel? Are you going to kill her too?' He had heard her irregular footsteps approaching, one shoe on, one shoe off. She was about to make an appearance any second.

At this point, the last thing that Charlie expected was the sight of Angel. She hobbled into the office carrying a shoe with a broken heel, and with a big grin on her face.

'Sorry, heel got stuck in ....' and then she too saw Charlie and the slaughter in front of her.

That settled it. Even if Charlie could pull the trigger for Redman, he knew he could not kill Angel. But he *could* give her the honour of feeling his collar, the collar of a mass murderer, and of breaking up the corrupt cell within her police force. If anyone deserved a break, it was Angel.

'Angel, before you do anything else, listen to what I have to say,' began Charlie. Redman opened his mouth and took a step forward to protest.

Phut!

A slug from the Beretta embedded itself in the wooden panelling behind him, stopping him in his tracks. Charlie then gave chapter and verse of everything that had happened since the day Tommy arrived at his house. There was no holding back. He told her everything, including Redman's relationship with Morrison. And Gavin Wright's. Redman's involvement did not surprise Charlie, but Wright's did. That was a devastating blow, given their friendship and history.

What Charlie had presented Angel with was the evidence that he had shot all three men and tortured one of them. All in cold blood. A planned revenge. He would even admit the other murders, although some of them might be difficult to prove, given that he was in no position to commit them. He would go down for life, literally, regardless of the provocation, so admitting the other murders was no great risk. Hell, it might even enhance his reputation. *Good old Charlie, who would have thought?* He explained what the books, DVDs and external hard drive would reveal.

When he thought he had covered everything, he offered the gun to Angel, grip first, and placed his wrists together in front of him, expecting to be handcuffed. He knew Angel had a thing for him, but even she could not ignore what was in front of her, especially with a witness present.

'I'm really sorry to disappoint you. You mean a lot to me, but I've blown it,' he said finally.

When Steve arrived at the front door, Angel had closed it. He turned the handle quietly and gently pushed. It opened easily without a sound. He stepped inside, taking care not to make any noise, and listened for movement. He tip-toed to the bottom of the stairs and steadied himself lightly on the bannister. The last thing he would have wanted is for the bannister to creak and give him away.

A glow was coming from the landing, and voices could be heard. There was no one in sight. They were all in the office. He began to climb the stairs slowly, one at a time. The glow intensified and the voices were becoming clearer. One of the voices was Charlie's. *He was confessing to the killings.* Steve subconsciously shook his head in disbelief.

As Angel took the gun from Charlie, Redman snatched it from her and took two steps backwards, pointing the gun at her. He motioned to her with the gun, to join Charlie.

'You're finished, Redman,' said Charlie, triumphantly. 'They'll throw away the key! Angel, do you want to tell him or will I?'

Angel thought about it for a moment. It was a risky business telling an armed, desperate man that you had enough evidence to put him away for a long time. But, surely, he would not shoot if he knew the same evidence was shared by a dozen cops investigating his corruption? She steadied herself.

'Redman, you don't know this, but several months ago, I was asked to spy on you,' she started. 'West Yorkshire Police were investigating allegations of corruption in our force and you were on the list. This little lot will blow you wide apart. And others besides!'

Redman smiled. 'From where I'm standing it's you who are in trouble. The books are going to disappear, and this lot won't be saying much, will they? It just leaves you two. Believe me when I say this, but it's the last thing I wanted.' He straightened his gun arm and took aim at Angel. She had to go first before she screamed the house down.

The shot from the silenced Ruger rocked Redman's head as Steve's bullet pierced the brain through his left ear. He dropped like a puppet with its strings cut. Steve put down the rifle and sprang to Redman's side, watched by the open-mouthed Angel and Charlie, then brought up the handgun, still in Redman's right hand, and with his finger on the trigger. He quickly looked along the barrel and squeezed the trigger. Twice. Angel dropped to the floor. Blood staining appeared in the area of her sternum, and blood trickled from a neat round hole in the centre of her forehead. Both wounds were fatal.

Charlie looked in disbelief at Steve, mouth agape.

'What the fuck?' he managed.

'I'll explain later, let's get out of here!'

Charlie dropped to Angel's side with thoughts of resuscitation. He knew it was pointless but he looked for vital signs, nevertheless, tears streaming. *Oh, God, this isn't happening!*

Steve allowed him a few seconds to say his goodbyes then grabbed him by the left shoulder and yanked him to his feet. 'She's gone, Charlie. I'm sorry, but we have to leave. NOW!' He pulled him forcibly away from Angel and dragged him out of the office.

'Compose yourself, mate, don't draw attention. Act naturally.'

'Act naturally? Are you for fucking real? Do you know what you've just done?'

'Behave yourself and settle down, you'll get it eventually.'

They both left, Steve dragging Charlie behind him. Charlie turned to catch a last glimpse of her. No matter what the angle, her accusing eyes appeared to follow him. Their brightness would soon be dull and dry. That would be his lasting memory of her.

Outside, Steve clutched the rifle to his side to camouflage it and reduce its profile in the street lighting. He pulled his mask up to look like a beanie hat, showing his face. There were no street closed circuit cameras along the route they would take, they had made sure of that, and as long as they played it cool, no one would notice them. A full ski mask would have drawn attention but now, to a passer-by, he would just look like a regular guy and it was too dark to be able to make a convincing identification. Charlie's ski mask was already on the top of his head. He had known that everyone he came into contact with that evening was going to die, so he had already revealed himself. He wanted them to know the identity of their executioner.

Steve took hold of Charlie and held him close to ensure that they walked at a pace that would not be noticed. Nothing was said by either until their journey was well under way. Charlie was too traumatised.

The car, a banger purchased that day with more of Charlie's money by Steve under a false name, was driven carefully so as not to raise heads. Steve would not risk the Merc, which he fancied for himself. Even if the police were taking an interest, they could not know about the car and there had been no time to plant a tracker or a listening device. It would be abandoned near to where the Merc was parked, some twenty miles away and outside of the police force area.

'Why, Steve? She loved me. The two women I loved have taken a bullet for me!'

'Stay focused, Charlie, don't lose it *now*. I couldn't get through to you on the radio to warn you so I came as fast as I could. I heard voices and made my entry. You *do* know that the guy was going to kill you both, don't you?'

'You can't be sure!'

'Can't be sure? Listen to yourself! Those books and her testament would have put him away for life! He had no choice! Besides.'

'Besides what?' asked Charlie, curious to know what other gem he had to offer.

'Nothing. Forget it, Charlie. You're right, I'm sorry, mate. Really, really sorry!'

'Besides what, Steve?'

'Charlie, just think about it.'

Charlie remained silent, staring straight ahead.

'You would have done the same if the shoe was on the other foot, mate. You haven't come this far to take such risks and that's the point I'm making.'

'What point?'

'She knew the full story. Thanks for keeping me out of it, by the way. You spilled your guts to her!'

'You heard all that?'

'Yes! What were you thinking of?'

'I thought I was finished and I wanted her to get the glory.'

'Charlie, this way I get another twenty-five years with the brother I love, as opposed to seeing him rot in jail. It's a no brainer. And what about young Mark? You won't do him any good inside, will you.'

'We'll probably be caught anyway, and Angel will have died for nothing!'

'We won't, trust me. Everything's going to be alright. Assuming you didn't leave any DNA?'

'Of course not, what do you think I am?'

'What about the tears?'

'Wiped them on my sleeve. Nothing dropped.'

'Well, if you're sure. It's a tragedy, and I'm really sorry for that, but we have to take the positives. I mean, the police are going to have a hell of a time unravelling this. Incidentally, apart from the last bit, how did it go?'

'All dead. Morrison gave me the books and stuff and I took the camera hard drive from tonight's footage. It was all switched off by the time Redman arrived. If the job's done properly, the books are sure to hang him out to dry.'

'Where's the hard drive?'

'Here, in my pocket.' Charlie patted his pocket to make sure he still had it. 'I hope the scenes of crime people are straight. I don't know how widespread the corruption is. When Redman walked in, I wasn't expecting that. I couldn't shoot a cop, even a bent one. Then Angel walked in and saw the gun in my hand. I gave it to her, surrendered and confessed to everything, but Redman snatched it. Complete cluster fuck.'

'Well, now it looks like Redman shot the lot. The only problem is, who shot Redman? The same guy that shot Hargreaves and company, I suppose. I don't envy the cops. It's going to be a total nightmare for them. It'll keep your pals busy for years, probably the length and breadth of the country. Do they know about your relationship with Angel?'

'Not unless she told anybody, but I think she's as anally retentive as me. Tells no one anything.'

'So, did these guys confess their involvement?'

'Kind of. Enough for me to put it to bed, anyway.'

'How did it feel?'

'Not sure, really. It was easy, I suppose. Maybe too easy. Mixture of body and head shots. Morrison got it in the elbows and suchlike first, though. I wanted him to feel pain.'

'Fuck me, Charlie, you can be a cruel twat sometimes!'

'One thing's puzzling me, though,' added Charlie, 'you followed the body shot with a head shot. That's police and army training, certainly for close protection in your case. We're already in the frame so, no doubt, they'll be knocking on our doors again. I'm the common denominator here, because I'm loosely linked with several events. It's a mess! Hopefully, the recording we made will give us an alibi.'

'Don't bottle it now, bruv! Even I know it's all circumstantial. Nothing's changed on that score. Don't over think it. Besides, it was the guy who shot Angel, not me, remember?'

Silence followed, but not for long.

'You didn't need to kill her, you know? With Redman gone, she would have concocted something.'

'Get wise, bruv, she would have eventually dropped you in it, either intentionally or otherwise. The pair of you just needed to fall out. Hell hath no fury, know what I mean? I couldn't take the chance. You wouldn't like prison food.'

'She wouldn't have, I know ....'

Steve interrupted. 'Listen, it's done, it's over. There is no one left to finger you. Practise what you preach. God knows you preach enough. No trails, you keep saying!'

More silence. Deep down, Charlie knew Steve was right. He was already forgiven.

'Yes, well, it's done now so let's get rid of the gear,' said Charlie, changing the subject and wiping the tears from his eyes yet again.

'Yes, if business is finished, let's get rid altogether,' agreed Steve.

'You're learning,' replied Charlie, quietly, still staring into space.

'And if we start up again, we'll use a new piece. I know the people.'

'Give it a rest, it's over,' replied Charlie. 'Now, drive and concentrate on where you're going!'

'One more thing, Charlie, give me your radio,' demanded Steve. Charlie obliged. Steve inspected it.

'I thought so, it's not even switched on! That's why I couldn't warn you!'

Charlie remembered he had switched it off momentarily as he crept up on the three men, but forgot to turn it back on. He closed his eyes in disbelief that he could jeopardise a major operation with such an elementary mistake. He, of all people.

'Sorry,' he said quietly, hoping that Steve would let him off lightly. Had he received the warning, perhaps neither Angel nor Redman would have died and he would have escaped before they stumbled across him. Had he just stuck to the plan rather than indulging himself, he would have been in and out within a few minutes. It was all his fault. 'Cluster fuck,' he repeated.

Steve kept his counsel. His brother was hurting and now was not the time to remind him of his operational shortcomings.

'Charlie, bruv, I'm only saying this because you're my brother and I love you, but you weren't thinking straight with that lass. It was far too soon after Julie. You would have regretted it in the long run.'

'Okay,' replied Charlie wearily. 'Just leave it!'

Over the next forty minutes they went over and over events to see if they had overlooked anything. They had no idea whether or when they would need to use the gun again, but they upheld their agreement to dispose of it once and for all. The main players, to their knowledge, were gone and the criminal fraternity would be left wondering who would be next. But if they had not finalised matters, someone could come looking for Charlie and it would start all over again.

They talked about what rival outfits would think. The strange theories they would come up with, their imaginations running wild. There would be mutual respect for some time to come as the gangs tried to work out what was happening. Some would deliberately up their importance by increasing the size of their payroll. It would be amusing to watch. For now, Steve and Charlie were finished. They could think of no more targets.

The press would be impatient for something to happen. Indeed, they would set away rumours just to get things going. The situation was strangely satisfying.

Within an hour, they had dumped the car in the Tesco car park in Newton Aycliffe and collected the Merc from the same car park. Their outer layers were removed and discarded into the Tesco charity bin. As usual, Steve dropped Charlie five minutes' walk from his home. He could see and hear more on foot.

There were no cars around, no bodies hiding in hedges, but he had not expected any. The police were probably just arriving at the scene and, surely, Charlie would not feature as a suspect, certainly not so soon. He quietly retrieved his i-pod from the coffee table in the sitting room and wiped it clean.

It wasn't until the midnight local news, that the story broke. Five bodies found shot in a South Shields nightclub. Judging from the number of blue lights on the television screen the circus had, indeed, come to town. That night, sleep would not come for Charlie until daybreak. Angel was gone and it was all his fault.

Days later, neither he nor Steve had heard anything from the police. To play it safe, Steve sold his Mondeo for scrap, probably complete with listening and tracking devices, to a faraway scrapyard.

TWENTY-EIGHT

Their bail date arrived, 15th January, and they both responded in Steve's Merc. They were admitted to the custody suite but were kept waiting in separate interview rooms. Their solicitors had also turned up and joined their respective clients. There was no news, no information.

Ninety minutes later, Detective Sergeant Hughes entered Charlie's interview room and profusely apologised that he had not been advised by letter that he was being released from bail, and that his attendance was no longer required. Steve was given the same news. Not a word was said about the murders in South Shields.

Minutes later, in the foyer, they both met and winked at one another, taking care not to be seen. Without a word, they got into Steve's car and drove back to Charlie's house. The Merc was probably neither bugged nor tracked but they could not take that chance and limited their conversation to small talk, and hopes that the police would find the killers.

Back home, Charlie went to the covert CCTV system he had installed a week earlier and switched on prior to responding to his bail. The cameras covered the front and back door entrances from the inside. The quality was reasonable for an off-the-shelf purchase, but probably not good enough to be able to identify faces. He inspected the activity. At 10.25am that morning the back door into the kitchen opened and in walked 5 figures silhouetted against the light. Two of them appeared to be carrying toolboxes. There was no more movement until forty-eight minutes later, when five figures left by the same route. There was no activity on the camera covering the front door.

He checked the two locations where he had found listening devices. They had been removed and the holes made good. The chances were that any other devices will also have been removed, but he would not take any chances. He and Steve would never again speak of the incident, either in the home or in a car.

Had Charlie's plan worked? Had the police been fooled by the audio alibi that he and Steve had recorded in The Balmoral? Perhaps they would never know. They heard no more from the police, but Charlie fully suspected that they would bide their time. The case would never close, particularly since it involved the deaths of two police officers. The police would continue to monitor their activity but, unless they found a new lead, the team would eventually dwindle to two, a detective sergeant and a detective constable. He and Steve would be the closest they would ever get to firm suspects, although that would never be broadcast. What little circumstantial evidence they had would be reviewed, put aside and reviewed again by different eyes. Maybe even different generations. It would never go away completely. Everything he would do from now on would be subject to scrutiny. To Charlie, it was now a game. If they had nothing on him now, their chances were hardly going to improve.

Exactly two weeks to the day that the grim discoveries were made at the night club, Assistant Chief Constable Gavin Wright's staff car arrived at the gatehouse of police headquarters at 7.45am. Unusually, the barrier remained down and the Jaguar XJ was forced to stop unexpectedly. There were not the usual smiling faces and greetings at the gatehouse office window. The usual occupants were conspicuous by their absence. Before the fact registered, Gavin Wright caught a glimpse of Detective Chief Superintendent Harvey Johnston and

Detective Superintendent Naz Hussein from West Yorkshire Police, walking briskly from the gatehouse door towards his car door. His head dropped. This was not a good sign. He instinctively knew that his run had come to an end. Why he had not quit while he was ahead would haunt him for the remainder of his life. Why he had embarked on the whole sordid affair in the first place, likewise. What had started as seemingly innocent gifts, had grown until he was making demands when the gifts dried up.

'Good morning, sir, would you mind stepping out of the car? We need to have a chat.' invited Hussein. Wright obliged without saying a word. He had no alternative but to comply.

In his wing mirror, the chauffeur saw his boss being handcuffed. Another officer, Detective Chief Inspector Trevor Nelson, also from West Yorkshire Police, opened the front passenger door and climbed in next to the chauffeur.

'Good morning Ron,' he said, as Wright was led to a waiting car behind the gatehouse. 'Your boss is in a spot of bother, as you might have gathered, and so will you be if you don't cooperate. I want details of everywhere you have been with or on behalf of him over the last few years. Will that be a problem?'

'Not at all, sir, except he's only been in office for about two years. I keep a log book and a pocket note book. The log book's here with my current note book. The old ones are in my locker. I'll get them now if you want?'

'I've already got them, Ron, but thanks anyway. Sorry for the intrusion, but needs must. By the way, you are not under arrest, but I do need you to cooperate, okay?'

'I'll help you all I can,' replied Felton.

The chauffeur was genuinely fine with the situation. It was not as if he was a personal friend. In fact, Wright was short on conversational skills and rarely concerned himself with how

Felton and his family were doing. He had no interest in anyone other than himself. He was not going to stick his neck out for a man like that.

'Have you any idea what this is about?' explored Nelson.

'Not really,' replied Felton, truthfully.

'You will have, by the time we get through all the questions.'

'I've got nothing to hide, boss. Bring it on.'

Two days later, after two nights in the cells, Assistant Chief Constable Wright was charged with a number of bribery and corruption offences, and appeared in court the following day. The entries in Morrison's record coincided with journeys undertaken in the Jaguar. Some of the CCTV footage was grainy but other sections were of sufficient quality to identify Wright. He would later be joined by a Detective Inspector Brad Allthorpe, when he returned from his holiday in Florida. The jungle drums would reach him long before he left Florida and it was not a homecoming to relish. Fleeing would be pointless. They would catch up with him eventually. Disappearance and a new life would take some organising and he neither had the time, the money, nor the will. Detective Chief Inspector Mick Redman had already paid his debt with his life. In the days to come, more arrests would follow.

One week after his remand in custody, the six o'clock news broke the story of Wright's further arrest on suspicion of being concerned in the murders of Malloy, Hargreaves, Harrison, Simpson, Redman and Angel Gallagher. Charlie immediately picked up his phone and dialled his brother.

'Have you heard the news, Steve? Gavin Wright's been arrested for all those shootings! What the hell's going on?'

'It probably has something to do with the murder weapon being found in the ceiling void of his garage with some of the books, DVDs and money that I lifted from the nightclub. It should have fingerprints and DNA all over it linking it to Morrison. I only gave him half of the stuff. The other half was in a drawer in the office, so it would look like he only took what he saw after he killed them, and missed the rest. I'm pleased they found them.'

'Bloody hell, mate, that's brilliant! It'll never stick, though, but I'm proud of you!'

'Maybe, maybe not, but it's the best evidence they're ever going to get. The threat of exposure could be the motive. It'll take some explaining, if nothing else.'

'When did you do it?' continued Charlie.

'A couple of days after the nightclub fiasco. I watched his gaff until he went to work, and when his missus left a bit later, I went in. I've got skills you don't know about, mate.'

'Forensics?'

'Pristine, mate. Absolutely nothing! In and out in under five minutes.'

'Well, all I can say is I'm gobsmacked. There's more to you than meets the eye, isn't there? Well done!'

Steve put down the phone. Finally, his brother had some respect for him. It would bode well for their future.

The multiple murder investigation was indeed in disarray. Now they had a strong suspect with opportunity and motive, but it was almost incredible that such a public figure could commit such butchery, yet the evidence pointed that way. Wright only had his wife as an alibi for that fateful evening. It would be a long time, if ever, before they could make sense of what had gone on. That pleased Charlie and Steve.

TWENTY-NINE

It was a Saturday morning and Charlie was reading the newspapers in the kitchen. It was now eleven months since the Morrisons' murders, and Wright had just been sentenced to twelve years on corruption convictions. He was still on technical bail for the shootings.

No one had knocked on Charlie's door in relation to the investigation. Steve obviously had not figured at all in police enquiries, unless they were saving him for later, which was unlikely. He had now gotten his head together and, with Charlie's backing, was now running his own executive limousine company. Just three owner driver Mercedes 'S' types and two Jaguar XJs to start with until he could fathom what the market could take, but business was already good and he was looking to double his team over the next three months.

Angel had been a big loss to Charlie, but it worried him that he had gotten over her so quickly. He had not set out to chase her. If anything, it was the other way around. Either way, that episode of his life was over. He indulged in a self-satisfied smile as he drained his coffee cup, before hearing a car turn into his drive. He had not been home long himself and had again forgotten to close the gates. The new gravel acted as an excellent early warning system.

He wasn't expecting anyone. He got to his feet and looked out of the window. A petite blond. He could only see her rear end but it was shapely and definitely female. She was leaning into the rear seat of a new silver Mercedes S Type, her grey small black and white hounds'-tooth skirt riding up slightly, but not high enough to take away her modesty. She retrieved a heavy shopping bag, straightened up, readjusted her skirt, closed the door, locked the car with her remote, and turned around. She walked slowly towards the front door, looking at the windows for any signs of life. As she neared, Charlie recognised Sue. Julie's sister. The good looking one. The frosty one.

What now? She never visits!

He did not wait for the doorbell to ring. He opened it and flashed a smile. They usually left business for their monthly board meetings.

'Hello, Sue,' he said, 'it's nice to see you. How've you been? We're not due another board meeting for two weeks, are we?'

She ignored his question, put her handbag and shopping bag down with a clunk and reached up to give him a hug, her arms around his neck. She planted a warm, slightly wet kiss on the left side of his throat. It was as high as she could reach without a step ladder. It was a real hug and she meant it, not the usual polite arms' length *mwah, mwah* he had come to expect. She held her pose for a good ten seconds before pulling her face away and placing her hands either side of his head, just behind his ears. She pulled his head forward and kissed him briefly on the lips before taking his hand and leading him back into the kitchen.

'Never mind me,' she said, 'how've you been? Sorry I've neglected you, but I wanted to give you space.'

'I'm fine. Things have settled down and I've come to terms with everything that's happened. Onwards and upwards I suppose. And you?'

'Hang on, I'll put the kettle on. Tea or coffee? Milk, no sugar I believe?'

'Coffee for me, please, milk, no sugar, thanks.'

She lifted the weighty shopping bag onto the worktop and pulled out two bottles of Bollinger.

'For later, if you fancy,' she said with a grin.

'Well,' she started, 'business is going extremely well, as you know. We've taken on those other two homes and we are going all out for some national excellence awards. We want a service second to none.'

'I know all that, I'm still a director and shareholder, remember? I get copied in to dozens of e-mails every day, mostly written by you,' he laughed. 'It's you I'm interested in.' Almost immediately he realised what he had said.

'You're interested in me?' she said. 'You always kept your distance.'

'You know what I mean. Anyway, it was you who always kept your distance from me, as I recall.'

'No, I was always up for cuddles when we met, but you would hide behind Julie.'

'I didn't want Julie to get jealous.'

'What do you mean?'

'Well you know what some women are like. You're very attractive and, truth is, there was some chemistry between us. At least on my part. I think Julie knew it and she would often test me. Whenever she felt down or a bit dowdy or her hair wouldn't go in the way she wanted it, she would say things like, *you fancy my sister, don't you?* And I would have to deny it to keep the peace. I suppose I avoided getting too close to you, know what I mean?'

'Well that explains a lot. Did you fancy me, then?'

'Come on, what sort of question's that?'

'Well, do you? Sorry, did you?'

'Well, you've always been a stunner. Any bloke would,' he said mischievously, knowing that it would provoke a response. He knew that all women liked compliments, and some weren't averse to a little harmless flirting. 'But I was with Julie, so it was a non-starter,' he explained, tamely.

'Would it surprise you to know that I had a thing for you, the moment Julie introduced us? I still feel the same way, I suppose. I can only say this now because it won't hurt her. Do you think I'm evil? I mean, it's only been just over a year. Is that too soon?' Her eyes were moist. It was a bold declaration and she knew it. One that could make their relationship go somewhere, or end it altogether. There was also a tinge of fear in her voice. She was now alone in the world, although Charlie was not to know that, and this was her make or break chance. It was nice to have pots of money, but money wasn't everything if you don't have someone to share the freedom it brings.

Charlie was shocked. She was not messing about. She was going straight for it, he thought, and he was beginning to realise that he may have been mistaken about the way she saw him. He was not prepared for this. He was unsure of what to say.

'Hold me,' she said, moving towards him without waiting for his answer. She took hold of Charlie's hands and placed them around her waist before putting her arms around his neck for the second time. Charlie complied and held her close to him. He was very comfortable and could have stayed that way for hours. He was short of affection, these days. She looked him in the eye then closed hers and provocatively kissed him on the lips, her tongue gently and patiently working its way into his mouth. It felt good and Charlie responded, slowly at first, then with escalating passion. He was just as exited and eager as she was. His hands slipped to the cheeks of her bottom and he squeezed gently. She responded by pushing her groin towards his, although the height difference meant that it was left to her lower stomach region to read the signs.

A minute passed before she again took him by the hand and led him towards the stairs. She could feel that he was ready.

'What about Brian?' he said, hesitating on the fourth stair.

'Brian? I kicked him out months ago. He's history. I'm expecting the degree absolute any day now, so never mind him. Here's something else you don't know,' she teased.

'Go on then,' he challenged.

'My Jenny and your Steve are seeing each other.'

'You're joking? He never said. How long?'

'Since the funeral.'

'Bloody hell! Is it serious?'

'Must be. I've been looking at wedding-venues with her. We haven't found anything yet so it won't be for a couple of years, though. Don't say anything. Act surprised when he asks you to be best man.'

Charlie was in shock and stopped in his tracks. 'I don't know what to say. I'm absolutely over the moon for him. And her, of course. The sly gits.' The corners of his mouth curled upwards in a wide grin.

'Anyway,' she said, 'we can talk about them later but, for now, can we please just fuck?'

Note to reader:

Thank you most sincerely for buying my book. If you have enjoyed it, please consider leaving a review on the Amazon Books website.

Kind regards,

Terry Atkinson

Printed in Great Britain
by Amazon